Praise fo

"*Lioness* is a darkly compelling portrait of an artist who evolves into a homegrown ecoterrorist. Mark Powell's brooding, twisty novel is packed with a distinctively American, highly explosive mixture of religion, art, sexual obsession, mental illness, and environmental menace."

—Tom Perrotta,
author of *Tracy Flick Can't Win* and *The Leftovers*

"Mark Powell's *Lioness* is a force of nature: moody, twisty, stormy, and supercharged with the fierce blue voltage of top-notch storytelling. It's a riveting ecothriller that's also a profound exploration of grief—grief for one another, and grief for the earth. What a powerful novel."

—Jonathan Miles,
author of *Anatomy of a Miracle*

"A thriller with quickness and elegance, *Lioness* asks tough questions about our responsibilities to the natural world and to one another. In offering no easy answers, it achieves something beautiful and haunting. Mark Powell has written a gorgeous, enthralling, immensely readable novel that will hook you until the very last page."

—Kayla Rae Whitaker,
author of *The Animators*

"Mark Powell's *Lioness* is an immersive rendering of the human quest for love and healing amidst a world on fire—a fire we have set and cannot tame."

—Annette Saunooke Clapsaddle,
author of *Even as We Breathe*

"*Lioness* takes the reader on a cross-country journey that is as much spiritual and psychological as it is physical. Mark Powell's powerful descriptions capture the grief, love, and despair of his characters as they move through a land that's been wrought by environmental degradation and an ever-changing climate."

—Jessica Cory,
editor of *Mountains Piled upon Mountains: Appalachian Nature Writing in the Anthropocene*

"In this haunting novel of passion and intrigue, Mark Powell takes on the environmental collapse coming at us and the people driven to action. Powell is a writer with mountains of talent, and here he creates complex and fascinating characters trying to figure a way out of grief and despair. Even love is sometimes violent."

—Janisse Ray,
author of *Wild Spectacle: Seeking Wonders in a World beyond Humans*

LIONESS

a novel

MARK POWELL

WEST VIRGINIA UNIVERSITY PRESS
MORGANTOWN

ISBN 978-1-952271-44-1 (paperback) / 978-1-952271-45-8 (ebook)

Library of Congress Control Number: 2021949733

Book and cover design by Than Saffel / WVU Press
Cover image by Morphart Creation / Shutterstock.com

for my Nana,
who told me my first stories,
(mostly in the porch swing,
mostly about Elvis),
and in memory of
Cliff James and LJ and Grace Powell

God will not have his work made manifest by cowards.

—Ralph Waldo Emerson

lioness

She finds it on the porch at first light. A Key deer, its neck bitten so deeply it clings to the body by the tea-colored weave of its pelt. Mara stands there for she doesn't know how long, stands there with her coffee and her fear while mosquitos gather around her ankles, and then goes inside to call the number printed on the magnet attached to the refrigerator. *Yes, dead. Very dead.* The other body she has seen—the other dead thing—was her mother, years ago. A childhood defined by gold Tory Burch flats and a .410 over-under.

Imagine that, she might think.

But she has no need to imagine, and instead hangs up and walks back to the single bedroom where the boy sleeps. If she needs sleep, she can lie on the couch in the front room. But she needs only to watch him: the delicate tracery of his eyelids, the soft slide of his philtrum, the tiny jade bird he clutches in one hand. She moves closer: the hint of sunscreen. It is suggested you reapply every ninety minutes, but at night she smells it on him even after he showers, its creamy glide never quite disappearing. Every day they volunteer at the bird sanctuary and every day it rains. In the evenings, they play chess while the thunderstorms break, and if he is bored or growing restless, he is also too polite to say.

But give him time, she thinks. He'll want out. He'll want away from you.

But not yet. Alone in this bungalow with its mold and tidal funk and the metal lattice beneath the outdoor shower—the piped water warm as soup—alone here, she has a hold on him. She tells him stories so that he won't realize how tightly. The ride of Paul Revere that is maybe 70 percent true. A story about Osceola in the Everglades that is completely made up. But about these things— the true versus the false—who can really say? Sometimes she reads up, takes the old laptop and tries to catch the Wi-Fi off the Marathon Courts Motor Inn two hundred meters away through the dense mangroves and hummock of pine and oak. Those nights she is left with a certain aloneness that isn't exactly loneliness, at least not yet, but like old milk threatens to turn without warning.

Perhaps it already has.

Just the same, she won't leave. The boy loves birds with an intensity she has never seen any child love any other thing: songbirds, seabirds, raptors. It is beautiful, this love, and she has come to believe it is her duty to preserve it at whatever cost.

That means staying.

That means hiding, and not only herself but the boy too, because somehow Mara has come to believe it's the boy they are after, the boy who is the point of all this and not the fire she imagines still burning five years and four hundred miles north. The boy who is the point and not Mara who still smells the residue of explosives on her hands and hair and in the weave of her cable-knit sweater.

They have spent their time here waiting, working, watching the nightly murmuration out on the dried lake bed that is akin to witnessing a miracle. Bronzed cowbirds that spiral into the trees. Thirty-thousand, but they move like one, a great black flash that, when it turns, is suddenly silver, suddenly alive. It's something she can't quite get over—the aliveness of the world—how it is around her at all times. She tries to remember as much, to live only in the present, though there are times she silently repeats a name, and then says it aloud just to prove she still can.

His name, mine.

She is still sitting when she hears the truck out on the shell drive. She walks out to the Key deer, this soft childlike thing with its lashed eyes and white-tufted ears, untouched but for the torn throat. But she doesn't feel any sympathy. All she wants is that it be gone. All she wants is that the boy not see it, and that she not have to touch it.

Touching would make it real.

Touching makes everything real.

There is talk of a last panther.

Not the stuffed mountain lion that had long since been donated to the museum back home. That lion, Chris's lion, was a relic. Sleek, dangerous, and like so much of her world, gone.

Here is an actual panther.

That is what the Fish and Wildlife officer tells her, standing by the loquat tree in his tan shirt on the crushed shell drive. There has been a roundup of the last cats in the disappearing Everglades, ear tags and radio collars, flatbed trucks to carry the caged things from the rising waters of South Florida to a preserve somewhere in Nebraska. But one has escaped, a mature lioness came south down the Overseas Highway, down along the shoulder, sometimes right out into the road.

"It killed a Rottweiler not two days ago," he says. "Caught it on a security cam. But the deer—"

"They shouldn't be here, should they?"

"No, ma'am. Normally Key deer are farther south down on Sugarloaf. But everything's mixed up these days, as I guess you realize."

There are still Christmas lights up, red and green bulbs strung through the trellis and along a clothesline that runs to the edge of the mangroves. She and the boy hung them weeks ago, just as the pumps were cut off in Key West and the waters left to rise unabated. She has heard there's a military cordon north of the Naval Air Station, no traffic in or out, and judging by the day's emptiness, she suspects that the rumors are true. All the panic is there. The demonstrations, the bombs, the man who transformed himself into a pyre of gas and flame in front of the field office of the US Department of Homeland Security.

There, she reminds herself. Not here.

"Just you, ma'am?"

"My son and me, yes."

"How old is your son?"

She never comes off the porch, never lets go of the neck of her housecoat. Not even when the officer wraps the Key deer in a blue tarp and drops it into the bed of his truck, wipes his hands on his pants and walks back over so that she looks down on him there in the yard. He is sweating, one dark smear of blood below his name tag and down the crease of his shirt. Behind her the window AC rattles on.

"Is that relevant?" she asks. "His age?"

"I'm just thinking a lot of boys like to wander out into the woods, playing and all. If he was out there at night, with a panther around."

"He won't be."

"Yes, ma'am. Well, if you hear something."

"Of course."

"Come across scat. See the print of a house cat, only twice the size." He shapes a track with his hands. "We have nonlethal traps. Big steel cages."

"I have the number on a magnet."

"That cat represents one thirty-seventh of the remaining population."

"I'll call."

"Yes, ma'am. That would be most appreciated." He turns for his truck but pauses to look at the house with its low roof and louvered windows. His name tag reads HOUSTON. "Is he inside there, your son?"

"He's sleeping."

"So he didn't see it?"

"No, he didn't."

"Yes, ma'am, thank you," he says, and this time he gets into his truck and drives away.

She stands on the porch until the truck vanishes into the dense green and then waits another moment to make certain he is really gone. Lately, she's found people moving slower than seems advisable, their souls spread a half step behind them, a mist, a granular smearing like a television in need of slapping. The old RCA in her father's house. Her mother with her Virginia Slims, ashing into a highball glass while *Seinfeld* goes to commercial. That last summer in North Carolina, back before it all fell apart. *Before* being in the days of Blockbuster Video and spray-on tans. *Before* around the time Bill Clinton was not having sexual relations with that woman. How old would Mara have been? In high school, alone on the green futon, sincere and angst-ridden. The idealist with the big broken heart. Her childhood spent wandering through a giant house of glass and stacked rock while her daddy babbled drunk on the couch and her mama went out into the woods to shoot herself in the face.

My God is bigger than that. That was her mother's line.

What comes next, honey? That was her mother's question.

What comes next is filling a pitcher with water and splashing it over the boards, the smear of blood thinning and then gone. She sweeps it clean and goes inside to smooth the damp pelt of the boy's hair. She had considered lying to the officer, but that seemed more dangerous than being honest.

No, I'm not alone. I'm here with my son.

So now the officer knows. But no one else does.

No one except me.

part one

your GPS is wrong

v

In September 2018, nine months after she had left me, and just over two years after our son Daniel died of non-Hodgkin's lymphoma, a bomb went off at the RAIN! water-bottling plant in southwest Virginia, two hours north of the home I shared—or once shared—with my wife. Whether Mara died in the explosion is unclear. What is without question is that she was responsible for the blast, carrying inside fertilizer and diesel fuel and a device the FBI believes to be blasting caps wired to a Tovex trigger.

The charge detonated within the actual opening of the well and set the fire that the Tazewell County fire department battled until late the following day. By that time, RAIN! had been largely reduced to ashes and the melted plastic of unfilled bottles, a cinder block shell in which machinery smoldered. None of it operable. Not that it would have mattered: the blast had collapsed the borehole, sealing it and whatever dioxins Mara imagined had poisoned our son.

The interior security cameras were destroyed, but a perimeter feed positioned near the cut fencing recorded five still shots of a figure making what appears to be three trips in and two trips out, body hunched, wiry arms pushing what appears to be a plastic Walmart garden cart loaded with the ammonium nitrate/fuel oil.

It was Mara, but also not.

What you have to do is construct an alternate life. Your life, but not quite, the distance between the two no more than the space between your thumb and forefinger. But make that distance everything, make that distance hum with what might have been. Mara had certainly tried. I've come to believe it was what she was doing those afternoons at the Ashe County group home, or those evenings sitting in the floor at the Kinzers: building a world of what might have been, a world that was nothing if not banal, a world where someone unloads the dishwasher or scrubs a carrot, all of it in the kitchen, in the evening half-light, with something on the radio you almost hum. A world of everydayness.

We'd almost had it.

We'd made bird feeders, pine cones smeared with peanut butter and sprinkled with seed, and the birds had come, cardinals, tufted titmice, a single hawk that circled above us on a rising draft. Beneath it—around us—the old barns in the bottomland and the new houses on the ridge, the giant triangular constructions of timber and glass overlooking herds of expensive Charolais cattle, white, muscled things that waded into the current. That we'd almost had it—I believe now that was part of what made her act, that and her failure to understand the stakes of saying *yes*. *Yes* means possibility, consequence. *Yes* returns to you in a way that is biblical, a way otherwise reserved for stuntmen and third-world theocracies, places where to light yourself on fire for an idea is to become something to someone, if only to yourself.

What comes next, Mara?

Here is what came first:

Mara and I spent the summer and fall of 2003 together with a man named Chris Bright, fell apart and came back together three years and two thousand miles away. We lived in Mexico, were married, were happy. Eventually, we bought a farm in North Carolina and Mara became a famous (relatively speaking) installation artist, represented by galleries in New York and London, profiled by *ArtForum* and *Juxtapoz*. She made herself into something hard, into something that mattered. Then it all fell apart, that hardness, that mattering. We lost our son and Mara fell into a depression so deep the idea of bottom must have felt theoretical, the idea of someday climbing out, impossible. Not that she didn't try. She looked for solace in art and in God but found it in neither. We did what we could to stay together, though it wasn't enough, and in January 2018 Mara left.

I thought at the time there was nothing unique about our collapse. It isn't uncommon for a marriage not to survive the loss of a child. There's a number I used to know, a statistic toward which we eventually added. It didn't happen at once. It took better than a year, in fact. There was an outpouring of grief, friends with casseroles and good intentions, folks sitting with us sometimes all night. The Facebook memorials, the well-meant invasions of privacy—a universe of maudlin bullshit for which I was profoundly grateful. We thanked people. We did our best. We went on and for a while tried to pretend everything was normal, or as normal as it might be.

It wasn't, of course, and by the fall after Daniel's death, Mara was desperate enough to be on Klonopin and Concerta. But she couldn't work behind them, couldn't paint, couldn't think, couldn't make art and art for Mara was, I believe, not an escape from the world so much as a way to thrust herself deeper into the world, a way to make the world bearable. The pills were a temporary fix, but—at least in that moment—a fix all the same, not unlike the way you might squeeze a smashed finger, cradling it, refusing to look. I've often asked myself why, when the pills failed, when art failed, she turned to miracle, to magic, to a god who wasn't listening. But it's a stupid question and even asking it makes clear that while Mara believed in truth and beauty, all I ever believed in was her.

Sometime after Christmas 2017, sixteen or so months after

Daniel died, Mara found my incomplete RAIN! file. The file was a piece of investigative journalism—a rejected piece—never finished. She read it all the same, and reading it must have realized that the three cases of water I'd brought home for her and Daniel's "Tree of Heaven" were quite possibly poison.

A few days later, she left me.

I shouldn't have been surprised. By that time, Mara had come to believe that wires had been attached to her, cables the width of needles that ran to her wrists and ankles and the base of her skull, each line anchored in bone so that there was a near constant tension. Which is to say she was exhausted. Which is to say she could no longer bear the weight of this world. Though to even say as much is a creamy cliché; the mindful hand-wringing, a luxury of late-capitalism in the failing West; a place where outrage has become decadence; to speak of anything, an indulgence. Which, maybe, is why she said nothing. Which, maybe, is why instead of painting it or sculpting it or contorting her body to represent it, she chose instead to destroy one small part of it.

(If none of this makes sense—the mystical causal chain, the branching decision tree of grief—then you occupy my position, minus, perhaps, the sorrow.)

She went to live with the old Mennonite couple, the Kinzers, where she erected two signs along their driveway—YOUR GPS IS WRONG, and, a hundred meters farther down the gravel: YOU ARE FAR FROM GOD. She went to the library where in her study carrel she read about dioxin poisoning. About Banks LLC purchase of a Tazewell County bottling plant and their subsequent no-bid contract with the religious NGO Global Evangelical Relief to provide bottled water to various camps and agencies in the African Sahel.

She watched the YouTube confessional of the former congressman turned GER administrator Richard Manley (R-VA). She read "The Health Effects of Dioxin Poisoning: A Comprehensive Review" alongside the December 2001 report by the Virginia Department of Health indicating "substantial contamination" of the bottling plant alongside the May 2015 report that indicated, miraculously, the absence of said contaminants.

She went far, far away from me.

She went to Chris Bright and assembled a bomb.

As for the bomb, it must have seemed more reliable than any poorly realized deity. As for the bomb, as for all that followed, I think of all the people who in the wake of Daniel's death assured us that everything happens for a reason, according to some great, if incomprehensible, plan. I've often wondered how they could have said that to us. How stupidly heartless, if well-intentioned, they must have been. Reason? There was no reason. The world had simply broken us, and Mara decided to go out and break it back. It wasn't rational. It didn't happen for a reason, and while I nursed my grievances, Mara carted a bomb across a Virginia field.

In hindsight, I suppose I wasn't surprised.

Violence has always been the lingua franca of America. There are countries in which you risk tsunamis or wildfires or drought; it's accepted. Here, we accept that eventually you will be shot at a concert or outside a house of worship, that your children will bleed out on the floor of their elementary school, or, perhaps, should they live, be sent overseas to make sure the rest of the world is fluent in the language of drone strikes and *Zero Dark Thirty*, in the Shock and Awe of televised death.

John Brown—the figure with whom Mara became so obsessed—understood this. He rode out with his sons first in Bleeding Kansas and later to the federal arsenal at Harpers Ferry. All Americans understand it, and while Mara is, or was, many things, she was most essentially American.

There is a great deal of literature surrounding the suicide bomber, though that literature tends to focus either on treating survivors or identifying potential bombers. The "implantation of biological material" is not uncommon, and survivors should be treated with both antibiotics and vaccines against tetanus and hepatitis B. Potential suicide bombers generally are not, as the popular imagination holds, unemployed or particularly depressed. They are, in fact, often highly focused and motivated individuals.

You're trying to find some unified field of belief, she had once said to me. *But what if we are put here only to recognize beauty?*

But what if we aren't?

The Kinzers—the Mennonite couple Mara moved in with—were veterans of the old peace wars, civil disobedience as part of the Sanctuary Movement, the anti-nuclear movement. Both had spent the 1970s and '80s in Central America, and it was at their house, at first idly, and then not so idly, Mara began to talk about doing something, about John Brown at Harper's Ferry, John Brown riding out to Pottawatomie Creek. This idea of a precipitating act. This idea that a bomb isn't so much about destroying a particular place or thing as much as a particular complacency. You set off a bomb and what follows is an awakening, what follows is something not unlike that time you looked up from your phone and were struck, if only for a moment, by the sudden realness of the world. Mara must have come to believe as much, to say as much. Sitting in the wood-paneled living room with books on the shelves and fire in the grate, the dog asleep on the rug and all at once the old Kinzer woman can't hear another word of it, all the talk of *doing something*, and she gets up and leaves so that it is only Mara, cross-legged on the floor, and the old Kinzer man in his glider.

If you wonder why she's so adamant about nonviolence, he says, *it's because we weren't always.*

You were violent?

Imagine the old man, glassy-eyed and far away. *You do what feels necessary in the moment. It's situational. It's emotional. But then you have to live with it.*

And that's what you're doing, living with it?

I don't mean to sound like I'm preaching at you. Lord knows.

Imagine Mara looking up. *But does He?*

Before she knew it, it was summer.

Before she knew it, someone had anchored wires into her wrists and ankles and the crown of her head. Someone, some larger thing, was controlling her, just as I have come to understand it is controlling all of us. Only Mara refused to look away.

"Walk us through that last day," the first FBI agent will say, "the day she left you. This would have been in January. Start early."

But it's her last day I find myself imagining, her last conversation with Chris before they got in the truck to drive north to the bottling plant. It would have been evening, a warm September evening, and I imagine him holding his hairless head in his thin hands, as if thinking necessitated breaking apart.

You can still go with us, she must have told him. *We can be in Georgia before the fire department shows up. Be in the Keys before they think it's anything other than a mechanical fire.*

And Chris, all exasperation, Chris all renunciation: *There's no us, Mara.*

She must have walked outside his trailer then, smoked, paced. She'd known him for two decades, but he wasn't who he'd once been. It was natural to change, but it was also somehow inexcusable. She smoked and paced and realized that it didn't matter whether he came with her after or not. They'd already assembled the Tovex trigger in a tent set up within the airless greenhouse out back, a good six-man dome with the rain fly snapped in place so that the temperature hung in the wet eighties. Gloves, hairnets, plastic painter suits bought at the Home Depot because sparks, dust, dirt, whatever—you just couldn't have it. The painter suits, three for ten dollars, right there by the checkout.

The ammonium nitrate/fuel oil had been only marginally harder to come by. They'd driven to a Feed & Seed in Hot Springs for the fertilizer, ridiculous, the both of them going, but by then Chris was so deep into his chemo he could neither go on his own nor be left alone. Mara must have driven, Mara must have paid. Imagine the woman at the counter counting change, barely looking up from her Sudoku.

They pumped the diesel at a Texaco in Hampton, Tennessee.

(Days after the explosion, the FBI will show me the grainy security footage.)

That was the ANFO. ANFO because the TATP Bruce handed them in New Orleans, instead of the promised Semtex, was too unstable, per Chris. Mara would have just carried it in as planned, wrapped in tinfoil and loaded in her backpack, but then again, by that point she must have already formulated her other plan, the private one that involved some sort of metaphysical restitution, though who could say for what? Certainly not Mara. About her own life, she was inexpert. About her own life, it never quite felt real. The art she had made, the decisions she had not. Her life being what had happened to her on the way to someplace else. But standing there outside the greenhouse with its broken panes, Chris having refused to join her escape, she understood that is as real as life can be, misunderstood, unappreciated, a series of habits and events that are worn like borrowed clothes: the actual self no more than circumstance.

"Start first thing in the morning," the second agent will say, the pale one. "You'd argued the night before. She had out some of your papers."

"Some research you had failed to complete."

18

Some research, yes. It would be the old Mennonite couple who would eventually return it to me. I visited two months after the explosion to find an envelope on the cot in their back room, waiting for me. The Kinzer woman handed it to me that storm-soaked afternoon, Mississippi John Hurt playing on a Fisher-Price stereo, and holding it, I began the process of understanding, or attempting to understand.

"We kept it hid," the old woman said. "When the police came."

I suppose I should have thanked her, but I didn't, and eventually she left me alone with the contents:

Mara's North Carolina driver's license, set to expire the following year.

A membership card to the Mint Museum in Charlotte (reciprocity with the Bechtler and the Harvey B. Gantt Center for African American Arts and Culture—she and Daniel liked to go).

A photo of Daniel at two: john-johns, blonde hair, our boy sweet and vaguely nautical.

Postcards from Jalpan de Serra, Mexico, and a pancake restaurant in Gatlinburg, Tennessee.

Mara's diary.

(But not the mini-cassette, not yet: it would be weeks before Toliver handed it to me in Chicago.)

I was leaving when the Kinzer woman stopped me. There was one more thing, a sheaf of papers Mara had titled "The Water of Life." The research I had failed to complete, now completed.

"She left this for you," the old woman said, with as much venom as disgust.

"For me?"

She shrugged.

"For someone."

I took it home and realized 2003 was the year she started keeping secrets.

It took a while longer to realize she had always kept secrets.

But already I'm getting ahead of myself.

Already I need to start over.

For years, Mara talked about mountain lions, and the summer after she left I began to see them everywhere. This was the summer we watched the country burn—wildfires in California called the Shasta, the Modoc, the Mendocino Complex. Political fires in Washington known, we came to realize, as an empire in the throes of death. At night, when I remembered to look up from the cooling ash of my own marriage, I would sometimes walk barefoot out into our yard, our dog, Banjo, behind me, arthritic and loyal, the owls in the trees above us, the moon above the trees. And above it all, perhaps, God—though I could make no accounting for God.

Mara had been gone for nearly a year by then, our son Daniel dead for almost two, but like the entirety of our life together, we existed in a state of flux so that it remained impossible to define what exactly we were—separated? finished? I could never quite say, and that not saying was, I suppose, the cloud that followed me so persistently I came to think of it as weather, a system as private as it was suffocating.

Mara and I had met in the summer of 2002, both of us in our mid-twenties, a time when the world was defined by possibility. I was a playwright—or would be soon enough—working the courthouse beat at the *Watauga Democrat* by day and reading Sam Shepherd by night. Mara was working for a nonprofit and painting landscapes, great canvases that were, thanks to the grace of her brushwork, both abstract and representational.

Given our current madness, it's hard now to remember the urgency of that time was something new. After the complacent '90s, we were suddenly caught between 9/11 and the coming war in Iraq. This was the time of anthrax and jihad, of government officials speaking of crusades and plastic sheeting, and what I remember most are the heightened emotions, the anger, the intensity of simply waking every morning into a world quickly becoming unrecognizable. I met Mara at a gathering of what, for lack of a better term, might be called the "peace movement," at least as it existed in the mountains of western North Carolina, and over the course of the next year we had an affair built around private lust and public fury. An affair furious and brief and very much of the moment.

Over the winter of 2003, the world seemed to have acquired a new velocity: Colin Powell spoke before the UN General Assembly about weapons of mass destruction while the Third Infantry Division massed in Kuwait. The 101st Airborne deployed, the 15th Marine Expeditionary Unit—there was an inevitability about it all, an anger, too. War was coming, and the people wouldn't stand for it.

Then it came, and they did, the thick apathy of Support the Troops poured over the "homeland" like cement. Suddenly there were no more marches, no more meetings, just Mara and me, and a few old women from Code Pink. Half the country cheering for that Yale cheerleader, the other half silent. But not us. Mara and I were loud, at least with each other. We'd wake naked and touching in her tiny Rivers Street loft, pots of water rattling on the ancient radiator, rage for hours—George-Fucking-Bush, Dick-Goddamn-Cheney—start drinking, start touching . . . a hopeless cycle that finally fell apart in late 2003. We had met Chris Bright by then—more accurately, we had been lured into his gravitational field, helpless to resist the undertow, not that we wanted to.

We moved out to his farm near the North Carolina-Tennessee

state line in the early summer of 2003, and whether that delayed or hurried the death of our relationship I've never been certain. Either way, it ended, and I moved west, hoping to string together magazine assignments while teaching myself to write. When Mara and I met again—almost three years and two thousand miles later—it seemed like more than chance. She had left Appalachia to study land art—Spiral Jetty, Walter De Maria's Lightning Field, Nancy Holt's Sun Tunnels—and we sort of just took to each other, drinking box wine and riding around in the convertible Sebring her father had given her a decade prior. It was purely physical then: there was none of the political talk that had defined our time in North Carolina, and that was a good thing. It was the talk that had killed us, the hours in camp chairs down by the river where, caught somewhere between night and day, the joy would turn to sorrow, and then, inevitably, to anger.

We spent a year in Mexico house sitting for an LA couple who were intimates of David Hockney—Toliver and the boyfriend we never quite met—drinking mescal and going to sunset parties while Mara painted. We were young and happy and decided to return home to North Carolina and marry. I could sense her slipping away from me, and rather than let it happen a second time I persuaded her that what she wanted wasn't change but stability, or something like that. Either way, Mara had received an offer to teach at the university back where we had met.

It was all, at first, a great success. We bought an abandoned farmhouse deep in the mountains where Mara began work on what would eventually become *Alone Beneath the Tree of Knowledge*—the work that, until the events of September 2018, defined her career—and I wrote. By May, my play was complete. In June it was accepted by the Bartram Theater, one of the oldest and most prestigious professional repertory companies in the country: it would be staged that fall. This was tremendous news, and we drove up one glorious summer day to meet the company director. He loved the play. He was already making some stage sketches, thinking about casting, thinking about promotion. We left him in an office crowded with wigs and tailors' dummies and had a champagne lunch we couldn't afford. We were driving home, sundrunk and listening to Cat Power and Tift Merritt when Mara told me she was pregnant.

It was winter when she told me about the mountain lion.

There were things I didn't know, of course. Most marriages are filled with gaps better left unexplored. Old lovers, childhood dreams—there are practical reasons for not prying. There is also the sense of mystery, the way in which your other appears glossed with a hazy furtiveness that can, if understood in the proper context, keep alive a certain magic. I always believed in such, which is why it took me so long to realize Chris Bright had reentered our lives. He was a few years older and known as something of a bohemian recluse, living with an aged aunt on a self-sufficient farm deep in the Appalachian Mountains. He was said to be magnetic, and that had proven to be true. Most of the rest wasn't. The stories of wild parties, of heathen excess—nothing could have been more distant from reality. Chris Bright lived with the discipline required of one existing outside the bounds of society. Like his hero, Wendell Berry, he farmed and he read. He liked bourbon, but not to excess. His wiry frame owed as much to his time as a distance runner as to manual labor. He was full of both good humor and righteous indignation, but not once did I ever see him lose control. I met him first, and soon enough brought Mara out to visit him (at least that was how I understood it at the time). I think neither of us was so much in love with him as we were in love with what he stood for, or what we believed he stood for.

Again: possibility.

In a world of mass-marketed death, he was life.

In a world of speed and corruption, he was slowest virtue.

He was also bearded and thin and appeared not unlike the portraits of Jesus we'd both seen growing up. Even back then, he was obsessed with what he called—what we now all call—our dying planet. Climate change. Rising seas. The Sixth Extinction.

A day will come, I remember him saying, when they are running pumps in Miami and Key West, in Mumbai and New Orleans and Guangzhou, China. Then, sometime later, a day will come when they turn the pumps off, and leave the waters to rise. The earth would shake us off, wash us away, and so on and so forth. You could tell how bad he wanted it, some days you could. Other days he seemed to want nothing so much as to lie in the sun, his toes in the creek sand. We'd float down the Watauga River in inner tubes, feet in the cold water, backs against the warm rubber, lazy, drifting, spinning, all of it glazed with tallboys and the great blue heron that kept pace with us, always just ahead, always just above, lifting on those broad wings you could almost hear. It was worship. We joked about it then, called it the Church of the Moving Waters, but I believe it was worship.

Mara and I spent six months living on his farm, but the intimacy was too much—here was the political talk that had killed us. I left before Christmas and was in Colorado the night 2003 rolled into 2004. Mara left sometime after, and come August was an MFA student in the Art and Ecology graduate program at the University of New Mexico.

I would occasionally think of Chris, but it wasn't until that fall so many years later—Mara pregnant and working manically on her tree—that I heard his name. It was Mara who said it and as hard as this might be to believe, she said it in her sleep.

Or did I say it in mine?

Either way, the next day she began to talk about the mountain lion.

Our house—I cannot yet conceive of it in any other way—sits at the end of a gravel thread that follows a creek for the half mile it winds off a secondary road that itself sits a few miles off a minor byway that runs the thirty miles between the university in western North Carolina and the deeper hollows of East Tennessee. We had bought the land for both the empty farmhouse and the gigantic barn Mara turned into a studio. It was secluded, and it was cheap. The mountains rise on all sides, the darkness of night marred only by the distant lights of the second homes along the ridge. Summer evenings you can sit on the porch and listen to the sound of the creek gradually give way to the rising cicadas and whip-poor-wills, the moon climbing from the net of trees to cast our narrow valley in a light as white as bone.

Since Mara had left, I was spending a great deal of my time on that porch, not exactly thinking about our son, Daniel, but not *not* thinking of him either. More like he was present, and though I was numb to his presence I was still, however dimly, aware of it, the way you might be aware of a draft in the house even as you sleep. Later, when I learned that as a boy Chris Bright had carried on long conversations with his dead father, I wondered why it had never occurred to me to speak to my own dead son. It was a failure of imagination, I suppose. Perhaps, too, some sort of inborn defense mechanism. I do know that I was drinking more than I should have been, though that is a pretty good descriptor of my adult life.

I was out on the porch that September night—the night it began—when I heard the phone go off. The cell signal here is poor and we had maintained a landline, something that I consistently forgot to take off the hook. It was after midnight, but I was perfectly awake, having become fully capable of running off Bulleit Rye and my coddled sense of injustice. So it took no great effort to rise from the porch rocker and lumber inside, our old lab, Banjo, following me while I called to the phone to hold on, I'm coming, Jesus.

Though I'd spent most of the previous months sitting on the front porch sweating the July heat into August and then September, I did write the occasional article for *Mountain Voice*, a regional magazine that focused on environmental issues in the Southern Appalachians. On the line was my editor, Bill Baker, a man I'd known since those early days writing for the *Watauga Democrat*. We'd started at the paper together, and while he had risen to become editor-in-chief of a weekly with offices in eight towns and a subscription base of ninety thousand, I had not. I think he probably suspected I was a better writer than him—I wasn't—and it was that guilt, coupled with nostalgia and pity, that led him to call every few months, requesting three thousand words on this proposed pipeline or that collapsing coal ash impoundment.

That night he sounded more agitated than usual, and though Bill was very much the proverbial pillar of the community—his had been an upward glide-path that leveled off with a five-thousand-square-foot house and a dependence on Wellbutrin—like most of us, he'd never quite been able to hear the music of unhappiness that scored his days. That night, I wondered if, like me, he hadn't sunk deeper into the rye than intended.

"Goddamn," he said when I came on the line, "I was afraid you'd be sleeping."

"No luck there."

"What's that?"

"Nothing. I said I'm not sleeping much these days."

"Right, right," he said, "of course you aren't. Sleeping's the last thing I'd expect out of you. But listen, are you hearing what's coming over the wires? Up in Virginia?"

"I've been listening to the creek."

"Jesus, David, and you call yourself a reporter." Which I never did. "Listen to this, all right?"

A fire was burning at a water-bottling plant two hours north in Virginia. It had been contained, but the damage sounded substantial. A HAZMAT team was present, and someone had been chattering over an open channel about the FBI.

"You know the place I'm talking about? It bottles for that company RAIN! You remember them I know."

I did. For the last few years, rumors had swirled around the company, and at one point I had pitched an investigative piece about the parent. They were owned by a local businessman and a Virginia widow, but the rumors held this was a front for several well-connected political figures, conservative darlings no longer in Washington but still tied to the establishment by strings of ideology and old-boy bullshit. They had bought the well at a bargain price: though the water had passed all the required tests, it had once been deemed toxic. Bill had shot the pitch down and after a visit to the office of RAIN! I had let it go. They seemed if not unimpeachable at least legitimate; they had also sent me home with three cases of water, which I had taken, if only to prove to myself how wrong I had been. This was the research—the conjecture—I had failed to complete. What was a matter of public record, however, was that RAIN! was in the process of fulfilling a lucrative contract for Global Evangelical Relief, a contract that was likely making the owners, whoever they were, obscenely rich.

"I want you to get up there first thing in the morning," Bill said. "You can do that, right?"

"Sure, yeah."

"Get on this, David. I swear to god, something about this doesn't feel right. Some first responder was jabbering over the scanner and then they just cut the traffic right goddamn off. You can get up there, can't you?"

"Of course, yeah."

"I got a feeling this is tied to some nefarious shit."

"Hey, Bill? Didn't I pitch something like this nefarious shit before?"

"Yeah, yeah. You were right and I was wrong."

"I just wanted you to say it."

"You're the tortured genius, and I'm the pitiful shortsighted manager, eyeless in Gaza."

"So long as we're clear on that."

"Get up there, David. I swear there's something more to it." He was almost panting. "Honest to god, it almost sounds like someone set off a bomb. First thing in the morning, all right?"

"Yeah," I said, "first thing in the morning."

But first thing in the morning found me late and hungover and I didn't drive to Virginia, not for many hours at least, and when I finally did, it was too late.

But then, in a manner of thinking, it had always been too late.

Alone Beneath the Tree of Knowledge was purchased in 2013 by a private collector in upstate New York, and despite its fragility I would occasionally hear of it on loan to the Whitney or the Broad. I'd seen it in person only once since the sale, at the High in Atlanta. That day, I was prepared for all sorts of emotions—I was prepared, frankly, to break down—but what struck me was how empty it appeared, how incomplete, without Mara naked beneath its naked boughs. Something about that sense of loss—the idea that such absence belonged now not only to me but the entire universe—was comforting.

Mara had found the tree just weeks after we had come back from Toliver's Mexican mansion to buy our farm and start what would be our married life, but she didn't begin the process of digging until summer. It was a lone wisteria tree that grew along an otherwise bare slope, perhaps fifty meters below the tree line of white pine and yellow birch, and I think it was that aloneness that made her hesitate. She showed it to me one July afternoon so golden the very day appeared some hammered alloy sheeted evenly across the length of the sky. We stood by the tree for a long time, wordless until I finally asked her what she was thinking.

Can't you see it, she said, only it wasn't a question, and I didn't attempt to answer. After that, she began to commune with it, to sit under it, to lay beneath its purple flowers. I would look up from my desk to see her out the window, back to its gnarled trunk. We were restoring the farmhouse—though most of my work consisted of standing at the elbow of Jaybird, a local carpenter who would eventually become a close friend—and I would put down the two-by-four I was carrying to see her on her back, body wreathed in petals, as if the tree were slowly burying her.

It was just after my play was accepted by the Bartram Theater that she began digging. She was in the first months of pregnancy by then but was adamant that she, and she alone, unearth its long, tapering roots. I relented because the work appeared more tedious than physically difficult, and because I was distracted. *High Water* had gone into rehearsals and there were proving to be problems. Entire blocks of dialogue that worked well on the page were failing on the stage. Panicked, I started making the hour drive to the theater, each time thinking it would be my last. But what was at first occasional, quickly became daily. Which meant I caught only passing glimpses of Mara out in the yard in work pants and tank top, sweating and filthy and following the line of a root with a tiny spade as if she were unearthing some long-forgotten creature. I would stay in Virginia late, nervous and frustrated with the rehearsals, and then go out for drinks with some of the cast to deal with my nerves and frustration. But those were impossibly long days, summer days, and no matter how late it seemed, I'd come home to find her in the shower, dirt running from her body in rivulets, so thick it sometimes clotted the drain. These were also happy days, and as often as not I would quickly strip and climb into the shower with her. After, we'd lie with the windows up, while Gillian Welch or Dwight Yoakam played beneath the whipping of the ceiling fan.

It was August when I came home to find her struggling to load the wisteria tree into the handcart we had found in the barn. Mara was just beginning to show, and I remember her Carhartt pants and dirty T-shirt. She smiled when she saw me. Like the day, she seemed to radiate life. I think she must have understood she was on the cusp of something transcendent, our child, this tree. Over the course of the summer, she had not simply dug it up—she had dug out every single root, following every tendril to its weedy end. Now it sat on the ground in its completeness, half tree, half spiraling root system, like some sea creature long thought extinct, now dragged back to reluctant life.

It was the golden hour, and as I walked toward her I felt something electric. Here was the world in its everydayness but made so strange, so new. Was it Joseph Cornell who said the world is beautiful but unsayable, and that's why we need art?

But all Mara needed were my hands.

"Just to get the trunk up," she said, and I helped her heft its surprising weight into the slatted bed, and then helped her pull the cart down to the barn where we unloaded it. It was all the help she ever asked for, and all the help she ever took. Thereafter, she worked in secret. I would see her come and go, filmed in sawdust and dirt, or smelling of varnish, smiling in tights and the old cable-knit sweater that swelled steadily over her stomach. She was always smiling, always happy, touching me lightly on the shoulder or the back of my neck as she passed. Meanwhile, my play limped toward its premiere. I had quit driving up every day. There were no more changes to be made, and though expectations were low, it was understood that while the play was flawed, there were also moments of genuine insight, flashes of dialogue that "gestured at some deeper truth" (to quote the promotional material).

A few days before opening night I had a last drink with the director. He drove a white Miata from the mid-90s I'd seen around the parking lot a few times, and that night, riding with him to a paneled cigar bar of Edison bulbs and cocktails from the jazz age, I realized that the car wasn't so much vintage as derelict with its torn upholstery and cracked dashboard.

"Listen, David, I want you to go into this with clear eyes," he said, and staring into the red-rimmed depths of his own, I realized that what I had taken to be artistic suffering was more likely alcoholism. "The play's going to have a mixed reception—okay, fine, that doesn't bother us. There are some flaws—yes, we know this. Chinks in the armor, cracks. But what's Leonard say? 'That's how the light gets in.' We aren't concerned with this. The important thing is that it shows great promise. You think you're a playwright now. But the truth is, you'll become a playwright about halfway home after the premiere. You're going to be driving back thinking through this and that, and there's going to be this great clarity, this just absolute sense of what you did right and what you did wrong. You have to step back from the mountain to see the mountain, my friend." Across the table he had taken one of my hands into both of his. "You'll start writing. It'll be so clear. You'll think: this is too simple, the dialogue, the plot. But then at some point you'll realize that simplicity masks a greater complexity." His hands were small and pink, and as he squeezed my fingers I felt overcome with a wave of compassion. "You'll understand what Ravel meant when he said 'complex, not complicated.'"

He signaled the bartender for another scotch.

"You are writing, of course?" he asked.

"Of course," I told him.

I wound up driving him back to his small apartment that sat up a flight of exterior stairs above the theater offices. Two rooms crowded with playbills and ashtrays and glitter, a kitchenette of linoleum and windows painted shut. He slept on a foldout couch, but I didn't bother folding it out, simply piled him onto the fabric, arranging him on his side.

"Keep writing, David," he managed to say, and tried to kiss me. I pushed him away gently and he collapsed onto the couch, his eyeshadow the lightest of blues.

"The writing is everything," he said.

But I wasn't writing. While Mara worked fourteen hours a day in her barn studio, I sat at my desk and stared out at the unmoving trees. There was a great wisdom in their stillness, and I told myself it was that wisdom I was after. But the truth was simpler. The truth is that like Mara I am not immune to periods of sadness. The apathy of lying in bed. The listlessness of sitting in a porch rocker, almost, but not quite, moving. It isn't so much depression as inertia, but, ultimately, what's the difference?

I might have stayed like that forever had larger forces not intervened.

In late August, Mara began teaching at the university, meaning she worked in the mornings and three afternoons a week drove the half hour to town where she taught four sections of Understanding Art. In late September, *High Water* opened. It was an eco-play that follows an orphaned boy who may or may not be the second coming of Jesus Christ, returned to resurrect not the quick and the dead but the birds of the air and the flowers of the field, to resurrect, in short, the planet. But, of course, it's too late: the planet is terminal. An environmental jeremiad, then, wrapped in all the trappings of the Old South. With great pretension, I took a line from Kafka as an epigraph:

The messiah will return when he is no longer necessary.

For a decade I had immersed myself in Tennessee Williams, in the gothic fiction of Flannery O'Connor and William Faulkner, and their influence showed in the ragged joinery of so many disparate elements: the abusive stepfather, the well-intentioned social worker, and, of course, the child who carries with him a magic talisman. In this case, a jade Carolina parakeet. Here, the boy has asked for a ride to rec league football.

WOMAN
DSS ain't no taxi service, son.

MAN (FROM OFFSTAGE)
What's he wanting?

WOMAN
Wants me to drive him to the ballfield.

MAN
Down to Chickapea? Have his ass walk.

And so on.

Mara returned from her work for opening night, hanging on my arm like a goddess, charming and hypnotic, laughing her full-bodied laugh, golden-skinned, golden-haired, and gorgeously pregnant. People kept coming up to us, congratulating me and fawning over her. The after-party was at an art museum in the antebellum mansion of a long-dead coal magnate, the house an exercise in historical fanaticism, the cabinets, the furniture, the andirons around the fireplace—everything period, everything authentic. Everything but the art deco pool around which servers moved great chafing dishes of food, while beneath the fairy lights four men in blue tuxedos worked through the opening bars of "Give Me Just a Little More Time."

It was nearing dawn when we drove home, the top down while Mara slept beneath a blanket someone had offered. She was five months pregnant and had been on her feet for twelve hours yet I swear she was smiling. The evening was such a success it was almost possible to forget that the play was not. It received a mixed review in the *Washington Post*, but outside of the local paper and a couple of theater blogs, was otherwise ignored. It closed in October. The director gave me a shoulder-hug and said he couldn't wait to read what was next.

"Complex," he said, "not complicated."

I went home to my upstairs office overlooking the valley and pretended to write.

Mara went back to her tree.

Fall came in all its failing glory. The silvering maples and purpling sweetgums, the way the light seemed to soften, as if the world might yet forgive us. In the evenings I made a fire in the hearth and rubbed Mara's feet, making a fuss over both because it gave me something to make a fuss over, some purpose greater than work, which I'd only been pretending at and which I no longer cared about. Our son was due in late January, Mara's project was almost complete, and if I squinted just right, if I chose to see the world through the cage of my lashes, all appeared well.

It snowed just before Christmas, and then one night, Mara said the name Chris Bright.

The next morning I came down to find her staring out the kitchen window.

"I think there's a mountain lion out there," she said.

The next day—the day I should have risen early to drive north to report on the fire—was a Friday. I woke around ten to the cicadas already screaming in the September heat. Out the window, the trees were full of tent worms, white nests in the dewy limbs, as if someone had flung plastic grocery bags into the green boughs.

When I sat up, I discovered I had left the front door open, the screen knocking against the frame as a welcome breeze moved down the valley. I lay in bed a while longer and listened to the sound of Banjo's nails on the hardwood floors. It was still very much summer and already you could feel the heat gathering in the atmosphere. By eleven it would begin to descend, wet and thick. By noon you would wear it like a scarf, a sloppy suffocation absent in these mountains a generation ago. I fed the dog and took a cold shower, dressed in jeans and an old fishing shirt, and walked barefoot into the yard to feed the chickens we—I—still kept. I was aware of Bill Baker's phone call, though only dimly. I knew I hadn't dreamed it. It was more that I didn't really care.

We kept a bag of Prairie's Choice chicken feed in a plastic garbage can, and when I rounded the corner I could see it had been tipped over, the lid dragged away along with a scattering of feed and the remains of the bag. A second later I saw what was left of the chickens. Over the years we had built a complex of coops, apartment buildings linked by wire-enclosed tunnels so that the entire thing looked like some Rube Goldberg aviary. It was torn apart now. Wire had been peeled and shredded, and in at least two places I could see the actual boards had been broken. There wasn't much left of the chickens either, feathers, a torn foot. The dog limped forward, sniffed a ragged body, and began to lick the bloody remains. A fox, I thought, but a fox couldn't do that to the enclosure. A bobcat maybe. There were no mountain lions left.

"Banjo," I said, and he looked up at me and went back to licking. "Get away from that. Hey!" I stepped toward him and he eased back, nose to the ground. "Let's go in," I said, because a cloud had just shifted over the valley: it was suddenly darker, cooler. Without meaning to, I looked up at where our son's old treehouse stood, no more than a platform now, and then looked away, back at the sky. It would rain soon. "Banjo," I called. "There ain't no mountain lions out here," I said, self-consciously overdoing the faux old-timer accent, but saying it all the same, saying it to calm myself. "Ain't no painters. No pumas or panthers. Come on, boy. Ain't no catamounts."

I left Banjo inside the house and stood on the porch. Above the still-green yard and the still-leafed maple, above what pasture lay beyond the white fence and Mara's graying barn, the wind was just beginning to snip and pick. I got into my truck and could smell rain and honeysuckle, and looked up at the wash-water of the sky just as the first drops began to bang against the metal roof. By the time I made it out to the blacktop, the rain fell in a long, slanting curtain.

I had met Jaybird that first fall back home. We'd hired him to do some plumbing and electrical and somehow what had started as a few odd jobs had grown into the more or less complete restoration of our home. He sang in a country-western band, The Heartless Bastards, complete with fiddle and pedal steel, and one night early in our return Mara and I had gone out to hear him at the Johnson County Ice House, a honky-tonk just across the state line. They played Merle and George Strait while the crowd drank dollar Buds and two-stepped in their shit-kickers, peanut shells on the concrete floor. Another week we saw him at one of the college bars in town. The crowd there was hipster, all beard oil and ironic PBRs, and that night they played Townes Van Zandt and John Prine covers. We became friends, the three of us, and that first fall he began to show up almost daily, sometimes to put in GFCI electrical sockets, sometimes to sit on the porch and drink cup after cup of black coffee. We paid him what we could when we could, which is to say poorly and infrequently, but he never seemed to care. He lived alone and frugally in a small farmhouse with asbestos siding and a tarpaper roof at the foot of a meadow where he kept two dozen sheep and a couple of luxury tiny homes he rented out on Airbnb.

By the time I made the fifteen-minute drive over to Jay's place, the rain had abated. It was no more than a drizzle when I pulled in, water dripping from the bright trees. His door was open and I called through the screen, but no one answered. A moment later I saw him coming down the hill, soaked and leading his flock of sheep toward the feed pen. I waited on the porch and by the time he made it to the house the sun was out, the world brilliant and steaming.

"Got caught in it, did you," I said.

He was in overalls, shirtless beneath, long stringy hair, graying and matted to the sides of his head.

"Microburst. Up on the knoll there with the sheep," he said, and shook my hand. "What say, David?"

"It was raining at the house, too."

"You loafing?"

"I guess."

"Let's get us a beer, why don't we?"

We sat out on the wrought-iron patio furniture the new girlfriend had bought him and drank Modelo Negra in the noon heat.

"Something got in my chickens last night," I told him.

"Like a fox?"

"I don't think so."

"Raccoon or something?"

"Something bigger than that. You should see the pen. You know that heavy oak door we put on? Completely torn off the hinges."

"Huh," he said and took a drink of beer. "Bear?"

"I actually think it was a mountain lion."

He smiled.

"Ain't no more mountain lions, partner."

"Exactly what I told the dog."

"This is grandpa talk. You know the guys that sit around outside the General Store?"

"I guess maybe I'm getting grandpa age."

"Shit. You're not even allowed to believe in them unless you're over seventy. Then you have to take some sort of oath, swearing allegiance."

"To the lions?"

"To the nonexistent mountain lions of southern Appalachia, exactly."

"Yeah, still though." I took a drink. "You should have seen that door."

He got us two more beers and two more after that. When he went back in again, he came back out carrying a twelve-gauge and an old .357 Magnum.

"Wanna shoot some?"

I downed my beer and nodded. We shot out behind the feed pen, hanging targets and a few rotten gourds he found in the weeds, pumpkins and acorn squash too soft to burst.

"You coming tonight?" he asked.

"Last one of the season, isn't it?"

He nodded, and slid his ear protectors back down. Every summer Friday a band played an outdoor concert at the Valle Crucis Park. The Heartless Bastards would be the last show before fall arrived. I had always loved those evenings, dragging Mara with me even when she was too exhausted to go. It was always a doing. Folks spreading quilts or fighting with complex folding tables. Drinking martinis in camp chairs. There were food trucks, but most people brought spreads of cheese and prosciutto, wine in stainless steel canteens. People liked to dress up. The women bare-foot and empire-waisted on the green grass. The gingham table-cloths and wicker picnic baskets. Everywhere children on bicy-cles, helmeted and laughing and waving sparklers. There would be a party at Jay's beforehand, his band, his new girlfriend. Bar-becue and beer, and then we'd all pile over to the park to do the sound check.

"My daddy's coming down for it," Jay said.

"Is he? I'll be glad to see him."

"He'll be glad to see you. He worries about you."

"Well."

"Excessively," Jay said, and took another shot.

We carried the guns back to the house and I sat outside while Jay took them in. He stuck his head out the screen door and asked if I wanted another beer. I didn't. I needed to get going. I'd see him tonight.

He nodded and when he came back out to sit, something in his face had changed. There was a solemnity there that I hadn't reg-istered before.

"You going to get any more chickens?" he asked.

"I don't think so."

"It was Mara who loved them, wasn't it?"

"Yeah. Mara and Daniel."

He walked with me out to my truck and lingered in a way that wasn't like him. Solicitous. Pensive. Both hands on the door as if he were there to stop me from shutting it.

"So you're coming back later?"

"I told you I would."

"All right," he said finally, and folded his hands in prayer. "Na-maste, brother."

I was halfway home before I realized I'd forgotten to ask him if he'd heard anything about the fire at the bottling plant.

The winter of Mara's pregnancy it had started snowing on December 23 and didn't stop until the sun broke over the trees Christmas morning. The sky cleared and the world appeared unmade, the land white, the air the clear blue of blown glass. There were nineteen inches on the ground, the roads impassable, and while I worried Mara might go into early labor and we'd be stuck here, she was at ease. Not yet, she told me. But what if it's time? I asked. I remember the way she looked at me, amused. She was sitting on the couch, her legs tucked beneath her, that same cable-knit sweater ragged and stretched and soft as chamois. I remember the way she took my hand into both of hers. But it isn't time, she told me, and as with all things, she was right. All things, I suppose now, but one.

For the next two weeks we stayed more or less in bed beneath a mound of heavy quilts, Banjo curled on the floor beside us, yipping and twitching in his sleep. I went out for firewood, and twice nursed the truck up the road and to the Cove Creek General Store for supplies. Otherwise, we nested. I read poetry to our unborn son—Daniel, we had decided to call him—my lips down by her navel. Mara dragged her laptop into the bed to show me paintings by Amy Sillman and Stanley Lewis, the performance pieces of Marina Abramović, the video installations of Bill Viola. She asked me to read *High Water* to her again and we talked about what I had done well, about what I would do better. We ate ice cream and venison and whatever else we found in the depths of the freezer. I rubbed her feet and calves and afterward spooned behind her to make the sort of slow meditative love that pulls afternoon into evening.

Then one morning I woke to find her sitting up in bed, leaned into the pillows.

"I had this dream," she said, "this nightmare."

"About what?"

"Something was watching us."

"What was?"

She shook her head and when I took her hand found it damp with night sweat.

Now and then she would talk about the mountain lion she believed lay hidden in the forest around us. Cougars, pumas, panthers—few animals inspire so many names—had disappeared from the Southern Appalachians nearly a century ago. But people were always claiming to have seen one. Inevitably it would be a bobcat or a dog or a fat tabby that lurked too close to a game camera. There were mountain lions out west and there were panthers in the Everglades, but in North Carolina they existed only in zoos and the minds of old-timers.

"You know what? We should get you a seat on the church pew out in front of the General Store. Everybody there talks about mountain lions," I told her that winter. "This is like the favorite discussion topic of old men."

"It's still true," she said.

"One of the top three, let's say. Gas prices and Obama's citizenship also being up there."

But she only smiled.

I had installed a game camera and in grainy black and white we saw deer and turkey and red fox, a single image of a bear, several of Banjo licking the aperture. But no mountain lion.

"You'll hear it sometimes," she told me over that long snowy time. "I mean I hear it."

I didn't ask about the name Chris Bright, if she ever heard that too, if she ever dreamed it.

I was, I suppose, afraid of an answer I already knew.

By early January the snow was mostly gone, piled in shadow and drift. Classes started, but Mara had arranged to teach online in order to be home with the baby. I went upstairs to my study where I pretended to write, staring out the window at the sky, the trees, a great murder of crows that sat down in the field, tiny splashes of ink on the otherwise white canvas of the day. I would hear Mara downstairs talking online to her students and occasionally catch sight of her bundled in blankets and trudging out to the barn. There was no use trying to stop her. She was so close, she told me. So close I can taste it, David. She was running off that proximity, fueled by it, always flushed, always exhilarated, calling me to where she sat at night in the claw-footed tub, nearly buoyant. Then one day in mid-January I came downstairs in the early afternoon to find her on the couch, red-faced and still in her heavy LLBean coat. Her boots had formed puddles beneath them and she appeared to be almost panting. When she looked up at me I knew exactly what she would say.

"I did it, David," she told me. "It's finished."

That night I fell into a sort of happy dreamless exhaustion, as if it were me who had finished something, sleeping so deeply Mara had to shake me repeatedly.

"David, wake up."

It was just after midnight.

"I feel something," she said, and when she stood, her water broke. Two hours later Daniel was born. They wiped him clean and lay him on Mara, and I stood there, touching them both. When I held him, I felt such tenderness, but such vulnerability too. It was as if the world had broken open, its interior revealed as both jagged and soft, part pomegranate, part shards of glass. I felt in that moment how vast the world had grown, and how it had constricted too. Seven years later when I again held my son, his body lifeless and broken, I went back to that moment, back to the sense that January night in the third-floor maternity ward of the Western North Carolina Regional Medical Center, where I had been given some insight that, while I couldn't articulate it, made so many things matter less, and one particular thing matter so much more.

But that was years in the future. That morning, I sat beside Mara as she held our son, touching her, touching him. Just after daylight, we all three slept. Later that day friends began to arrive, Jay and his girlfriend, colleagues of Mara's in bright scarves and long overcoats who came in flushed and smiling. It was a parade of glad welcome, all handshakes and hugs, while Mara nursed Daniel and we all dozed between visits. That evening Mara asked me if I would drive back to our house to get a few things she had forgotten and to check on Banjo. I left them reluctantly, but once I was outside walking to the parking deck, I felt an overwhelming exhilaration. Here I was, on this cold turning earth, with such purpose, even if it was no more than bringing back a hairbrush and an old nightgown that had belonged to her mother. I drove home, stopping once at a McDonald's for coffee, and ran into the house, letting Banjo out to pee and refilling his water, scattering his food across the linoleum. The toiletries and nightgown were easy to find and within minutes I was ready to return. But something held me.

In the months since I had helped Mara load the wisteria tree into the trailer and unload it in the barn I had seen nothing of her work. She had given updates, but they were always vague, and while I knew she didn't want me going in there, I decided to go anyway. What I found—I don't know exactly how to describe it. It stunned me, the beauty of it. But it also unnerved me. It frightened me, I suppose. The wisteria tree floated in the center of the room, its intricate root system suspended and spreading around it the way a dress will lift and hover when you step into water. It was as if I was looking at the tree in the ground, but the dirt made transparent, made invisible, and it took me a moment to realize everything hung from hundreds of lines of clear filament tied to the trusses of the barn. The entire tree had been sanded and finished in a clear varnish. The leaves were lavender. Crepe paper cut into ovals, I realized when I touched one. They were laced in the boughs, but also scattered on the concrete floor. When I saw the long indentation I knew she had been lying there, beneath the tree, cradled in a drift of the softest of purples.

I stood there for a long time, longer than I intended and would have stood there longer still had I not heard Banjo barking. I didn't know exactly what to think of this woman I loved. I did know that she had brought something wondrous into the world.

Two things—I told myself. Two things.

I came home from Jay's to find Bill Baker had called three times and left two messages. I didn't need to hear them to know what they would say—was I on the road yet? Goddamn it, David, why haven't you checked in?—and deleted both without listening, turned on the ceiling fan and let Banjo out, remembering the dead chickens as he shot across the yard.

"Don't," I called, but he was already gone, nose down and sniffing.

I opened all the windows and then my laptop.

There was a brief notice about the fire. Just before midnight a call had gone to the Mountain View fire and rescue: someone reported smoke over the horizon. Mountain View and three neighboring stations had responded. The fire had been contained and the sheriff's department was on the scene. There was no sign of arson, and no mention of the FBI. A routine mechanical fire then, contained, finished. I still had a file upstairs on RAIN!, the information—the hearsay—I had collected way back when I first pitched the idea to Bill Baker and he dismissed it with a shake of his head. *Think lawsuits, dumbass.* I was in my office, trying to find it in the swamp of papers that littered the room, when I

44

heard Banjo barking. I could see him from the window. He was out at the coop, just outside the torn door, his body rigid. I opened the window and called to him but he never looked up, just stayed fixed on whatever was inside.

I walked downstairs.

From the porch, I could see that he was scared, and suddenly I was too. I couldn't say why, only that something fundamental seemed to have changed. But it wasn't something visible. The day was still and bright, the air hot. I walked past the neglected gardens, the raised beds left to weeds and rot, the crucified scarecrow with his pie-tin face. There was a hawk up in a dead oak, its broad form silhouetted against a sky sun-dogged and glimmering. Everything glimmering, lighted, it seemed, with a certain predation. It hit me then what I felt: I was being watched. There was something in the coop. Probably a raccoon or even a vulture that had hopped its way in. But also, possibly, something else. What had come for my son and my marriage. What would come, eventually, for me.

I walked slowly, calling *Banjo, come on, boy,* softly, cooingly. When I reached him a cloud slipped over the sun and we were cast into a cool darkness. *Come on, boy,* I said. *It's okay.* He seemed to relax a little into his haunches and I reached down and stroked the back of his neck. We were walking back to the house when the sun slipped its halo of thundercloud and all at once everything became blindingly luminous again, violently so, the world sharper than it needed to be. I pulled Banjo inside and shut the door. He limped into the kitchen to lap up nearly a bowl of water. When I heard him ease onto the floor to sleep, I walked back to the window and stared out at the coop.

Not long after Daniel was born, I'd woken one night to find Mara standing over his cradle. She wasn't touching him, wasn't moving, she just stood there in the cold dark.

"You okay?" But she didn't hear me, and startled when I touched her wrist. "Hey, you okay?"

"That dream," she said.

"Come back to bed."

We crawled back beneath the sheets and she told it to me again: something was watching her, coming for our boy. She must have dreamed it a dozen times, she told me. "Remember right after the play closed, maybe a week after? You went to see Bill Baker about that pipeline story, and then Jay came by that night with that blueberry cobbler he had made? That was the first night."

"But it's over now," I told her.

She was shaking.

"That was the first night I had the dream," she told me.

It was only weeks later when it came to me: that night, the night she first dreamed of being watched, was the night she'd said his name. Chris Bright. He had reentered our life. I just hadn't been willing to deal with it.

Now, Banjo was asleep in the kitchen, exhausted, it seemed. Certainly no longer concerned with the chicken coop. But I couldn't quit staring out at it. I stood there while the phone rang in the other room. I stood there until the ringing stopped and the answering machine came on, and then for some time more. The feathers, the blood. At some point I'd have to clean it up.

But not yet.

The year Daniel turned seven we decided to spend May in Florida. The winter had been harsh and we wanted sun and sand and the smell of Coppertone, as evocative to me as the scent of a baby's head. Mara had gone to a gallery opening in Miami in February and taken Daniel with her. He'd had a sickly winter—fevers, chills, something like a lingering flu though it wasn't—and we both thought the warm humid air would be good for him. In hindsight, these were the early symptoms of non-Hodgkin's, something that despite his persistently swollen lymph nodes neither we nor his pediatrician had realized. But that was all later. After the gallery opening, they'd driven south and rented a bungalow on Marathon Key near a bird sanctuary where they spent several days volunteering. Except for a panic attack on the last night—Mara had called me the next morning, clearly shaken by what she called her "panther nightmare"—it had all gone well.

Mara called it a "scouting trip" and planned our May itinerary: we would drive down and spend a few days camping in the Everglades. We'd take an airboat ride. We'd go to an alligator farm. After that, we'd drive to Largo and take Daniel snorkeling at the Pennekamp Reef. Finally, we'd go to the bird sanctuary on Marathon. That would be the highlight of the trip—a week volunteering just as he and Mara had. We'd finish in Key West and then spend two days driving home. It would be touristy and silly, but also warm and fun.

"We'll vacation like normal Americans," Mara said, only half joking.

That would be a good thing, I thought. To give Daniel a taste of American normalcy. Normal was not a world in which we trafficked. In the years since his birth, Mara's reputation as an artist had grown. *Alone Beneath the Tree of Knowledge* had sold for a very respectable six figures (that it was soon appraised by the new buyer's insurer for seven bothered Mara not in the least). She was teaching only one class now, and in the past year had taught herself the art of glass blowing. Her habits had changed. Or one had, at least: she no longer worked alone, the great solitude that had characterized the months she spent on her tree replaced by the presence of Daniel. Daniel in the BabyBjörn carrier, Daniel on her hip, Daniel tottering behind her, fingers streaked with the paint and Elmer's glue he used for his own "projects."

All that spring, Mara and Daniel had worked together on the "Tree of Heaven," as they came to call it. They'd started making trips to a scrap yard and from an array of bicycle frames, pipes, metal tubing, and a length of flagpole, Mara has fashioned a tree, welding the parts and anchoring the frame in concrete. The birds—seabirds, songbirds, raptors—were made from empty water bottles that might otherwise have choked them. When you turned the iron trunk, the plastic took flight, the birds assuming the shape of a murmuration not unlike the ones Mara and I had seen years before living in Mexico. Mara and Daniel took the water bottles from recycling bins, trash cans, the side of the road. I brought home three cases from RAIN! but that was breaking the rules, Daniel told me. We were supposed to take plastic out of the world, not put more in. Still, Daniel and Mara took the cases I'd brought to their studio and Daniel drank the water over the coming months, dutifully downing one after the next so the bottles could be used.

If the project was a bit sentimental, a bit of a cliché, it was also beautiful and meaningful, not just visually, and not just knowing what it meant to Daniel. He had come to love birds, and, as he put it, heaven was the place where all birds would gather, a great nesting of color and shape, and if that is a cliché, it's the sort of cliché that makes life worthwhile. But what I loved most about the project was that it showed a softer side of Mara. So often her work revealed a sharp edge, an anger. But not this. She cut the shapes and Daniel painted them until beneath the tree hung seven hundred birds, three-dimensional and, when the tree spun, turning on filaments of wire. It was a beautiful thing and fit perfectly in the measured chaos of our backyard.

Our house was all old dog and art books and a confetti of construction paper. Wilco or the Delines on the stereo. Lucinda Williams singing "Are You Alright?" We had a circle of eccentric friends, artists, of course, but also people who had gravitated to the mountains in order to be outdoors. Climbers with day jobs in retail. Photographers and trail runners selling insurance or brewing beer.

The previous Halloween we had trick-or-treated up King Street where, so many years before, Mara and I had marched against the Iraq war. That day had ended violently—tear gas, arrests, the pepper spray in Mara's face—but it no longer felt like the same place. The autumn light was lavish, so golden it appeared from a different star, and we walked drunkenly, happily with a dozen other parents and their children, everyone in costume. I was Tennessee Williams in white suit and giant glasses. Mara was Wonder Woman. Daniel, a scuba diver in long black underwear, a plastic three-liter bottle painted silver and strapped to his back, goggles on his forehead.

The Heartless Bastards were playing at the pub on the far end of the town and we were a happy parade, making our unsteady way there, the street closed to traffic and everywhere folks in costume, laughing, greeting friends. Daniel was just ahead of us, and we watched him buzz into storefronts for candy like a bee to pollen. I put my arm around Mara and we walked like that for a while. Finally, she leaned in to kiss my jaw, and what it felt like was a sort of admission of contentment. Here we are, she seemed to say, and how wonderful it is to be here.

For my part, I was writing, mostly articles for *Mountain Voice*, but I was scribbling bits of dialogue too. Things overhead, things remembered. I wasn't exactly writing a play, a screenplay maybe. Something magisterial, I told myself. Ross McElwee for the twenty-first century, Werner Herzog in southern seersucker. But I wasn't exactly doing that either. I made notes, imagined scenes. I was doing enough to at least maintain the illusion of progress, even if no one but me cared. And why should anyone care? We were happy, the three of us, always together, eating at the big farm table we'd found at a yard sale, sitting on the porch swing in the evenings. There was some money now, and besides the occasional trip to the Guggenheim in New York or the Tate in London, we stayed at home or in the woods, walking the trails we had built through the National Forest.

By April we were preparing for Florida. We had booked the camp site and airboat ride, the day of snorkeling, the condo overlooking the gulf in Islamorada. Three days before we left, we hiked up to Orchard Falls, a waterfall that descended through a series of pools choked with rock and logs, everything mossy and green and damp. It was our favorite hike. We would take our shoes off and walk in the shallows, finding driftwood and the tiny moonstones worn smooth as glass by the current. It had rained the night before and the falls thundered, all white foam and rain. It's hard for me to recall so many things about that day but I do remember the water. I remember how raw and green everything seemed, a primal day of ferns and sunlight. I took off my shoes and shirt and walked onto a rock on the edge of the widest pool, just upstream from where Mara held Daniel's hand as they knelt and felt for stones. I was looking up at the falls, the roar of it all in my ears, when I heard Mara scream Daniel's name.

I spun around to find he stood behind me, shirtless, and covered with a constellation of bruises that hadn't been there just hours before.

There's nothing quite like late summer in the mountains, the sky a broken peach, torn and split and spread the length of the horizon as if for no other reason than the beauty of it all. It was after five now. I had ignored another message from Bill Baker and drank a few Shiners in the kitchen. I'd wanted to sit outside and had even carried a beer out onto the porch, but only briefly. The truth was,

I was scared, but of what? Of a mountain lion? No—at least I told myself I wasn't. Either way, I had walked back inside and sat at the kitchen table. By the time I got in the truck, the day had softened, revealing such warm give it seemed ridiculous to fear anything.

When I arrived, the party was in full swing.

The yard was crowded with all Jay's goodtime buddies, the cars and pickups, the Prius and Nissan Leaf. The ancient F-100 with three-on-the-tree and a bumper of peeling stickers: LOCAL FIRST. EVOLVE. BOONE DOCKS MMA. The Flying Burrito Brothers were on the speakers set up on the deck. I saw Jay out by the grill and his girlfriend through the kitchen window, people drinking on the patio furniture and drinking up in the meadow with the sheep. A watermelon sat halved and gleaming on the picnic table. Jay's dad was in a camp chair beneath a willow tree, the old retired cop drinking liberally from a flask.

After Daniel died, I started riding with Jay out into the further reaches of the county. Sometimes I rode along while he played a gig or talked to a bar manager, but mostly we drank and got in fights, or I did at least. As a man told me one night in Ashe County, my face bloodied and pressed to the condom machine in the men's room, I shouldn't have been out looking to start shit. But shit has a way of starting on its own, and I felt helpless to it. I rode out 321 into Tennessee one night to Zudy's Place, a convenience store with cheap beer, hot dogs, and a sign that read EBT ACCEPTED HERE. The honky-tonk sat beside it. The only woman in the place was Zudy's daughter, or maybe his granddaughter, her arms sleeved with tattoos, one side of her head blonde, the other black, the part down the middle absolutely precise. I drank Jack and Cokes and got into it with two good ole boys barely out of their teens. They kicked the shit out of me and then, in an act of mercy, propped me in my truck where I woke a few hours later to drive home, lip split and mouth dry. Another time I got into it at a fish fry outside the American Legion—stupid. Once on the steps of a house with the hot water tank beside the washing machine, both out on the porch—again: stupid, but the point was stupid.

It went on for several months, and I don't know why I did it. Or I do, it's just not an answer I'd prefer to give. To say you'd rather feel physical pain than despair is a cliché, but I suppose it's a cliché for a reason. To be able to point to a busted face is somehow preferable to pointing at a ruined life. Refuge in pain—as pathetic as that sounds.

As for the pain—

After we buried Daniel, something changed in both of us, but Mara especially. A certain zero-sum ruefulness had entered our lives. For me, it came as sadness. But I think for Mara, it was disbelief, as if she simply could not comprehend that one life had traded out with another, and in this new life there were no more bedtime stories or art projects. In this new life, there was no more Monopoly. No more chess or Ticket to Ride or Axis & Allies spread over four afternoons and two-thirds of the farm table. No more dancing in the kitchen, cooking breakfast while NPR played softly or some Prince-tribute CD roared at ninety decibels. *For NPR News in Washington, I'm Nora Raum . . . I'm Jack Speer . . . I'm Lakshmi Singh and this is what it sounds like when doves cry . . .* But not anymore.

Mara went back to work, barring herself in the barn where she painted relentlessly, but it felt somehow different. Less like she was trying to create one thing than attempting to destroy another. The past would be the easy answer. Whatever it was she was trying to do didn't work, and when that failed—as it eventually did—she started attending a tiny Pentecostal church out in Ashe County where they spoke in tongues and were slain in the spirit. But then that failed too, and one day I came in to find her upstairs in my office, my incomplete research into RAIN! spread before her on the floor.

"What are you doing?" I said, taking the pages from her, but still she didn't look at me. "Mara?"

"You knew," she said finally, and it was like she had woken to find herself here, in that room, in that very particular life. "You knew and still you brought that into our house."

"Please."

"Why, David?" she asked. "How?"

The next day she was gone.

You brought that into our house. It took me days before I realized she was talking about the three cases of water I'd brought back from the RAIN! bottling plant. Appalachia has consistently been drained of resources, polluted, shit on. But there was absolutely no evidence the water was anything other than what the Virginia Department of Health declared it to be: pure.

I looked at Jay's dad who smiled and waved me over. I waved back, motioned like I was getting a drink first, but instead got back in my truck and drove home. There was another message on the machine, but I had to drink a great deal before I could listen to it. I knew already it would be Bill Baker and knew already what he would say. *Jesus Christ, David, where are you? I was right. It was a bomb. Call me as soon as you get this. I need to—just call me, all right? David, listen.* And I swear, from where I stood swaying in the hallway, hands planted on the drywall for balance, it almost sounded like he said: *It looks like Mara was involved.*

Sometime after that I must have passed out.

Daniel had died in the green heat of summer on an otherwise ordinary September Thursday in Durham, North Carolina, the air above the parking lot of Duke University Children's Hospital hot and thick when we finally stumbled out into the blinding sun. It had happened so suddenly: his decline meteoric, his body resistant to every form of treatment from chemo to steroids to prayer. There had been no false hope: in hindsight, we realized his doctors had been preparing us for what they must have known was inevitable from the first time they saw him.

We hadn't believed them—what were we supposed to do besides not believe?

We hadn't believed and hadn't believed, and then came that bright Thursday when not believing was no longer possible, and we drove home to our old life, except that life no longer existed.

I am a small man, vain and petty, but just smart enough to conceal myself from most. I realized this early on, at approximately the same moment it came to me that Mara contained multitudes. Perhaps that was why I couldn't understand. That she was larger than life—there is such a thing—and that largeness, that largess, is often as confusing as it is infuriating because it isn't the simple narcissism or fragility that drives so many of us. We don't recognize it and react with fear, rather than awe, and while watching Mara grieve Daniel, I will admit there was some awe. But more than that, there was fear.

For my part, I was drinking, more than usual, but not, I thought, excessively. Just enough to keep acquainted with detachment. Just enough to keep me suitably numb. The summer after Daniel died, the summer before Mara left, was a summer of staggering heat and we moved in and out of the house like birds through the cavities of a dead tree, doors open, windows up, everywhere the finest of dust. A honeysuckle heat, a maddening dry heat, as sharp as the air was granular.

Evenings, I would fill a Nalgene bottle with bourbon and walk past the chickens and into the forest. Daniel's treehouse was no more than a platform with rails, but it was solid. I had made it myself, and though Mara had teased me about its lack of sophistication, it was well built. I would climb up and sit there and stare at the house or at the mountains or, often enough, at everything and nothing. One evening I came out to find the netting we had added as a sort of roof had torn. Another day I found a rail dangling. I left it. I wanted it to fall apart as the world saw fit, depreciation at the accepted rate, nothing rash, nothing premature. I wanted it to grow old slowly. It seemed a reasonable wish.

What I didn't know at the time—what I wouldn't know for a long time—was that Mara had started walking the length of the river down below Orchard Falls, and sometime that spring, standing by the pool where we'd first seen the bruises on Daniel's tiny body, she watched a young boy emerge from the river. He was with a group of children swimming in the placid water downstream, but had somehow made his way to the falls. His name was Cory and she recognized him immediately. A few weeks prior there had been a notice in the *Watauga Democrat* of a benefit— hot dogs, gospel music, seven dollars a plate—for this boy who was suffering from the same disease that had killed our son. He was ten years old and lived in a group home not far from us. But to Mara, he was something else entirely.

To Mara, he was magic.

That summer she started driving over to the group home to see Lucille Duncan, to sit in her living room while the boy named Cory and an undersized boy named Martin sat outside on the concrete stoop.

"You say you're researching something?" the woman asked.

"I am."

A girl came from the bedroom, hair uncombed, shorts too short, a teenage boy following her out, both looking sleepy and oversexed.

"I don't want no trouble," the woman said. "If Jeb were to ask—"

Jeb was her husband, a long-haul trucker away more often than not.

"If Jeb were to know—"

And Mara, already frantic, already worried she would never see the boy again, taking a thousand dollars from her purse and almost shoving it at the woman.

"I can pay you. I'm happy to pay."

So she did. Textile money. Her grandfather's money, her mother's money, Mara's money. Untouched for nearly two decades, it was now a down payment on a ghost.

Like Daniel, Cory had about him a calm so deep Mara suspected it was imagined. She visited him once at school, another time down at the softball field where he played football on the red dirt of the infield, started following him everywhere, really. Told them she was with Child Protective Services, told them she was an aunt. When he died a little over a year after Daniel, well, she hadn't been prepared for that exactly. She hadn't foreseen such. She'd been shut out. She'd paid the woman to let her see him, but then Cory was in Duke and the woman wouldn't answer her calls. Mara drove down to Durham—it must have been so much like before—even walked the oncology ward until she was standing outside his room and the woman, looking wildly up and down the hall, wanted to know what the hell she was doing here, *I told you to stay away.*

You can say I'm your friend. You can say I'm his aunt.

But the woman was afraid and wouldn't say anything and so it was left to Mara to break into her house and take the boy's clothes and the small jade parakeet wrapped in a T-shirt.

I, of course, knew none of this at the time.

In hindsight, it must have been just after Cory's death when I climbed down from the tree house one autumn evening to discover the smell of marijuana drifting over the yard. It was dusk and the house was cast in not the lazy depths of afternoon but the deeper shadows of night. I called Mara's name, and though she said nothing I knew she was near, the heat off her body, the scent off her skin. The resinous smell of marijuana was thick. I stepped into the living room and she began to materialize: a vague shape in the far corner, sitting on the floor and slowly assembling into something like a body, one long leg stretched before her. It was only when she spoke—"Stop right there, David"—that I saw the barrel resting beneath her chin. Her father's gun. The .410 she'd kept for I couldn't remember why. And then I did. Of course, I did: it was the gun her mother had used. Mara had never said as much, but suddenly it made a sort of twisted sense.

"Mara." It sounded like I was testing the name, as if I had spoken from some deeper uncertainty. Which, I suppose, I had.

"Stop right there."

"What are you doing?"

"I'm just." There was something almost dreamy in her voice, something lost. The genie out of her bottle, unable to find her way back in. "Hi, David."

"Mara."

"It's okay. I'm just resting a minute."

I took another step.

"Where did you get this?"

"The closet."

"Can I have it?"

She seemed to consider this.

"Not yet," she said finally.

"Mara."

"It's loaded," she told me in that same dreamy voice, as if this were something almost beyond possibility. "Those home defense rounds or shells or whatever they are."

"You loaded it?"

"It wasn't hard to figure out."

"I want you to give it to me, all right?"

"Sit down, David." She looked up from where the metal fed into the skin beneath her jaw. "Please sit."

I lowered myself onto the floor, close enough for our feet to touch, hers bare, mine in old dress shoes I'd ruined walking in the woods. Our feet then: but only that. She was in a nightgown, silver and made more silver by the gloss of her pale skin. It was something she never wore. Her mother's nightgown, I realized. The one I'd gone back that night from the hospital to fetch. She'd dressed up, and, realizing as much, I felt some deeper channel open, a sluice as deep as it was cold.

Mara, I started to say, but was afraid to. How long we sat like that I don't know. She had her back to the wall, her legs in front of her, and slowly, slowly, I reached out and touched one of her ankles. When she didn't pull back I let my fingers encircle it.

"I just needed to know what it felt like," she said, and handed me the gun, her fingers a pale bracelet around the barrel.

Months later, after she had sat in my office floor and asked *how could you?* after she had taken the RAIN! file and left, just *after*, I suppose, I sat there in the same spot, the barrel beneath my own chin. But I had no intention of killing myself. Like Mara, I just needed to know how it felt.

It must have been earlier that year that Mara started attending a mountain church of what I thought then were hard-shell Baptists but proved to be Pentecostal. It had happened without notice.

One Sunday she was simply absent, and then another, and then one day I noticed a flyer left in the kitchen for a Wednesday evening homecoming service at Open Arms. Mara had said nothing to me about going, and that day I said nothing to her, just waited until she had left and then found the address online.

The church sat deep in the country on a winding gravel road gouged with runoff and made blind with sudden switchbacks. I passed trailers and A-frames and now and then, through a gap in the pines, a monstrous house sitting atop the ridge like a chalet. The building itself was white clapboard siding with a block stoop and a narrow steeple—all of it no larger than one of the small farmhouses strung along the road. There were maybe a dozen cars and trucks nosed around the church—a Buick, a few pickups, a worn Escort, Mara's Sebring—and seeing it I had a vague sense of recognition. Then I realized I had seen the church before. It had been years ago, and Mara and I had been hiking on Beech Mountain with its wine bars and giant second homes, everywhere exposed beams and tartan prints, chandeliers assembled from antlers. All the men with eye jobs and expensive watches, all the women in furs and leggings. The contrast should have been startling. Instead, it felt exactly right. We'd driven from richest Appalachia into poorest. From Mercedes parked outside cigar shops to the flock of ducks outside a moldering camper shell where a big shepherd mix ran the length of a clothesline past the pink four-wheeler and the man vaping on a porch glider.

That day, coming from Beech Mountain, the church had stood out with its perfect symmetry—the clean lines, the mown yard—and I remember Mara saying something, though I can't remember what exactly. Surely something anodyne. *What a pretty church* or, perhaps, *how lovely*. Noting, perhaps, its Shaker simplicity. Nothing more. An elderly couple had stood in the yard, giant people it appeared, ridiculously tall and dressed in somber black and white, the woman's head covered with a bonnet. Mennonites, Mara might have said. Nothing more.

It was no different the day I followed her.

I parked as far from the building as possible and sat in my truck until I was sure the service had started. When I stepped out, I could hear music coming through the walls, the old hymns, the ones that won't go away. That old rugged cross. I shall not be moved. I slipped into the back and stood along the wood paneling. I only wanted to see, to confirm, I suppose, that she was here, that she was coming not only without me but without telling me. I realize now how possessive that must sound and can only say that at the time I felt that sense of possession. I felt it violated our relationship and it made me want to wound her. It made me want to comfort her too. But I lacked the strength to do either.

The church was a single room, a few pews angled toward an altar. Behind it, a baptistery that looked like a kiddie pool framed out with two-by-fours. Christ was on the wall. His brown eyes and long straight hair. Knocking on a door with no handle because He has to be invited in. I looked for Mara and saw her near the front, seated in the pew, her back to me. She was singing. They were all singing. The preacher was in short sleeves and Dickies pants. Stocky, about my age. Balding but with long sideburns and a face given to reddening, like a cut of meat. The crowd—maybe thirty people—were older, a room of Walmart greeters, a few children underfoot. I slipped out and drove home, more bereft than at any moment since the day we left the hospital without Daniel.

It was months later, just after the New Year, when I found her with the RAIN! file.

When I put out my hand she recoiled as if it were a snake.

"Why, David?" she had asked. "How?"

I didn't answer, and the next day she was gone.

That was January.

It must have been March when the woman from the church came by. She hadn't seen Mara in months and was worried. I had nothing to tell her, nothing to say to her.

"I want to help if I can," she said.

"Who are you?"

"My name's Lucille," she said. "Lucille Duncan. But most people call me Nana. I run the group home out on 421."

"How do you know Mara?"

"We met at church and then she come out to the house a few times. I foster some kids, boys mostly. Mara, she liked to just come sit and watch 'em. But I ain't seen her now since Cory passed."

"I haven't seen her either."

"But you're her husband?"

"I am."

She nodded, as if not quite believing me, but not quite willing to contradict me either.

"If you see her, tell her I come looking for her," she said. "And if you want to talk about anything."

"Thank you for coming by."

"You want to talk, I work most days at the Dollar General."

Then she reached forward and took both my hands.

"Will you pray with me?" she said.

"I think you need to go."

She nodded, as if she understood this, then put back her head and shut her eyes.

"Dear Jesus," she said.

"You need to go."

"Dear Jesus, we stand before you today—"

But I was already closing the door in her face.

I woke in bed, washed up somewhere between dusk and daylight, the room silvered with the sort of moonlight that seemed to whisper, but bright enough to see a shadow. The dog was standing by the shut bedroom door, completely silent but completely still, his thin body rigid. *Banjo?* I whispered. *Go to sleep, boy.* But he didn't move. *Banjo?* I started to say again, but then I heard it. Though my head felt broken, swollen and split like a melon forgotten in the sun, I was certain: something was in the house, on the other side of the door. I sat up and gently put my feet on the floorboards, the room, warm and thick with the winey musk of my own sweat. *Easy, boy.* When I touched him he whimpered but otherwise didn't move, just stood there in what I realized was a shallow pool of his own urine. We could both hear it, whatever had torn into the chickens. It was in the living room, moving on the giant pads of its feet, swinging the great lantern of its head. I could almost see it through the closed door, and eased away to get back in bed. I didn't pray. I got in the bed and shut my eyes, the room so bright I could see everything, even when I squeezed them tight.

When I got up the next morning, I found the living room destroyed, lamps broken, book shelves spilled, dishes shattered. Banjo's urine a long streak along the uneven floor. I fixed nothing and was drinking a cup of coffee when I heard someone coming down the gravel drive. Through the curtain I watched the car park, a black Crown Vic, unmarked. The men were in suits, just as you'd expect them to be. One stood by the car while the other wandered out into the yard. When they both came up the steps a few minutes later, Banjo retreated to the bedroom and began to whimper. It was only when they knocked that I realized the door was still locked, latched and bolted from the inside.

They had their badges out, field agents from the FBI's Roanoke office. They had driven down that morning. The photo they had of Mara was from her website, taken at a gallery show in Los Angeles about a year before Daniel died. I couldn't date the photo of Chris Bright, only to say that I didn't recognize him. But then I hadn't seen him in fifteen years. He was bearded and still thin, though the lean athleticism of so long ago had been replaced by a gauntness: he appeared sick. *When was the last time I saw Mara?* Months, how many, Jesus, nine months it would have been. *What was our last communication?* Our last communication? *What was the last thing she said to you, sir? Do you know where she'd been staying?* No, I didn't know where she'd been staying, though in that moment it occurred to me exactly where she had been: she had been with Chris.

They left a card.

"We'd like to be in touch again," one said.

"Okay."

"Sometime over the next twenty-four hours. And, of course, if anything comes up."

"Yeah."

"You'll call."

"By the way," said the other, "what happened out in the yard?"

"Our chickens," I said. "My chickens."

"Fox in the henhouse?"

"Something like that."

"What about in here?" he asked, pointing through the half-closed door at the mess inside. "Fox get in the house, too?"

The other smiled and nodded formally.

"Thank you for your time, Mr. Wood. And if anything whatsoever comes up."

"Yeah, I'll call."

But I wasn't going to call.

I watched them walk to their car, look back once at the house, and drive away.

When they were gone, I went upstairs and looked a last time for the file I had on RAIN!

It was gone and I knew then Mara had taken it.

I drank three glasses of water and swallowed four ibuprofens, eased Banjo and a bag of dog food into the cab of the truck, and started down the drive. When I turned onto the road I saw a panel van sitting near the curve on a pull-off meant for the power company. So they were watching the house. It didn't matter. I drove straight to Jay's and was hefting Banjo down when he came out, shirtless and barefoot in jeans, coffee in his hand.

"Hey, bud."

"Can you keep Banjo for a bit?"

"Sure," he said, and reached down to rub him. "You going somewhere?"

"For a little, yeah."

"Why don't you come in for a minute first."

"I can't."

"Come see Dad a minute. We got worried about you last night."

"I really can't."

"I came by after the show, but you didn't answer the door."

I set the bag of Purina on the ground.

"David," he said, something changed in his voice. "Talk to me for a second, okay."

"I'm sorry." I got back in the truck, and fired the engine. "I wish I could."

He was still standing there, following me with his eyes, when I made the curve and took the right onto 421 toward Virginia.

This is a love story.

For a long time, I thought it was mine.

But my GPS was wrong.

I was far from God.

part two

ain't nothing but a
stranger in this world

On the 20th of March 2003, on the first day of the first war in the new millennium, we marched on the federal building in Boone, North Carolina, which, admittedly, housed only extension offices for the Departments of Agriculture and Internal Revenue, but that wasn't the point. The point was that war was needless and foolish and the people were angry. Angry and assembled and coming up King Street, three thousand strong with their bongos and giant puppets of Bush and Blair and Cheney, the papier-mâché heads bobbing above a sea of dreadlocks and gauged ears, the men and women and boys and girls who chanted and danced and beat on the glass of the USMC recruitment office in the strip mall by the Town Tavern.

No blood for oil!

Regime change starts at home!

That was how it started for Mara, she supposed later, with wave after wave flowing down the highway between the ski shops and coffee shops and the chamber of commerce, a few tourists caught unawares and staring out through the plate-glass windows of Dancing Moon or Mast General Store, the snow, plowed and browning in the shadow of apartments. It should have been spring, or at least some vague representation of such, scattered sun, new buds on the trees. But the wind was blowing and noses were running, and there was a recklessness, a restlessness that seemed to gather as we approached the Broyhill Federal Building and the ranks of police with their Plexiglas shields and collared dogs, the TV trucks from Charlotte, aerials extended. All waiting as we began to fill the plaza, and, yes, we were singing and stomping and beating drums, and, yes, we were marching without a permit (the city having refused), but we were also college kids, by and large white kids, soft and well-intentioned, so they let it go, the mayor, the police, the federal agents who stood on the edges, video recording the faces as they passed. They let it go right up until the moment someone sent a rock toward a rank of state troopers and then, only then, did those motherfuckers wade in.

Yes, Mara would think later, the march, the rock.

That was how it started for her.

At least that's the story I told myself back then, back before I knew the rest.

She was maybe a third of the way back, a quarter mile from the front, walking inside the puffed warmth of her North Face parka, Chris nowhere to be seen, but I, reluctant and pissed off David, I was beside her. She held my right hand with her left, and while she wasn't exactly dragging me, I wasn't exactly coming willingly either. Her right hand was stuffed deep in her pocket, clenching the balled tissue she brought out to swab the nose that absolutely would not quit dripping because that was where she was health-wise, strung out and tired, eyes bagged, sinuses possibly infected. She could feel the chill behind her eyes and it was almost like dreaming, her head a lazy balloon from the Sudafed and espresso taken to counteract the beer and weed taken to counteract the violent indifference of the greater Western world. We'd been up late the night before, arguing in council until after midnight and then arguing in private, just the two of us, sitting on the frozen fire escape outside her apartment complex, leaned together for warmth, both down-spiraling off the failing alcohol and adrenaline. Alone with the cold starlight and passing cars and someone shouting down by the green dumpsters.

"What would it look like," she had asked me, "if we didn't go? If we didn't march?"

"Fuck what it looks like. It's theater."

"I don't care if it is theater. I'm not arguing that. I'm just talking about general solidarity with the peace movement."

And me throwing back my head as if I might howl, as if I'd finally reached the end of some seemingly endless metaphorical rope and was ready now to drop.

"There is no peace movement," I told her that night. "There's just us. People like us. People willing to act."

She might have said that was exactly what marching was: a form of action. But she knew it wasn't the kind of action I meant. We have screamed for a solid year—this was my line, my approach to all conciliatory gestures. *We have screamed for a solid year and who has listened? What has it accomplished? Absolutely nothing. They are still bombing children in Afghanistan, and soon enough they'll be bombing them in Iraq. They are still leveling mountains not a hundred miles from here. They're still poisoning our water, our soil.* (I would stand then, look around whatever dim basement we occupied, the pizza boxes and hookahs, look from person to person, maybe gently prod one of the beanbag chairs where they sprawled, but never, *never* bother to sweep the marijuana smoke from my face so that I was wreathed in sorrow as much as dope.) *What has it accomplished?* I would ask again, and then I would answer: *Absolutely nothing. That's what talking has gotten us. So how long do we keep talking? How long do we keep with the bullshit marches and online petitions? How long until we actually, you know, do something?* And everyone, of course, was for action, everyone was for, you know, doing something. Except actually they weren't. There were twenty or so serious activists in their group—Christian anarchists, Marxists, would-be monkey wrenches lacking only skill and anything resembling balls—but the truth was there were only two people actually willing to act and that was one reason why Mara and I had gravitated to each other. That was why we were marching now, hands held, or at least hands grasping in the way of two people whose connection was greater than self. If deep could call to deep, surely desperation could do the same. And that was what we were, we were desperate.

We were also older.

In a room of nineteen- and twenty-year-olds, Mara and I were an elderly twenty-four. She'd gotten her art degree at Pratt, hung around New York, and eventually come home to the mountains to work for SAP, Southern Appalachian Patriots, an eco- and social-justice organization whose inefficiency had thus far justified the acronym. I was working for the *Watauga Democrat* and writing a story (a story that never ran) about the peace movement at the university. It was at the second council meeting of the "League for International Peace, Community, and Justice" where I'd seen Mara and more or less fallen immediately in love.

Later, she told me that I had kind of floored her too, big and decent-enough looking, I suppose. Able to ramble a bit about art. A playwright who could both dunk a basketball and casually discuss the "bogus infantilism" of Jeff Koons and Damien Hirst. The six-three former high school power forward obsessed with Tennessee Williams and *The Cremaster Cycle*. I'd grown up in Charleston, South Carolina, and she must have imagined me a sort southern Julian Schnabel, had Julian Schnabel grown up listening to Radiohead and playing with his back to the basket. That this was a complete facade mattered not at all. At the time Mara had been obsessed with Mazzy Star, trying to affect her best Hope Sandoval, all ribbed tank tops and moody indifference, wearing gauzy peasant skirts and refusing eye contact. Which is to say she knew what it was to try on a self as casually as someone else's coat.

As for the League for International Peace and so on—Mara could never bring herself to call it that, but it was their name, arrived at by democratic means, so who was she to argue?—it was a small collective that had been meeting a little over a year. She had helped organize it, setting up an information table on the campus green, a web page, a mailing list, and it had started with such high hopes. People were organizing, right? People cared, didn't they? Well . . . people drifted in and out, skipping the river cleanup, failing to show for the march against domestic violence, never bothering to sign the anti-MTR mining petition. Eventually, the group had stabilized into a small, if essentially committed, core. Though in truth, it was mostly the two of us.

We had met—really met, as in something more than me ogling her across a room overstuffed with third-hand couches and some old school Rage against the Machine—the previous spring at the Vietnamese place off campus. She had gone there to meet friends but when she pushed open the door to stomp her feet and brush the rain from her bare arms, she had seen me instead, this noncollege-aged man who had shown up at their previous meeting to silently brood, as if both disgusted and entranced by the sing-song optimism. But that night I wasn't brooding. That night I was out with my lone friend and fellow reporter, Bill Baker, celebrating something, though I can no longer remember what. That night the restaurant was packed, folks at the high-top tables, in the booths, three-deep at the bar, everyone loud and happy. Mara had wound up peeling off from her friends to sit with us, the three of us getting magnificently shit-faced and arguing over the efficacy of foreign aid, something we knew absolutely nothing about, which was maybe the point.

Eventually, Bill had passed out at the table, his head tipped forward in a comically slow fall. He snored all the way back to his apartment where we lugged him up the stairs and onto his couch. His dinner we boxed up and took to Mara's place, an extravagant plate of grilled pork and rice noodles we ate on for days. Three days to be precise, because that was how long I had stayed in her apartment, which was more or less how long we had stayed in her bed, staring up only occasionally at the unfinished landscape paintings leaned against the block walls.

We'd sat up only to argue, to debate, to fact-check on the internet or in whatever volume of Chomsky she had lying around. We had argued and argued. Not because we disagreed, but because it brought a certain frisson to things, an excitement that was belly deep and far more interesting than the fact that we were on the same side.

The war.

The destruction of the environment.

The whole bullshit materialist consumer capitalist-crony setup.

We'd argue and have sex, our touching charged with everything said and thought and felt, lie tangled in the damp sheets with the window AC blowing the sort of dry air that scratched our eyes. Then we'd start touching again, already submerged in the pattern that would define that first year together. That had been our great revelation: that we believed in the same things. Chief among them democratic socialism and our mutual enjoyment of crawling naked into her cotton sheets. But by the time we marched, even that had begun to fail.

I had drifted into a sort of funk, a listlessness that she traced to my meeting Chris Bright.

Chris—she must have reminded herself as we approached the federal building—Chris who was not here. Chris—she must have convinced herself—who was surely the chief generator of my recent apathy. Chris who was surely the one who had fed me the *no more talking, time for action* stance. I had met him, but she didn't know how or where. I was always vague about it, deflecting the question while implying to push the issue was the sort of naive pose she was surely above, but the truth was: I had sought him out. I had heard rumors and gone to find him. But that seemed a bit too fanboy to admit. What Mara knew—or what I believed Mara knew—was that Chris was slightly older than us and a longtime activist of some unspoken renown. But it was a whisper campaign, the sort of thing where everyone acted as if they knew all about him so that, in the end, no one knew a damn thing. Still, she caught the edges, the wild, often contradictory rumors: Chris had been in Seattle for the WTO riots in '99, had fought with Earth First! torching timber headquarters and sabotaging bulldozers. He'd operated in the coal fields, destroying giant draglines with the very explosives intended to destroy the mountain. They called him the Mad Farmer (he did love Wendell Berry), and he'd been clubbed, gassed, cuffed, and beaten. One Easter Sunday, he'd chained himself to the front gate of the New London, Connecticut, submariner base. The next year he'd taken a mallet to the nose cone of a B-52 (to hammer it into a plowshare, of course). At a pit mine in Harlan County, Kentucky, two men had held him down while a third spat wintergreen Copenhagen in his eyes. He'd done that, he'd survived. He'd done everything, it seemed, except given up.

That much was true, the not giving up part. How much of the rest was, she didn't know. Mara knew only that I had come under his spell, traveling out to his cabin deep in the Cherokee National Forest every weekend to do god only knew what (possibly nothing, she reminded herself, possibly drink myself senseless among the white pines). I had been after her to join me for weeks, and in the late summer of 2002 she finally had, riding out Highway 321 and onto a series of gravel and fire roads, eventually crossing a meadow on foot to find a neatly kept cabin and several outbuildings tongue-and-grooved into the dense forest of rhododendron and mountain laurel. And Chris was impressive. She had come a little under his spell, too. But not so deeply as to do something rash. And that was the feeling she had gotten that day from both Chris and me: that something rash was in the offing. That something rash was exactly what we had in mind.

Which was what she feared most.

Despite her true commitment, despite her fervent belief, there was still a part of her, a very basic, very Sunday school part of her that wanted control, and to wreck something, to burn something, to attack something was to lose any semblance of such.

She didn't want us to coerce her into some violent scheme. As it turned out, we didn't want that either.

Ultimately, it was Mara who would change.

Ultimately, it was Mara who would do the coercing.

But that was much later.

The weekend Mara "met" Chris, we took my Tacoma up a gravel road as winding as it was steep, the switchbacks trenched with runoff so that the gray road wore long streaks of tawny mud like ribbons in a girl's hair. Near the ridgeline the road simply ended, dissolving into a meadow of butterflies and three deer, a doe and two fawn, who stood for a moment in the clearing, heads cocked, backs spotted, before slipping like brown ghosts into the tree line.

"Did you see that?" she asked me.

"Every time I come out here," I said, smiling. "Every single time."

We walked to the ridge, a wide bald where the view opened on what appeared to be endless mountains, a slow rising and falling of green. The forest was full of blowdowns, giant white pines cracked at the precise same height by the straight-line winds that had gusted through the previous week. She stood by a snapped fir and inhaled the sharp scent of Christmas. She had resisted coming out—why would I want to meet the object of your utter and absolute affection? she kept asking, only half joking—but I could tell she was already being won over, which is, I suppose, evidence of how naive I had been.

"You're smiling," I said.

"No I'm not."

"You don't want to, but, yeah, you are."

She didn't want to, that much was true. It seemed to me she had decided early on that her visit was a formality, the punching of a clock required to help shake me back into the person I had been, which was, if she got down to it, her passionate angry sex-drunk boyfriend who liked to talk about the play he would probably never write. But yeah, she was liking it. Hard to admit, but actually she was loving it. The long drive in, the road hugging the Watauga River, the Elk River, passing the general store, the leaning barns and old block silos. The disk plow pulled beneath a rock overhang. EGGS FOR SALE. FIREWOOD. Herefords grazing the ridiculously inclined slopes. Brick houses, as plain and reliable as old aunts, sitting by the collapsing grandeur of the homeplace with its hewn logs and well-turned balustrades. Trailers clustered along a creek, the underpinning, half obscured by lattice and a few gray propane tanks.

The way the sun-starved understory would, here and there, open into a spectacularly clean light—she loved it. The way the trail wound down the back of the slope and eventually straightened to follow the narrow creek that threaded the bottomland— she loved that too. The way the forest was dark here, wet, but ahead was a meadow of light, revealing the shapes of a house and barn and beyond us the white clapboards of what appeared to be a tiny church.

"Where are we?" she asked me.

"We're here."

"Is that a church?"

"Sort of."

"So yes or no?"

"It's church-ish, I'd say."

The church had surprised her. Everything about that first visit had surprised her. Maybe she had expected some Unabomber recluse living in a damp cave, but here was a sunshiny openness.

That was part of it.

The other part was Chris. That he had an aura about him, a certain presence she sensed as much as saw—this cannot be denied. He had this entrancing calmness—neither of us could deny it any more than we could resist it. He was scything a field when we walked up because, really, what else would he be doing?

Mara stopped in her tracks.

"Think he's been waiting on us all day, standing out there with that thing like he's out of a Tolstoy novel?"

"You know I love this side of you."

"I'm asking an actual question."

"The cynical bastard side. I never get to see it."

But that day she was prepared to show it. Except she never got the chance. She was too busy being pleasantly surprised. Tall and lean, Chris was wound with the sort of muscle that comes from what we once called "manual labor." Instead of a harem of glassy-eyed virgins, a clutch of Manson girls like Mara had imagined, he introduced her to his aunt, an old Appalachian granny who sat in a porch rocker with her black coffee and arthritic hands.

There was also his mountain lion.

Mara must have found it as she wandered from room to room while Chris and I sat drinking Elijah Craig. The mountain lion sat in his bedroom, mounted and occupying the better part of one wall. Seeing it, she didn't quite know how to feel. It wasn't sexual, but it was surely the sexiest thing she'd ever laid eyes on. The lean, muscled frame. The white mouth and kohl eyes. It looked like something from either the ancient past or the distant future, a relic, or a thing not yet realized. She must have stood there until she heard us calling. Otherwise, she might have stood there forever.

We had dinner together—the four of us counting Chris's aunt—biscuits and okra and tomato slices. Silver queen corn. It had all come from the garden, the food simple and delicious. The sort of meal that would soon be labeled farm-to-table and cost thirty dollars in town, but here it was just food. We didn't talk about it. We talked about Mara. She hadn't intended to, but soon enough found herself telling us about her life, her family, her time in New York, even about her art—something she'd barely shared with me. She kept telling herself to stop, to shut up, but found she couldn't. Or more likely wouldn't. Chris and his aunt were so open, so interested, and she must have realized it was the first time in years she had spoken personally to anyone. Must have realized how desperate she'd been for it. There had been endless conversations about Liberation Theology or the efficacy of online activism, but had she ever uttered the name of her late mother? (Her name was Anna.) Had she talked about the hymns they'd sung that summer she'd walked alone to the church in Blowing Rock? (Her favorite, sentimental as it may be, was "The Old Rugged Cross.") But she talked about them that day, talked about them at the table and then on the porch after Chris's aunt had gone to bed. She talked about everything. (Or so I thought at the time. Had she revealed the chief thing, the very reason she had come, I wonder how different our lives might have been. But then I doubt there would have been any *our* left.)

It was mothy dusk by the time Chris drove us in his old Galaxie convertible out the gravel road and back around the mountain to my truck.

"You mean we could have driven there?" she asked me when we were back on the highway.

"And missed that great walk?"

She said nothing and I put my hand on her knee.

"Next time," I said, "we'll drive in."

She hadn't argued. She must have known already there would be a next time. She must have sensed how much she was looking forward to it. (Was what she was withholding part of that pleasure? Did she think of that on that frozen day, marching and chanting?) In the months since then, she'd been back she didn't know how many times. A dozen? At least a dozen. Not as often as me, but often enough. She loved the visits. We would work in the garden or walk barefoot in the creek in summer, rake leaves in fall, cut the Christmas tree come winter. There were discussions of God and justice, but mostly there was good food, bourbon, kindness. Van Morrison singing about being a stranger in this world. The three of us getting drunk on the porch while the fireflies sparked. The rectangular corn patch in the bottomland. Distant porch lights. The creek after a heavy rain, brown and foaming with pockets of sticks and trash and that single plastic bag in a fallen tree, straining and flexing like a lung. She felt close to the earth there, close to God. Closer, she realized, than she had since her mother died. There was something elemental here, something authentic.

We helped cut firewood, Chris and Mara stacking it under the porch eaves while I plowed the road with the Kubota. If she was a little in love with Chris, she didn't see any need to say it. In a certain way, I was a little in love with him too.

Still, she kept waiting for *the ask*. This lingering sense that all this basic human kindness was a prelude to coercion. Let's go blow up a dam. Let's go shoot the president. One of her fears was that she would say yes. The other, perhaps greater fear was that she would say no. But it never came, and instead of coercion we got winter. Chris was either retired from activism or, in the old spirit of John Brown, conspiring with no one but his God. It was something we didn't talk about, and now, in the absence of spring, marching into the plaza at the Broyhill Federal Building, I have to imagine she regretted our silence since within that silence something had wedged itself between us. Maybe it was paranoia, maybe it was jealousy. But lately she had come to believe that Chris and I were plotting something, something huge and something that very thoughtfully left her out.

I suspect she hated us for it. Just a little but it was there, the anger, the hurt of being discarded. But then that was ridiculous: she had made very plain to me that she wanted no part in anything that might remotely be construed as violent. Civil disobedience was one thing. But violence—no, don't tell me, don't include me, don't even hint at it. She was an artist; she wanted to make things, not wreck them.

You're trying to find some unified field of belief, she would tell me the coming summer. *But what if we are put here only to recognize beauty?*

But that was months in the future.

Now, marching, she squeezed my hand, hard, and I returned the squeeze, glanced at her, and actually smiled. She was trying to hurt me, I think, and when I squeezed back, gently, lovingly, she dropped my hand and put both fists in the air. A chant was going up—*No more war! No more war!*—and she joined in, loud enough for her voice to ring in my ear.

The entire spectacle was somehow embarrassing, and when my face fell a little she must have felt happy. She might have felt childish too, but she couldn't deny the need to hurt me. She couldn't deny something was changing in the crowd too. The air had prickled. A group of frat boys standing on a hill waved an American flag and threw hot dogs at the crowd, water balloons, a single brown shoe. Meanwhile, the chants for peace sounded more like a call to war. Someone was on a bullhorn, some official robotic voice made grainy and disjointed by the noise of the crowd. *Disperse . . . illegal gathering . . . in violation . . .* She couldn't make out all the words, but she detected the fear. The plaza was now a sea of brightly colored toboggan hats, posters and puppets and raised fists. Police stood on both sides of the crowd. Not the local police so much as soldiers, state police, an army of face shields and body armor, of big shotguns modified to fire beanbags and tear gas canisters. She saw a pumper truck from the fire department, its water hose unfurled. She saw the TV trucks, cameras raised and waiting for whatever came next, the quiet dispersal, she supposed, the moment when, having made our point, everyone went home to warm up. Only that wasn't happening. Rather than dispersing, the crowd had taken up another chant.

Fuck the police!

Fuck the police!

She reached back and found my arm, went to pull me closer, as if my closeness might signal something—her disdain, her need to leave—only now I was chanting too. She pulled at me, but I was lost in the moment, eyes rolled back in a way she might have recognized from all those days and nights writhing in bed.

"David. *David*?"

She told me later that when I looked at her it seemed to take me a moment to remember who she was. She looked back over the crowd. It was tightly packed, but also possible to shimmy to the edge and escape.

"I think I don't like this," she said.

"This was your idea."

"I know but I didn't think—" She motioned around us.

"Didn't think what? That people at a protest would actually protest?"

"I just—I made a mistake, all right? I think . . . something's going to happen."

"Yes, exactly, we're going to make our voices heard."

"No, something bad. Something we don't want."

I turned to her, bent to her, just as the first rock flew. Later she would have a clear memory of its high arc, the way it lofted over the crowd to clatter its way onto a riot shield. She knew this was impossible. She hadn't seen it. What she had seen was, perhaps, the third or fourth or fiftieth rock, because by the time she looked up the crowd was shifting, undulating. There was a wild panic and she would have fallen had it not been impossible, held up as she was by the bodies around her. There was screaming. She heard the bullhorn. She heard what she would later identify as the dull thump of a tear gas canister being fired. When she finally did go to the ground—I jerked her down, pebbles of asphalt grinding into our palms—she saw through a forest of legs that people were falling, people were being beaten. It rippled through the crowd, the falling, the thunk of clubs. Then she felt me being pulled from her, she felt the sleeve of her coat tear, her sinuses and eyes burning as the tear gas misted over her. Someone had her. A face-masked man. He had no face. He had a family, a life, probably a wife at home, maybe a son who played football at the rec fields. But he had no face.

Someone else wrenched her arms behind her, and, seated there on the asphalt, she felt her wrists constrict.

She was crying.

All around her people were crying, screaming.

She felt her hands being pulled so that she collapsed backward, face open to the gray sky.

The man with no face put one gloved hand behind her and tilted her head back farther. It was almost like she was receiving communion, the way her mouth fell open. With his other hand he expertly flipped her eyelid back. She could feel her wrists bound in plastic. She could smell the latex of his gloves. The day, gray as it had been, was suddenly very bright and she realized then what was coming. She knew better than to move.

"How can you do this?" she pleaded. Beside her a girl was screaming, curled into the fetal position, hands zip-tied behind her, body shrimped into itself, alone with only her suffering.

How can you do this?

The girl's legs were pedaling the air, one foot occasionally gaining purchase on the asphalt so that she turned in a lazy pirouette, a motion as pointless as it was slow. Mara looked from her curled form into the barrel of the mace dispenser, its dark eye like something predatory, a shark just before the white membrane drops.

"This isn't right. You shouldn't use violence on nonviolent protesters."

"Shut up."

(Did he say this? No, he said nothing. He was a robot—looking back he was a robot.)

But in that moment, he was a human being. She reminded herself of this. He had a dog and a mother. He was probably a Baptist.

"This is wrong," she said. "This is immoral."

"You're getting what you wanted," he said, or she would, at least, remember him saying.

"You should be ashamed of yourself."

She felt her head stretched back so far she thought her neck might break.

"You should be—"

"You're getting exactly what you wanted, bitch."

And then he shot the mace directly into her right eye.

The mace, of course, wasn't imagined.

The oleoresin capsicum, a lacrimatory agent meant to induce tears.

The mace was very real.

I didn't need Chris Bright to tell me the mace was real.

I found him that September day in 2018, two days after the explosion, at the Evans Haynes Burn Center in Richmond, Virginia, suspended in a nest of tubes and gauze. He had third-degree burns over 20 percent of his body: hands and arms, face and neck, parts of his chest. The fire had burned away his beard and eyebrows. But the larger issue was his eyes: the blast wave had blinded him, and propped in the hospital bed he appeared a wounded prophet, suspended in a cocoon of bandages and morphine, his wounds as severe as they were self-inflicted. I got just inside his room by claiming to a nurse and an indifferent security guard I was his lawyer, but no farther: a deputy from the Henrico County Sheriff's Department sitting inside the door asked for identification. When I told him I was a reporter with *Mountain Voices*, he told me to wait outside and started down the hall, speaking into the mic on his shoulder. When he rounded the corner, I walked back out to my truck and called Bill Baker.

"I'm here," I told him. "At the burn center."

"Jesus Christ, David. You might have been in touch. Has he talked to anyone?"

"He's completely sedated. He looks bad. Also, Bill, it looks like maybe he was blinded by it, the fire I guess."

"Not the fire," Bill said. "Have you not seen what they're saying?"

"I've been driving."

He let go a long sigh.

"Get online and then call me back."

"All right."

"Think you can get in to see him?"

"Maybe. I got ran off by a deputy, but I'll try again."

"All right. I'll make some calls and see what I can do. Just don't ghost on me again, okay?"

"Yeah."

"And, David," he said, just before I hung up. "I'm sorry as hell."

It was all over the internet. What they'd been calling a mechanical fire was now being called an act of terrorism: a bomb had been set off inside the bottling plant of RAIN!, a subsidiary of Banks Water LLC. Christopher Bright of Bethel Community, North Carolina, had been found at the scene and was in critical but stable condition in a Virginia hospital. A second suspect, Mara Wood of Sugar Grove, North Carolina, was believed to have died in the explosion, though authorities were currently listing her as a person of interest and seeking information.

I sat in the truck for some time, staring at the screen of my phone, all the weight of what I'd read, all the weight of *believed to have died* shifting inside me and around me—it felt disproportionate, that so much could be carried within my phone. I kept sitting there and eventually it went off—it was Jay calling—but I let it go to voicemail. When I called Bill back he was quieter, reserved. He said I could go up tomorrow, though they doubted Bright would be in any state to talk. I thanked him and hung up.

I got a room at a Super 8 and read everything I could, but it was all the same: a bomb had gone off, one man was injured and in custody, a woman was missing and presumed dead. There was nothing about the plant itself, nothing of the information I had gathered in the file I no longer possessed. No rumors of political intrigue or poisoned water.

Around dusk I walked to the Sportsmen's Club, a windowless

bar in a strip mall with a hair salon, Mexican restaurant, and Verizon store. A sad, dusty place, concrete floor, no light but the digital jukebox. The kind of place I'd spent months getting my ass kicked in. It was mostly empty, a few older men attached to the bar, a couple in a distant booth. I got a beer and then another, and by the third was thinking of Mexico, of the year we'd spent there before returning to North Carolina. It was in Jalpan de Serra that Toliver would eventually tell me that Mara had first realized she was pregnant. I had never known this—she didn't tell me until we were back in North Carolina—and why she had withheld it wasn't clear. But then again, it was quickly becoming evident to me how many things were never clear, how many things I didn't know about her. *Didn't know*, not *hadn't known*, because I realize now that in that moment, sitting there in the windowless Sportsmen's Club, I was convinced she was still alive, and the answers weren't so much lost as waiting. Everything was waiting, I had only to be patient.

At some point I switched to bourbon. I could feel my phone going off in my pocket but didn't touch it. The jukebox was playing an old Randy Travis song and then an old Clint Black song and I was dutifully cataloging what I did and didn't know about Mara. That her mother had died, yes. But why?

(You can surmise alcohol and varied benzodiazepines as rationale—you might also surmise the Devil—but whatever her motivations, it did nothing to change the fact that the year Mara turned sixteen her mother walked deep into the woods where she placed her gold Tory Burch flats on a rock not far from the FLORA & FAUNA sign erected by Boy Scout Troop 819, put her back to a tree and the barrel of a .410 over-under into her mouth so that the gunsight must have pressed into the soft of her palate.

It was the wrong gun, but then again it must not have been.)

I knew Mara had lived for a time in New York—"my Pratt

phase," she had called it—but that was all I knew. What about her time with Chris after I left? Or her time at the church after Daniel died, or in her studio, or in a thousand different places? What did I know of her mountain lion? What did I know of her sorrow?

When the room shifted, I fell off my stool and someone was pulling me up by one arm and the bartender was ordering me out. I must have said something because a moment later he had a baseball bat, but whoever was helping me along was saying *it's all right, I got this, I got it*, and then we were out in the parking lot, the day still blazing, the rush-hour traffic stalled by the stop-light. The man leaned me against a brick column and looked me up and down. He was wearing a blue vest, the puffy sort of thing you see in REI catalogs, and a watch cap, despite the heat. Gaunt with a gray two-day stubble. Or maybe he had just shaved poorly: there were wiry patches on his Adam's apple, beneath an ear. He looked sick and I realized he was prodding at my pockets asking me where I'd parked.

"I didn't fucking park," I told him, and started toward the highway.

"Wait," he called.

I fell and came up with bits of gravel on my knees and in the soft of my hands.

"Wait a minute."

But I got up and kept walking, just sober enough to get to my room and fall asleep face down on the bed.

I had no trouble getting in to see Chris Bright the next morn-ing. Whatever favors Bill Baker had called in had worked. I was met by the same deputy from the previous day who along with a doctor escorted me to a changing room where we pumped hand sanitizer and I put on a yellow gown, mask, and gloves. I would be allowed in alone but only for ten minutes. When his dressings were changed, I would have to leave.

The room was empty but for his bed and monitors, the drip bags running into his swaddled arms. The deputy stood on the other side of the observation window, glaring, but the doctor was gone. It was difficult to say if I recognized Chris. So much of him was covered, but I thought I detected something familiar there, some holdover from before. He appeared to be sleeping—he appeared, actually, to be dead—but then his eyes popped open, that same glacial blue, but milky now, almost translucent.

"Chris," I said very quietly.

When he spoke, it was a whisper, and I had to move beside the bed to hear him. He had said a single word. I thought he had said my name. Then I realized he had said hers.

"They're looking for her," I said.

His voice made me think of the dried palm fronds in Mexico, brittle and fallen and raked along the sidewalks.

"Can they hear us?" he asked.

I looked at the window. The deputy was gone.

"We're alone."

He almost shook his head.

"They're listening," he said.

"There's no one here. Tell me what happened."

"Mara."

"What happened, Chris? They're looking for her."

"They won't find her."

"Where is she?"

"She kept talking about him."

"About who?"

"She thought . . ."

"Is she alive?"

"She was crawling. She just got it in her head somehow and then . . ."

"Tell me where she is."

With the two swollen fingers that curled fat and blue from his bandages, he motioned me closer.

"Chris, please," I said. "They're looking for her."

"They won't find her." I could barely hear him. "She went down into the well. Because of the boy. She thought it was a trap."

"Because of Daniel?"

"I told her it was her imagination, but she thought it was some sort of karmic thing. Like they had baited it. These dead birds."

"Something about Daniel?"

"She was supposed to leave it there and get out. I was outside and then she never came. She never came and I knew something was wrong, but I didn't think. . . . She got down in the bore hole, I think. I was running back when it went off."

"She died?"

"They won't find her."

"Is she dead?"

"She had this plan. Remember our plan?"

"What plan? Where is she? Is she alive?" It was only when they came in the door, the doctor and the deputy and two male nurses, that I realized I was yelling, realized I had grabbed his arm, and the nurses were grabbing me and the doctor was saying *that's enough, I said that's enough.* Then I was back in the hall, marched to the elevator and back to the parking lot. I was in my truck, panting, when I saw the man watching me. The man from the bar. The same puffy vest, same watch cap. He was standing near the service entrance where the fencing opened onto two green dumpsters. The same man. I was almost certain.

It was late afternoon by the time I got back to Jay's. Banjo was fine, loping his arthritic self out to lick my hand. Jay came out more slowly, measured, shirtless in jeans, a beer in his hand.

"You heard, I guess," I said.

"Impossible not to. You want to come in a minute?"

I followed him into the kitchen where we sat at the table, ceiling fan turning, cans of Bud sweating. I think Jay must have talked to me about Mara, but I don't remember what exactly he said. He must have assumed she was dead and I must have allowed him to go on believing such. I do remember asking him if he could keep Banjo a few more days.

"You know I'm always glad to have him," he said, "but I need to ask you what you're up to."

"Just clearing my head."

"Just clearing your head?" He wiped one finger along the side of his can. "Daddy said I should keep you here, by force if necessary."

"He said that?"

"He thinks you might be prone to some rashness."

"He really thinks that?"

"I guess he's seen it," Jay said, "in his line of work."

I nodded. The can had come not from the refrigerator but from a cooler on the porch, so cold it burned my fingertips when I touched it.

"Just two days," I said. "I'm not doing anything stupid. I just need some time."

"I understand."

I picked up my beer.

"You think I could get one more of these?"

"Of course."

"I'm going to hit the head here," I said, and stood.

He watched me for a long moment and finally turned for the porch.

I walked down the hall and stopped outside the bathroom until I heard the screen door slap. Then I walked to his bedroom where in the second drawer of his nightstand I found the .357 we had fired just days ago, the pistol cleaned and loaded and wrapped in an oilcloth. I shoved it into the waistband of my jeans where it rested cold and heavy against my lower back. I pulled my shirt down as best I could, and walked back into the kitchen. When Jay came inside with two Buds I told him maybe I better be going, that I'd be back for Banjo soon.

He followed me out to the truck but said not a word.

I started it and, just before I dropped it into reverse, gave a little wave, my goodbye.

She got down in the bore hole, I thought as I rolled down the gravel. *I was running back when it went off.*

So that was how it ended for Chris.

But I had to go back to how it started.

Which would have been decades ago, and with such subtlety, such kindness. There was always that, his kindness. As a boy, Chris Bright was kind to everyone, but it wasn't something he thought about. It was who he was, achingly tenderhearted, his aunt and uncle said. His aunt and uncle who raised him from the time he was three, his parents having crossed first the centerline of I-40 and then that bright crystal sea that separates the quick and the dead, and it was his aunt who thought maybe that wound opened his heart a little more than everyone else, that maybe losing his mama and daddy let in that certain slant of light not present in most.

Chris didn't think it was true.

His parents were ghosts, less than ghosts, not memories but a whisper campaign of sad remembrance. They were the stories he heard on the porch swing hung in the carport, swaying on July nights with a glass of sweet tea, Ronnie Milsap on the radio. Fireflies down in the kudzu. His uncle whittling a length of walnut while his aunt broke beans into a washtub. His grandfather was a block of crumbling limestone named Burl Bright who lived alone at the end of Burl Bright Road, an old timber man with a stubbled neck and hands the size of bear paws. Chris would go rabbit hunting with him, and the old man would tell him about Chris's daddy and his uncle as boys, working that bottomland or hiking up that knob, going off to Nam together for no better reason than the pure hell of it. They even got married the same day, same ceremony by old what's-his-face down at the Primitive Baptist church along the river. Ate red velvet cake and fried apple pies and then everyone went home to get drunk without the preacher seeing. *Them boys was something, the two of 'em together. And your mama was the sweetest thing you ever met. Could cook. Lord, that woman could cook. The stories I could tell you,* and he did, the old man told his stories. But that was all Chris knew, so when he overheard his aunt saying their absence was the reason he was so gentle he wanted to tell her it wasn't that. It was who he was and that was enough, and if it wasn't enough, it didn't matter anyway. It was all he had.

His aunt and uncle in the kitchen at night with okra and tomatoes, hands on the Formica table, worrying over him.

"He's got a good heart." His uncle saying this.

Then his aunt: "It ain't the goodness of his heart I'm talking about. I'm talking about the world walking all over him."

"He's all right."

"He's too much like his mama is what he is."

They had no children of their own. It wasn't something they talked about.

91

They lived in the mountains of Watauga County, North Carolina, just this side of the Tennessee state line. A farm community called Bethel that still had its general store and post office and volunteer fire department. The local Ruritan club with its Friday fish fry. A backstop and baseball diamond cut in the grass along the river. Chris was a southern boy, a good boy. A mama's boy, if only he'd had a mama. His uncle worked at the Erwin Fossil Plant moving coal ash in a Caterpillar D10, the job an hour's drive into Tennessee. His aunt had worked in a textile mill making towels for Kmart until the arthritis in her fingers got too bad and not even the BC powder helped. Not that it mattered. By then they were busy closing the mill and shipping the whole operation to Thailand.

Chris rode the bus to school, seven winding miles along the highway that threaded the valley past the farms and old homeplaces, the sediment of days washed away so all that was left was what could not be moved. The stone chimney. The brick foundation. That leaning corner of the barn, collapsed into the locust grove. He was so quiet they put him in self-contained until the third grade when he took the North Carolina Basic Assessment and scored in the top 1 percent, and then they tracked him into every gifted program they had, which meant he got half an hour twice a week with a woman with two degrees from Chapel Hill. But he didn't speak, not any more than he had to. At home he helped in the garden and played alone in Cove Creek, building little sand dams where the pincered crawfish would maneuver through the mica dust. In the evenings he sat on the porch swing, his uncle listening to the Braves on the station out of Johnson City, his aunt staring out as day smoothed into night and the owls came out of the trees as silent as starlight.

They made sun tea in the window. They canned green beans

and chow-chow. The toilet had a padded seat, the foam just beginning to crack. When they went to the Dairy Queen in town, his uncle let him eat the hot fries out of the bottom of the bag.

That was his world.

The way the Chips Ahoy! went soft in his aunt's cookie jar.

The way they collected the Smurf glasses from Hardee's.

Summers he played little league on the field behind the firehouse, roamed the woods, worked the garden pulling the dark roots of this or that, dirt beneath his nails, beet juice staining his fingers. He liked to go to his granddaddy's and walk down to Old Watauga River Road where he'd roam for hours only to come back to find the old man on the porch right where he'd left him, spitting Red Man into the yard. *I'm hungry as a tied dog. Come in here and I'll heat us a can a soup.* He'd fry steak with chicken gravy and together they'd ride in his Ford Galaxie with the bench seats the color of raspberry Kool-Aid. Rambling along the gravel road, the river unwinding itself in time to crash down the spillway by the old lumber mill. *Place was hell on a Friday night. I was bad for the drink back then. Fighting too. Hell, son, I was bad for everything back then.* At home, Chris would walk for hours, pastures, meadows, cemeteries tucked beneath the ridge, walk and watch for hawks and deer, the barbed wire still clenched around a claim otherwise long forgotten.

Fifth grade was the year he started vomiting his milk, barely making it from the breakfast table to the toilet. His aunt and uncle thinking he had a stomach bug, thinking he was lactose intolerant, thinking maybe he was just guzzling it too fast. Nobody ever thinking he was nervous, the way people looked at him, talked about him not behind his back but right there in front of him as if he were deaf and blind. *Quare,* they called it.

The boy's just quare.

Not queer, quare: odd, strange.

See how quare he acts? My mama said just leave him be. It's how he is.

The blonde hair flying over his ears and too long one year. Buzzed too short the next. The hand-me-down jeans and V-neck T-shirts he wouldn't dare tell his aunt and uncle nobody wore. The Velcro on his shoes. *My mama said he ain't retarded. I guess he just likes them kind of shoes.* So the walks got longer, he was alone more, though not exactly lonely. Though now and then there was that, there was loneliness, at least the aftertaste, the sense of it lingering at night in bed, the windows open to the whip-poor-wills and cicadas, the aunt and uncle snoring in the other room. Those nights he lay awake for hours, sometimes praying, sometimes speaking silently to his parents, telling them about his day, what had happened and what had not. And then a long litany of blessings and mercy. Please Lord be with my uncle. Help him not get too tired at work. Please Lord be with my aunt. Help her fingers not hurt too much. Be with my mama and daddy in heaven, Lord. Be with me.

They went to church three services a week, Bethel Baptist, a white block building, charmless but for its position on the ridge overlooking the valley. But in between the services there were constant returns so there was less a line between the worlds of spirit and flesh as a hazy uncertainty that in a moment could turn and then turn again.

Sixth grade he started running down along the river, jogging at first, just to see more. But then quicker, more focused. He wasn't waiting on anyone, after all. It was only later he realized the mistake he'd made, that if he'd stopped running he might have addressed his loneliness. But by then it was too late: once loneliness is realized, once loneliness becomes the bedrock of your life, there is no other referent. Your life is built around the absence of others even if others are there.

The next year he saw his first bird—saw, he meant, with his true eye—a little male northern cardinal with its red body and black mask and if he was running, all at once it was without any connection to the earth, he was above it. He was, at least for those moments alone in the fields and pastures and woods, flying. He saw a Carolina wren a few days later, identified from a book he checked out at the Sugar Grove library. Then a red-tailed hawk, a barred owl.

One Saturday morning he sat at the table while his granddaddy drank coffee from the cup of his Stanley thermos.

"You like watching them birds?"

"Yes, sir."

"I always did too. Look here."

He left the table and came back with a pair of Zeiss binoculars.

"I carried 'em in the war. I hope you enjoy 'em more than I did."

Chris ran through the woods. Even when he was still and silent—and he was often still and often silent, down on his stomach watching a blue jay feed its young, or a hawk riding a thermal—he was running or flying through the world, untouched, alone but for the birds he watched.

Animals, too. A doe and her fawn he walked up on one day. They were grazing blackberries along the side of the road and he seemed to see the mother just as she saw him so that both stood for a moment, reverent, hushed, and then the mother and her young dashed into the woods and were gone so quickly they became less creature than belief. He started trying to run like a deer, silent, pausing to listen, ears cocked. He saw red fox and wild turkeys and squirrels and rabbits. He wanted to see a mountain lion.

"There used to be panther all in these mountains," his uncle said.

"There's still more than a few," his aunt said. "I've heard 'em."

But Chris never did. He saw broad-winged hawks and ospreys sweeping over the river, fishing for trout. He saw a black bear in a tree and deer moving through a corn patch like gleaners. He saw turtles and snakes and kingbirds and hummingbirds. But he never saw a lion.

At church—he was in the youth group now—they were studying the Book of Job, of God's answer out of the whirlwind, and what struck Chris was that all the world's bitter wisdom seemed to rest with the animals. It was they who had been present for the building of the world, the laying of the foundation. Everyone was busy telling him what was and what was not, except the animals. It was the animals that kept silent counsel, emerging and disappearing back into the world, and it was the animals, he realized one day, who were dying.

"I don't want to eat deer no more," he told his aunt one night at the table. "I don't want to eat any animals."

She stood in the kitchen, hand gloved in an oven mitt.

"Well, I hope you're ready to be hungry."

"I can eat biscuits and hot dogs."

"Boy, what do you think a hot dog is but pig meat?"

He found the deer stand one fall day on the edge of a clear-cut a half mile off Rush Branch Road. It was a metal platform winched to the trunk of a maple and overlooking what had become a slope of brambles and briars and the occasional dwarf pine netted in kudzu. He climbed the ladder and examined the thing, the old lawnmower seat bolted to the lattice, the torn camouflage netting, and then he went home and found his uncle's socket set. He started at the top and worked his way down: took off the seat, slashed the netting. When he released the winch he felt the stand sway, held to the tree by nothing but gravity. The ladder was harder. He loosened the bolts as he inched down, the rungs bouncing, the ladder beginning to lean. When he stepped off, he gave it a hard push and it crashed into the brush.

There was a great echo Chris felt inside him, a great interior humming that vibrated up into his eyes until he realized his eyes were crying. There, he said, because it seemed something should be said, and then he walked back to the house.

But a week later he found the deer stand resurrected and what he felt was an anger so intense for a moment he couldn't see. He had never experienced anything like it. This time he took the stand down without tools, loosening the winch and bungee cords (there were cords now, bound around the trunk), and pushing the tower over. When it crashed, he ran.

That night he lay in bed and listened to the wind rub its way along the house, against the windows and beneath the eaves, through the dormant field and through the empty tops of trees, and then he felt it rub its way inside him and it moved there and then he was the wind, sweeping over the valley and the mountains, above the heads of the hawks and songbirds, the northern parula and wood thrush, until he had reached the mountain top and there, on an outcropping of gray rock, stood a mountain lion, waiting on him.

The headlights woke him. His uncle going to work before the slightest blush of dawn. Then he realized the lights weren't going away from the house, but coming toward it and at that moment the wind that had moved inside him stilled. He was not on the ridge, but in bed, cold beneath the piled quilts and still very much a little boy.

He didn't need to hear his grandparents' voices to know it was the man who owned the deer stand. His aunt's raised voice, his uncle quieter, but no less firm. Chris waited until the headlights brushed past his window and disappeared up the road before he came out.

His uncle sat at the table, smoking, the sixteen gauge across his lap.

His aunt was in the kitchen, standing over the stove, and when he emerged from the bedroom her head popped up like a turtle and she crossed the room in three great strides to where Chris stood with his matted hair and Star Wars pajamas.

"Boy, was you raised Christian or not?"

"Grace," his uncle said.

But she already had Chris's ear, was already pulling him toward the table where his uncle's ashtray sat mounded.

"Did you go on that man's land? Don't you lie to me."

The man was Cabbage Jones, a beefy red-faced bachelor who owned a muffler and air conditioning shop in town. Chris went to work for him on the Saturday after Thanksgiving. That was the agreement: four Saturdays of labor to make up for his vandalism.

Jones met Chris on the porch in long johns, a can of Schlitz in his fist. The morning cold and overcast, a thin gray eyelid drawn over the valley.

"You gonna cut that field, boy." He motioned at the corn patch, at the brown and withered stalks that should have been cleared months ago. "When you get it gathered, you're gonna dump it down at the edge of the pasture and then come back up here and I'll set you to something else. You understand me?"

"Yes, sir."

"You got a knife? Get one out of the kitchen if you don't."

He turned back into the house and Chris stood for a moment on the front step. In the yard sat a Chevy Silverado, its bed full of crumpled tallboys. On the porch stood a washing machine and a bushel basket of more cans.

He got to work.

The corn was a half acre Chris cut with his Old Timer, one row, another, down on his knees in the cold mud, the shadows skimmed in an ice that had caught spider webs and silk worms. His fingers hurt. His nose ran. It took him a good forty minutes to cut a third of it, working his way down one row and up another. He stood to stretch his back, his knees wet, tennis shoes clotted red. When he fingered his pocket knife, he found it was dull, like cutting with a piece of gravel. A line of smoke went up from the chimney, but otherwise the house was still. He decided to get a sharper knife from the kitchen.

He knocked the mud from his Keds and slipped inside. The house was a mess, an old console radio and a red-patterned couch, more beer cans. A potbellied stove and Eddie Money on the hi-fi. But above it all, tacked to the wood paneling, were animals. Three bucks, a rainbow trout, a mink, a red fox, and standing in the corner, occupying the entire corner, the tawny body of a female mountain lion, its tail stretching from the corner past the stove to the couch. Amber-eyed, ears flat. The round paws and thickly muscled back legs. Its coat was shabby and patched, but for all its worn shine, it was no less regal. He took a step closer. It was looking at him, the lioness, its head cocked though not in surprise. Its head cocked as if it had been waiting a long time for Chris's arrival, never quite believing he would come, but never doubting it either.

"My uncle shot it. That would have been sometime in the thirties."

He turned to find the man behind him, the long johns dirty and stretched over the swell of his gut. There was another beer in his hand and he cracked the top.

"That might well have been the last panther in this valley."

The man's eyes drifted down to the linoleum.

"You got mud on my floor."

"I ain't sorry," Chris said.

The man snorted.

"Your aunt said you won't eat meat."

"No."

"You don't know shit about the world."

"I ain't sorry," he said again. "For none of it."

He stood for a moment staring at Chris's muddy tracks and then shook his head in disgust. "You get on home and don't come back. I catch you by that stand again, I'll have you mounted, you little son of a bitch."

He reached for Chris, stumbled, and Chris shot beneath his outstretched arm and made for the door, running all the way home and saying not a word to his aunt and uncle. They didn't ask, and he didn't go back. And he wasn't sorry. He was free.

It was March when he saw the advertisement for the camp in Wolf Laurel. Bird banding on the open expanse of Big Bald, the treeless crown of a six-thousand-foot peak along the Appalachian Trail. He was sitting in the tiny Sugar Grove library, copying the information onto his hand from an issue of *North Carolina Wildlife* when the librarian came up behind him and said, "You can take it."

"Ma'am?"

"The magazine. You can take it if you like."

The camp was six days and cost two hundred dollars but there was a scholarship. He wrote the essay and mailed it off. When the congratulatory letter arrived, he wasn't surprised. Strangely, he wasn't even grateful. It seemed more fated than that, as if he had been found.

He lied to this aunt and uncle that it was a sleepaway camp, and lied to the camp director that he would be staying with family in the area. His grandmother, he said, she lives just a mile or so away. Then he packed his tent and sleeping bag—everybody just camps, he told his aunt—and his uncle drove him the ninety minutes south down I-26.

It was there he found his people, thirteen-year-olds obsessed with red-winged blackbirds or American kestrels or the migratory patterns of ruby-throated hummingbirds. Shy girls who would spend hours sketching Queen Anne's lace. Hulking boys who cared nothing about SEC football and everything about woodpeckers. They were rich, the children of privilege, that was the one difference—a not insignificant one—but so long as they were in the field it seemed not to matter.

It was trickier in the evenings. The camp was based in a giant summer home that was more English country lodge than house. Leather upholstery and Audubon prints. The green shaded lamps, the coppery quiet, all of it beneath a patina of fine dust. The house perched two-thirds up a mountain in a gated community, and when the other parents arrived to pick up their children, Chris smiled and said his goodbyes. Did he need a ride? No thanks, his grandmother's house was right down there. He would start walking and then duck into the forest and begin the half-mile trek toward the summit of Big Bald, the top sheared bare so that the view extended farther than Chris had ever traveled. He pitched his tent just off the slope in an area of scrub called the Scratch. He'd thought after the first day to leave it up, but that Tuesday the camp had hiked up to set mist nets and he knew discovery was inevitable. He took it down every morning and stowed it in his pack.

If it sounded like a burden, it wasn't. It became, in fact, everything. Alone at night the world opened to him in a way he had never known, and he went through the woods like some long-ago mystic. The self-anointed. The made-holy. If they would not lay hands on him, he would lay hands on himself.

He didn't need sleep.

He would set up his tent and wander up to the summit where

passing hikers watched the sun set in a great bleed of color, the mountains turning the dark felt of an aging pool table. When it was gone, he walked the dusky trails and then off the trails into the denser forest, into the darkness. The darkness held everything. There were deer bedded in thickets, fawns so young they had not yet lost their spots. Rabbits flicking through the underbrush. Turkeys and red fox. He moved past them. Came to barbed-wire fences rusted and gouged into trees, stepped over the bottom strand, felt the staple give and then hold. He was something else, this nocturnal thing who changed with the darkness, and changed back when that darkness receded.

The last night he sat watching a mist net set up to snare northern saw-whet owls for banding, elusive birds no bigger than his fist. The owls everywhere, it seemed, except here. He could hear birds in the deeper forest, the yips of coyotes. But here, nothing. Here was silence, the breeze ticking the high grasses of Big Bald, and then, out of that low whispering, someone speaking to him.

What do you see, son?

Whose voice? His mother's?

No. It was his father's. He thought of him now and then, his father skimming the jungle canopy. His father, dry-mouthed and sweating as a fleet of slicks descended on a Laotian clearing, the elephant grass laid over into great whorls as the tracer fire began to come out of the tree line, the AKs and the heavier Soviet-made DShK. The war. The thing his uncle never talked about and which might not have existed were it not for the Class A uniform, plastic-bagged and nearly hidden in the coat closet, the patch of the First Cavalry Division (Airmobile) on the shoulder. Like the advertisement for the camp, he had found his father in the pages of the Sugar Grove library. Or what passed for a father, which was, in the end, little more than Larry Burrows's photographs in a series of *Time-Life* books.

About his mother there was only hearsay.

What are we watching for here?

He was beside him now, his father. Chris's eyes were forward, focused on the darkness he knew to hold the mist net, and he forced himself not to turn. As long as he didn't look, he knew his father was beside him.

There's a net up there.

What are we trying to catch?

These tiny little owls. Northern saw-whet owls.

We aren't going to hurt them, are we?

Oh, no, Dad. Just band them. Then we'll let them go.

Good, good. I wouldn't want to hurt a living thing.

No. Never.

They waited.

Anything? his dad asked.

Not yet.

Well, we've got plenty more night.

Yes, sir.

Above them, patterned light, the high cirrus clouds stretched to near nothing so that stars were blown across the great dome of sky, so clear he could see the failing slant of the Milky Way. The world before the world was made. The world before it knew itself.

Dad?

Yes, son?

Is mom with you?

She's right here.

Why can't I hear her?

She wants you to know that she's right here.

Will I ever see her?

I don't know. But she wants you to know she loves you. She's so proud of you, of how good you are. She says no matter what, don't lose your goodness.

It was only later, when the light began to assert itself, that he woke with a start to realize the great gray eyelid that had closed over the world that morning, cutting cornstalks for Cabbage Jones, had lifted. He started to tell his father but his father had disarticulated himself. His father was now a helicopter, forever descending in a jungle clearing. His father was a coat, forgotten in the closet, a voice. A hand reaching for his wife as they both hurled toward an I-40 embankment, tires losing the catch of the asphalt.

Chris sat alone, looking down at the greening world so intently he almost missed the shape of the mountain lion, paused, as it was, on the scattered gravel of the trail before it ducked into the forest and back out of his life.

But not before he tucked it into some deeper pocket of self.

That fall he started ninth grade at Watauga High, riding the bus out of the valley for what felt like the first time. Now he was no longer among just the country kids, the redneck kids, picked up from where they stood cluttered by the roadside like mailboxes. The children of rural routes. The folks cleaning the houses of the university professors or roofing the second homes. Now he was among the townies. He kept to himself, as he always had, but where at the Bethel school he had been understood as no more than "quare," now he was understood as odd, the weirdo, the little faggot who don't say boo, do you, boy? and what he got for that were the wedgies in the locker room, the noogies against his blonde head, the shoves against the trophy case in middle hall.

At home, his uncle was not well, aging, failing, always coughing into his armpit. His white hair had thinned, his back had begun to hump. *Naw, I'm all right, son. Just getting a little older, that's all.* But it was a brutal decline. Not the graceful silvering of the temples, but the kind of aging that scrapes away life, pruning the body.

That got-damn power plant is killing him, his granddaddy said. But it wasn't just the plant. His aunt showed it, too. Her fingers, gnarled and thick as sausages. Forearms mottled with liver spots. At night, he watched her take out her false teeth, the way her mouth collapsed into her face and with it all the defiance, all the fierceness that animated her. When she took her teeth out, she looked like a tired old woman, and that was exactly what she was.

He tried to help more, to work in the garden, to push-mow the lawn. He did the laundry and the dishes. All the while his aunt and uncle complaining. *Don't fuss over that. Your job is your studies.* But he saw they needed the help, saw how much they appreciated it. And school was easy. He had no trouble with his classes beyond the stares, the lone poor kid in gifted and talented, the lone country boy wearing his Dingo boots in a class of townies in their acid-washed jeans and Members Only jackets. He spent less time in the woods, but thought about it more until soon the greater world of forest and creek and the barbed-wire fence nailed to the locust posts existed inside the walls of his mind. It was limitless there. Sun. Sky. Tree. Populated by birds and deer and prowled, somewhere just beyond the edge of seeing, by the lioness he had seen first mounted in Cabbage Jones's living room and then down along the trail beneath Big Bald. He ran there in his dreams, he ran there at night when he lay beneath the quilts in bed, and he ran there during class while this algebra teacher or that history teacher droned on explaining what he already knew.

Then one day a man approached him and asked if he'd ever considered running. It took Chris a moment to realize he meant truly running, as in physically, legs and feet and lungs.

"I coach the cross-country team. You ever think of coming out?"

"No, sir."

"You live out in Bethel, don't you? I saw you jogging last Saturday."

Except he hadn't been jogging, at least not in any conscious sense. He had finished what had to be done at home and he was running down toward the river where he would lope for hours, slowly picking his way along the road that mirrored the Watauga all the way from the dam with its abandoned sawmill down to the park in Valle Crucis where the tourists bought expensive pottery.

The next week he went to practice in the same worn Keds he wore to school, the soles flapping until he duct-taped them, and then came home to find a new pair of white Adidas cradled in tissue paper. He stuck his nose inside each and inhaled the new smell, knowing his aunt and uncle couldn't afford the shoes but knowing nothing made them happier than seeing them on his feet.

They came to his first meet and he wondered at it. It was impossible to imagine them anywhere but church or home, working in the garden or the kitchen, his uncle on his old Cub Cadet or heading down the gravel drive to the power plant. Yet there they were.

The race was five kilometers around the school athletic fields and Chris cruised easily to the front, staying just off the shoulder of a senior who was the fastest boy in the county. Chris finished a step behind him, hands on his hips, barely panting.

"Why didn't you pass that boy?" his aunt asked him on the way home.

"I don't know. I didn't know if I should."

But he did pass him the next week, easing ahead at two miles and steadily speeding up until the look on the senior's face changed from surprise to wrenching exhaustion. Chris won by thirteen seconds and that fall finished fourth in the state AA cross-country meet. Everything changed then. Suddenly he was popular, people said hello, people noticed him.

The summer before his sophomore year, a girl from the cross-country team invited him to the Sunday service in town. One June morning, Brandy Jones picked him up in her Plymouth Renault, the upholstered seats so yellow they appeared lemon, a cassette of Wham! in the tape deck.

"Don't you look nice," she said when he got in.

"Thank you. So do you."

"Fancy. Very fancy."

He had run eight miles along the highway shoulder, finishing before seven so that he could shower and iron the shirt and tie he wore. It was only when they pulled into the First Baptist parking lot and he saw the other kids in shorts and tank tops that he realized that her *very fancy* wasn't admiration so much as disbelief. Everything was disbelief: the youth service was held in the darkened gymnasium. Someone played an electric guitar and someone else played the drums. No one mentioned the Devil and no one mentioned sin. The world, for all the talk of the youth pastor, was in no danger of ending any time soon.

After the service, Brandy Jones kissed him across the front seat, the car pulled onto the gravel shoulder, her hair brushed behind her ears, her hands gripping his wrists.

When she picked him up the next week, he wore jeans and a T-shirt and she seemed quietly relieved.

"Ready for some Jesus?" she asked.

This time they moved into the backseat of the car and he found his hand inside the buttons of her blouse, against the lacy cup of her bra.

"Easy," she said, but leaned closer.

That fall he won first the region and then the district championships and finished second at the state meet behind a senior headed on scholarship to NC State. But it was the rides home that mattered. He sat with Brandy in the back of the dark bus, the windows down to let in the autumn cool, a blanket over their laps to hide their hands. Outside apple trees and cemeteries and the mountain roads switching back as the bus ascended through Linville Gorge.

It was astonishing, this new way of being, and soon enough it became everything to him: running, Brandy. The cross-country spikes on his feet, his hands on her body. He still went into the woods but less often. He did what had to be done at home, but he did it quickly and sloppily. His aunt and uncle didn't seem to notice. They occupied a tighter circle that began to shrink from the fields and barn down to the kitchen and porch and bedroom. His uncle still worked at the power plant, but it seemed more shadow than act, the habit hanging on long after the spirit had fled. Chris would wake to find them both still asleep, the fire out, breakfast unmade. They slept long and sound, exhaustion hanging about their shoulders the way fog hung over the river. Their only connection to the larger world was Chris, his running, his life the only window left to let in any light. When he thought of this, it moved him. But he didn't think of it so often. He saw less of his granddaddy.

I hardly recognize you, boy. Come here and sit for a half a second.

But half a second was all he could spare.

Junior year he won the state championship by nineteen seconds, missing the state record by a few strides. He and Brandy were still making out but less so. At church she quit sitting by him in the bean-bagged dark, pushing his hand out of her lap when he moved close. It didn't really matter to him, and he hardly noticed when she broke up with him. There were other girls, plenty of girls, and when he wasn't running he was making out at Trash Can Falls or skinny-dipping at Snake Pit. He bought hair gel and sat in a front row beanbag at First Baptist where he beat a tambourine against his thigh simply because he liked the way he looked holding it.

In the spring, he won the state two-mile in track and started to hear from college coaches. He started to notice Brandy again, too. She had withdrawn from the world, the once popular girl— *very fancy*—with her Swatch watch and Madonna tapes, now quiet and alone, as if through so much touching they had reversed lives. At youth group she was one of a small group who huddled in the corner and prayed while the others played ping-pong and ate pizza. They were working Monday nights at the homeless shelter on King Street and planning a mission trip to a youth conference in Daytona Beach. Just before school let out for the summer he saw her walking alone downtown. He was in his uncle's pickup— more and more it was his pickup—and pulled alongside her.

"Brandy!"

She had a notebook of some sort pressed to her chest, a stack of them, he saw, Trapper Keepers like third graders carried.

"Hey, Brandy!"

When she turned to him, he asked if she needed a ride.

"Not really."

"Where you going?"

"Down here."

"Down here where?"

"Just down here."

"Well, let me give you a ride."

Behind him a horn honked.

"No, thanks."

"Come on. I'm holding up traffic."

He pulled in by the Ag extension office and she seemed to get in reluctantly, as much to avoid a scene as anything else.

"It's good to see you," he said.

"Sure."

"Tell me which way."

"Just right up here."

He drove her to the Watauga County Offices, a monolith of Cold War concrete and smoked glass where decades later I would be interviewed by the FBI.

"What's here?"

"Social Services."

"What are you doing there?"

"Volunteering," she said.

"Why?"

"Oh, I don't know, maybe to help people."

"Really?"

"Of course, really. Thanks for the ride, Chris."

She popped the door and crossed the parking lot, same denim jacket, same acid-washed 501 jeans, but very much a different human being, and watching her go he felt both longing and jealousy because that was who he had been, who he should be still. The kind one, helping people. And for the first time in months he thought of all those days he had spent alone in the woods, the birds, the deer. He thought of dismantling Cabbage Jones's deer stand. He thought of his uncle and aunt at home on the porch, just as they'd spent every evening of the last two decades, only now without him.

He thought of his father's voice.

He hadn't heard it in years.

He didn't go straight home, but instead drove the backroads, Rush Branch to Bethel to Old Watauga River, all the roads he'd once seen only from the shoulder or the adjoining fields and it was strange seeing them this way, the angle changed, the world slightly off plumb, but it also felt like he was returning to something he only now realized he had left. He drove until dusk began to creep from the peaks, the shadows fingering out from the white pines, and then he turned for home, catching, as he made the left onto 321, something brown and quick moving through the brush beside the creek that was maybe a large dog or maybe a small horse, but also, maybe, a mountain lion, loping beside him as if keeping watch.

He called Brandy the next morning. All night the mountain lion had lurked along the tree line of sleep, occupying the place he could no more see than he could take his eyes from. Sometime before dawn he had realized it was taking his measure, and finding him lacking.

"I want to go on that mission trip," he told her. "The trip to Daytona Beach."

"Is this a joke or something?"

"I'm completely serious."

"So you can laugh at it or something? Play your tambourine and make fun of people."

"Please, Brandy."

She sighed.

"It's not up to me," she said finally.

"I know it isn't. But I'm still asking."

They left in late June, the church van gliding through dislocations of heat. He sat alone and stared out the window as the land flattened and the air grew thick with honeysuckle and diesel. The endless traffic lights, the fast food and Quik-Marts and Circle Ks. Charlotte to Columbia to Savannah to Jacksonville, though all they really saw was the highway. Two stops for Gatorade and Funions and lining up for the bathroom. The Black men congregating outside a Jet Express in Orangeburg. I-95 from South Carolina through Georgia into Florida and finally into Daytona Beach.

They drove past the Speedway with its steel girders and

billboard faces—Richard Petty, Mark Martin—all the way to the Breakers Hotel where the parking lot was full of buses and vans and sleepy teenagers piling out carrying duffel bags and pillows. The girls in cut-offs, pockets pasted to thighs. Boys in high-tops and tank tops and mirrored shades. The day was bright beyond belief, the sky blue, the clouds an idea not quite realized, all of it so open. He couldn't get over that, the openness, the green stars that proved to be the crowns of high skinny palms, the traffic, constant and loud.

In the afternoon a storm blew ashore and he walked out to the beach where the world had gone a sudden gray. He had imagined the ocean as a vast blue and it was almost disappointing, as if he were seeing something else, something almost but not quite. Yet he knew it was there. Beneath the gulls and the failing light was this great wash that extended around the planet, farther than he could begin to imagine.

That evening they attended a rally at the convention center, three thousand screaming believers, the stage all fog machine and flashing light, all electric guitar. Around him people were weeping, swaying, hands raised, and he raised his hands too because he wanted to feel something, to experience the current that very clearly was traveling the smoky air. Just before the altar call he caught Brandy looking at him, and when she stepped into the aisle he stepped out too and started down the steps behind her. But people were streaming forward and they were separated and it was just enough, that separation, to justify his stepping not toward the altar that the stage had become but away from it. He ducked out a side entrance past the concession stands selling Snickers and Cokes and PRAISE HIM! T-shirts, crossed the highway, and all at once he was more or less alone on the beach.

It was dusk and he felt oddly protected by the falling night as he walked past the hotel pools overlooking the sand, the smell of oil in the tiki torches, the empty lifeguard stands. He stood in the surf and felt the tide pull the beach under his feet and between his toes. Everywhere dead jellyfish embedded in the wet sand, gelatinous, bursting with mites. The clouds were low and more gray than silver and he walked as far as a tidal channel before he turned back for the hotel. It had been hours, and his roommate was asleep, exhausted and, so it appeared to Chris, blissfully content. After the rally, they had handed out flyers in the parking lot of a dance club called Razzles and from such work seemed to have been made content. The sight of such simple happiness was more than Chris could stand, and he went back outside to the pool. It was after midnight, after curfew, but still warm, and he sat in a deck chair in the shadow of the palms, more or less out of sight, when the voice found him.

"You aren't supposed to be out here."

He didn't see her at first.

"What?"

"The pool's closed."

She was sitting in a deeper shadow over near the lanai and he had to stand to see her, this girl he didn't know. He walked over to where she sat on an identical chair, a bottle on the tiles beside her.

"If it's closed," he said, "you shouldn't be here either."

"Sit down."

He looked around, not quite comprehending, until she nudged the chair beside her.

"Sit, idiot," she said. "Before someone sees you."

He sat, the vinyl straps giving, and slowly the night sounds began to reassert themselves. The traffic on the highway, the hum of the pool filter. The way the breeze shifted so that sometimes he smelled the ocean and sometimes it was just gas and heat. Then for a moment the night smelled of chlorine, an exotic smell.

"I saw you walk out," she said. "You didn't go to the club?"

"Did you?"

"People went to clubs all over town. You're from Boone?"

"Near there."

"I'm from Blowing Rock."

He said nothing. She was no more than a gray shape in the grayer night and if he looked straight ahead she was nothing at all. She was a voice.

"Some girl was looking for you afterward."

"How do you know?"

"Because she asked me if I'd seen you, stupid. She asked everybody."

"Brandy."

"Brandy," the voice repeated. "I didn't tell Brandy you were walking on the beach. Here. Look at all the fun you missed."

He felt something touch his arm. It was one of the flyers they had given out and read IF YOU DIED RIGHT NOW ARE YOU 100% SURE YOU WOULD GO TO HEAVEN?

"Well," she said, "are you?"

"What?"

"One hundred percent absolutely unequivocally sure, stupid."

"Are you?"

He heard her exhale, maybe shift in the plastic chair.

"My God is bigger than that," she said.

"Here," he said and tried to hand back the flyer but she didn't take it.

"I think that if you say the name of God," she said, "you'd better be ready to do something."

"Like what?"

"My name's Lana."

"Lana. I'm Chris."

"I know who you are."

And then he felt something touch his arm, her hand, her fingers curling around his wrist and then the brush of her hair against his face. When she kissed him it was slowly and deeply and he tasted her strawberry lip balm, felt the fine particulates of sand grained there, tasted wine. Realized it was wine she was drinking.

"Lana," he said, when she had eased back from his face.

"I have to go to bed," she said, and that was all. He reached for her, started to call her name, but she had already crossed the patio and was gone, just the sounds of her footsteps and the sound of the wine bottle going into the trash and what he was left with were the same night sounds as before.

On the second night he went back to the pool hoping to see her but she never came. He was disappointed but went back the third and final night knowing, somehow, she would be there, which she was, knowing too, somehow, they would wind up back in her room, which they did. For all his touching, it was his first time, and at dawn, his second. He slipped back into his own room just before daylight. His roommate woke him a few hours later to tell him to hurry up, they were already packed.

He was carrying down his bag when Brandy cornered him down by the ice machine. They were in an alcove of damp carpet and vending machines and she took both his wrists.

"What's going on with you, Chris?"

"What do you mean?"

"Tell me what's happening."

"I don't know," he said, and that was the truth.

"Chris!" the youth pastor called. "Come on!"

"Hold on," he called back, dropped his bag and ran up to find Lana's room.

The door was open. Inside a maid vacuumed the carpet.

"Where is . . ." he started to ask.

The woman looked at him, headphones wired to the Walkman clipped to her waist.

"Chris?" someone called, and he looked from the balcony to see the youth pastor in the parking lot. "Come on for gosh sake. We're all loaded and waiting."

Riding back, he reassumed his seat by the window, looking away from the passing highway to find Brandy staring at him, looking away as quick as he caught her eye. He knew she wanted to talk to him, knew she cared for him, but some small selfish part of himself couldn't convince the larger better part to take the empty seat beside her. By the time they were back in Boone she was looking at everything but him, her face porcelain, smooth and perfect, but harder too, set with some permanent indifference.

He didn't see her the rest of the summer. He ran. He worked at home and at his granddaddy's. He found himself quiet in the way he had once been. He found himself back in the woods. The church of the forest. The church of the moving water. It seemed like worship enough.

Now and then he would think of driving over to Blowing Rock and finding Lana but something kept him from it. He thought of her kiss, her touch, he thought of her God, deeper and wider than anything he might imagine, and he thought sometimes that though he could surely find Lana he doubted whether he could find such a god.

Senior year he became a monk, silent, head bowed, running. He broke the state records in both the 5K and two-mile and had scholarship offers from nine different schools. His aunt and uncle wanted him to go away somewhere, Duke or Chapel Hill, get the best education you can get, son. But he knew he couldn't leave them and enrolled at Appalachian State, fifteen miles away. There,

116

he was a philosophy major, but mostly he was a runner. He grew his hair to his shoulders and ran one hundred miles a week because that was what they all did. Drank cheap Pabst and on Saturday nights after meets smoked cheap bud because they did that too, and they were meant to be indistinguishable, the runners, the dirt bags piled into a single two-room apartment where they slept on mattresses and ate Ramen off a hot plate.

They did stupid shit, intentionally, he and his teammates. As in *let's go out and do some stupid shit.* Riding on the roof of some Ford Explorer with a boxy VHS camera so old you had to carry the VCR with you in a shoulder bag. Climbing water towers. Running hours through the night—eighteen, twenty miles—then hopping the fence to swim in the city pool just as dawn broke.

A senior ten-thousand-meter man named Bruce, who wore his hair to his waist, gave him a stack of worn paperbacks, and Chris read Black Elk and Sartre and Merton. He was nineteen years old. He tried to meditate and then thought of his uncle at the power plant and the life he had lived. At nineteen his uncle had been at a firebase up near the Cambodian border, his father, too. His granddaddy had been in France, wading ashore to the sound of German 88s in shrill decline.

What was he doing?

In this moment, he meant. In this life.

He had no answer.

Which was another way of saying everything seemed largely pointless, an indulgence in which he'd lost interest. So when his teammates went west to spend the summer working at resorts and running at altitude, Chris stayed home, rising early to run for hours along trails and fire roads, then coming home to cut grass or work in the garden for an hour before showering and driving his pickup to town where he worked for the county cutting more grass or cleaning municipal pools. At night his ears rang. He felt the vibration from the weed eater in his hands, the scorch of pool chemicals on the dry tips of his fingers. Flecks of greenery adhered to the damp skin behind his ears. Life narrowed. There were the books he read and the body he moved. There were his aunt and uncle and grandfather. There were his teammates. He grew quieter still, more monkish, more withdrawn. He began to dream again of Cabbage Jones's mountain lion and there were days he became the lion, loping through the forest, silent, tireless, moving on the big pads of his clawed feet.

His uncle retired from the power plant the summer before Chris's senior year and with that Chris knew it was time to leave. After graduation, he packed his truck with his running shoes and sleeping bag. He was going west, Colorado maybe, Seattle. People seemed to assume it was so that he could train in the company of faster runners, and he was content to allow them to assume as much. The truth was he had no more idea where he was going than why he was going. Just away, just west. Just somewhere other than here.

He passed through Denver in May, sleeping beneath his camper shell in national forests and truck stops. Boulder, Steamboat Springs, Telluride. His training was sporadic—he would run twenty miles a day one week straight and then nothing the next—his training wasn't really training at all. He needed it to right his mind, these endless trail runs. He was in mountain lion country, and there was always the thought he was courting his other self, the self he both was and might yet be.

He kept wandering.

Wyoming in June, Idaho, Montana.

The summer wildfires. The great assemblies of natural gas pipe laid across reservations with their casinos and stray dogs. The mountains so much sharper here, serrated or snowcapped, the entire earth lifting. So unlike the worn hills of home. He kept moving, passed ski resorts and right-wing compounds with barbed wire and warnings about FEMA conspiracies, slipped through small towns and past the untended ranches of millionaires.

In Bozeman, he met a group of Freegans at the food co-op and followed them to California and the massive redwood forests, these mossy places that extended north. July in Portland: working at an assisted-living facility off North Williams. Drinking Rainier beer and running along the Willamette River, back and forth across the bridges. September on Whidbey Island, foraging for mushrooms, trying to figure out what it was he was doing in this town/state/life. Drifting on the edge of a community encamped, at least until they were evicted, in a forest belonging to a local Waldorf school. Maybe two dozen men and women dumpster diving and smoking weed, taking the ferry to Mukilteo where they sold their plasma, hitching rides to Seattle where they busked and begged down around the university. Free and easy wandering, Chuang Tzu had called it.

Just drifting, he told us that summer after the march on the federal building.

Drifting.

Adrift.

Back then we were all adrift, I suppose, sitting in camp chairs by the river, passing the bourbon as the heat faded and the stars emerged. The summer and fall of 2003. The golden hour not just of the day but—I say it at the risk of great pretension—of our lives. The summer of bottle glass, the great curved shards we found along the riverbanks, the way the world appeared through it, warped, but softer too, forgiving, as if we were none of us ourselves, and better for it.

"We live under an umbrella of violence," Chris would say, but not with any real conviction.

Back home from seeing him in the Virginia burn center, I sat on my porch, remembering all of this, not necessarily surprised by how much I could recall. It was more like I was frightened by it, that I could bring back all that Chris had confessed to us so many years prior. There was a way in which Mara and I had hung on his every word, a way in which everything he said had been pressed like flowers into a book and a part of me wondered if in imprinting Chris's life into my memory I had effaced my own.

I thought of that there on the porch.

I'd driven over from Jay's to find what I suspected was the FBI van, parked on the highway, gone. There was little left of the chickens either. Animals had gotten to them, raccoons, vultures, and now the carnage was marked by a few scattered feathers and darker splotches of damp earth. But the house was still a wreck. It was hard to recall what had happened, only that something had. The lion in the house, Mara's lion. It was part of the reason I had the gun. But not the only one.

I opened a bottle of Elijah Craig and turned on the TV to let Judge Judy address the emptiness. That same deadening stillness I'd felt out in the yard with Banjo had descended and I needed the noise, even if it was game shows on the NBC affiliate out of Bristol. When I felt calmer, I raised the windows and slept on the couch. I wanted to invite it in. Jay's pistol was on the floor beside me, and I wanted to settle things, I wanted to see it. But nothing came, and I woke in the predawn cool, the room a haze of blue half-light, the day not yet gathering itself, but soon enough.

I called for Banjo but of course he wasn't there.

Finally, I got up, dressed, and left.

I was back in Richmond by noon, drinking gas station coffee in the burn center parking lot, the pistol on the seat beside me. The asphalt quaked with dislocations of heat that were turning the day wavy. It was a soggy warmth and I had sweated through my shirt so that it stuck to the upholstery. Now and then the sun flashed off the silver of the pistol. I didn't know what I was doing, I didn't know what was expected of me, and eventually I just got up, stuck the Magnum in the glovebox and walked through the automatic doors into a wall of hospital air conditioning. I passed the receptionist, the dispensers of hand sanitizer, crossed the seafoam green carpet to the bank of elevators. No one seemed to remember me. No one seemed to care.

The fifth floor was hurried and overlit and I walked to the observation window outside Chris's room only to find it empty. No deputy by the door. No one within. I checked the room number and walked to the nurses' station. The patient in 519? She checked a chart.

"I'm sorry, sir. He's no longer with us."

"What do you mean he's no longer with us?" I asked, but already knowing. "I hope he's dead."

"He's—sir."

"I hope he's dead," I said again.

She looked at me for a long moment.

"He passed away last night."

"Last night."

"What's your name, sir?"

She had picked up the phone, but I had already turned to go.

"Sir?" she called. "Hey, stop!"

I took the stairs down and stumbled out the fire exit into the staggering heat, trying to breathe, to gather the self I felt spread down the stairs like a dress's train. From the side of the building I watched the front entrance for cops, but no one came and eventually I walked back to the truck. Did I really hope he was dead? I don't know what I hoped. I do know that it didn't matter.

I was back on the highway when I saw him behind me, following clumsily in an old Ford Escort. The man from the bar. The man in the puffy jacket. I took the pistol out of the glovebox and left it on the seat, feeling something inside me shift. Not fear, I realized, but anger. I turned toward the Super 8 I'd stayed in and pulled behind it. I got out quick, passed the ice machine and the vending machine, the wet carpet, took the gun from my pants and waited around a blind corner. This wasn't me, but it wasn't someone else either.

When he rounded the corner, this thing that was almost me got my left arm around his neck and the pistol into the soft of his throat. He started to twist then went amazingly still.

"Who are you?"

"Relax, man."

"Why are you following me?"

"Relax," he said calmly. "Move the gun, okay?"

"Tell me why you're following me."

"Just take the gun off me, all right? Somebody's going to see us."

"I don't fucking care." I was shivering, freezing, exhausted. I didn't care.

"The thing about pointing a gun at somebody," he said, "that's usually how accidents happen. Put it down, all right?"

And I did, if only because I could no longer raise my arm.

"Let's go talk somewhere," he said, straightening his shirt. "Let's not be out like this."

"I'm not going anywhere."

He looked around the edge of the building, out toward the parking lot, the filled-in pool now a rectangle of concrete, sunlight flashing off the metal piping of the rail. The motel office appeared deserted behind closed blinds.

He was a greyhound, lean and silvered, his skin ashen. He looked at me and shook his narrow head.

"He said you might be this way," he said.

"Who did?"

"Chris," he told me. "Who else?"

"I met back up with him on Whidbey Island," he told me. "I don't know what I was doing, busy playing Gary Snyder, I guess. Busy playing the Beat poet."

We were sitting in his room at the Dee-Luxe Inn, drinking bourbon and ice out of the plastic cups I'd found by the sink. The curtains drawn and the ancient air conditioner spewing glacial air. His name was Bruce. He was the ten-thousand-meter man who had run cross-country and track with Chris at Appalachian State and then headed west where he dropped out of the graduate program in Indigenous Studies at Berkeley. He was working as the gardener on the Whidbey Island estate of some computer genius barely out of his twenties when he saw Chris again.

"Chris was a few years behind me," Bruce said, "and was doing more or less the same thing. Loafing, fulfilling our manifest destiny, if you will." He took a drink. "What'd you bring the gun for?"

"I'm not sure," I said. "I saw something the other day."

"You saw me."

"Yeah. But not that. I think I saw a mountain lion."

"Jesus." He smiled and for the first time I noticed he was missing several teeth. "You too?"

"What happened to him?" I asked.

"To Chris? Secobarbital."

"You gave it to him?"

"I got a package a few weeks ago in the mail. The letter said that should I hear about certain circumstances et cetera, et cetera . . ." He made a little motion with his free hand, like something trying to hold steady in a current of air.

"How did you get to him?"

"It doesn't matter, does it?"

He took a cupful of ice from the plastic bucket and poured bourbon over it.

"I can't say that I was surprised," he said. "Getting a letter like that. The level of detail. The level of preparation. Apparently he got it from someplace he used to work at in Mexico. Chris had it all worked out. When I saw it in the news, I got in the car. I must have got here just before you."

"What did he say about me?"

"Just that you'd be coming."

I had taken a chair from the concrete stoop and when I rocked it onto its back legs I felt the plastic begin to give.

"Did you ever meet Mara?"

"Just once. We had a sort of consult in New Orleans back in the summer. June it would have been. She was sort of lit. Internally, I mean. The kind of glow you don't know where it's divine or just plain crazy. Like maybe she's just clinically insane. But it's there, you know? You were out of your depth marrying her."

"I know that. What sort of consult?"

"Punching way above your weight."

"I've always known it. Tell me about the consult."

"Chris had never used anything but ANFO. They needed something lighter. Semtex, TATP, whatever." He looked at me, his cracked lips spreading into something very near a smile. "Ammonium Nitrate and Fuel Oil. That's your Oklahoma City shit right there. Powerful, but not the sort of thing you'd want to pack in. Not for the kind of job they were considering."

"So you're what, the explosives guy?"

"Not really. I know just enough to be dangerous, I guess. More than Chris."

"Chris had done this before?"

He looked up from the ice in his drink, took the bottle and topped his cup.

"I don't actually drink," he said. "Going on fourteen years until this happened."

"He'd done this before?"

He swirled his cup.

"You didn't really know him, did you?"

"I guess I didn't."

"I hadn't seen him in years till we met up in New Orleans and the change just about staggered me. Clean-living Chris—Jesus. He'd lived in Mexico for a while. Got locked up for a while. Got clean and sober just as he found out he was sick. Living with his addict girlfriend Tammy something. Then I guess your wife shows up and it's like bam. It's like he's reborn. Still sick, but reborn, sitting outside at some café in the Marigny and looking around like he's watching the whole place underwater."

"How sick?"

"Cancer. He had it everywhere by then. It was why he'd got that Secobarbital in the first place. He was dying."

"But she wasn't."

"Shit," he said, and looked at me with those faded eyes. "Is that what you think?"

Bruce was still running, had gotten serious about rock climbing. This must have been '96 or '97. Bruce alone, Bruce doing his forty-days-in-the-desert thing, and here Chris shows up and more or less attaches himself to his old friend's hip.

"You know how it can be when you're young, the whole dirt-bag thing, and here I was a few years older. Wiser, he probably thought. More settled. Here I was all clean-shaven and, at least when my hair wasn't tied in a bun and tucked beneath my CAT DIESEL hat, clean-cut."

"American," I said.

"Yeah, American. A certain kind of American." He let his chin float up and down. "I was working hard at it."

They started running together that fall in Washington State, Chris a half stride off Bruce's right shoulder in that show of slight deference one runner gives to another.

It was October when Bruce asked Chris if he needed work. The computer genius was hiring.

"You'd get a room, decent money."

"For doing what?"

"Who knows, really. Keeping the place up, I guess. He's one of those internet gurus worth however many millions. He just sold everything and he's moving out here full time. He says his work is done."

They were walking along a trail through a forest of hemlock and Douglas fir and Bruce stopped to face Chris. Past them the trail wound from sight, the split-rail fence that marked it thick with a fur of moss.

"So what do you think?"

Chris took the job and gathered mushrooms, worked in the garden and the flowerbeds. It all smelled like Christmas, like living inside a tree. The swishing of wind—never had he so often mistaken the sound of wind for rain, both so elemental. And then there were the trees, the giant Sitka spruces.

"God is a giant tree," he said to Bruce one day when they were walking.

"Yeah," Bruce said, without ever looking at him, "I guess he probably is."

The main building looked like the Zen retreat centers Chris had seen coming up the Pacific Coast. Timber beams. A great upthrust of vertical lines and white light. Walls of glass letting in a melt of rainy sun. A giant gong pushed against the wall like an embarrassed guest. Inside the house were Futurist paintings, a Lucian Freud. A Francis Bacon triptych beside a signed Steve Largent jersey.

When Chris wasn't working or running, he wandered the grounds. The trees were taller than he'd ever seen. The way the tops swished in the wind—you could it hear it gathering in the distance and then it was on you, as if the world itself had come loose. Moss everywhere. Tiny cottages scattered in the dense fern beds. Foot trails between them. A sign read:

Out beyond ideas of wrong doing and right doing,
There is a field. I'll meet you there.

Past the buildings, a labyrinth was arranged in an open field. A circular path, constantly doubling back on itself. River stones. Cedar chips. The small placard said the design dated back to at least the thirteenth century. It was modeled on the labyrinth on the floor of Chartres and was meant to bring some sort of spiritual clarity. He walked it faster than he should have, but he walked it just the same. When he got back to his room he called home and got his aunt.

"Your uncle's been sick."

"Is he all right?"

"All right enough, I reckon. But I know he'd like to see you. You plan on coming home for Christmas?"

"I don't know. I'll come if I can."

But instead of going home, he went with Bruce to Utah.

"I want you to meet some people," Bruce had told him.

They traveled south to Moab, Chris in his pickup following Bruce down the rainy coast and then east through the dry mountains. Just outside town there was an empty Airstream on the edge of a watermelon patch on the edge of an organic farm and they stayed there, Bruce in the single bed and Chris on the floor, except nights when one of the women passing through town to bike or climb or just passing through came home with Bruce, and Chris would sleep in a hammock between two acacia trees in the otherwise bare yard. It felt like an idle time, though he was running every morning with Bruce, long predawn treks through the suburban streets or into the starlit desert. He would come home and eat oatmeal and peaches and sleep until ten. He would buy dried beans and quinoa from the bulk bins at the food co-op in town and then spend a few hours doing farm work in exchange for his room and the occasional meal. He cleared brush with the eighteen-inch bar of a Stihl chainsaw, came in smelling of sawdust and gas, machine oil grooved along his fingernails. One day he and Bruce cut and stacked five cords of firewood and then collapsed in the truck, hands raw, hair full of shavings.

Evenings he read. More Thomas Merton. Edward Abbey. Wendell Berry. Terry Tempest Williams's *Refuge*. Emerson's "Self-Reliance." Whitman's *Leaves of Grass*. Dorothy Day, Simone Weil. Bruce had a small library of Buddhist texts and he worked his way through those.

"In the future," Bruce told him in the lawn chairs one evening, "in the future you're going to see little groups of people making themselves crazy, fighting these pointless fights against the world, against the Buy Me's, the land takers, the weapon makers. It's going to be utterly pointless, this resistance. But I'm with them. I want to love things. That's the only way I'm willing to live."

Chris was quiet.

"Shit," Bruce said. "I know you didn't ask for a speech."

Chris said nothing.

Chris moved the small flock of goats between pastures.

Winter came, the nights clearer and colder than he had ever imagined the desert could be. On Christmas Eve, he used the phone in the farm office to call his aunt and uncle and grand-daddy, but all that did was make him lonely. He was idle; he was alone. There was no more farm work so he ran in the morning and most days stayed inside reading or, if the day was unusually warm, read in a patch of sunlight. Bruce would come and go, as would Bruce's friends, this one back from hitchhiking to Tierra del Fuego, that one returning from a Fulbright in Thailand. There was much talk of carbon footprints and resting heart rates. Bruce left in January. Chris ran, read. He had some money saved from working at the estate on Whidbey Island, not much but enough to last, but last until what?

He couldn't say, and felt himself growing listless. He felt certain there was some fragile miracle within him, only he could never be still enough or quiet enough to realize it.

In February he called his aunt and uncle for the first time since Christmas Eve.

"How are you?"

"We're lonely," his aunt said. "The two of us."

"Well, y'all should get out. Do things. Nobody says you have to sit at home."

"Oh, honey," she said, and he imagined her standing in the

faded wallpaper and linoleum of the kitchen, everything scrolled and peeling. "It's not that kind of lonely."

For days he considered going home if only to sit quietly together, collected again into a family. It felt holy, this longing, and he wondered if it could be that God is our collective unexpressed love? He'd heard this somewhere, read it, but couldn't recall where. That the things we cannot say, might those alone gather into the Cloud? It would mean the ground of being was simply our calling out to each other, unvoiced. The world kept afloat atop a sea of unshed tears. Which meant—

Which meant he was maybe going stir-crazy.

The running didn't help.

Despite the great openness of the sky and the hours he spent moving beneath it, the running didn't help. The Buddhists speak of *beyuls*, dream spaces only open to the spiritually aware. He found them everywhere. Yet he could never enter.

One night in March he drove to Salt Lake City and ran the hollowed streets. He had a hunger for people, not to speak to them, but to simply be among them. But somehow—maybe it was the late hour or maybe he just picked the wrong part of town—somehow he saw no one. Only the blowing ghetto trash and iron security grilles. He kept thinking he would round a corner and find the glass lighted like a fallen star and it would be some storefront congregation. A church without denomination. An unlettered preacher who worked with his hands. No theology but the Blood. But he found nothing beyond feral cats and vegetable rot and the man crawling from a mass of wet bedding, busted pallets made into sleeping quarters for the beautifully insane. His knees hurt, but he ran until dawn and drove back to Moab, arriving as the sun came up.

He was sound asleep—maybe for the first time in months—when Bruce shook him awake.

Something was wrong. That was his first impression on seeing Bruce above him, shaking Chris with one hand, a mug of coffee in the other.

"I've been waiting on you all morning," he said. "I can't wait any longer."

Chris opened his eyes not to grainy morning but the brightness of afternoon. His hamstrings were tight and he felt dehydrated.

"What time is it?"

"I've been sitting here for hours. Drink this," he said, and forced the coffee into Chris's hand.

Chris sat up, the warm mug in his hand.

"What the hell did you do last night?" Bruce asked. "You get hammered?"

"I ran."

"I figured you were stoned."

"When did you come back?"

"I figured you'd been sitting in here hitting the pipe for the last two months."

"I went to Salt Lake City to run."

He picked up his wristwatch from beside the bed, a Timex Ironman he'd worn since high school. The chronograph read 5:42:36; he had covered approximately forty-six miles. Bruce took the watch from him.

"This is last night?"

"I guess so."

"No wonder you look like shit."

Bruce brought him a banana and stood for a moment with the heels of his hands planted over his eyes.

"Eat that and drink some water," he said. "I need you for something."

But he wouldn't say exactly what. Not in the trailer and not a half hour later when they were driving north on 191. In Crescent

131

Junction they got on I-70 and back onto 191 through Woodside and Wellington and Price. Chris had the backpack Bruce had asked him to bring: a flashlight, bottled water, a thermos of coffee, a light rain jacket, and three Powerbars. He was dressed for the cold, wearing hiking boots, just as Bruce had asked. Beneath the tarp in the bed of the truck were several sealed five-gallon plastic buckets and a can of spray paint.

In Castle Gate they headed east on roads gradually narrowing until they were on a one-lane asphalt path that led through the juniper and pinyon and what appeared an expanse of wilderness. He pulled off the highway just before an iron gate and a sign that read PHASE TWO CONSTRUCTION: TRESPASSING ON A CONSTRUCTION SITE IS A FELONY OFFENSE.

"I wouldn't have you here if this wasn't important," Bruce said. "But everything is set to go and we've had someone drop out."

"Drop out of what?"

But Bruce only gestured toward the sign.

"Trespassing is a felony offense," Chris read.

"Exactly."

"So we're here to trespass?"

"I am. You're here to watch."

Bruce turned and what Chris saw was a face that had hardened in the same way the face of Brandy Jones had, and he wondered for a moment if somehow he was managing to live his life just a half step shy of adulthood, anchored in late adolescence while the rest of the world raced on to its serious business.

"But only if you're okay with that," Bruce said.

"Okay with watching?"

"You'd be a lookout."

"A lookout for what?"

"Just yes or no is what I need from you."

"This is something illegal?"

"Just yes or no, Chris. I won't say anymore."

"All right then. Yes."

They drove to a coffee shop back near the highway. There were tourist shops with T-shirts and racks of postcards and cafés with HIKERS BREAKFAST!, but the place they went was a truck stop, out front the tankers and rigs, inside the flannel shirts and steak-and-egg specials. Men running on White Crosses and Willie Nelson cassettes.

"Eat something," Bruce said. "I've got to meet some people, but I'll be back in forty-five minutes, an hour tops. You have some money?"

"So I just sit here and wait?"

"I won't be long."

When Bruce was gone he ordered coffee and toast, eggs and bacon and then got up, his legs still stiff, and began to hobble toward the bathroom. He was by the front window when he happened to see Bruce. He was directly across the road, sitting in a diner with another man and a woman. The man wore a skull-cap and was gesturing wildly while the woman nodded in agreement, her thick dreadlocks bobbing around the pale oval of her face. Chris stood watching them, feeling as if he was propped on crutches. The woman looked familiar. The man he couldn't place, but he was almost certain he recognized the woman from the Freegan encampment on Whidbey Island. Then the man looked up and for no more than a half second they made eye contact through the two panes of glass and across the street.

Chris turned and lumbered into the bathroom.

When he came back, the booth across the street was empty.

He ate his breakfast and was sitting in front of the coffee the waitress kept needlessly topping off when Bruce came back in. It had been closer to two hours than one and he looked pissed.

"You finished here?" he said, gesturing at the table.

"Just let me get the check."

"I'll be out in the truck."

"People think they can do whatever shit they want," Bruce said when Chris was beside him. "They think that's the definition of freedom: let me hate whoever I want. Let me tear shit up."

"Who were those two?"

"You shouldn't have stared like that. You scared the shit out of Leif."

"I recognized the woman."

"She recognized you too."

"What is it we're doing, Bruce?"

"We'll drive out at dusk and I'll show you."

And at dusk they did, back down the same narrow lane to the same gate. The sun was setting magnificently, all golden light over the scrub and the larger cottonwoods that gathered along the creek bed. You could hear the wind sing along high-tension lines somewhere to the south.

"This is BLM land," Bruce said, "but the Clinton administration is busy handing over every possible parcel to industry. In this case, a spa slash hotel slash ranch. A two-hundred-acre footprint, and that doesn't take into account the infrastructure that'll come with it. Just imagine when this is a major highway, imagine what crops up along it. The same shit as everywhere else, the gas stations and hotels and bullshit trinket stores. This used to be hunting grounds for the Hopi, a sacred space. Land is either sacred or desecrated."

"That's Wendell Berry."

"That's human wisdom. The only thing that's still sacred in America is shopping."

"It looks like nothing's happened for a while."

"It's tied up in court, but it won't be for much longer. That's why we're here. We're here to settle things."

Around ten he drove Chris down a side road of rain-cut gravel, the truck bucking slowly, headlights off, driving by the light of a moon Chris only now noticed was full. They moved downhill for a half hour, stopping when the land leveled. Chris saw plastic-wrapped pallets of brick, a bulldozer parked beneath a makeshift shed, a small portable building that might have been toilets but might also have been an office. Around the perimeter of the field—he saw now they were in a field, the land graded and cleared—stood heavy machinery, a couple of dump trucks and skid steers, a scraper.

Bruce cut the engine and they stepped into the night.

A creek ran from a large drainage pipe, erosion barriers sheeted around it.

"No one's been down here for weeks and there's absolutely no reason to expect anyone will be," Bruce said. "But there's always the possibility of a random security check. You know how to work this?"

He extended a walkie-talkie to Chris, almost cartoonish in design with its blunt antenna.

"Channel 3," Bruce said. "That's the signal key there. What I'm asking is simple. Find a place overlooking this road—I'd suggest maybe back in those trees—and just wait. If anyone or anything passes this point, key the radio three times, wait ten seconds, and then key it three more. Then wait."

"For what?"

"For me. It might be daylight—if someone happens to come through it will almost certainly be daylight—but I'll come for you. You have the backpack?"

"In the truck."

"Almost certainly no one will show."

"That's all someone's private property, Bruce."

"The land?"

135

"The tractors, that shed. It's a crime."

"So how do you feel about the Boston Tea Party?"

Chris said nothing and Bruce touched his upper arm.

"Almost certainly no one will show," he said. "And I'll be back for you in a few hours."

They walked to the truck.

"You're okay with this?"

Chris nodded.

"Get back in those trees," he said. "And whatever you do, don't fall asleep."

But there was no danger of falling asleep. The adrenaline, the way the night clawed and wept. He heard the creek, but gradually he began to hear other things. Owls, starveling deer coming out of the forest to graze along the clearing's edge. The moon was shoaled in gray cloud, the land dark, and then suddenly the moon was free and the field was lit in a milky ghost light. He sat on an embankment maybe fifty feet off the road, his back against a cottonwood, his butt wet. It was cold, but not unbearably so. A good scouring chill just above freezing. He felt alert, his nostrils and ears raw. He drank the coffee and waited, but just as Bruce had said no one came.

Bruce was down the road somewhere, Bruce and the woman he recognized and the man he did not. Leif, Bruce had said. Doing what? Settling things, Bruce had said that too. He tipped his head back. The moon was netted in the bare branches of the cottonwood so that the ground was laced with shadow, an intricate maze that folded over his lap and legs and arms and face.

He stood and tried to shake the stiffness from his body, flexed his hands, his fingers, brittle needles, but all of it a good hurt, the kind of hurt that made him present. He thought this was maybe what he'd needed all his life, to be out in the world like this, responsible, watching. He got up and down every twenty or so minutes, sipped coffee and water and ate a Powerbar. It was one in the morning and then it was two.

And then he saw the lights.

He was standing at the time, glancing back up in the direction they had driven in, and it took him a moment to register what he saw. Then it clicked: headlights, bucking slowly down the same road, rising and falling and negotiating the bend in the road so that they swept the tree line and right then an owl flew, low and silent and gone.

Chris sat down and fumbled through his backpack for the radio, found it and put his thumb to the signal key. Then he noticed the truck was just sitting there, coming no closer. It was still a good hundred meters from the clearing, from *this point,* the point at which Bruce had said to signal if anyone passed. But they weren't passing. They were just sitting there, and he thought for a moment they were looking to turn around.

When a door opened he felt his body pull tight, as if preparing to receive a blow. The cab light revealed two men and a single flashlight moving toward the trees. One man was taking a leak and Chris felt something drain from him too, the fear he hadn't realized was balled within him. It was fine, but just as quickly it wasn't. Walking back to the truck the man must have seen something because a moment later two flashlight beams began to swing over the roadbed and stop on what Chris knew without seeing were the tracks he and Bruce had made driving in earlier. When the men turned for the truck, Chris grabbed the radio and keyed three times, counted to ten and keyed three more.

A second truck was coming over the rise and easing down behind the first.

He keyed the radio three more times, stuffed it in his backpack, and stretched out on his stomach, face inches from the damp ground that bore the imprint of his sitting. He realized his legs were no longer tight. In fact, he found his hamstrings and quadriceps loose, ready to move. His heart rattled and he blinked slowly, keenly aware that four men were now out of the trucks and moving along the road. Voices but no sense of what they were saying. Just carrying sound. Footsteps, talk. They gathered around the tire tracks and separated, swung their flashlights around the construction equipment which sat untouched, grayer shapes in the gray dark.

Chris looked behind him. Bruce had said to wait, but waiting wasn't an option. What he had identified as focus morphed into fear. Still, it was possible to just wait. They would find nothing. They would get in their trucks and leave. He looked into the forest behind him, dense and lightless and where would he go? It didn't matter. They would get in their trucks and leave.

Except they didn't.

One of the men stood in the glare of the headlights and talked on the radio. A few minutes later the forest began to glow and another truck topped the hill and began to wind its way down to the clearing. He knew then he had to go. No idea where. Deeper into the forest. West. Highway 191 was west. He guessed it no more than fifteen or so miles. Fifteen miles of broken country, but he'd covered far more in his life. The moon was up. So okay, here's what you do. Slip into the forest. Move west and make the highway. Put some miles between you and these men. He could do that. He thought he could do that. He worked to control his breathing, quick shots of oxygen taken through his nose, mouth closed. It was like racing. Be calm. Be in control.

He slipped the backpack around to make sure it was secure. The idea was to hug it to his chest for the first hundred meters or so, long enough that no one would hear the rattle. Then slip it on, get on level ground, and run. He could hitch a ride back to Moab. Or maybe lay low for a few days in one of the hotels along the way.

He felt into his bag for the thermos, the uneaten Powerbar, checked the radio and saw—oh god—saw the channel indicator was turned not to 3 but to 0. Only he was sure it had been channel 3 when he sent the message. Only he wasn't sure. He felt panic make its oily slide down his backbone, a very physical, very real sensation. It was possible he had hit the channel indicator when rifling through the bag. It was almost certainly the case. He held the radio with two hands and looked out at the clearing. The men were on the far end, their lights running over the shed and the skid steers. He kept his eyes on them while he smoothly clicked the radio from 0 to 3, put his thumb on the signal button, and depressed it three times in quick succession.

What happened next made no sense.

The sound was like something misheard, three quick bleats his mind couldn't make sense of, like a dying sheep there in the desert night. It sounded impossible. Only it wasn't. Only the lights had suddenly swung in his direction, bouncing in his direction. Men were running, yelling, still it made no sense. Then with a sinking sense he realized he had dialed not the channel indicator but the volume.

He began to move then, everything began to move.

The land was uneven and he ran blindly, briars and limbs grabbing at his arms and legs and slashing his face so that he ran head down, one arm shielding his eyes, like a man advancing into a steady rain. He fell, got up, fell again, felt something hot flash up his right shin and fade to the cool numbness of motion. He ran for what seemed hours but also seemed seconds. In truth it was likely four or five minutes, not long, but long enough to put distance between him and the voices. There was only the sound of his breathing now. No one was behind him. He had no idea if he had traveled west or not but no one was behind him.

He walked for another twenty minutes along a dry creek bed

and cut up the crumbling bank onto the mesa. He was on flat land now and to the east he could see the glow of the gathered trucks circled like wagons. Beyond that was a greater glow—the fire he knew Bruce and the man and woman had set. So they had done what they had come to do, and he had helped. Making him an accomplice, an accessory, a something. He didn't know how he felt about this, and it didn't matter, at least not in that moment. What mattered was getting out of the desert.

He checked the waning moon and realized he had indeed traveled west. He sat on the ground and drank some water. The radio, he saw now, was on channel 3 and had been all along. He felt stupid but also grateful: he had signaled Bruce, and along the horizon he could see beads of light moving along the bracelet of Highway 191. He wouldn't have to use the radio—not that he even knew how. It was three-forty in the morning and he thought he could make the highway a little after dawn.

But when he stood up, he knew he couldn't.

The pain radiated from his right ankle up his shin into his knee, boring into the socket of his hip with a pain that made his eyes water. It was like walking into an ocean wave, that bright and swift and total. He yelped and crashed onto his butt, lifted his pant leg and saw that his right ankle was blue and so swollen his boot was pushed outward, the laces straining.

His ankle was broken, or at the least badly sprained.

It was the realization more than the pain that overcame him, and he put his head back and wept, alone on the open mesa with his throbbing leg. When the grief and anger expired as quickly as it started, he shut his eyes and fell asleep.

It was daylight when he woke and attempted to stand. The gasp that came from his lips was nearly inaudible, spittle and breath, almost airless. His vision blurred and he collapsed flat on his back with his mouth open and dry, his leg a dull of pain of discomfort.

He let the air come back into his body. How long it took he didn't know, but by the time he could see clearly it was after nine and he felt seared by both wind and sun. He was on perfectly level ground, open but for the patchy mesquite and pinyon. 191 was lost in a haze of ozone and dust, a macadam river vanished in a morning fog of exhaust and distance. He drank the last of his water and realized how stupid that was. He had the Powerbar and ate that and when he was left thirstier than before realized that was stupid too.

The sun was bright and heatless, and eventually he eased himself onto all fours and as gently as possible stood on one foot. He tested his ankle but it couldn't support his weight. He hopped for a moment and went back down onto all fours.

He'd need a walking stick.

He'd need to be the opposite of stupid.

Either way, there was no use waiting, and he pulled on his backpack and began to hobble west.

He kept falling, kept coming across something he could lean on only to find it was prickly or crooked or too narrow to be of use. He slid down the mesa's edge to crawl through damp seeps and dry arroyos, tore the knees of his pants, felt his palms cut by thorns. There were mule deer down near a creek bed and they watched his slow approach, this ragged thing, half hopping, half dragging his busted leg, and went back to their grazing, untroubled. When he got to the creek he drank deeply, flat on his stomach, the cold water soaking his face and shirt. He had been walking for almost three hours and guessed he had covered no more than a mile. Now he was in a deep ravine that followed the winding calligraphy of the creek bed and had no idea how he'd get out.

A juniper tree stood downstream and he crawled toward it. He could find a walking stick maybe. There was the radio but earlier he'd heard a helicopter overhead, not passing but hovering.

The sheriff's department, he thought, and if not the law then a TV crew filming the blaze, or what was left of it. Up on the mesa he had smelled the carrying smoke, but down in the ravine he smelled only the bright flash of the cool water.

He had to crawl and he did, on toward the juniper, dragging his leg over the bedded river stones, smooth ovoid shapes of brown and tan and eggshell. He stopped when he saw the track, the print of a housecat, except it was wider than his hand. He knew they were here, of course, this had once been mountain lion country, but he hadn't thought about them in months.

He was suddenly cold, suddenly shivering, and crawled not toward the juniper tree but away from the creek onto the sandy wash where he could sit with his back against the canyon wall. The lion had come down the ravine, paused to drink, and continued on. The cat was not what should concern him, but it did. The great muscled back legs. The clear eyes. He remembered the tawny blaze he'd seen along the road's edge so many years ago back home. The lion down beneath Big Bald. Both had surely been imagined, but this was surely not.

He tipped his head back against the rock face, the sky above a ribbon of pale blue. He was cold. He no longer felt his leg. It was possible his body was in shock and he needed to not be stupid. That was what he kept telling himself: don't be stupid. Likely the desert was full of law enforcement and reporters. Helicopters would be in the air. Jeeps on the ground. He needed to be patient and he was, eventually shutting his eyes and falling asleep.

He woke to its face, its eyes so yellow as to appear golden. The pupils a glossy black, his own skinny image balanced in the wet center. He could feel the weight of one of its front paws pin the backpack that lay beside him, still looped over his right arm. He shut his eyes again. He was dreaming. Then two sharp whiskers grazed his face. Its breath was wet and humid and smelled like meat. When he looked again he saw the kohl ringing the sloe eyes, the tuft of white fur around the mouth. Its tail curled around its body and Chris felt it against his thigh, sliding, curious.

He was dreaming.

It stepped back.

He was dreaming because he heard his mother's voice telling him to get up, *get up, Chris, get up, honey*, and he thought even then to remember the sound because, although he knew this was her voice, he had no idea what her voice sounded like. It was buried in him, though, somewhere within him it had imprinted.

Chris?

The lion stood by his feet and sniffed his damaged ankle.

You have to get up now, honey. You have to walk.

Then it turned and slinked through the shadows and into the sunlit creek where it paused once to look back at him, and he knew if he was to get up, now was the time. *Go on, Chris. That's it.* The lion waited beside a thicket of pinyon and then disappeared into it. Chris followed.

He was moving quickly now. Cacti and pinyon pulled at him, but he couldn't feel it. He couldn't feel his ankle either. His vision narrowed so that he walked through a dim tunnel lit only by the lion that loped ten or so meters in front of him. Chris began to lope too, the rhythm of motion settling into his body, into his bones, like he had known it all his life, which of course he had.

They climbed out of the canyon onto another mesa at dusk. They kept moving. The lion steady, tail erect, never stopping. The descent of the mesa wall was technical, precarious, but Chris moved without pause. The right step, the right step—he kept putting each foot exactly where it should be.

Then it was not dusk but full dark and they were running across the flatland. How fast they were moving he couldn't say, only that he was sprinting, hurdling over scrub and the remnants of a barbed-wire fence he never saw. It was the voice that told him, his mother's voice, but also, perhaps, the voice of the lion. *Jump, Chris. Now, higher. Good, good.* By the time he saw lights moving along 191 somewhere in front of him, he was beside the lion, its long body in full extension, ears back. He could feel the wind in his face and rippling through his hair. Thirty, forty, fifty miles an hour. He had never run faster, no one had, and a part of him knew no one ever would again. The lights grew closer. He could hear the long approach of cars, the air compressing and expanding in the cones of headlight.

The lion was saying *yes, yes, go*, and he did, he went, and then he was alone along the highway's shoulder. The lion was gone. Where was it? It was beside him and then, all at once, it wasn't. He walked through the breakdown lane, transfer trucks downshifting as they entered the curve ahead, and then a van stopped. It happened just like that: a van stopped and he got in, two boys and a girl drinking box wine, passing the plastic bladder between them. The rear seats were removed and he sprawled across their skis and piles of dirty clothes.

"What kind of shit you get into?"

They were laughing.

"What kind of shit did you find, my brother?"

They let him out at dawn on the edge of Moab. His ankle was just beginning to pound again as he passed the Super 8 and headed toward Swanny Park where he saw the newspaper in its square dispenser. The headlines of the *Times-Independent* read, "Investigators Rule Fire at Future Resort to be Arson." He read to the fold: The fire that engulfed the future Pinyon Canyon Resort & Spa was set. Investigators suspect ammonium nitrate fuel oil. Spray painted on a storage shed were the words: *land is either sacred or desecrated.* That was all. The local and state authorities were cooperating with the FBI. The resort has been the subject of much debate with opponents claiming the location on sensitive desert habitat would—

The rest continued below the fold. Not that it mattered.

He started walking in the direction of the organic farm, started walking home.

It was late morning when he saw Bruce's pickup in front of the Airstream.

He pushed open the door. Bruce sat in a camp chair holding a champagne flute and a Reese's Peanut Butter cup. On the floor was a copy of the newspaper. He started to speak but something kept him from it. His bourbon floated halfway to his mouth and held there. He smiled.

Chris said nothing, just hobbled past him to collapse onto the trailer floor.

"His mountain lion," Bruce said there at the Dee-Luxe Inn and lifted the bourbon.

"No," I told him, taking the bottle from him. "Mara's."

He nodded and waited patiently for me to pass it back.

"In the end, life takes everything," he said finally, "and it gives you back clarity. It strips you down but you begin to see that the world isn't ephemeral, you dig? The world *is*. When you see that, for some, things change. You stop wasting time. For some, you see what's in front of you, and you act."

"Is that what they did?"

He raised the bottle almost in salute but then lowered it and shook his head sadly.

"It's childish to resent it, David. That's lower vibration. It's human, I get it. But it's also bullshit is what I'm saying."

The rest I pieced together later.

How Chris had spent the spring recuperating. How he had run thirteen miles on a broken ankle but miraculously the ligaments were intact. Bruce had a doctor friend, a climber, sympathetic to the uninsured, who set and plastered the ankle in his office after hours. That there was no permanent damage seemed a miracle, and Chris suspected it was. Bruce stuck around for three weeks, tending to him, until Chris was hobbling with ease. They stayed inside as much as possible, out of sight, tracking the fire in the newspaper. The fire was set, the construction site destroyed—but beyond that there was nothing.

The Pinyon Canyon development cashed its insurance check and pulled out.

The authorities did not come knocking.

We did it right, Bruce said, and then he was gone, his harness and a coil of climbing rope around one shoulder, off to the Wind River Range. Chris hadn't told him about the mountain lion, not at first. Mostly he didn't believe in it. But there were hours, sometimes days, that he did. Those days passed slowly. He hobbled around, started driving into town to eat, suddenly overtaken by the loneliness he hadn't considered over the previous months. The money that had held out for months disappeared in a few weeks and all at once it was hot, the sun forever white and forever overhead. The tourists arrived with their Jeep tours and mountain bikes, and he sat in the Airstream listening to Townes Van Zandt and Willie Nelson and Van Morrison's *Astral Weeks*, that acoustic warble that sounded like what it was he was living, how contingent it all was. How something was going to change. He felt this. Day after day something was on the verge of changing, but day after day that change failed to arrive. April became May and May became its own season of light and heat, like stumbling onto some brighter planet that stretched without limit.

He was squinting into that light, waiting for Bruce to return, waiting for the police to show up, waiting for something, when he got the letter from his aunt. It had been forwarded from Whidbey to Moab. How it arrived in his mailbox he had no idea, only that it was dated three weeks ago. His uncle was dying in the VA hospital in Johnson City.

We ain't heard from you since after Christmas but he don't know that. I'm busy lying to him while you're busy doing I don't know what. Telling him, yes, Chris is fine. Yes, I just heard from him last week. But I can't lie to him no more. If you get this I believe I'd think long and hard about quitting whatever it is you're doing that can't or won't let you call your own family and come home. Family is blood, Chris. Family is everything. I know I don't need to tell you that, but then again maybe I do.

He used the phone in the farm office to call. He got the answering machine, but when he called back an hour later from the road his aunt answered.

"How is he?"

"I reckon you got my letter."

"How's he doing?"

"I had my regrets after sending it. It was maybe harsher than I meant it to be."

"Is he . . ."

"Dying?" she said. "He's coughing up blood if you want to know the all of it."

"I'll be there day after tomorrow."

"I reckon the Lord'll forgive me if I say I'll believe you when I see you."

He drove straight through, eighteen hundred miles on coffee and protein bars. Denver to Kansas City to St. Louis to Nashville to Knoxville, then up I-81 to the glass and red brick of the James H. Quillen Veteran Affairs Medical Center. His granddaddy sat in the waiting room beneath a buzzing fluorescent light, arms piled into a tan Carhartt barn coat too heavy for summer. Boss Hog on the TV as he lumbered out of the chair, and Chris realized he had been sleeping, his chin balanced on the pile of his chest.

"Come here, boy. Let me look at you a minute."

When he pulled Chris into him, his grandfather smelled of all the things Chris had known and forgotten: mown hay and 3-in-One oil, laundry drying on the line in the cool of the day.

"You been in there yet?" his granddaddy asked.

"I just got here."

"He was sleeping before, but go in. Your aunt's fit to be tied."

The room was dim. Light seeping through the window blinds. The curtain was pulled to obscure his uncle, but when Chris stepped around it he saw that same light poured through his body. He was translucent, arranged in the inclined bed, but only just. There was so little left of him was the thing. A skeletal system and a bald head cankered with scabs. He had an IV port in his neck and was surrounded by a small city of machines and pumps with their LED screens and the sound of his mechanical breathing.

"Hey," he whispered, and touched the parchment of his uncle's right arm. "It's Chris. I'm here now. I'm here with you."

He walked with his granddaddy out to Chris's truck and pulled onto the highway.

"Make a left down here."

They passed the strip malls and gas stations and fast food.

"Pull into this McDonald's and I'll buy you lunch," his granddaddy said.

"I don't eat that."

"What, lunch?"

"McDonald's. I don't put that in my body."

"Because you think you're pure. Well, let me tell you something," his grandfather said. "Pure or not, you're home now."

They sat with quarter pounders and the smell of the fry-trap grease. Children running wild on the playground on the other side of the glass.

"That power plant killed him," his grandfather said.

"Pretty much."

"Ain't no pretty much to it. Coal ash. Ain't nothing but arsenic. Mercury. Lead. Ain't no pretty much to that."

When they were back on the highway, his granddaddy directed him past the hospital.

"Pull up here just a bit," he said. "We'll see your aunt soon enough. I been coming up here most days just to sit and stew."

A few miles past the VA stood the low-slung headquarters of Erwin Power. The building was corrugated metal with a brick portico added to the front. They sat just beyond the guard shack along the chain-link fencing, the truck idling.

"Yeah, I come here some days and just sit." He motioned at the building, the sign, the khaki-and-Dockers crowd moving in and out. "You go study them chicken-fuckers you want something to fill your heart with daggers. If I was a younger man . . . ," he said.

"You'd what?"

"I don't know," he said. "Drive on."

"If you were a younger man, you'd do what?"

He shook his head.

"Drive on before I get sick just looking at the bastards."

His aunt was waiting for him at the hospital. He had expected her wrath, but instead of anger it was tears. She fell into him and he felt her go limp, felt her soften in a way that signaled not just age but resignation.

"He's awake now," she said. "He wants to see you."

He was indeed awake.

"Chris, come here, son. Them doctors are saying it don't look so good for me."

"They could be wrong."

"I suspect they ain't. It's all right though. I ain't complaining."

Thereafter, it seemed he was always awake, always alert. Though his body was being erased, his mind was still sharp, and if Chris kept his eyes on the television he could almost imagine they were back on the front porch and his uncle's raspy voice was a throat made sore from work and weather rather than the tube they'd rammed down it.

They watched the Braves and then the Falcons, summer greening beyond the double-paned windows and the rattle of the air conditioning, summer fading.

"It ain't as bad as it looks," his uncle said. "I mean, I know I ain't walking out of here. But it ain't so bad really. I knew one fella had close-air drop napalm right on the wire. Airlifted him to Okinawa. Nineteen seventy that would have been. It took seventeen years in a burn unit before it killed him."

His uncle was fifty-one but appeared seventy, a scarecrow scavenged from the corn patch and propped in the inclined bed. Chris came every evening. He was living back at home with his aunt and hanging and finishing drywall, arriving at the VA with the mud damp on his fingers and bristled in the hairs of his arms. He'd stay till visiting hours ended and then a little longer because the nurses all liked him. It would be nearly eleven by the time he got home, and his aunt would be up in the kitchen drinking Folgers. They'd sit in silence for a moment and then Chris would go to bed. By the time he was up at six-thirty, his aunt would have already left for the hospital.

The first Saturday in September, when the days were just beginning to cool, he drove through an evening fog back to the gates of Erwin Energy and felt his heart fill with daggers, or felt the daggers already there. He sat there and sat there and then drove to the hospital and they watched the Volunteers hammer Middle Tennessee State by four touchdowns. A week later he found himself outside the headquarters again, and then a few days later a third time.

"The power plant is what killed him," he told his aunt that night in the kitchen. "Erwin Power."

"You been listening too much to your granddaddy."

"I've read up. Coal ash is pretty much nothing but toxic chemicals. They're murderers."

She shook her head over a plate of dry toast.

"It don't matter if they are or if they aren't. Every last one of them is sitting in high rises in Charlotte and Atlanta. Murderers or not, you'll never see 'em. You can't even find a body to spit on."

He cut firewood for his granddaddy, brought in the garden, and planted for winter. Turnips, pumpkins, cucumbers for pickling.

He drove his granddaddy around in the Galaxie, the top down and the old man in the passenger seat drinking Jack and Coke in a plastic cup that read GUT BUSTER.

"I've driven back by the Erwin building a couple of times," Chris said.

"What's that?"

"Erwin Energy."

"You got to quit that," his granddaddy said.

"You know how many deaths each year are attributed to coal ash?"

"You got to let all that go."

"It's in the water, the air. It gets in birds and fish and pregnant women."

"I shouldn't have took you by there. I was just so damn mad."

"And you're not anymore?"

His granddaddy took a drink from his cup and went back to watching the roadside, the barns and fields and signs for the Friday Fish Fry at Cove Creek Baptist. When they passed the General Store his granddaddy motioned at the old men sitting on the bench out front.

"You recognize him?" he asked.

"Who?"

"Drinking Yoo-Hoos cause they quit bottling Chocolate Soldiers."

"Who is?"

"You remember Chocolate Soldiers. You always loved a Chocolate Soldier."

The man on the bench was Cabbage Jones and Chris thought of that morning cutting corn. He thought of the stuffed mountain lion in the living room and then the spirit mountain lion in Utah.

"I shouldn't have said nothing before," his granddaddy told him later, "about if I was a younger man and all."

They had Thanksgiving dinner in the hospital room, the four of them, turkey and dressing and cranberry sauce and fried okra. All of it packed into Tupperware.

That night he drove his granddaddy home. He meant to just drop him off, but the old man asked him to get out for a minute. "I want to show you something."

The Galaxie was in the carport.

"I want you to take it," he said and extended the keys.

"Your car?"

"I ain't asking you. Only thing is," his granddaddy said. "This is a mountain car. You got to stay local with it."

"Yes, sir."

"I mean I guess you could take it to Myrtle Beach or somewhere, but it sure as hell don't belong in no California."

A few weeks later Chris and his uncle sat and watched the riots in Seattle, the marchers dressed like sea turtles and carrying bongos, the police like robots with their pepper spray and billy sticks.

"What's this about?" his uncle asked.

"The World Trade Organization."

"Shipping jobs to China I'll bet you anything. It's how they've always done it," he said, and then was asleep again. He was sleeping more. When he was awake, his mind was still sharp but he was awake less and less, and Chris watched the protesters smash the windows and the police smash the protesters with his uncle snoring beside him. Then the nurse came in to pump Glucerna into his feeding tube.

"Visiting hours ended an hour ago, hon."

"Yes, ma'am."

"He'll see you tomorrow."

But the next day Chris didn't drive straight to the VA but to an internet café he'd seen down by a Church's Chicken and a martial arts dojo. He read everything he could find on the riots, watched the video clips. A woman was interviewing a group of black-masked men and women who appeared to have arrived from some Central American battlefield circa the Reagan years.

"How do you respond to people who say you aren't attacking the capitalist system, but destroying private property?"

"I would disagree," the black-masked man said.

"Private property that people have worked very hard for."

"I would perhaps ask them how they felt about the Boston Tea Party."

He tried then to detect the shape of Bruce beneath the ski mask, the curve of his skull, the way his hands hung loosely at his sides all those hundreds of miles of running the sun into the sky and then back out again. It was maybe him or it maybe wasn't.

Either way, Chris found himself outside Erwin Energy for the first time in months.

He was finishing a basement when his uncle died, cutting chair rail in a miter box, and didn't find out until he got to the hospital. They had tried to call him, they were sorry. He's still in there if you want to go see him.

He did, and then regretted it. Though he looked no different, as starved and worn as he had all that fall, he was also changed, reduced. Chris imagined the chemicals leaching from his body to stain the bedsheets.

"I'll fix this," he said to his dead uncle.

Son, there ain't nothing to fix, his dead uncle said back.

"Just the same," he told the drip bags and ECG and all the useless machines ushered into the corner. "Just the goddamn same."

They buried him two days later in the churchyard and Chris drove his pickup to Asheboro to buy the fertilizer at a feed store. The diesel he got down near Brevard. He put both in the barn with his old pickup and after that only drove the Galaxie. He wanted people to see him in it.

It was February when he drove the Galaxie to the Ruritan club, parked out front, and went inside and ordered a draft Bud. "Keep the tab open, please," he told the woman at the bar, and slipped out and in falling dusk ran along the river back to his aunt's house where he got his pickup out of the barn for the first time in months and drove north into Virginia. Turned out the murderers weren't all in high rises in Atlanta and Charlotte. The CEO of Erwin Energy had a summer home just outside Abingdon less than an hour away. Turns out there was a body to spit on.

The house was at the peak of Hawk Mountain, a rising of glass and stacked rock that put him in mind of the estate on Whidbey Island. He put on painter's coveralls, latex gloves, a swim cap, and a surgical mask. He had prepared the timers that morning, working inside a tent set up in the barn, following precisely the instructions in the manual he'd picked up weeks ago at a used bookstore in Asheville.

When the five-gallon buckets were prepped and spaced in the basement, he took a moment to walk through the upstairs. There were perhaps surveillance cameras, but it didn't matter. He had enough ANFO to burn the house to its foundation twice over.

He took his time.

There were photographs on the mantle, the man with his wife and daughter and son. At a wedding. Skiing on what looked like Lake Norman. An attractive family, a Duke University family, a lacrosse and field hockey family. In the refrigerator was Chardonnay and brie, ketchup and a box of Arm & Hammer. In the bathroom were pills for heartburn and a shampoo called Silver Fox. He didn't need to linger; he needed to go. There was the sense he could have spent the rest of his life in this house that was not his, this life that was not his, but was built on the sacrifice of the world he inhabited. The bones of his people ground to fertilize the flowerbeds. The land raped to pay for the satellite TV and ski boat. The people poisoned to—but no.

He set the timers for six hours and left.

When he got back to his aunt's, he parked the truck in the barn and burned the tent, coveralls, mask, cap, and gloves in a small pyre in the back field. Then he showered and walked back to the Ruritan club. He had been gone a little under three hours. His tab was still open.

He drank two beers, talked to everyone he could, and then drove the Galaxie home.

The next day the fire made national news.

He spent the following year building a life and several outbuildings around the main house. There was some money from his uncle's death benefit and he used part of it to rough out a greenhouse and what he thought of as the small chapel Mara would notice the day we walked in. His aunt seemed happy, sitting in her rocking chair watching him frame the walls and run the wiring. He was home, he had purpose. She never said anything about the fire and neither did his granddaddy. He had grown quieter and Chris suspected that was as it should be. He'd lost both his sons, lost his wife. He was deep in his eighties and while age had so long been kept at bay, now it drew close enough to fog his eyes. His back began to hunch, his big frame thinning and collapsing, as brittle as broomstraw. Every Sunday the three of them had dinner together and afterward Chris drove them in the Galaxie through the mountain roads, the top down, the heater on high when winter came.

He was running again, though there were days he felt a stiffness in his ankle that took miles to loosen. When Cabbage Jones had a heart attack in the parking lot of a Wilkesboro strip club, Chris bought the mounted lioness from Vilas Antiques and put it in his room so that it was the first thing he saw on waking. There were old men who believed there were still cougars in the mountains, old toms that roamed in hopeless search for a mate. Chris believed them, or at least wanted to. But he never saw them, not even the day they buried his granddaddy in the churchyard near enough his wife and two sons to keep watch, all four below ground now, but reconstituted into something like a family.

Meanwhile, the farm grew. He had this idea—you would never mention it to the old-timers sitting in front of the general store for it sounded like some woo-woo hippie shit—but this idea was that you could live in harmony with the land, that if you loved the land it would love you back. He cultivated ten acres of bottomland and then fifteen acres, and soon enough he was working twenty-five acres, running a row-hoe between asparagus plants or heads of romaine, digging potatoes and picking okra.

People came. He didn't want them to, but they did anyway. They built their tiny homes around the clearing's edge, worked the fields, shared the food. A blacksmith, a farrier with his horses, people who had passed through this or that addiction only to come out on the other side. Chris worked all day, and at night he read his Gary Snyder and his Wendell Berry. His Chomsky. His granddaddy's King James Bible. Bill Baker came from *Mountain Voices* and asked if this was a commune. *Don't bullshit me, please. What is it you're doing out here?* A TV crew came from Charlotte and called it *an intentional community.*

People came though they were never invited. I don't want disciples, Chris told them. I'm trying to *be* a disciple. But they came anyway. The Mad Farmer living down along the river without internet or phone, not that you could get service anyway. He farmed with animals. He prayed, though no one seemed exactly sure to whom. He read and he ran. He had nothing to say to the papers or radio or TV or the professor down from Cornell researching a book on contemporary monastic communities. He didn't make statements. He didn't write manifestos. He lived his life simply. But no one lived that way anymore and that meant something. It frightened people, it moved people. The masses with their eyes and hearts buried in the screens of the phones buried in their right hands buried in their getting and spending and their sad summer timeshares and their bored sad children and their tiny sad pills they all swallowed so as not to die of sadness. And here was this man plowing in the traces of a mule, hands raw, the sun on his face. Someone claimed to have heard him singing.

Beyond the farm, the world turned and turned again.

Planes hit the Towers. Someone sent anthrax spores through the US mail.

Meanwhile, out in the garden he argued with himself. He'd burned a house to the ground. He was a terrorist, too, wasn't he? In the coming years, we would all be well schooled in terrorism, from Charlie Hebdo and Theo van Gogh to bombs in nightclubs and subways and men opening fire at this Walmart in Texas or that mosque in New Zealand. But at the time, there was a certain frightening novelty to it all—it was a scourge, and we were going to eradicate it. It would be years before we came to understand that there was no moral arc to the universe, and even if there were, it sure as hell wasn't bending toward anything like justice. But back then, if you can believe such, we Americans were even more naive than we are as I write these words.

So, he asked himself, was he a terrorist?

He'd attacked a symbol, hadn't he? He'd attacked the system, an ideology.

But terrorists kill people. Did anybody die?

No.

Then that ain't terrorism.

Well, what do you call it?

I don't know. I call it justice.

A year after the Hawk Mountain fire, Erwin Energy denied the presence of heavy metals in the drinking water of a community in East Tennessee. A month later the EPA measured contamination at a thousand times the legal limit. But by then a baby was already dead and several women were having hysterectomies.

Chris waited for the last of the disciples to leave, until it was only he and his aunt. He had learned patience and that was a good thing as it took him months to collect enough ammonium nitrate to burn their office park outside Johnson City but he did burn it, and when the vice president of Regional Operations appeared on television to decry the fire as an act of domestic terrorism, no different than the actions of Al-Qaeda, he found the address of the VP's office and he burned that as well.

Then he put in his tomato plants.

If they chose to wage war on the earth and her people, he would wage war on them.

Then one day a would-be playwright showed up having read Bill Baker's newspaper article, one day I showed up. A few months after that, I brought Mara, and it was Mara who asked, as if asking about no more than the weather, What if we did something?

We moved out to the farm in May of 2003. The Farm, the commune, the whatever it was. The *intentional living community*, which made it sound not terribly different from the upscale gated community where Mara's mother had walked into the woods to die. We took up residence in one of the buildings that clustered along the river a few weeks after the disastrous march on the federal building in town. It was a time of such promise that the news around us barely registered, the war, the death, the shiny bomblets picked up by children. Everything was remade, and in that renewal Mara seldom thought about her parents, her dead mother, her ineffectual father—or at least that was what I believed. In her happiness (in my naivety), they had been reduced to easily comprehensible roles—dead mom, broken dad—and it made it a little easier to accept that her old life no longer existed.

The march had changed something. In hindsight, I see that as the hinge, the point from which we swung from that life to this. It was small at first, it was hopeful. I was outlining a play, sketching scenes, jotting down dialogue, doing everything short of actually writing it, but that would come soon enough. Mara quit her job with SAP. No more organizing for Mara. No more beating her head against the great wall of apathy. We had decided we would take the year off from societal expectations (we said things like that back then, "societal expectations"). Which meant that for the next year we would live on the farm—it quickly became The Farm—spend the summer in the garden, read, meditate, winterize the cabin in which we would live. In the fall, we would plan some grand protest, something beyond getting pelted by frat boy hot dogs and pepper-sprayed by fascist cops. Something of importance.

But what?

That had been my question the evening the three of us sat by the fire ring, the river curling past, close enough to smell the water, the dirt, the new grass along the bank. It was April and if you were hopeful you could sense the first scrap of summer, and Mara had most certainly been hopeful. Though the campus march had taken place weeks prior, her eyes had only now ceased to itch. Despite the Visine, despite the cool water, the saline, the prayers, the anger, despite it all, the burning had lasted for days, slowly giving way to swollen sinuses and the sort of manic twitch that seemed to shudder across her face when she least expected it. That twitch had lasted the better part of the week, until only the itching remained. But now even that was gone, and here she was in the spring dusk with these two men, while behind us the river went golden and then dark, and in front of us the coals of the fire seemed to expand, weeping light.

We had been coming out every weekend, Saturday and Sunday, and then started sleeping over, pitching a tent one weekend and returning the next to find Chris had swept out one of the abandoned cabins and carried over a mattress and box springs. The place was otherwise empty: just Chris and his aunt, two horses, a mule, six laying hens, and a rooster. The lioness, of course. The mattress had been an invitation: look at all this space I have to myself. But also, look at all this *work* I have to myself. But the work was no deterrent. If anything, it was an attraction. This was something Mara and I had talked about repeatedly over the last year, the extent to which so much of our engagement with the world was mediated, theoretical, sitting around *talking about things*. But to do actual useful work, to grow our own food, to sit in the evenings by the river by the fire? When Chris invited us, we accepted immediately, though it took Chris weeks to return to Mara's initial question: what if we did something?

"Like what?" I had wanted to know.

But Chris had only spread his hands wide.

"I'd prefer not to be pepper-sprayed again," I said.

"I understand that," Chris said.

But Mara didn't understand—was I saying I was done? that risking any sort of pain was simply too much?—because it wasn't for her. Jesus, no. They could spray her or beat her or lock her up and she wouldn't stop, because stopping—

"I just mean," I said, "that if it comes to that, I want to be the one doing the spraying. What do you think?"

"I think yes," she said.

"Yes what?"

"Yes to everything."

Yes to everything because what she had come to realize was that she wasn't some dewy-eyed pacifist. She believed in righteousness, she believed in power. The Jehovah of the Old Testament. The Voice out of the Whirlwind. She'd watched the bombs exploding all over Iraq and Afghanistan and Gaza, the JDAMs dropped from planes, the Tomahawks launched from sea. So while we unloaded our bags and made the bed and worked in the garden, she allowed her mind to float to possibilities. There is a great American tradition of resistance, of acts of civil disobedience, and she fingered that history like prayer beads. Acts against Halliburton, against Kellogg, Brown, and Root, against the federal government, the state government, against . . . While I fell in love with Mara, Mara fell in love with John Brown. In truth, I was never going to do anything. As I said earlier, I'm a small man, and like all small men I found myself lost in the moment, saying things I didn't really mean, overpromising. Fooling everyone but myself.

Though in my defense, it was easy to be fooled because for all our talk of acting, we spent our days playing. We took long walks through the woods, climbing Elk Knob and driving to Roan Mountain to walk for hours through the foggy Appalachian highlands. When the days warmed, we jumped off Trash Can Falls and tubed down the Watauga, planted lounge chairs in the creek that ran past the farm and sat there in the afternoon sun when our work was done. Feet in the water, bourbon in our veins. Mara would sit in her bikini and feel the sun on her shoulders and arms and face, a paperback tented in her lap. It was a dreamy time of touch and taste, of wet peaches and warm skin and the sun-dogged heat. She had so much energy. Sleep was so deep and restorative that she barely needed it. She could make love to me at dawn, spend hours in the garden or searching the woods for the gilled mushrooms she was learning to name, eat lunch and make love to me a second time, legs hooked around my skinny waist, nails clawing my skinny back with an urgency we had never known. Then get up and spend the afternoon painting or sculpting or walking or reading or swimming or some glorious combination of all five. Evenings we ate dinner with Chris's aunt, bid her goodnight, and sat by the fire ring or at the edge of the creek, sometimes swimming, sometimes simply stretching out on the sandbank, stripped to our underwear and goose-bumped in the cool of the day, passing some bottle of something, head swooning with a boozy grace. It was as if she was this new thing and what had come before—had anything come before?

She thought that something had, some other Mara in some other existence that must have been gray and sad, but she could barely remember anything from that before, not her parents, not her time in New York. The protest march had surely happened to someone else, and she kept catching herself turning suddenly, as if something were creeping up behind her. She suspected it was her actual life, the one she would make, the one she was *making* at that very moment. That it might go on forever seemed an article of faith, something so basic there was no sense in even considering its transience.

It was beautiful and endless and she knew this.

(Or am I talking about myself? Projecting some wished for past with such focus I can no longer separate fact from fiction?)

Either way, one autumn day Chris knocked early on our cabin door—we were naked and dozing beneath the sheet, sweat-stuck and raw—to say he had an idea.

The idea was a privately held zoo just outside Gatlinburg. The town wasn't even a town, just a collection of farms and trailers and two Baptist churches arranged in the slow southward curve of the Pigeon River: a little outpost of rebel flags strapped to the aerials of pickups, trampolines, and Trans-Ams in the dirt yards.

A local man named Tugg Wilson kept animals in the wire enclosures that dotted the back of his property, and though it wasn't something officially open to the public—Tugg Wilson felt a deeper kinship with the animals, something that extended past the possibility of financial gain but stopped well short of actual kindness—the public, should the public stop by, were generally free to roam the property so long as they stayed out of Tugg's way.

Chris had been there twice as a boy, once with his third-grade class and once with his Sunday school. It had been decades ago, but Tugg was still alive, and so were many of the mangy animals, including—Chris had just learned—a mountain lion said to have been trapped in South Dakota the year prior and sold by a dealer said to supplement his business running prescription drugs and firearms with the occasional sale of an exotic cat.

"A female," Chris said that evening when we gathered by the fire ring. "I didn't think it was true, but drove over anyway, and sure enough there it was, maybe two or three years old."

"You saw it?" Mara asked.

"Walked right in. He was on his tractor and told me not to put my hands in the cages, but otherwise that was it. He has bears, a wolf, a—"

"When can we go?" Mara asked.

She was anxious, excited, but scared too. I remember the way she leaned forward into the firelight. I remember the way Chris was leaning forward too. I remember it because I thought then—or at least remember thinking—that it marked the end of something, if not of that life, at least of that summer.

It was only later, only when we were in bed that I told her it was stupid and small-minded and needlessly dangerous, not only for us but for the animals.

"Setting them loose?" she wanted to know. "How is freeing them dangerous?"

"Because what happens when they're free? When there's a panther running wild, Mara. What happens then?"

"Nothing," she said. "It runs, and so do we. We're in the Keys before they even know what happened."

"That's idiotic. They shoot it is what happens."

"No one would shoot it."

I laughed at her, and if there is anything I regret about that time together it was how I laughed at her. We argued about it for the rest of the fall and on into winter, but it was a proxy fight. The truth was, whatever we'd had together had flamed out months ago. It was only moving to the cabin and the illusion of new life that had kept us going. That summer she had touched me to keep the summer alive. But now summer was over. I refused to be involved with the zoo. It was stupid, it was reckless, it was irresponsible. Mara pleaded but I cut her off, and when the weather turned cold, I turned inward. We slept under three quilts. We quit touching each other.

We fought through the fall and just before Christmas I left.

I was in Colorado by January, in Utah by February. By March I was freelancing for an outdoors magazine, stringing together just enough to live happily if cheaply. There were a few girlfriends but nothing that stuck. Mostly there was the night sky, the mountains, the days paddling rivers and the evenings sleeping by them. I didn't talk to Mara or Chris and as much as possible I tried not to think of them. This, I told myself, was an act of self-preservation, and in this, I was correct.

Two and a half years had passed when I saw Mara again. I was in New Mexico to interview an environmental studies professor for a story on public lands when I saw her name listed in the campus paper. It was an advertisement for a graduate student art show.

I saw it.

I went.

We wound up spending the evening together and then the night, and it wasn't so much like no time had passed as all time had passed, and here we were, having emerged into some new universe with only a twinkling awareness of the one we had left. A few months later, we were living together at Toliver's casa in Mexico. What had changed? Me, yes. Mara, certainly. But that wasn't it, not exactly. We had both grown up, but I realize now we had grown up in the worst sort of way. Which is also the necessary way. We had buried that rawness that had once fueled us. We had grown thicker skins. We were both ready to compromise. Which is adult, of course, which is necessary. But also sad. I didn't know then anything of what happened with Chris or the zoo. I was ignorant, but perfectly content to live in that ignorance.

And I did, I did.

Right up until the day Daniel slipped out of our life and Mara walked out into the sun to weep and rage and, ultimately, push three garden carts of ANFO across a Virginia field.

I left Bruce outside his room at the Dee-Luxe Inn in Richmond. He was driving back to Moab the next day and I knew I wouldn't see him again. He'd done what he'd come to do, he'd said what he had to say.

"You know you could come down to North Carolina if you needed to," I told him there in the parking lot. "Rest up."

A tiny dreamcatcher hung from his rearview mirror, like a basketball hoop hung crooked and thus useless.

"I think I'm going home."

"Okay."

"I think I'm declaring this is over and out. I think you should too." He took a step closer and touched my shoulder. "Is there a bad vibe coming off you, like a lower vibration?"

"Like I might do something rash?"

"Maybe I'm imagining it."

"Maybe so."

(I left him there in the parking lot, though later I would wonder if it was his face I saw online getting fire-hosed at Standing Rock, just one face, and for only a moment. Which says something, maybe, about my powers of observation, or more likely says something about what happens when a relatively large white man sees a relatively small brown man in pain—there is guilt and sympathy, though neither helped me to actually *see*. But that was later.)

At a Scotchman, I got a fountain Coke, filled it halfway, and topped it off with what was left of the Elijah Craig we'd drunk in his room. I-81 was a brilliant haze after that, the sort of high-bandwidth green that signals life. The wind in my ear. The sunlight. The Flying Js, the Stuckey's, the signs reading PRODUCE 4 SALE. The battlefields and truck stops. I came home to find someone had cleaned the house. The broken dishes had been swept away. The furniture righted. Even the sink shone. It filled me with some gratitude, but not enough to change anything.

I was hungover but sober when the two FBI agents knocked the next day. This time, they wanted me to come with them, just some questions, just a few minutes of my time. I considered saying the things one might say, asking if they had a warrant, if they were arresting me, and so forth, but none of it seemed worth the trouble. Instead, I got back in my truck and followed them downtown to the Watauga County Offices. We came in through the back, past the clerks, past the license plate office, and though I saw any number of people I knew well no one seemed willing to make eye contact. Finally, we sat down in a conference room of beige carpet and gray walls, in the corner a giant television on a rolling cart.

"You should know up front," said one agent, "we have material evidence linking your wife to the bombing of the water-bottling plant in Virginia."

"Just so we're clear on this from the start," said the other agent, his skin so pale as to be nearly translucent. "Have a look."

He put a tablet in front of me and on it I watched the grainy footage of Mara pumping diesel in Hampton, Tennessee.

"She's getting gas," I said.

He nodded. Bemused, might be the word.

"What about this?" he asked, and proceeded to swipe past five grainy images of Mara pushing her garden cart back and forth past the perimeter fencing. "Look like she's getting gas there?"

"We know you haven't seen your wife since January," said the first. "We know the two of you had had a fight just before she left. What I want is for you to walk me back through that day. Start early."

"Start first thing in the morning," said the second one, the pale one. "You'd argued the night before. She had out some of your papers."

"Some research you had failed to complete."

"I want my lawyer," I said.

I got that bemused look again.

"No, you don't, Mr. Wood. Because what that means is that everything escalates and that's not in anyone's interest. Not in yours and certainly not in your wife's."

"Where is she?"

"That's what we want your help with."

The second stepped forward and opened a folder in front of me. "Take a look at this."

I could see CHRISTOPHER BRIGHT in all caps across the top.

"Go ahead, Mr. Wood," said the first agent. "Indulge yourself."

And I did, though only for a moment. The file contained page after page linking Chris to fires in North Carolina and Tennessee and Utah. It felt like a contagion, and I slapped it shut, leaned back in my chair, and crossed my arms. I wanted to stand but was suddenly so dizzy I thought I'd fall over if I tried.

"I want my lawyer."

The pale agent sighed and the other shook his head like a disappointed father.

"All right," he said, "get a lawyer. Meanwhile we'll get a search warrant and seize everything your wife might have even looked at. Her stuff, your son's stuff."

"Can I go?"

"That's going to be fun, Mr. Wood. Watching us haul out your sons' toys."

"Can I go or not?"

"By all means go, Mr. Wood. By all means."

It wasn't until I was back in the hall that I felt my balance return. It was then that I saw Bill Baker and his wife, huddled on a bench and no doubt awaiting questioning. They hadn't seen me and I turned in the other direction. That way was longer and suddenly I was dizzy again, but I couldn't face them.

I put one hand on the wall and in that manner made it back to my truck.

That night, I slept beneath sheets I hadn't changed since Mara had left and woke the next day to knocking.

A woman stood at the door. About my age, though worn. Plastic Crocs and a flannel shirt over nurse's scrubs. It was the DOLLAR GENERAL tag pinned to her shirt that gave her way. Lucille Duncan. The woman from the church who had come looking for Mara months ago. *We met at church and then she come out to the house a few times,* she'd said. *But I ain't seen her now since Cory passed.* She sat on the couch reluctantly, pink hands in her lap until I brought her a cup of coffee.

She put out stock, boxes of Lucky Charms, Dinty Moore in the new pop-top cans. Rang up earbuds and hair barrettes and Tide pods and Mucinex. Her husband Jeb was a long-haul trucker, gone again in his Peterbilt.

But here she was.

"I hope you don't mind," she said, looking around the room. "The door was open and it was such a mess and I thought . . ."

"You did this?"

"I thought maybe someone had come and vandalized things."

"You cleaned the house?"

"I'm sorry," she said. "I've had some time on my hands with Jeb away and all."

"This is the nicest thing anyone's done for me in a long time."

"I doubt that's true. But that ain't why I come by." She looked down at the floor. "There's some things you need to know, Mr. Wood. About Mara. Some things I didn't say before. I've been watching the house. They told me to wait until the government folk were gone."

"Who told you to wait?"

"If you'll just listen a minute."

She told me the rest then: how Mara had seen Cory just below Orchard Falls, how Mara would stop by to visit the group home Lucille ran: how Mara watched the boys playing, and one particular boy named Cory who was slightly older than Daniel would have been, but small. Just a little shrimp of a thing and she just sat there and watched that boy, watched Cory, tears welling up in her eyes though she never would actually cry.

"I knew y'all's boy had died," she told me. "I didn't know then it was non-Hodgkin's, same as Cory. But then Mara started acting a little . . . I don't know. She showed up one night at the ballfield where he was on the football team. Another day she came to the school, acting like she was social services. It's like she just needed to see him at first. But then the more she saw him the more she had to—I don't know. The more she needed him. Then when he died . . ."

"He died? This boy?"

"Cory. It was back last year and Mara she just . . . she just sort of lost it and . . ."

I was no longer really listening when she said, "I think you need to come with me."

"I'm sorry?"

"I said I wish you'd come with me."

"To where?"

"To the church," she said. "There's some people I think you should meet."

"Right now?"

"Yes, right now. It's Sunday."

"Sunday," I said, and it was.

She pushed herself up off the couch.

"Sunday," I said again.

I hadn't realized.

I followed her to the church, eyes fixed on the GOD'S BEEN GOOD sticker peeling off the bumper of her Buick Skylark. The yard was full and the service already underway when I followed her inside. I sat alone in the back pew while she walked up front to sit at the end of a row of boys with their heads shaved to stiff fuzz—the foster children Mara had spent her days watching.

The same preacher I'd seen before was holding forth, stomping his feet, gasping, crying out to the Lord. *And they found the stone rolled away,* he gasped, *and they entered in, and found not the body of our Lord Jesus Christ.* His face was red and panting. His Western shirt soaked beneath his arms, the pearl snaps strained. *And it came to pass, as they were much perplexed thereabout, behold, two men stood by them in shining garments. Behold!* he cried, and went down on one knee like a football player, resting. *Behold!* Hands were raised, palms open to the heavens. A moment later they began to file forward, coming out of the aisles with walkers and canes, in Reeboks and work boots, the old and infirm, the unchurched. The boys appeared restless. A man laughed and then began to cry and then began to spit up into his hands. *Behold!* What pulled me forward I don't know, only that I began to swim that same subterranean river you travel as a fevered child, the world real yet disproportionate, time recognizable but no longer functioning. It dragged me forward, that current, that Holy Ghost, until I stood at the center of things, before the altar, before the preacher, their hands on me, steadying me, righting me.

Holding me.

Right up until the moment I felt it hit me in my guts and collapsed in a heap onto the burnt orange carpet.

Outside was a black rain. I woke on the front pew, someone's shawl thrown over my chest, Lucille Duncan holding my left hand. When I opened my eyes she stepped back. Standing by her were two giants, a dour man and a woman of impossible height, the Kinzers, the Mennonite couple I'd seen outside the church so many years ago when Mara and I had passed.

"Mr. Wood," Lucille said. "I think these are the people you want to see."

I rode in the back of their truck, an old Land Rover that appeared airlifted out of 1980s Africa, crowded between boxes of clothes and a plastic laundry basket full of loaves of Bunny bread they delivered to their neighbors. Their house sat in a hollow of shadow and white pine on a gravel road that switched back twice across a creek running clear and fast with the rain.

A sign read, YOUR GPS IS WRONG.

Then another, YOU ARE FAR FROM GOD.

They parked under a carport and got out without a word, the storm deafening on the aluminum roof. The house was dark and warm and crowded with books and records and more boxes. On the wood-paneled walls hung paintings and tribal masks and a photograph of Oscar Romero shadowed by the Kinzers' younger incarnations. I sat in the living room with the man while the woman brought coffee, and Mississippi John Hurt sang *Here I Am, Oh Lord, Send Me* on a Fisher-Price stereo. They appeared to be in their seventies. Neither had said their names, neither had said where they were from, though it was clear from their voices they weren't from here.

"We started as missionaries in Nicaragua," the man said when his wife finally sat.

"I guess she knew that," the woman told me. "That we'd be sympathetic to her—I don't know how you'd put it."

"Her ways," the man said. "The way she saw the world."

"We sat here and talked to her. She was hurting so bad. Talking about the boy you'd lost, talking about how he'd been poisoned. Many nights we sat here talking, and many nights," the woman said, "we just listened."

"I'm sorry," I said. "I don't understand."

"When she was staying here," the woman said. "Or didn't you know?"

"I thought . . . "

"You thought she was with that man."

"I don't know what I thought. I guess I did."

"No. She was here, until the very end."

She stood and her husband rose beside her.

"You should probably see this," she said.

The room was off the back of the house. It appeared to have been an office once, barely large enough to contain the cot and the desk beside it. Windows opened onto the back pasture where I could just make out the dark shape that marked a barn, the wood almost blued with age, the door open on a gaping space darker still. There was sudden sunlight and then another shudder of rain, the light failing, the day dimming, so dim, in fact, I could barely make out what lay out on the neatly made cot.

"The FBI came," the woman said.

"They took some books she'd made notes in," the man said. "One she had about John Brown. Her clothes. They took her car, took pretty much everything she touched."

It was the woman who handed it to me.

"Everything," she said, "except this. We kept this back."

Inside the envelope, I found her license, the photo of Daniel, her membership card for the Mint Museum in Charlotte, the two postcards, and her diary.

I scooped it up and was about to turn and go when the old woman stopped me.

"She left this for you," the old woman said.

"For me?"

She shrugged and handed me the sheaf of pages marked "The Water of Life."

"For someone," she said.

part three

the water of life

david1976@pop.email.com
To: joseph.baker@mountainvoice.org
Sun 11/18/2018
The Water of Life

Bill,

Please find attached the article we discussed.

D

Attachment: TheWaterOfLife.pdf

joseph.baker@mountainvoice.org
To: david1976@pop.email.com
Tue 11/19/2018
Re: The Water of Life

Can we talk about this in person?

joseph.baker@mountainvoice.org
To: david1976@pop.email.com
Th 11/19/2018
Re: The Water of Life

David, seriously, can we please talk in person?

joseph.baker@mountainvoice.org
To: david1976@pop.email.com
Th 11/20/2018
Re: The Water of Life

you getting these?

joseph.baker@mountainvoice.org
To: david1976@pop.email.com
Sun 11/21/2018
Re: The Water of Life

Okay, so I wanted to talk face 2 face, but you're obviously ignoring me. I'm trying to be as sympathetic as possible, David. I'm trying not to be an asshole. This is a way to deal with things. I get it. But wtf, man? You know good and well I can't publish this. We'd both be sued seven ways from Sunday.

Look, I have no doubt about your accuracy. These are not good people. But nothing here is substantiated. You've invented dialogue—did you even talk to anybody? You've imagined thoughts. You've impugned actual people on the basis of what—your grief? This isn't journalism; this is a hit job. I'm sorry to be so blunt but there it is. I'm deleting this file and I suggest you do the same. You needn't bother contacting me about this.

You know the GODDAMN FBI INTERVIEWED MY WIFE!!!!!!

> Save me, O God; for the waters are come in unto my soul.
> Psalm 69

She drove down on a glorious May morning, and had she not already known she was leaving God's country she would have suspected she was entering it. Kathryn Banks had woken in an angle of light, the early sun falling through the bedroom window of her Loudon County estate, and, for the first time since her husband had passed away the previous June, felt what might be called happiness, or, if not happiness, purpose. Her daughters were away for the weekend—Maddy a junior at Hollins, Jocelyn, a high school sophomore, sleeping at a friend's—so Kathryn walked alone through the paddocks and out to the stables. The horses appeared as luminous as the day, though she suspected that was simply the product of her mood. She had coffee and spent twenty minutes doing a series of intense body-weight exercises (planks, push-ups, bicycle kicks—she had an app on her phone) and another twenty in the half lotus, attuning her breath. She showered and dressed, matched a Hermès scarf to her Eileen Fisher pants, and, sometime around eight, got in her Lexus and started down her driveway past the two stone horses that marked the edge of her property. She glided through Middleburg, took I-66, and turned south on I-81.

The bottling plant lay on 176 acres in a forgotten corner of southwest Virginia, rolling hills, grazing Herefords. Farther east began the coalfields, the gutted seams and striated rock, but that was miles away. Here, it was all apple orchards and bike trails, the farm-to-table restaurants by the clapboard churches, and beneath it all, a water as pure as the day.

Credit card receipts indicate she stopped once for gas and a bottle of Lion Heart Kombucha (BEV $4.19) in Wytheville.

Cellular records indicate she made no phone calls.

It was just after lunch when she met the realtor, Monty Drudge, at his downtown office in Mountain View. Drudge's office, like the town, might be described as "fabricated quaint." A fish-scaled Victorian, it had Federalist furniture and a La Marzocco espresso machine. The town had gaslights and a microbrewery. All of it intentional—the shabby chic the product of a Richmond consultancy—and all of it animated by the sort of civic pride that arises at the intersection of affluence and affectation.

Though he acted as if he knew nothing of her, Drudge had done a minimum of due diligence, which is to say he had googled Kathryn Banks. So as they sat down to coffee and croissants on the wrought-iron chairs in the triangle of courtyard behind his office—it really was a glorious day, all peonies and promise—Drudge would have known that when her husband had died the previous summer of a heart attack outside the US District Court in Oakland, California, he had left his wife with sole proprietorship of a water-bottling consortium that stretched from Rialto, California, to Enterprise, Florida, and was valued at roughly $147 million dollars (Mr. Banks had consistently disputed this figure, thus his appearance that day in court). Drudge would have known that following her husband's death, Kathryn and her daughter Jocelyn (Joce to her friends) had sold the family home in Santa Clara County and moved east to be nearer her older daughter. Had he accessed public records easily available online, he would have known she had recently purchased bottling plants in Michigan and Minnesota. Were he particularly diligent, he might have even known that the Bankses, husband and wife, had been especially generous to Republican candidates at both the state and national levels, had contributed lavishly (and unsuccessfully) to California Proposition 8, and twice had been guests of the Koch brothers at their strategy sessions at the Esmeralda Renaissance Resort just outside Palm Springs.

"Mrs. Banks," he might have said, hand extended. "What a pleasure."

They made small talk on the courtyard—she'd seen the theater coming in and asked about the summer season: they were staging *Shrek: The Musical*—and then got into Drudge's Tahoe and drove north.

The bottling plant sat thirteen miles out of town, the land ascending, rising from the valley into the rolling hills, everything green, everything alive. What poverty there was—trailers, concrete stoops crowded with washers and dogs—appeared more as authentication than blight. They passed a fledgling vineyard and a fading billboard—HOW DO YOU LIKE YOUR ETERNITY? SMOKING OR NON?—and parked on a gravel fire road beneath the beech and white pine, ahead of them a gate pulled shut.

"One moment and I'll just . . . "

But when Drudge went to open the gate, Kathryn Banks said she'd rather walk, see the land, get a sense of things.

"You sure? It's a quarter of a mile."

"I don't mind," she said. "A day like this."

They wound uphill through the dense forest, the road overhung with white pine and cut with the runoff of spring rain, but at the switchback it opened onto a long sweep of pasture, the path lined with sunflowers. The building appeared in a fold of land, block walls and a metal roof, like an airplane hangar removed to a landscape painting, the Hudson River School gone postindustrial. The bottling plant had closed in March 2003, a victim, according to bankruptcy filings, of heightened security requirements after 9/11.

"But everything's intact?"

"Like the day they left it. I've seen it myself."

He was right, of course. The raw tank and the booster pump, the quartz and carbon filters. The winding belts that led from the filling and capping machine on to the shrink-wrap—it was all exactly as it had been left, functional and clean. Cleaner, in fact, as Drudge had hired a service to pressure-wash the interior, flushing out the dust and grime and a family of field mice so resilient he'd debated hiring a falconer.

"I'll have to have someone check the condition of the machinery," she said.

"Of course," Drudge said, smiling his bright smile.

"I could get a team down here by, say, middle of the week."

"I can be here at your convenience."

"They'd need to check the transfer pump, a few other things. Is there power?"

"I can certainly get it on."

She stood nodding, bottom lip caught between her teeth.

"It might be useful to find a local partner," she said.

"I can look into that if you like."

"Someone with a good sense of the business climate, local knowledge."

"I can certainly look into that, absolutely."

She turned then, no longer nodding, no longer biting her lip.

She had, it appeared, decided.

"And the price?" she asked.

But she already knew the price. It was the price that had drawn her: 800K. Absurdly cheap, even if the machinery was no longer operational—though she could tell by looking at it that it still was. Her husband had taught her that much at least.

"Let me make a call," she said, and walked out of the cool, dim interior into the warm sun.

It was all, they were both thinking, too good to be true.

And it was, and they knew it.

That was Saturday.

Sundays Monty Drudge kept the Sabbath, driving south from Mountain View to Abingdon Baptist, an octagonal arena of sound and light where three thousand parishioners met over coffee and crullers to celebrate the resurrection of both their Lord (via God's grace) and the greater fossil fuel industry (via the grace—and subsidies—of the federal government). Abingdon was the legal hub of the region's coal companies and was littered with lawyers and executives and former legislators who had retired here in order to drink bourbon at Morgan's while their wives got their mani-pedis at the Martha Washington Inn. You could drive around the countryside in your vintage Aston-Martin thinking about the founding fathers while antiquing for stoneware or another corner cupboard. Monty Drudge made the half-hour drive for reasons economic: the church provided a gateway to his moneyed clientele, and more often than not he stuck around for lamb and roasted potatoes in this or that paneled dining room.

So it was that two weeks after Kathryn Banks's visit, he found himself having Sunday dinner in a Main Street bistro with Jeff Morgan. Morgan owned a chain of interstate Bojangles, thirteen restaurants spread north along I-81. He had spent two years as a missionary in Sierra Leone and while he had found salvation, he had lost his wife, Carol, who left him at the Freetown Radisson to return home and take up with a North Carolina carpenter known to his eight thousand followers on Instagram as "The Wood Shaver."

"Except he doesn't even build houses or barns or whatever," Jeff said. "It's god-dang 'wood art,' or 'wood sculpture,' which, excuse me, but that's just bullshit is what that is."

The previous week Banks had sent down both a lawyer and a mechanical engineer. The machinery had functioned exactly as it should and now the papers were being drawn up.

When the waitress—Drudge recognized her from one of the local theater productions and made a mental note to stop back later in the week—brought out a torte for Morgan and a coffee for himself, Drudge switched the conversation to the bottling plant.

"You finally selling that son of a bitch?" Morgan was all chocolatey teeth, powdered sugar in his beard.

"Like you didn't hear?"

"I heard some little old lady from California bought it."

"From Virginia," Drudge corrected, "by way of California. Just to be clear."

Morgan smiled. "Well, good for you, brother. What's the commission on a deal like that?"

"What are you up to these days, Jeff?"

"Ten percent of what? Seven, eight hundred K?"

"Cause a little bird told me you were spending your days driving up and down the interstate bugging the fry cooks."

"A little bird told you that?"

"Checking the sweet tea for sugar. Checking the bathrooms for toilet paper."

"It's called quality control."

"It's called boredom. You really love biscuits that much?"

"I love profit that much," he said. The tines of the fork came out of his mouth gleaming. "How 'bout that?"

"How 'bout that, indeed. But listen for a minute."

The woman, the California Yankee via Virginia via wherever the hell she hailed from, needed a partner, someone local, someone with area contacts.

"Ah." Morgan had the chocolate smile thing down. "So that's

what this was about. She wants how much, a third of the stake, half?"

"She doesn't want any money."

"Don't tell me two-goddamn-thirds."

"Zero. She's buying local knowledge."

"Local knowledge."

"She wants someone onboard who's from here, someone who can manage the day-to-day."

"Thus the invitation to lunch." He attempted to wipe the chocolate from his face. "Look, I'm flattered, but I'm not interested."

"I don't believe that."

"I appreciate it, but I'm not. This thing with Carol—"

"Jesus, Jeff."

"This thing with Carol. Seriously. It just sort of took the starch out of me."

"Would a 20 percent stake put it back in you?"

Morgan took his napkin from his lap, inspected it, quartered it, and, finally, draped it over his dessert plate as if it were a fallen comrade.

"Twenty percent?"

"So you're listening?"

"I'm listening."

"Or maybe you just can't get away long enough from all that chicken and biscuits and dirty rice?"

"Goddamn, brother. I said I'm listening."

Ownership was transferred on June 2, 2015, and while Banks LLC held a controlling interest, a minority stake (25 percent after negotiations) fell to Morgan Enterprises. Two days later Jeff hired a secretary and set up an office on the premises. A week after that, water samples were taken from Morgan's kitchen sink and shipped to Richmond for testing. This wasn't so much obfuscation—the water was pure as a Christian's heart—as convenience: the pumps would take a few days to get operational and there was no sense in delaying.

Jeff called a friend with Dollar General to see if maybe they were interested in a distribution deal and sure, maybe, we'll see.

Three days later revival began.

Revival in the southern church goes back as far as the brush arbor. The circuit-riding preacher arrives via horseback or Edsel—or in the case of Abingdon Baptist, a Land Rover driven south from Roanoke— to drive membership and quench a collective thirst for the water of life. While tradition called for a week of prayer and repentance, market forces had compelled the church to consolidate to a single night, that night being Sunday, June 8. The preacher in this case, Dr. Michael Fuzzeli, was not so much a Soul Saver as a political organizer currently on leave from his own church (Baptist, mega) and spending a year as a research fellow at the Heritage Foundation. It was known that Reverend Fuzzeli had the ear of the Republican Party, and the presence of such a Beltway heavyweight brought out the area's business and political elite, including, but not limited to, former congressman Richard Manley (R-VA). Manley had served two terms in the halls of power but then, more taken with his own electability than the electorate, lost a bid for governor, polling, alas, in the single digits. There followed a period of soul-searching involving affairs with both a staff intern from UVA (nineteen and perfectly legal) and low-grade opioids (Oxys, 10 mg Percs—but only occasionally), ultimately culminating in twenty-eight days at the Wildflower Recovery Center and a YouTube confessional where he tearfully apologized for his misdeeds and announced his intention to reenter public life as the Servant-Leader God intended him to be.

But God had other ideas, and the night Manley arrived to hear

Reverend Fuzzeli deliver his sermon "Gifts of the Spirit," he had put aside all plans of returning to office (the focus groups were less than positive) and accepted a job with Global Evangelical Relief, a religious nonprofit with an annual operating budget of nine figures. It was a sort of sinecure, he supposed, but a good job, and he was excited, maybe a little scared. He needed comfort. In a week, he'd be in Rome organizing aid efforts in the Sahel, and overcome with a certain sentimentality, had come, he supposed, to say goodbye.

Looking back, Manley would come to believe that winding up thigh to thigh in the pew by Jeff Morgan could only be viewed as God's inscrutable will. That they fell into conversation, Manley revealing his imminent departure—"goddamn, Rich, Rome?"—could only be seen as, well, a Gift of the Spirit. And then Africa came up.

"Africa?"

"I'll be working in the Sahel. Mali, Niger, Chad—"

"Jesus, man, I know the Sahel. I spent the two best years of my life in Africa, Carol and me. Tell you what, let me buy you a drink."

Manley didn't drink anymore, but he did accept the invitation, so that they wound up at the Tavern on Main, leaning forward over glasses of Woodford and a Diet 7UP, no ice, but yes, a straw, please, plastic, because he was sick of those tree huggers telling him what to do. Manley had spent the weeks since accepting the position wishing badly for a different life, so when Morgan confessed how jealous he was—"I'd love to be you right now, brother"—Manley was willing to hear it. Eventually, the conversation turned to Morgan, his divorce, his fried chicken, and, a mere afterthought at this point, his water-bottling venture.

"Hey," Manley said, "are you for real?"

"About the water? Completely."

"You know we deliver water to Africa. All over the world, actually."

"I did not know that, my friend."

"At least I think we do. You know?"

"Yeah."

"Hey, if something were to ever come up."

"Sure, yeah," Morgan said, now drunk and unable to imagine anything past those days in Freetown, Carol on the balcony of the Radisson in giant sunglasses and a gauzy sarong. "Keep me in mind."

But the only thing Richard Manley could keep in mind was how much he hated Rome. It was dirty, it was hot. When he tooled around the Palazzo delle Esposizioni in white Nikes and fanny pack, the locals treated him like he was some dumb American, which, obviously, he so was not. He liked Africa better. He was spending two or three days a week in Niamey or Bamako, flying down on a baby blue Hercules to oversee the distribution of this pallet of grain or that crate of tractor parts. He'd started keeping a blog called "Dispatches from the Dark Continent," then, realizing he was in violation of both departmental policy and good taste, had started simply emailing his reflections to his old friend Jeff Morgan. Though Morgan only responded to every third or fourth post—"Good stuff, buddy!!!"—Manley was grateful for an audience. In his darker moments, Manley refused to entertain the possibility that Morgan was his only friend, but, if you got down to it, not really a friend at all. But Richard Manley's one true talent was ingratiating himself in places he was otherwise unwelcome, so when he found his department on the verge of opening the bidding on a new contract ($7.5 million to distribute one-liter bottles of water throughout the Sahel), Manley very casually—it involved no more than a single click of his mouse—changed the bidding status from "open" to "closed." Then, in what he would later describe to the Inspector General's Office as a fit of temporary insanity brought on by the heat and a nascent case of (undiagnosed) Typhoid fever, inserted a 2 in front of the $7.5 so that the figure became $27.5 million.

Then he picked up the phone and, despite the time difference, called Jeff Morgan.

In July, Kathryn Banks attended the Spring Cup in Middleburg where both her daughters were participating in the individual dressage (both were said to be horse crazy, and a look at the Instagram pics of the Dorado riding boots lining their closets like soldiers in a North Korean parade would seem to attest to as much). It was to be a grand day, announcing, as she imagined it, her arrival in Virginia society, a regional trumpeting of her wealth, taste, and gathering influence. It was a classy affair and the last person she wanted in attendance was Jeff Morgan—she had met him twice, both times equally under-whelmed, and since then had given no thought to her new bottling plant. But she had a member's box, so when he asked, repeatedly, insistently, what was she to say but yes, come, of course. He had good news, he said. She supposed that with the grace of God and a sufficient quantity of gin she could handle as much.

The Spring Cup is arguably the oldest horse race in the United States. As such, it holds its attendees to a standard of dress that makes most derbies appear as receptions at the local Hampton Inn, all-business casual and a party tray from Chick-fil-A. But here, the landed gentry of Old Virginia dressed in seersucker by Thom Browne and sun hats by Etro while rubbing well-moisturized elbows with the Beltway elite, the retired three-stars, the lobbyists, the blonde with the high cheekbones and a spot on *Fox & Friends*. It was not so much the world Kathryn Banks preferred so much as the one only one she acknowledged.

So when she saw Jeff Morgan coming through the crowd in khakis and a golf shirt that read—good Lord—18th Annual Bob Evans Charity Golf Classic, she felt herself go brittle, a sharpening of her already sharp features. She met him down by the infield fence, away from anyone she might recognize, and exhaled with great deliberateness. She would give him two minutes.

"I just saw a man in a pink suit," he said.

"How lovely."

"Had the sort of frilly collar if you know what I'm talking about."

"You'll see those now and then."

"He looked queer to me but I'm bad about those things."

"What exactly did you want to talk about, Mr. Morgan?"

"Like ruffles is what you'd call them. A grown man, I'm talking about."

He held a champagne flute, a single raspberry having sunk to the bottom.

"Business, I presume," Banks said.

He downed the champagne, hesitated, and then ate the raspberry.

"Yes, ma'am," he said, "Business, indeed."

Somehow those two minutes turned into ten, and then twenty, and then Banks was escorting him up to her box, oblivious to the expensive clamor all around her because Morgan had said the magic words. Morgan had said, "Twenty-seven point five mil, ma'am."

"And this man?"

"Richard Manley."

"This Richard Manley. He's a friend of yours?"

"So to speak," Morgan said. "I mean yes, so far, I guess, as he has friends."

"Don't we already have a deal to distribute through—where?"

"Dollar General. But this is different," he said. "This is another order of magnitude, profit-wise."

They leaned against the open window of the box, around them Kathryn's new friends, her daughters' friends, around her the world she would shortly come to rule through not so much the heft of her bank account as the force of her will.

"And this is legal?" she asked.

He shrugged. "It's just a contract."

"For $27.5 million."

"I'd say we'd turn 21, 22 mil in straight profit. But the thing is, we'd have to ramp up production."

"What would that entail?"

And with this he took not a business plan from an attaché case but a single sheet of notebook paper from his pocket. On it, he had diagrammed the layout of the RAIN! facility.

"We drill a second well just down the slope here," he said. "Pump the water back up to the bottling facility. Up-front costs are maybe two mil but the return—Lord."

"Couldn't we just up production from the primary?"

"Unfortunately, no. We couldn't meet the contract demand."

"You're sure of this?"

"You can send your man down if you like, but I've looked at it ten different ways."

"So a second well."

"Yes, ma'am."

"And you can do this?"

"We'd have to have it tested, approved, all that legal shit."

"That's nothing."

"Water samples and so on."

"That's a mere formality." She looked out at the track where the horses were being led from the infield tunnel, beside them small men in bright jumpsuits.

"So . . . ," Morgan said.

"So call your so-to-speak friend back. Sign the papers."

"Yes, ma'am."

"Get that well in the ground."

"Yes, goddamn, ma'am," he said, and slapped the notebook paper against his thigh.

"Oh, and Mr. Morgan," she called to him as he was leaving.

He paused and grinned his big cracker grin.

"Next time," she said, "wear a tie."

Phone records indicate Morgan called Richard Manley that night. It was early morning in Rome and Manley picked up. Two days later, they began to drill the second well just down the slope from the primary borehole. It was three weeks later that Manley called back to let his old pal know that the contract had now made its way through the bureaucratic tangle that was Global Evangelical Relief and was ready for a signature.

Richard Manley's call went to voicemail. Not that Jeff Morgan was avoiding him. It was more that Morgan suddenly found himself sunk in a mire of his own trouble. RAIN! had pumped its first samples from the second well and, per state regulations, submitted them to the Department of Health and Environmental Control. The A and B samples were bottled and labeled and sent off to the state office in Richmond. It had happened without his consent—in a fit of initiative his engineer had sent them, but while Jeff would have preferred once again submitting samples from the well that pumped cool mountain water into his house, he wasn't worried. It was a formality. They'd be flying water into the Sahel by autumn. But then Morgan got a call from Ben Johnson, a distant relative he now and then ran into at family reunions beneath the picnic shelter at Grayson Highlands State Park, the big shelter, he meant. Morgan was head of

Dairy, Soft Drinks, and Bottled Water (this is what was meant by "local knowledge") and called with some very troubling news.

A week after sending the samples, Johnson phoned to say that the water he had just tested contained unusually high levels of dioxins.

"That can't be."

But somewhere far away in an office park Johnson swore it was.

"Jeff, I'm telling you, you've got chlorinated hydrocarbons running out the ying-yang."

"I got what?"

"Aldrin, dieldrin, DDT—"

"DDT's banned, I thought."

"It is. But these things have hell of a half-life, cuz. Where'd you bottle this again?"

"North of Mountain View," Morgan said. "In a goddamn pristine place. You can see the info there on the form. This absolutely can't be."

"I don't know what to say except sorry."

"Did you check the B sample?"

"The results are right here in front of me."

"But we checked out before. What the hell?"

"But that was a different well."

"Like two hundred meters up the slope."

"Up the slope, you say?"

"Yes, up the goddamn slope, where else?"

"Well, I'm guessing you've got runoff, cuz."

"Bullshit we've got runoff. We've got reverse osmosis is what we've got. We've got carbon filtration. I watched a fucking wiki-How probably eighteen times. Hired some hydrologist out of fucking Atlanta."

"But did you look at your soil mobility?"

"My what?"

"Your soil—"

"Look. Just sit tight. I'm driving up there."

"To Richmond?"

"Has anyone else seen this?"

"Just the lab tech, but there's no identifying info on it, so—"

"All right. That's good. Look, just sit tight and don't do anything till I get there."

"You really driving up?"

"Don't call anyone."

"I gotcha."

"Don't even look at anyone. I'm fucking serious, Ben."

"I gotcha. Relax."

But there was no relaxing. What there was, was Jeff Morgan making the five-hour drive in four so that it was early afternoon when he sat on the brushed-steel counter of the lab that adjoined Ben Johnson's office, report in one hand, his bursting head in the other.

"So I did some research," Johnson said and raised an open palm when his cousin looked up in panic. "Didn't talk to anybody, don't worry. But I looked up the file on your bottling plant. Take a look here." He handed Morgan a sheaf of pages, dot-matrix–printed down the center, three-hole punched in the corner.

"Why did you tell me they closed?" Johnson asked. "Back in 2002."

"I never said. But it was security costs after 9/11."

Johnson tapped the sheets Morgan held.

"I think you better read that."

He did, the sinking sensation quickly giving way to nausea.

"Pesticides?"

"Like I said, running out the ying-yang."

"How the fuck did they hide this?"

"Did you ask for the papers?"

"I don't know."

"This is all public record," Johnson said with a shrug. "I had to know where to look, but it's all out there. I guess no one bothered to track it down? Or maybe no one cared?"

Either way, the papers revealed that while the bottling plant did indeed cite security costs as the reason for declaring bankruptcy, they had failed to mention that water tests conducted in December 2001 had revealed the same elevated levels of chlorinated hydrocarbons that were now showing up in Well 2 and likely would have been found in Well 1 had that sample not come from Morgan's kitchen sink.

"I'm guessing once the water tested dirty they went and closed preemptively," Johnson said. "Avoid potential lawsuits, keep regulators out."

"You mean people like you?"

Johnson shrugged.

"They probably tested it in-house. By law, they had to release the result, but since they had already closed, it just slipped into the public record."

"You found it."

Again, Johnson gave a shrug.

"Yeah, but I knew where to look."

"And it's still there," Morgan asked, "in the water?"

"Half-life. It just takes forever for that shit to go away."

"But there's nothing up there. Trees and grass and blue sky. I just don't . . ."

"Read the bottom."

Morgan did.

"An apple orchard," he said.

"I'm guessing they sprayed pretty heavy back in the day," Johnson said. "Pesticides, you know? That stuff seeps, cuz."

"Runoff."

"I'd say you got lucky with the first well. In fact, I'm betting if we tested it again you'd get some elevated number there too. In fact, I'm betting what you supplied was maybe not what you labeled. Were they, Jeff?"

"Jesus."

"Were they?"

Morgan nodded his heavy head. What had been a low thrum behind his eyes was replaced with the buzz of action. What was 25 percent of 27.5 million? He had 6.875 million reasons to do something.

"Can I take these?" he asked, thumbing through the papers.

"Sure," Johnson said. "I just printed them off the internet."

"This report too?"

"Well—"

He went for the two water samples so quick Johnson found himself jumping back. Morgan was hunched forward, papers and bottles clutched to his chest. But even hunched forward, he was a big man.

"Actually, Jeff, the water I can't let you take—"

"I'll be in touch, all right?"

"The samples are kind of state property now."

"I'm sorry," Morgan said. "I'll be in touch."

"Jeff?"

Morgan made it as far as the door before he stopped and walked back over. But something had changed. He stood upright now and his eyes had acquired a clarity that would have frightened Johnson had he not known that—actually, he was flat-out scared.

"Not a word about this, all right?" Morgan said. "These samples never happened. You understand?"

Johnson made his body as still as possible.

"Nod if you understand?"

Johnson made his head nod. If it was slight, it was also all he could manage.

That night, Morgan's phone continued to flash, but, sunk deep into gloom and four glasses of Woodford, he didn't bother to listen to the voicemail. So it was the next morning when he heard Richard Manley sounding particularly tinny and chipper.

"Hey, buddy! I got a contract sitting right here in front of me. I think you're gonna want to give me a call soon as you can."

That afternoon Morgan drove north to visit Kathryn Banks.

It was August when Monty Drudge got a call from Jeff Morgan inviting him to lunch. Drudge had been seeing the waitress/actress he'd met months ago and hadn't heard from Morgan since putting together the water deal, as he had come to think of it. But business is a web or a spiral, or some other tacky tangled thing, so when Jeff called asking Monty to join him and his cousin Ben Johnson he wasn't the least surprised.

They met at the Mountain View Country Club and migrated from the zinc bar with its Edison bulbs and dapper barkeeps to one of the tables that overlooked the fairway.

Morgan appeared sunburned but happy.

"Yeah, old Ben here," he said, and slapped his sheepish cousin on the back, "had a dear aunt pass away—didn't even know her really, did you, Ben? But here she up and left her entire estate to him. Now he's looking for a nice piece of property down here to retire on. Aren't you, Ben?"

Monty found him a twelve-acre estate with a stream, a salt-water pool, and a long view of green mountains. 642K of which he earned 6 percent. He took his waitress/actress to South Beach to celebrate. Around the time RAIN!'s first shipment of water was loaded onto pallets and slipped into the belly of a C-141 Starlifter at Pope Air Force Base, Ben Johnson bought a membership to the country club and a new Kubota tractor. His wife was reading Yelp reviews, searching for a local landscaper, though Ben would have rather done things himself. He thought some manual labor might ease his nerves, now that he'd taken early retirement from the state. Still, he was happy. Periodically, he reminded himself to be happy. There had been some misunderstandings regarding water quality, and periodically he reminded himself he was glad to have sorted them out. Everything was fine. He had the house, the wife, the barn with the gorgeous rafters from which, a year later, he would climb into and, reckoning their construction solid enough, tie off the nylon rope he would use to hang himself. But that was months in the future. That day, he just needed someone who knew his flowers and shrubs.

Meanwhile, Jeff Morgan had dug his passport out of the drawer—the very act dredged up painful memories of Carol—strapped into a jump seat on the plane, put on a pair of noise-canceling headphones and swallowed an Ambien. A few hours later he watched the cargo door ease open onto the searing brightness of the Ouagadougou airport and the silhouette of his old friend and new business partner, Richard Manley.

"Hey, buddy!" Manley called into the hulking interior of the plane. He slapped a pallet of shrink-wrapped water and laughed. "Are you thirsty?"

part four

here i am. lord, send me.

In the end, life takes everything and gives you back clarity.

But what happens when it takes everything all at once?

And what happens when all you can see is absence?

Mara had grown up in a giant home in Blowing Rock where everyone they knew spent their days acting as if they were landed gentry, her parents included. Her father was an eccentric man. Her mother one of those women seemingly born astride a horse, a collector of expensive animals, among which she must have numbered her daughter. Heir to a textile fortune that had long since migrated to Mexico, there was too much money and too little to do. Mara had books and music and horses and everything bucolic, everything proper, everything that feels like enough right up until that moment you realize it isn't, which—I know only now, years after these events transpired—came to pass the year Mara turned sixteen.

Later, she'd tell herself she'd left that time behind her, her mother's death, her father's slow dissipation. Except she hadn't. Two years after her mother died, Mara had made a go at the same university at which she would eventually teach, but it wasn't to be: she'd dropped out before she could flunk out. She spent a last Christmas with her father and over the course of those gray weeks decided to go to New York. Her father paid for the Amtrak ticket to Grand Central Station and by January there she was: Mara heading north, Mara leaving her father, leaving her books and memories and her mother's LPs of Emmylou Harris and Gram Parsons, the Stones and John Prine. Leaving everything.

Her arrival in New York was followed by that first night sleeping on the edge of the Sheep Meadow in Central Park. Sleep, or what passed for sleep. It was more exhaustion than rest, jerking awake at some passing sound, thinking hours, days had passed only to see by the bright dial of her Timex it was a matter of minutes, bunched and stumbling and then, near dawn, hurrying past in a fit of dreams that carried her into morning.

That was New York for her.

She met boys.

She started painting and dancing and shoplifting from the Duane Reade.

She also started going to art parties in Chelsea lofts and brownstones by Morningside Park, this gorgeous naive thing with the southern drawl who would drink a bottle of champagne and fall asleep in someone's guest bed only to wake in the afternoon, the house empty of people but filled with paling sunlight. They let her sleep, let her stay. They were all charmed by her, grateful to have her in their kitchens eating blueberries and reading yesterday's *Times*, borrowing this shirt or that dress. This was the start of her Mazzy Star phase, all demure sexiness and dark eyeliner. She was something unsettled, something not yet decided, and maybe that was what they loved about her: that virgin fluidity, that soon-but-not-quite. It was a magic time, it seemed, even if these did prove in hindsight to be the moments that she began to think of her own mother, of what it meant to disappear with such precision you left behind barely a ripple, just a broken skull and a pair of dirty flats abandoned at the edge of a creek. She stayed "lost" for seven months, though it felt much longer. Whether her father thought her abducted, dead—she no longer answered the occasional letter—she didn't know. Yet she did, actually, she did know: he thought Mara her mother's child. And that was explanation enough.

By fall of 1997 she'd had enough and moved into a dorm on West 14th Street, painting at Parsons, something she thought her dead mother's money might have had a hand in arranging. She bought her supplies at a craft shop in the East Village, bought books on Georgia O'Keeffe, Rothko, Pollock, became fascinated with the photography of Garry Winogrand, the nudes of Edward Weston, the man "as he stood in his world" of Dorothea Lange (exactly as her mother had not—or was that *exactly* what she'd done?). Mara had discovered her gift of making things, of making art. Which is another way of saying she had discovered herself.

She got her degree and came home. A year later we met in that campus basement, and, a few months later still, I took her out to Chris Bright's farm for the first time.

At least that was how I'd always understood it, and it was true—so far as it went. But it was the next day—the day she went alone back to Chris Bright's farm—that matters most. A day about which I knew nothing until I discovered it in the diary the old Kinzer woman handed me. Here is how Mara puts it in her leaning script: *I don't know why I went back the next day to see Chris. I mean of course I know why.*

Had Chris recognized her that first day?

Probably not. I have the sense that had he, it would have taken some of Mara's pleasure out of her return. She doesn't describe it in her diary; we have to imagine it.

"It's nice to see you again," she might have said.

"You too."

"I mean after so many years."

And then the look he must have given her, confusion slowly giving way to something dramatic, something that belongs on a daytime soap, something like: "wait, you're . . . Lana?"

The year Mara turned sixteen was the year she started keeping secrets.

The year she started going to church.

The year her mother died.

It was also the year—the summer, really—she decided to call herself Lana.

No idea why except it was another self. No idea why except she liked the sound of it, so close to her own name, so close to her own life, and yet not. That year she spent the summer in the Blowing Rock house largely alone, her parents traveling, checking in, showing up with groceries, which was unnecessary—there was a woman who brought them every Monday. Or asking about laundry. Also unnecessary—there was someone for that too.

So she was alone in that giant house of stone and glass with its stacked rock and view of the mountains so vast that on a clear day you could see the sun flashing off the Bank of America building ninety miles away in Charlotte. It was a welcome thing, that aloneness. She loved her parents, but they were exhausting, and she was happy for some distance. Her overbearing mother with her three Carolina textile mills shuttered and shipped to Irapuato. Her ineffectual father with his bourbon and books. But they weren't here. Only Mara—Lana, she decided—was here.

How did she spend her days?

Reading in a hammock, I imagine. Listening to her mother's records. Roaming the vast open spaces of those five-thousand square feet. Though the house felt completely isolated, it was a short walk to downtown and I picture her sitting alone on one of the benches, while around her children ran on the expensive playground with its fresh mulch and the tourists came out of restaurants and ice cream shops, every last one of them laughing. All but Mara. It must have been a time of withdrawal for her, a time of collecting herself, an idle time. She had one year of high school left but had long since lost interest in such. What she did take an interest in was the local Baptist church, a fundamentalist outlier in moneyed and mainline Blowing Rock, a relic. She walked past it and walked past it and then one day she walked in and something happened, something opened inside her.

She went every Sunday after that, and while it wasn't yet a secret it felt like it could be, were anyone to ask. The church belonged to an older incarnation, what the mountains had been before the second homes went up and the meat and threes gave way to the antique emporiums and pet boutiques, the shops selling hand-tied trout flies and Orvis waders that cost a week's salary. At the church, it was all fire and brimstone and power in the blood; it was all consequence. At the church, the lovely give of wealth gave way to the certainty of judgment, and that possibility, that surety of the first becoming last, infected her. At least until the Sunday she came out of the church door, flushed and excited, Bible clutched to her chest, to find her mother sitting on the bench out front, a Virginia Slim burning down in her left hand.

She looked up only once, her mother.

"I didn't know you went there," she said.

"Mom, I didn't know you were home."

"We just came in and I went for a walk and I just . . ." She made a little spinning motion with her cigarette. "I wandered in and I saw you and . . ."

She looked tired, her mother. Dressed immaculately, of course. Hair coiffed above a Burberry scarf, gold Tory Burch flats on her feet. Immaculate but very tired. Even behind the giant sunglasses Mara could see how exhausted her mother appeared.

"What did you think?" Mara asked.

"What did I think?" She looked away, as if the answer waited in the middle distance. "Darling, I think it's spiritual terrorism, what they are telling you. I think . . . I think my God is bigger than that."

"Well, I love it," Mara said, because Mara did not.

"Oh, darling."

"I believe it," Mara said, because it wasn't true.

That Chris Bright was doing the same twenty-five miles away is not lost on me. That they wound up attending the same summer mission trip in Florida. That Mara—that Lana—slept with him there in a Daytona Beach hotel. None of this is lost on me.

It must not have been lost on her mother either. Something was written on Mara's face, enough so that when she came in from that mission trip her mother looked at her and knew everything.

"What comes next, Mara?"

What came next was the all-consuming fire, arriving on the fall Tuesday when her mother disappeared, only to reappear, headless and sprawled. The gold Tory Burch flats, her "sensible flats," left on a smooth rock, Mara supposed, as she crossed the creek over to the stand of white pines where, seated against the trunk of one, she put the barrel of her husband's .410 in the soft of her palate.

Mara spent the year after her mother's death doing whatever needed to be done, which was a year too many for she had known everything she needed to know within the first hour of her mother's absence (if there was the lure of the all-consuming flame, there was also the lure of the self-extinguishing). Her mother's long blue-veined hands, the green eyes above a shadow of mouth, the sudden intake of breath, not unlike a fish gasping in the shallows. She knew the hesitations and had known them from the moment memory found purchase: she needed no schooling in grief. Mara was now alone with her father and her mother's albums, the music accompaniment to a life now accompanying exactly nothing. Accompanying, she supposed, her father's steady dissolution, a sight so reliable that in August of the following year she moved the ten miles from Blowing Rock to the university where she shared a suite with three other girls.

She could have commuted from home but she didn't want home. She was excited and barely thought about home, at least at first. But by late September the weather had changed and by October she felt buried beneath an early winter, alone in her room watching movies while her roommates went to frat parties or did Jell-O shots on Hippie Hill. She had been invited at first, but had refused often enough that soon the invitations had stopped and she was treated with a polite diffidence, the overtures of friendship turning to indifference turning to *what's that weird-ass girl's problem?* Her problem was, well . . . she had thought at various points she was simply homesick or lonely or, for the better part of a week, dying of an obscure blood disease. It would be years before she realized it was neither more nor less than simple depression, the blues she could only vaguely recall hanging above her mother like a sky that would not clear.

She generally avoided her father.

When she ran out of Lean Cuisine or Crystal Light, she would call him and he would promise to take her to the grocery store. Eventually, she would catch a ride home to find him passed out in bed, covers to his chin, three o'clock in the afternoon. She would shake him—*wake up! this isn't fair, this isn't how you're supposed to be*—and feed him dry toast and instant coffee because that was the only thing she could find in the cabinets.

Mara would catch another ride back to her dorm if the mood struck her, sleep in her childhood bed if it didn't. By Halloween she was skipping her classes and then failing her classes, not that anyone bothered to tell her and not that she would have cared anyway. On some level she knew, of course, and felt it at worst a sort of passive sabotage. At best, it was a declaration of independence: refusing to let her schooling interfere with her education. She had more or less moved back to the Blowing Rock house by early November and had effectively quit school by Thanksgiving.

It was Thanksgiving that ended it for her. *It* being her experiment of being in the presence of her father as refracted through the absence of her mother. The holiday nothing so much as a festival of grief and shared recrimination, buoyed on a sea of turkey gravy and Maker's Mark. The Wednesday before came a bright thaw so that Thanksgiving Day broke warm and dripping, the sliding glass door beaded and fogged, while inside her father drank his way through the Macy's parade and on into the Detroit Lions' game.

In hindsight, she would remember that Thanksgiving as revelatory.

It had come to her that things were slipping past her, and while she was fine with letting certain things like grades or would-be friendships slide by, the thought that her life was moving with a glacial yet inevitable slowness toward something not unlike her mother's scared the hell out of her. Scared her enough, in fact, to bum a ride to the Ingles in Boone where she bought frozen turkey loaf, potatoes, and a can of cranberry sauce. It was easier than she'd imagined. Can opener. Microwave. Add water and let sit for three minutes. But she wanted it to be more, she wanted it to be *something.* She thought about the meals that had once involved armies of women baking elaborate cakes decorated like brides-to-be while she did nothing more than open a bottle of wine and *stir vigorously.* Refreshed her father's drink—*oh god, he's already through another?*—and set the table with the cloth napkins untouched since her mother's death.

In the end she imagined steam: the food was soft and steamed, the kitchen felt steamed. Everything steamed with the funk of overcooking so that they slumped above their plates like wilting flowers. They fed themselves and just about the time she tucked into the steamed—*I can't even run a damn microwave right!*—green bean casserole, she started making plans to get out.

It started with that.

It ended with Mara and her father on opposite couches, her father glazed with bourbon and meat, Mara's eyes on a AAA road atlas.

"Happy Thanksgiving, Dad."

"What, baby?"

"I said 'happy Thanksgiving.'"

But he was already dozing and she already knew she couldn't do it again. Not ever fucking again, she remembered thinking, in that artificial dramatic flair it had taken months of near homelessness to dispense with.

Christmas came and, alone with her father, she played her mother's *Some Girls* and *Beggars Banquet* over and over until she no longer heard them. Her mother's milk-thick *Grievous Angel*. Memories flooded back, filled her to such an extent she didn't know why she was put on this earth, to live life or to recall it. At times she was aware of her father, alone, of her mother, headless. But more than that, she was aware of Mara, trapped.

She had to go, and she did.

Her father pleaded with her to stay, knowing she wouldn't. Instead of insisting, he bought her a ticket at the Amtrak in Charlotte. She knew he was worth so many millions she couldn't begin to imagine, an inheritance he was simply holding for her. It was hers for the asking. Leaving wasn't necessary. But it was actually. She was going to be a painter. She already knew grief. Now, she told herself, standing there on the Amtrak platform without a hint of self-awareness, it was time to transform that grief into art.

She spent the next eight months living in a squat. This was

the aforementioned time of shoplifting and art parties and "borrowed" champagne. Of weeping in front of a Rothko and having fire hazard sex in a condemned Ports Authority warehouse. Then came school at Parsons, and with it, a new Mara so that when she returned to North Carolina four years later she was a different thing, or so she thought. Twenty-three years old with a BFA in Studio Art, yes. But more than that she was focused, serious. She took a job as a community organizer with Southern Appalachian Patriots—it gave her time to paint, it mattered (maybe)—and then one evening in a stuffy basement she met a journalist from the *Watauga Democrat*, she met me. A few months later I took her out to meet Chris Bright.

The next time she went alone.

How much did she tell Chris that day so many years later when she returned to the farm without me? Maybe nothing. Maybe he figured it out, recognized her. What accommodation they worked out I have no idea. The summer and fall we lived at the farm, Mara and I were barely out of each other's sight, barely out of each other's arms. It seems impossible to me to imagine there was anything between them at the time, or, I should say, impossible to imagine they *acted* on anything at the time. But then, so much I've imagined impossible proved to be not just possible but true.

That Christmas, Christmas of '03, pissed off and fed up, I drove west to try to make a living writing for magazines. We had spent that fall arguing about direct action, about Tugg Wilson's zoo, about *doing something*. The very thing that Mara had been so opposed to having become the thing she wanted most. The change must have started the day she was pepper-sprayed, and I imagine it is too much to compare it to a form of contemporary baptism: the first violence, the first laying on of hands.

Even then I knew the fight about the "zoo" (Mara's air quotes) was a proxy fight, a way to euthanize the relationship we both knew was as good as dead. So we fought. I left and Mara stayed.

Mara decided to do something.

Gray wolves, black bears, a single mountain lion—the zoo was just outside Gatlinburg and, though it had been popular in the '80s, it had fallen into grave disrepair, Tugg Wilson grandfathered in under less humane laws. The animals were mangy and caged, the county indifferent—the idea was a raid. The idea was to set the animals free in the name of justice and mercy and then to flee to the Florida Keys for a few weeks of happy debauchery. But it was always just that: an idea. At least until I left.

How did their accommodation change after that?

Sometime in the weeks after I left, Mara must have moved into the cabin with Chris. They hunkered down. It was a winter of deep snows and maybe it was there—in bed, weighed beneath the quilts, the fire burning in the grate, or, having made love and sweating atop the quilts—that they began to sketch their plan. It must have still seemed unreal at the time. It must have seemed like an impossibility what with the roads buried and schools closed. But the winter went on and they kept talking, the abstract steadily becoming concrete, becoming specific, the bolt cutters, the maps. *If you take Sand Pit Road and turn right here where the asphalt turns to gravel down near the old rock quarry. Look, Chris, there's a Forest Service fire road right up to the back of the property.* It was all idle talk, winter talk. But then it was no longer winter. It was spring and the talk became a single question, the talk became *What are we going to do, Chris?*

Not this, he must have told her.

But he must not have meant it either.

I imagine it must have felt like a referendum on their own

goodness. I know that sounds grandiose, but didn't they feel some guilt? Didn't they feel some remorse? They'd kept secrets, or one big secret at least. Possibly, they had snuck around behind my back. To do something would recategorize things. They were together because they were bent on action. I was gone because I was not. The desire to do good in the world, or at least to fight the bad, having died right out of me, or maybe me out of it.

So what are we going to do, Chris?

What they are doing to do is get a room in Gatlinburg, with its window AC and worn carpet and narrow balcony overlooking the Pigeon River. What they are going to do is tell the desk clerk they are newlyweds. They are going to drink Bacardi on that sliver of balcony, chairs tipped back, feet on the railing while beneath them the clear water runs over a bed of stones. You can hear the traffic but only just, the sounds of fly fishermen upriver barely audible. They get drunk, get in bed. Wake at dusk and eat in the one of the pancake houses where Mara slips a postcard off the rack and into her jeans pocket, a little memento, a little something to carry with her. They had registered as honeymooners after all. Mara must have almost believed it.

Then it is time.

They leave the parking deck just after ten, skirt town, and eventually turn onto Sand Pit Road—exactly as they have planned. The road goes from asphalt to gravel, and just before it ends at the county rock quarry they turn onto the Forest Service fire road Mara had found weeks ago on the map. The road cuts two hundred meters up the back of a mountain before ending abruptly in a stand of pine and the unfinished shell of a new house, all cinder block and mud. It's after eleven by then, and when Chris cuts the engine a startling quiet descends. After a moment, Mara hears the wind swish through the boughs of the firs and white pines higher on the ridge, but even that sound only deepens the silence. There's the smell of sawdust, of raw lumber. Outside the house a dumpster is packed with pink frills of insulation, broken gypsum board, a blue electrical box. From what will be the living room, they can see Tugg Wilson's zoo and for a moment they stand there in this future home of the tasteless, of the vulgar, of the sickeningly rich. They let the night settle. They are ready. They have the heavy bolt cutters. They have the lightest of fogs. It must have been almost magical. It must have been cold.

They put on work gloves and Chris takes two face masks from the truck and hands one to Mara.

"Seriously?" she says.

"Have you done this before?"

"Have you?"

"Just put it on."

Imagine them moving down the slope, gloved, masked, the zoo coming into view. Imagine the quick clicks as Chris cuts a hole in the fencing and they slip through. It looks more like a barnyard. It feels more like a high school prank. When Mara starts to move, Chris puts out a hand to still her. "Not yet," he says, and they crouch there just beyond the cages, waiting. There are no animal sounds, no howling. Just the sound of their pacing, their tired insomnia, their worn nails clicking on the concrete floors beneath the buzz of the halogen security light. It's a large fenced enclosure with a barn, tractor shed, and seven metal cages, each too small for what they hold. A porch light shines by the house but the windows are dark, the night still. A windmill, imagine the windmill turning. Imagine the fog lifting and Chris looking at Mara, both staring into the eyeholes of the other. He nods. They move.

Imagine it is all motion now, scrambling to the first cage where Chris clips not the lock—it's too thick—but the wiring, Mara peeling it back and looking in at the golden eyes of the mountain lion. Stumbling back because, Jesus Christ, what are we doing?

But Chris is already off to the next cage. Seven cages, seven minutes. It takes no more than that. And still Mara is planted there in front of the lioness, maybe five feet of space between them, the animal awake but unmoving. Mara awake but unmoving. Yet something is vibrating. The air is vibrating.

She's still there when she feels someone pulling her sleeve, Chris saying *come on, let's go.* And she does, she goes, remembering to breathe, catching her coat on the fencing but remembering to back up slowly, to take care that nothing tears, that no traces are left. They move up the steep hill grabbing at small trees, pawing at the ground, moving too fast really but how else is there to move? The panting, the oh my god oh my god oh my god. At the top, they pull off their masks, still panting, while below them all is still.

They look for a moment back down the slope, and then laugh and laugh.

They crawl the truck down the fire road with the lights off, leaned forward, Mara taking a pint of Elijah Craig from the glove box, barely able to get the cork out but then she does and they are drinking, passing the bottle, still laughing. They fall into bed, muddy and exhilarated, all tangling limbs and wet mouths. They did it. My god, Chris, we did it. The sliding glass door is open to let in the breeze and the sex, the sex is furious at first, almost dangerous, but then slower, calmer as the night settles around them in all its softness, the blousing curtains, the river in its bed, the barred owls in their trees.

That's how I imagine the night.

Day is something else. Day is Chris sitting on the balcony, a glass of what is left of the rum by the chair leg (there is no more Elijah Craig), the newspaper in his hands. That look on his face.

"What?" Mara asks, and he gives her the paper.

Says nothing, just hands it over, because it's right there above the fold. How the man came out to find all the cages cut open, but the animals, docile, senile maybe, unmoved, sitting in their caged filth. All except the mountain lion. He found the lioness prowling the edge of the fence, green eyed and wandering. She turned on him and he killed her with a 30.06. He had no choice. The photo shows the dead lion. Standing over it, the man weeps.

"We're so stupid," she says, drops the paper and begins to pack what little there is to pack. "We're so goddamn stupid."

That was April.

By May she is in Albuquerque, registering for fall classes in the University of New Mexico's Art and Ecology Master of Fine Arts program. Done with Chris. Done with the past. Immersing herself for the next two and a half years in her work. Tireless. Focused. Immensely talented. And then by chance I see her name in the program for an art show. Graduating master's students and there is Mara. This is the spring of 2006 and I haven't seen her in nearly three years but somehow it's like no time has passed, or maybe a lifetime has passed because the air has cleared, the mood is different.

"David," she says, and we spend the evening together laughing and talking as she leads me around the gallery and then to a bar with her friends in Nob Hill.

It's August when she invites me to Mexico. She's housesitting for a man named Toliver. An entire casa, a compound. "Come on, David. Go with me."

And I do.

Of course I do.

I go with her to Mexico.

I go with her everywhere, right up until the day our son slips from our hands. And then Mara slips from mine.

She must have thought it would save her, repentance, salvation. Or maybe there was simply nowhere left to go. Either way, Mara's memory was the same as mine: a simple whitewashed church along the thread of a gravel road. Imagine she woke up one morning remembering, hoping, and then she realized it was Sunday: that sudden awareness like a new breath—Sunday, the Sabbath. Imagine she got into the aging Sebring her father had given her before her mother died and her father failed.

Imagine she got in and went.

She met the Kinzers on her second Sunday at church when they invited her back to their house for dinner. There were different, outsiders, though they had lived in the mountains for nearly thirty years, and they must have recognized that same displaced searching in Mara, and not just her stranger-in-a-strange-land bewilderment. More so, I think it was the radical openness of her exile that tasted so familiar. They had come individually to the mountains in the '70s as VISTA volunteers, met, married, and spent much of the rest of the next decade in Central America. Born and educated in the northeast—Jersey, Philly—not that it mattered. They were from "off," which was to say anywhere that wasn't here, which meant they could spend a half century terrace farming their hollow and still wouldn't be considered local. Mara must have sensed that. She must have told them everything, Sunday after Sunday, and at some point—around the January day she found my RAIN! file and left me, let's suppose—around that time they must have asked her to stay. The little clapboard room off the back, the one piled with books and a desk and the cot on which she'd read David Reynolds's *John Brown, Abolitionist.*

And where was I during all this?

Drinking in the treehouse, or drinking in the truck, drinking and disbelieving. That summer with Chris at the farm there had been the bourbon and weed and Ziplocked edibles—all of it communal, all of it celebratory. The doors of perception and so forth. But my descent was now private, all brown liquor and grief, nothing to celebrate, no rooms left to unlock. An off-the-rack sadness as plain as it was real. Mara must have said something to me at some point, she must have seen me in the treehouse, rocking unsteadily on the pressure-treated platform our dead son would never again occupy, the camouflage netting a torn flag, the rail dangling by a single ten-penny nail. She must have seen me and decided she would have to go.

She did stay with me through the holidays, through Christmas and the New Year, though there was no Christmas, no New Year, just as there hadn't been since Daniel had died. What made her stay, I don't know. It might have been nothing more than logistics. But I like to think she was tugging at some final thread that bound us, testing its tensile strength to determine if there might be enough to rebind, to repair the damage done. Whatever the case, I came home that winter day to find her on the floor, the pages of my RAIN! research spread before her.

"Why didn't you tell?" she asked.

The next day she was gone.

The next day she was reborn as the Kinzers' child, and like all good parents, they sat with her, listened to her. At night, when she argued out her life, her justifications, her rationalizations, her mistakes and regrets, they said nothing. They simply sat there, so still they appeared as statuary, as something against which she might shatter what was left of her being. They argued about violence, or she did, at least. The world is constructed from the suffering of others and so on, and they must have comforted her, assured her that she wasn't alone in the nightmare of the world. All day she read online at the library about Banks LLC, arriving at the very real possibility that I had, through my blind negligence, poisoned our son just as the boy named Cory was poisoned, just as children were being poisoned all over the Sahel.

It must have seemed fitting.

That was the winter of landslides and shithole countries and Stormy Daniels. The season of troll farms and Robert Mueller indicting Russians. She argued it all. How the world is bricked from indifference, the mortar cruelty. The Kinzers didn't disagree with her, but the point wasn't to agree or disagree. She didn't need affirmation or debate. She needed someone to hear her and at this they were expert. To listen, to genuinely pay attention, then to set about making things right—that was the measure of their days, the pattern out of which the Kinzers had beaten a life. They had been in Nicaragua—pacifists up around Matagalpa—in El Salvador, Honduras, Mexico. They had sat vigil with the dead nuns, the dead Romero, walked by the side of Subcomandante Marcos, all the while hemmed in by assassins trained at the School of the Americas, or pinned down by ordinance made in Ohio or Pennsylvania or at the Rock Island Armory, which came all that way to fall through the canopy and along the dirt roads to shatter cows and children and the old woman who took a single fragment of shrapnel just above her right eye, the slot there four inches deep but appearing as no more than a paper cut.

They weren't naive. They were educated, well-read, well-traveled. Members of the Sanctuary Movement in the Southwest when there had been such a thing. Veterans of marches in Washington and New York and outside the razor-wired gates of Fort Benning. They'd survived Chiapas, Managua, San Salvador. Knew their Merton and Yoder, their Tolstoy and Gandhi. Their Chomsky, their Zinn, their Naomi Klein.

"Let me fix us a fire," John Kinzer would say, or a glass of tea or a bite of this or a taste of that. Putting another record on the Fisher-Price stereo. Dorothy Love Coates or the Reverend James

Cleveland. "Hold on," he'd say, "listen." And then it was Sam Cooke and the Soul Stirrers singing *when I've gone the last mile of the way*...

But the old woman wasn't listening.

The old woman was without compromise.

"Sit down, John," she would tell him.

The old woman sitting resolutely in her rocking chair, hair in a bun, hands in fists. Mara down on the carpet, sunk in the pile like the child she had become.

"I'll be right back."

"Sit down. No one needs a thing except to sit here and listen."

No one needed a thing except Mara. Mara needed everything. Solace, comfort, red wine, and those vitamin B12 melts that tasted of cherry. The surplus cot set up in the back room John had nailed on when the first Bush was in office. Except she really needed none of it, and came to suspect she had held on to such things—her health, her sanity, her iPhone—simply so she could let them go.

As winter greened into spring, that was exactly what she did: she let go. When there was nothing left, she would—well, she didn't know exactly what she would do. But that was okay. What she found herself in, what was happening to her—she told herself it was temporary, a holding pattern. If life is a spiral, to descend in one moment meant one was merely gaining momentum to ascend in the next. To race down implied the inevitable race up.

So she stayed.

She read.

Philosophy, sacred texts, all the things she had missed, and there was so much she had missed. The Upanishads. The Gospels of Thomas and Judas and James. Plato and Hannah Arendt. Kierkegaard. Simone Weil becoming lean as a needle. John Brown severing heads from bodies. Mara sat in something that might have approached meditation, had the vacuum of her thoughts not created a space into which drifted those she had lost—her mother, our son, the boy named Cory. But if it was memory, what did it matter? Memory is a story we tell ourselves. Memory is simply the acknowledgment that the failing candle of our life was once greater, and now it has diminished, and now it has diminished again.

She tried to make sense of it.

We all want our suffering to mean something.

The Principle of Sufficient Reason holds that everything happens for a reason. There is no such thing as simple tragedy: someone, somewhere, is always responsible, if only God, if only the Devil. Mara explained it to me once at home. We were unloading the dishwasher, just the two of us, working quietly, and she asked me if I believed in such.

I didn't know what to say.

I thought probably I didn't.

But I believe Mara did.

She believed in causation.

She believed in culpability.

And, in the end, she must have found herself culpable.

I believe that is what he was doing that night in Virginia.

What she was doing at the public library was calling up public records. She examined the tax filings of Banks Holdings. Searched Jeff Morgan and found his string of interstate Bojangles. Watched Richard Manley break down over and over on his YouTube confessional (13,200 views, 251 thumbs-up, 368 thumbs-down). *I know I've done wrong, but I know the Lord's forgiveness is big enough to wash over me. I know His love is big enough to cleanse. . . .* This repentant, godly man weeping at his kitchen table, the camera tilted at an angle so that you saw the dark hollows of his nostrils when his head pitched back. They were all Christians,

Soldiers in the Army of God, strapped beneath the Breast Plate of Righteousness. That they were possibly poisoning children in the Sahel just as they had poisoned our son, an unfortunate footnote. Because she found that too. She found the contamination reports from December 2001. Aldrin, dieldrin, DDT. Her husband—I, me—had found everything but that, everything but the essential thing.

It wasn't hard to pity me.

She didn't necessarily want to, but it wasn't hard. Born ordinary in the worse sense. A man given to dandruff and sugaring his coffee. A man fascinated with his own reflection, as if aware that he went no deeper. My one skill had been adhesion: I'd clung to her. All of which signaled a certain pragmatism as surely as it singled a lack of imagination, or worse still: a failure of discipline. *He has no plan, no approach.* By which she meant—she had no idea what she meant. But what was it that T. S. Eliot had said about it being not the conviction but how deeply the conviction was held? Not that she was making any sense. Not that she cared. If she was in a holding pattern, if she was spiraling down, it was only because she was coming to understand what was next.

She talked and read and waited, and one day began writing, and one day not long after that started thinking because suddenly what was before her was this *what if,* a little atmosphere of possibility. What if she stopped it? Not: I will stop you from poisoning another child. That reason was certainly there—it was the reason she would use to convince Chris Bright. But it wasn't the reason she used to convince herself. It was more like this opportunity, something that hung out on that border where the life you have thus far lived brushes against the one you might still.

"We were in El Mozote," John Kinzer would say, or, "Out on the Mosquito Coast. You remember, honey?"

And his wife, nodding.

"I remember." Her eyes shut, rocking chair moving so slowly it was almost imperceptible. "I remember the brown people had the land and we had the Bible. Now the brown people have the Bible and we have the land."

"Monsanto has the land."

And his wife, eyes still shut, tsking at her husband.

"What's the difference?"

What's the difference? By which I imagine she meant: everything we did amounted to nothing. But maybe also meant: yet we did it.

In March, two or so months after leaving me, Mara decided she would drive to Florida, retrace the trip we had never made together. The airboats and snorkeling. The milkshakes outside the Robert Is Here fruit stand. She'd rent the same cottage on Marathon she and Daniel had shared, sit on the same porch. Vacation: the great American narcotic as rated and appraised on TripAdvisor. But the truth was, she wanted to see a panther. She had continued to believe a mountain lion prowled the woods around our farm, occasionally descending to steal one of our chickens or, across two ridges, one of Jay's sheep. But it was gone now, and it wasn't just that she no longer thought she saw it at night, out on the edge of the tree line. It was that she no longer felt it. It had left her, or she had left it. Either way, she was alone. By that point, I think she knew what she would eventually do. By that point, she must have felt called forth by God. By that point, she must have been thinking of not only John Brown but the Mississippi John Hurt that had been playing the day the Kinzers gave me her diary.

Here I am, oh Lord, send me.

It was October, five weeks after the bomb went off, when I flew to Chicago to meet Toliver. The Art Institute was holding a retrospective of his work, and we met in the rococo bar of the Palmer House Hotel, all gilt and gold and potted fern, even if outside the day was gray and cold, even if Toliver was gray and cold, all but the pink nose he kept wiping.

"I had heard something," he told me. "I wasn't certain but then I thought, of course it's her."

"So you weren't surprised?"

"Were you?"

"I don't know. We'd lost our son."

He nodded slowly, fingers templed. "I heard that too. I'm sorry."

"I think her grief—"

"But it wasn't her grief."

"I think after Daniel died—"

"It wasn't her grief, David. It wasn't even her anger." He leaned forward. "Listen to me. It was her vision."

He was dressed just as I remembered from Mexico: the scarf and smoked glasses, the beaded silk shirt, something airy about him, just as there had always been, as if he wore not clothes but a single pleated cloud. Only he was older now, the hair receded, the ears gigantic—there was no hiding it. I had read online that his partner had died two years ago. I told him how sorry I was and he nodded in a very perfunctory way. Though we had spent a year living in one of his houses, he was always Mara's friend, Mara's champion, his love for her striking me as that of a protective uncle, a believer in her talent, an enabler of her aspirations.

"Pneumonia," he said, talking about his partner, Elliot.

"I'm sorry."

"I don't know that you ever met him. In San Miguel, I mean."

San Miguel de Allende. Mara had met Toliver at an opening her final year of graduate school, and when he asked if she would be interested in spending the following year as caretaker of his place in Mexico, she said yes without hesitation. The house was in the Linda Vista neighborhood, a great walled compound of yellow stucco and red tanagers nesting in the orange trees. Three stories. Two balconies. A rooftop of mosaic tile and a hot tub that was seldom used because the weather was so warm. The two acres of grounds were immaculate: succulents and the purple blossoms of bougainvillea climbing lattice, fountains scattered around the cobbled walks that snaked through palm trees strung with fairy lights. In one corner sat a raised pavilion. In the other sat Toliver's studio, a bare room of concrete floor and paneled windows so dusty as to be translucent.

Toliver had started life as a figure skater, winning the bronze in free skating, or, rather, losing the gold, at the '76 Olympics in Innsbruck. Afterward he had studied at the École des beaux-arts de Montréal, and by the time Mara had met him he was a fixture in the art world, a respected painter, but also something of a curiosity, the dean of the culture vultures, cutting a wide swath through the wealthy retirees from Los Angeles and Dallas who had bought up the mansions that perched above the Chorro Steps. The dark glasses worn inside and out, the Liberace suits—it was a shame, really, that his persona overtook his talent. He was a gifted painter, but people would always know him first as the skater-cum-bon vivant. He must have known this, and rather than fighting it, rather than becoming bitter, he leaned into it in much the way of Tennessee Williams in Key West. He was successful, he was known, and behind the facade of *ne plus ultra* sophistication and disenchantment, a remarkably generous man, offering Mara use of his house and very nearly convincing her she was doing him a great favor. What that favor was, was never clear. But we lived there for a year amid the Rosenthal dishware and pre-Columbian artifacts, Mara painting, me doing something that almost approached writing. We saw Toliver only twice that year as he whisked through town, once for a gallery show and once for a sunset party he insisted we attend.

We were happy to comply.

It had been almost three years since Mara and I had parted or broken up or whatever it had been there by the creek behind Chris Bright's farm, and all the attendant gravity, the hand-wringing and neediness tied to *action* and *violence* and *politics* had evaporated in the desert air. It was 2007 and it felt like the last year on record.

Allow me to invoke it:

The surge. The drone strikes in Somalia. The dead soldiers in Baghdad and Karbala. So much dying. The champion racehorse Barbaro was dead. Anna Nicole Smith was dead. Kurt Vonnegut was dead. That spring thirty-three would die at Virginia Tech. The economy was crawling to a standstill while the Jolie-Pitts adopted the malnourished of the Third World. Suffering was everywhere and somehow that was a good thing. It made me feel less alone, as if it was communal, this sickness, this peculiar brokenness of being American, as if the entire nation were in palliative care.

And yet . . .

And yet it seemed not to touch Mara at all, and soon enough, as with all things, I followed her into a sort of grand ignorance. Ours became carnal, a return to our earliest state, the bliss we'd found in her Rivers Street apartment, only without the arguing.

In Mexico, we were oblivious.

In Mexico, we ate pozole and flautas served with guacamole and sea salt crushed with a mortar and pestle. We sat on the balcony and drank Toliver's wine, slept in his four-poster bed. We spoke only of necessities, supplies, logistics. It was understood we were involved in matters of intellect and depth—painting, writing—draining matters that left us ready for nothing beyond touch and taste. I felt—hoped, if I ever thought even that abstractly—we

229

could go on like this forever. If Mara didn't think forever, she at least thought we could go on a bit longer.

But there's no such thing as forever, is there? And it was there in Mexico, holding on to whatever it was we had, that Chris Bright crept back into our life.

I knew none of this at the time (how many times will I say such a thing?). How the first time Mara saw him it was purely by chance (though of course it wasn't). How we were at a rooftop party watching the sunset when Chris Bright "emerged" (my word, though I imagine it hers as well) onto the tiled deck to look out over that city of hovels and saints and masonry walls topped with teeth of bared glass. How she watched him, not quite believing, yet also knowing, knowing without the slightest doubt that the man with the thick beard and glasses—how childish, those glasses, thick frame, no prescription—was Chris Bright, the man neither of us had seen in almost four years.

We'd been in San Miguel long enough to have settled in, moving along the cobbled streets past the city buses and beneath the roof dogs. The fireworks and the traffic along the *autopista*. The way the Americans never moved off the sidewalks; the way the locals always did. We made trips out to see the Zapotec ruins, drank margaritas, and saw films at the Pocket Theater. In hindsight, I imagine her as bored, restless with what she hadn't yet identified as unhappiness but would soon enough. And here was Chris.

She watched him, telling herself it couldn't be.

Then something woke in her, and she knew it was. Her work was online. Her bio identified her as an expatriate painter working in Mexico. Toliver had connected her with a local gallery. She realized it wouldn't have been hard for someone to find her, and realizing as much she found herself alone in a corner of widening shade in the Bajio Mountains of Central Mexico. She found her-self both sad and ridiculous but also, for the first time in a long time, excited.

She looked at him again, put down her drink, and left.

When she saw him again, she decided to walk away, just as she had before.

This was exactly what Mara had told herself she wouldn't do. She had planned to approach him, confront him, demand from him an explanation because the only explanation possible was that he had tracked her here. He had followed her.

Yet there he was, and here she went, excusing and extricating herself. Ridiculous, she knew. The sun hadn't even begun to fall and this, after all, was yet another sunset party—what do we do here, she sometimes asked herself, besides watch the sun set while some underpaid boy circulates with a tray of Veuve Clicquot? At least there were the birds, she thought, the murmuration she would watch those nights when there was no party.

But that night there was a party.

Toliver was in town for the week; this was the party he had insisted we attend. The house was just off the *jardin* and the in-tricate sandcastle of the *parrocchia*, a rooftop of rattan and glass that looked out at the mountains and in at the sandals and open-backed dresses. A different life in a beautiful place, he told us, with perhaps a trace of sincerity.

And it was beautiful, she had no trouble acknowledging its beauty.

But that didn't mean she wanted to stay.

She watched Chris lean against the rail, alone, waiting, watch-ing. And instead of a man, she saw memories, regrets, and what else I can't say, only that eventually she saw me. Found me actu-ally, laughing in a cluster of gray heads, these aging industrialists with their second wives. The men all Sunbelt pink. The women all cheekbone and leg, spray-tanned and botoxed into the future.

Lately, she hadn't been painting, and I suppose I should have noticed as much, that gathering restlessness that usually found outlet on the canvas. But she'd worked relentlessly for better than three years and was now, I assumed, in a fallow period, latent, gathering. We'd been in San Miguel several months, and while it would be a cliché to say those months had been freeing or liberating or some other descriptor implying the absence of patriarchy or expectation, they had been. More to the point, Mara had experienced a sort of settling, as if she'd been stirred and every day she felt the grains of self drift back into her center, collecting there until what had gathered was this thing justifiably called Mara. Yet another cliché, I know. Not that she felt capable of doing anything about it. She only knew that in my company, in the company of her future husband, she felt those grains of self to be disturbed. Disrupted in a way she didn't like. It was visual.

But that night, seeing Chris Bright, it was physical. It stirred her, frightened her, she felt the self she had spent the last few years becoming whirl.

She put her drink on the rail—within the ice cube a nopal slice suspended perfectly—and told me she was going, the dry air, her sinuses. I said I would go with her, but no, she didn't want that.

"Please stay. I'll catch a taxi on the street."

"You have the address? It's written down?"

"Memorized."

"And the keys?"

"Right here."

Around us men smiled indulgently.

"I really think," I began.

She stopped me with a hand.

"Please just stay. Enjoy yourself. I'm fine."

The house was modernist in design, walls of slate and glass, falling water. She descended a staircase of black marble, past the potted cacti, past the heavy gate that separated the house from the street. It was only when she had passed into that outer world that Toliver followed her.

"She hadn't seen me," he told me that day in Chicago. "I don't believe she had seen anyone but Chris."

"She'd told you about him?"

"She'd told me everything. Eventually, at least."

Toliver had been inside, standing beneath a Mondrian print, when she hurried down the spiral stairs, oblivious and flustered.

He waited until she was near the *jardin* to catch up to her.

The shops, the motorbikes, the old women.

Everywhere were dogs and all appeared female, all appeared to have recently given birth.

He followed her closely.

"It was clear something had happened," he told me. "Only I didn't know what. If I had seen him, I would've known, but I hadn't. Only Mara, running out, frightened in a way she never was."

"You were worried."

"I loved Mara, too," he said, and removed his dark glasses. "We all did. But worried? No," he said. "You struck me, David, forgive me, but you struck me as intelligent, forthright, and thoroughly uninteresting. I thought . . . I suppose I thought she was bored."

Around the *jardin* were tourists and souvenir stalls, a mariachi band, children kicking a ball. Toliver kept following her. And watching her, he began to wonder if perhaps this was the first time she'd been out alone. There was little in the expat community besides the expectedness of it all, the banality. The women with their iron-gray corkscrew hair and leather sandals lurking around the *biblioteca* with their ethnic griefs and well-intended condescension. The men, all capitalists, all indifferent, shuttling back and forth to corporate parks in Houston or Atlanta, buying sombreros and shot glasses in the airport gift shop. Was he, perhaps, witnessing her first moment of freedom?

Toliver did not speak to her that night, only followed her as she ignored the taxis and walked the two miles home. I imagine her as a sort of fuse burning up Ignacio Allende all the way to where, behind a wall topped with sea-green glass, she quietly exploded.

The house and surrounding walls were yellow. The view from the balcony unobstructed. She sat there shaking, drinking a bottle of Argentinian red, trying to think until the only thought was that the bottle was gone, and she was drunk, if only a little. When I came home, we made love with an urgency I hadn't felt since those years on the farm. I slept happily, deeply. But Mara was restless.

She stood on the balcony in her robe and continued to shake.

That it was dark didn't matter.

That night would soon give way to day—irrelevant.

All that mattered was that she'd now seen Chris Bright twice. She was certain of his identity. It was his intentions that were unclear. Imagine her standing there, vibrating. She'd made trips to Guanajuato to see the murals, to Mexico City to see the museums. To El Charco del Ingenio where she sat in a sweat lodge until she had to be dragged out. She'd grown bored here but suddenly she wasn't.

The next morning I woke to find her staring at me.

"Hey," I said. "You okay?"

Toliver leaned toward me.

"That night," he said.

That night she went alone to watch the murmuration, the birds that swirled in a sort of choreographed cyclone over the dry lake bed. Churning and impenetrable, but then everything shifts, the black wings silver, and what is defined as a cloud becomes individual birds, feathers, eyes. Patches of sky are visible when they become a scatter of themselves and then the sky disappears again as the birds reassemble. The thought had long been that one bird moved and that movement passed through the flock in a split second—it was all reaction, as if, like her, they were pulled by steel wires. But high-speed photography has revealed they are moving independently, only at precisely the same moment. It isn't reaction. It's synchronicity. Which makes it something else.

Chris was here.

It felt like the realest thing she'd ever known, standing in that dark cloud as the birds came down. There were people up on the cliffs among the cacti and along the washed-out trails, but she stood alone on the lake bed, out by the reeds where the Bronze-headed cowbirds that had arrived in a long train would drop in a sudden flush. Chris was here. She was going to see him. The reeds shook with the weight of ten thousand silhouettes, the cawing, the last thump of wings. What the hell was she doing, going to see him?

I tell you again: I knew nothing of it at the time, living, as I was, in a sort of sated ignorance. What I know now is what Mara told Toliver months later at a café called La Serena Gorda, drinking sangria and hating herself. *I shouldn't be drinking like this.* She'd been to a doctor that morning who had confirmed her suspicions: she was pregnant. She told herself she would terminate the pregnancy immediately but knew she wouldn't. Whether she had agreed to meet Toliver out of desperation or guilt, he wasn't certain.

He did know that she was lonely.

And while I am convinced Toliver told me any number of lies that day in Chicago, on the question of her loneliness I believe him completely.

"The better part of my life has been a study in loneliness," he told me, reclined on couch cushions and staring at a Venetian palace of commodities traders and Lincoln Park wives.

"To recognize it sitting across from me wasn't difficult. I suggested we walk—it was a glorious day—but she preferred, needed, I believe, the darkness of the café. I didn't argue. I admit freely I was somewhat amused by it, the drama, the operatic quality that felt so earnest and naive. Yet lived in, absolutely lived in." By the time she had finished her story, she had moved on from sangria to the first of what would be several margaritas. I shouldn't be drinking like this, she kept saying. My god, what am I doing, drinking like this? "Then she asked me about sadness. I remember this with great clarity. Sadness, David. Are you aware of the way in which sadness manifests itself physically? Syrian refugees going catatonic. Japanese teens unable to leave their parents' basements. It didn't seem totally real to me, what she had told me. I thought she would outgrow it, live past it."

"You mean live past me."

"How childish it would be, David." And he gave me a look that must have been similar to what he offered Mara that day: open, yet with a recognizable sternness. "How childish it would be if that bothered you, here so late in the day."

I looked away from him until I felt a little more stable. "What did you say to her?" I asked finally.

"I didn't say anything."

He listened to her.

He knew better than to speak.

In time, she began to talk about Chris Bright, exactly as he had known she would.

It hadn't been hard to find him. She asked around, and a few days after watching the murmuration found him in a house on Alameda, ten rooms of mahogany flooring and natural light that belonged to an American woman who was Chris didn't know where—LA? New York? There were no theatrics, no yelling, no accusations. She knocked on the door. She asked what he was doing there. He was here because he felt the need to disappear for a while. Seeing her was pure chance. She didn't believe him, of course, it was ridiculous—*chance*? Jesus, Chris—but she didn't argue with him either. What she did was start spending her days with him, leaving in the morning and walking the cobbled streets until eventually, as if by accident, Mara found herself coming inside. Talking, drinking, touching. Naps in the absent woman's bed. A shower in the vast master bath. That's where she was maybe three weeks after finding him, in the shower, the smell of Aveda— one of her mother's smells—so thick, the water so warm that she was nearly asleep on her feet. That's where she was when Chris stepped into the walk-in shower with a video camera held in front of him.

She rinsed the soap from her eyes, turned—Chris. What are . . . are you filming?

"God. Turn that off."

"Smile."

"Turn that off. Where did you get that?"

She reached for the towel.

"You don't need that," he said. "Just step out."

"I'm wet."

"Just step out."

"Turn it off, Chris."

"Step out of the shower, Mara. I'm serious."

She did then, no idea why, but she did, moving steadily forward, braids of water falling from the gleam of her naked body, conscious of Chris as he backpedaled, smiling, eyes fixed on the display screen.

"Look at this," he said and flipped the screen, swiveled it so that she saw her full length, miniaturized and inverted. The gloss of the water beneath the bathroom light made her appear phosphorescent.

"Walk this way," he said. "Just follow me."

He backpedaled out of the bathroom and down the long hall, Mara following, trained in the pinprick lens of the camera, aware of the wet footprints flashing and lifting, dissolving off the floor behind her. She didn't know what to do with her hands. The instinct was to cover herself, the instinct was to look away from the black aperture that held a crescent of reflected light.

"Act natural," he said. "You look beautiful."

"I feel gross."

"You look amazing. How could you feel gross coming out of the shower like this? Everything about you is alive."

The long hall led past a series of windows, the park, the churches, the cisterns scattered and stacked on buildings like antique toys. It was peripheral—she kept her eyes forward.

"Beautiful," he kept saying. "You want to be an artist, but what you are is art itself. This is amazing."

The hall led to what she had learned to call the media room: three rows of stadium seating down to a plush couch that sat in front of a flat screen. She saw now that the couch was covered with a white sheet. Chris's doing. Another camera, this one much larger, sat on a tripod, angled down from the second row.

"Lie down on the couch," he said.

"I'm cold."

That was true. But what he said about her being alive—that was also true. The water lay over her in tracks, silver ropes visible only when she moved, a web of convergence that would separate, run free, meet again. Pool. But there was no pooling left now. The water appeared part of her, as delicate as lace, but somehow absorbed, as if her skin carried both memory and scar. She sat on the couch because there appeared nowhere else to sit.

"Wait," he said, "one moment."

He popped out the mini-cassette and what had appeared as tiny on the camera display—her shrunken inverted shape, caught as if in the bowl of a spoon—was suddenly realized on the giant flat screen. The image was nearly as large as she. She thought it someone else.

"It'll play on a loop," he said, and began to take off his clothes.

For the next week, Chris lay in bed and watched the video of their lovemaking. Mara refused to watch it and then, one afternoon when he was out, finally did. In the background was the large screen, her naked self, dripping up the hall, moving as if through water or a dream of such, so slow and measured her arrival. It was not her, but someone who had only just surfaced in this world, someone so new the contours of her shape were not yet familiar.

This is my hand.

Yes, this is my hand, *here*.

This is my face, *there*.

In the foreground, between the camera and the screen, they made love, and this was her, this messy panting self she recognized as the girl walking alone through downtown Blowing Rock, the girl by the pool in Daytona Beach, the girl trying to stay awake all the way north in the coach car of an Amtrak train. The girl staring into the eyes of the caged lioness. When he faced her, when he came around unclothed—that's how she thought of it *unclothed*; never naked—and she could no longer pretend she didn't understand his intentions she had willed herself to be uncomfortable, itchy and restless. But it had not taken. In truth, the presence of the camera, the presence of that other gliding body, had allowed her to lose herself. It was a physical thing that became psychic, squeezing every muscle so tight there was nothing left but contraction, and then that point where the universe threatened to implode, where everything she had ever known or would ever know risked folding in on itself. Instead of panic or fear, there was release and she burst outward, scattered into the panting, the fold of her legs around his back, the sound of the casters as the couch skated its way along the floorboards.

Chris directed her with a clear, cruel eye. That rumored sliver of ice buried in his heart, exactly as Kafka had promised. She didn't care. It felt addictive in a way no drug had ever been. There was enough video equipment to project around them scene after scene so that the tapes took on a texture that both called up the past and made necessary the need to move beyond it. If there was abandonment—and there was—she felt it bound her to a higher calling: the necessity of depravity. They were saying something important, the tapes a document of transcendence. Not sex but performance art, her first performance.

Those days she came back to me in the early evenings exhausted, slept twelve hours, woke happy. We were still so young then, young enough for Mara not to bother attempting to deceive me; young enough for me to be blind to it all. She simply came and went as she pleased. Not that I needed deceiving. I was both delighted by her sudden happiness and lost in my own private world, the nature of which I was coming to understand as literary ambition proscribed by the absence of literary talent. I spent a lot of time feeling sorry for myself in a particularly affected way, drinking shots of espresso and cans of Victoria in cafés, seeking out obscure mescals and reading in a slant of sun by the potted succulents at the biblioteca. Disappointed, but no less happy for it. Scribbling *Notes on High Water* in a Moleskine. Meanwhile, Mara came and went, sometimes singing the Stones or Gram Parsons yet always catching herself because that was a part of her past Mara couldn't yet enter into.

I sat there in the banquette as Toliver told me all of this, absorbing it like radiation which is to say feeling not a thing, but knowing nonetheless that damage was being done.

"This would have been around the time you two started making trips together," I told him.

"What trips?"

"To Mexico City, Oaxaca."

He shook his gray head.

"Oh, David. We never made any trips together."

"I thought—"

"They were together."

"I see."

"All the time."

When he reached into his coat, I half expected him to pull out a gun, as silly as that sounds. I'm not sure it would have been an unwelcome thing. Instead, it was a small mini-cassette, the sort of thing that had existed between VHS and digital. She had left it in his house, tucked on a shelf behind the china. Kept the baby, left the tape.

"You don't want this," he said, but immediately I did.

"Give it to me."

"You don't want it, David," he said, and put it in my hand.

The road south from San Miguel de Allende is ribbed with speed bumps as it travels through patchy hills, as slow and winding as it is frustrating. But I doubt they were frustrated. They must have been laughing. What day exactly Mara and Chris left together on that last trip I can no longer recall. It was May, I do remember that much. She had told me she was meeting Toliver in Mexico City to see an exhibit at the Palacio de Bellas Artes and I, of course, believed her. She was always going somewhere to meet Toliver. *We never made any trips together.* She would stay over for three, maybe four days. *They were together.* Did I want her to bring me anything? Only yourself, I said, and kissed her nose. That's not an expression: I actually kissed her nose, standing there outside the car rental on Calle San Antonio. I don't remember watching her drive away but I suppose I must have. That night I met friends at Tacos Don Felix and drank excessively there among the caged birds, the African grays and cockatoos. I remember crawling into bed late, the windows open to the fireworks and roof dogs, but none of it audible beneath the roar of the fans. I remember the white noise of the fans. I remember feeling content.

Mara, of course, didn't go to Mexico City.

By the time I was walking back to our house, she was with Chris in a hotel room in a tourist town called Bernal. The pueblo is built at the foot of a giant rock, a porphyritic monolith known as Peña de Bernal that many believe emanates a healing energy. Mara must have felt it. She must have been drawn to it. Imagine them walking hand in hand through the streets, the Land Rovers and kiosks selling turquoise jewelry, the Chileans, the Colombians, the Germans, the families with crying children, strollers trapped in the deep grooves of the cobbles, the beautiful couples up from Mexico City, straight off the set of a *telenova* and sending the whole thing out over Instagram.

They ate on the patio of a café with a view back toward the rock, its sheer faces bathed in the soft whites of moonlight— wine, candles, all the trappings—then went back to their room.

Did they think of that night in Gatlinburg when they had set free the animals? Was there some sense of distance traveled, not just geographically but emotionally? Did they think of it the next day when, high in the Sierra Gorda mountains, they saw the images of the black panther that had just been photographed on a game camera? Did Mara see something in the animal's eyes?

They had left Bernal to drive into the mountains of yucca and sycamore, everything windblown, everything bent and scattered along the edge of the narrow roads with their ridiculous switchbacks, the trucks and buses roaring down, the smell of their burning brakes, not a guardrail in sight. Mara had heard of a place called Puente de Dios, the Bridge of God, and somewhere in the mountains they turned onto a dirt road down into the green valley.

"This can't possibly be it."

But of course it was.

A clear blue river rushing down the mountain to thread the jungle floor—it was jungle here, the valley as lush as the high desert had been dry. By the river sat a gravel parking lot with signs for guides. I would go there the week after meeting Toliver, when it became evident my life could not move forward unless it first moved back. Renting a car in Mexico City and driving the same roads, I eventually walked those same wooden planks made slippery with algae and moss, the river beside me, ahead of me a veil of waterfall I moved beneath to enter what I can only describe as a chamber of smaller waterfalls. I angled past them and emerged to find the bluest hole imaginable. Around it high green jungle and a wash of falling water so fine it appeared to hang in place. Families were swimming. Couples taking photographs. It was clear this was an enchanted place, but its magic wasn't mine. I was excluded, and I knew it.

"Do you want to go on?" my guide asked.

I did not.

It was back in the parking lot that I saw the photographs of the black panther. The images were printed, laminated, and tacked to a wooden board. Though washed out by the sun, I could still see the sleek body, the luminous eyes. The first photos were taken from a game camera. The last few were after, and when I saw the panther had been captured and killed I felt physically sick. Still, I made it almost back to the mountain highway before I had to hang open my door and vomit.

When I got back to the road, I turned left for Jalpan de Serra. Just as they had.

I could only guess at the hotel, but it must have been the Casa Cielo, the House of Heaven.

It was a rundown town with a beautiful, filthy square cobbled out around a Franciscan mission and the Casa Cielo looked out over it all, the dogs and old women, the men selling cut flowers and baggies of corn chips. The hotel offered a simple, elegant room of stucco and tile and a balcony of wrought iron.

Toliver had told me everything he knew. I thanked him for his time, and though he stood reluctantly, I could tell he was relieved to be finished with me. We wouldn't be seeing each other again and shook hands by the door.

"This cassette?" I asked him. "It shows?"

"I'm sorry," he told me and got into a cab.

I found a viewing room at the Harold Washington Library, signed into the ledger as a guest, and took a seat at a wooden carrel, the screen in front of me not much larger than my hand. There were headphones, but I didn't bother with them. My vision tingled with the sort of black lights boxers talk about. I fumbled with the mini-cassette. There was the sense that I had to hurry, the sense that I might pass out. All the way over I had asked myself why hadn't she destroyed it instead of leaving it at Toliver's casa where he would eventually find it? There was only one possible answer: she couldn't.

"It must have been there in Jalpan," Toliver had told me back in the Palmer House bar, "that she realized she was pregnant."

Days later Mara had told him the rest back in San Miguel de Allende, back from the doctor, drinking sangria and then margaritas at La Serena Gorda. *My god, what am I doing, drinking like this?* How back in Jalpan she was suddenly overcome with something, guilt, shame, fear—who could say?—only that she had to get out of that hotel room.

She must have pulled on her dress, her sandals. She must have made an excuse. Another bottle of wine, another something. Chris must have tried to convince her to stay: *it's so late, if we need something, let me get it.* She would have made promises. *Soon. I'll be right back. No, no. You just wait here.* He must have done so reluctantly. In the bathroom she stuffed her passport and several dollars and pesos into her purse. She had a small bag of clothes and toiletries but left them. She had to get out and she did, pausing in the lobby only long enough to take the postcard I would find years later on the bed in the back room of the Kinzers.

By then, night was creeping toward morning. Imagine 2, 3 a.m., and here she is standing outside the Casa Cielo, looking up at the lighted window that glows softly behind the iron filigree of the balcony. She's going, but doesn't know where, just starts walking, heading up the cobbled street past the signs reading MI MERCADO and CAJAS AUTOMATICAS.

Nothing open.

Dogs in the street.

She turns a corner and there are a few people, old men, she

thinks, lurking around a doorway. She feels suddenly vulnerable, as if she's walking to some other fate, as if she's chosen something irrevocable without ever actually choosing, and then realizes that feeling is recognition of another life, the one growing inside her. She turns, turns again, walks until she is beneath the overpass of the freeway, trucks blasting by, banging over the speedbumps.

Up the steps then, across the caged pedestrian walkway, the graffiti, the chain-link peeled back in long curls. Farther down the street a man is working through the cool of the night, shoveling sand through an open window. She moves between the pools of streetlight. She feels, perhaps, like her mother must have felt, walking that day away from the house, the shotgun in her hands, leaving those gold Tory Burch flats positioned perfectly on a rock, a little arrow that everyone will fail to follow. Everyone but her daughter.

She thinks of her time in New York, conjuring her Hope Sandoval/Mazzy Star vibe: the pouty insouciance and gauzy dress, the world as too much. That night falling asleep in the apartment down on Avenue A. That morning walking across the Brooklyn Bridge alone at daybreak—my god.

But it had all been affectation; now it was real.

Now it was—

She keeps walking.

She's going downhill now. FARMACIA. A face stenciled on the wall, the words EL SILENCIO MATA sealing its mouth. A boy begins to tail her, what does she want? *What you want, lady? Taxi? Drink? I get you anything.* But she doesn't want anything. She wants to go home, but where is home? Home is not here. That much she knows.

Ahead is the glow of the square and she heads toward it. Above her roof dogs barking, laundry strung and sagging. The concept of day seems theoretical, but already the sky is lightening, black giving way to some intimation of blue. Lights ahead, noise. A wedding procession, she realizes, revelers headed back to their hotel after the night's celebration. Papier-mâché bride and groom, a goddamn accordion. They are singing, jubilant, and passing and gone. Now there are two boys beside her, now three. She starts to jog. Where is she going? She is going toward a new life, the one she already has. She is coming back to me. There is no other way, really. That's what she tells herself. They have taken everything else from her. What is left is within her. What is left is this child.

She will live only for him now—already she knew it was *him*. Her child, she keeps repeating, *my* child. Everything else has been taken. Everything else—this false life with Chris and whatever it might have yielded—everything else is finished. She will become a different woman. Arrange a life with rugs and curtains and good wine. Not expensive wine, simply good. It's one of those things you can give yourself if you allow it: her days like the cabin of a small boat: everything in its place. You can measure this sort of life. Put passion in an anteroom, lock desire inside with only itself to blame. You could thin the thing out until you saw through it, whatever the thing was.

The lights ahead appear no closer. The boys around her jabber, what does she want, what does the lady want? Above her a girl of no more than three stands by a roof's edge as if capable of flight.

She keeps moving.

She can do this. She will do this. Wear this grace like perfume. And it is grace, it has to be. She will marry me and we will have a son, and whether he is my son or not he will be *my son*. We'll go home, buy a house, take him to Florida to see the manatees, to Tanglewood to hear Shostakovich, and all of this will happen, all of this will become true. The smell of fabric softener in the bed sheets, the way the earth thaws in spring. Putting up the chow-chow and the canning, the bulbs of black garlic and tins of sardines—our pantry barely able to contain it all, our *life* barely able to contain it all. For seven years it will be this bourgeois dream of vacations and ski trips and art projects in the barn. We'll plan trips to London and New York and on the radio they'll be discussing the weather and then the markets, the Nasdaq, the Nikkei, sober voices relating news of stocks and commodity prices. All the while our son will sit with his contented eyes an inch from the window. Yes, yes—she would arrange this, she could. This simulacrum of the everyday. And it will matter. Do you believe me when I tell you all of this means something? Seven years in the middle of a life *is* a life. Do you believe me when I say that it was mine to witness, mine to have and to hold right up until the moment it was taken from us?

Life was clever, but Mara was clever, too. She could have it. She *would* have it precisely because this old life, the one receding behind her as she ran toward the bus station and away from Chris, that life was over. She kept repeating it until it became a mantra. It was over. It was over.

She needs to go home.

She needs to go home because she can't help thinking that her life isn't so much lost as waiting for her, her new life, the one she is coming back to.

The boys around her no longer speak, simply keep pace beside her, a half-dozen vagrants, barefoot, unwashed, smiling. One of them wiggles a loose tooth.

Around her a maze of stair-stepped brick buildings, black water tanks atop each.

Dogs barking.

Birds singing.

An antenna on a distant hill.

A blue neon cross on a church

The mountains are all haze.

When she finds the bus station, she gets on what proves to be the local rather than the *directo* back to San Miguel. A thousand stops, constant stops, men and women getting on and off to package cut flowers and work sewing machines and mow the lawns and change the babies of the rich. It's morning, actual morning, when she arrives in San Miguel, exhausted, the money still in her purse. Her eyes are dry. Her eyes throb, her whole body throbs, so much so that when she sees the jacaranda tree outside the bus station shedding its leaves, Mara can do nothing more than collapse into the purple carpet beneath it. And there she remains, alone beneath the tree of knowledge.

Three days later she will tell all of this to Toliver.

Two days after that we will leave for North Carolina.

Chris stays behind in Mexico, working at a healing center. Chris knows nothing. But then he must know something. He comes home a year later, just after my son—or is it his son?—is born.

So maybe it's me who knows nothing, maybe it's Mara.

Either way, years pass—this thing otherwise known as *our life*—and it's January 2016. She and Daniel are nearing the end of their project, the plastic birds nearly gathered in the murmuration that is the Tree of Heaven, the bottles of RAIN! water—my contribution—long since drunk. In three days Daniel will turn seven. In February, he and Mara will go to Miami for a gallery opening. In May we will all drive south to vacation in Florida like normal Americans, at least that's the plan. Daniel has been in the midst of a sickly winter, but she can sense the end of such: the warm weather, the clear sinuses.

As for Mara, she will be in a place without nightmares.

As for me, at least that January night, I'm in a Motel 6 outside Lynchburg, Virginia, reporting on a proposed pipeline that, if approved, will come south from the Marcellus Shale to cross the Appalachian Trail. There are protests and counterprotests, rallies in Richmond, tree sitters who refuse to come down so that the state police have taken up position, though whether to protect the sitters or remove them is unclear. "It's going to the courts," a local organizer tells me, "nothing's changing any time soon." I have two thousand words, but my editor, Bill Baker, says to stay with it. I call Mara: one more day, I tell her, and she's all understanding, all, "Yeah, of course, just be sure you're here for Daniel's birthday." Of course, of course. I wouldn't miss it. She sounds dreamy and sweet and I hang up and drive back out to John's Hollow where a giant banner that reads WATER IS LIFE * WE WONT BACK DOWN has been strung between the winter trees.

At home, Mara opens a bottle of red, fills her insulated cup, and—dreamy and sweet—puts Daniel in his booster seat and starts east. The drive into town is the long stretch of Highway 321 that parallels first the Watauga River and then, above the confluence, Laurel Creek. The road bends into 421 by the roller rink, an aluminum hangar of hairspray and middle-aged men in rollerblades and white jeans swishing by clouds of preteens with their braces and bubble gum. Beyond the rink is the long climb to Boone, a steady incline past the QT and Randy's Alternator & Starter Shop, past the Dollar General where years later I will stand with Lucille Duncan. *I figured those old Mennonites had set something in her head*, she will say. There is Vilas Antiques where years prior Chris had bought Cabbage Jones's mountain lion. As the road declines, there are clusters of apartment complexes where students gather in distracted knots and wait for the AppalCART to drop them off outside classroom buildings.

Mara made the drive twice a week to teach her classes in the Art Department, but that night it appeared differently, not so much newer as softer, the hard edges round, the sharp air warm. Maybe it was the wine, maybe it was Daniel's birthday or their approaching trip. Their nearly completed project must have given the sense of a milestone, the sense of contentment. But something had made her want to get out—something we did rarely—and once she was out, stay. She was happy, calm, a sleepy contentment that went well with the early sunset, the snow brushed from the road and sidewalks into the gutters or piled beneath light poles.

"Are you hungry?" she asked.

Daniel was in the backseat, fingering a smiley face on the window.

"What, mama?"

"Hungry, baby?"

"A little."

A little, not a lot. So she decided to drive just a bit longer, through the university and down the strip of fast food and big box stores, the Boone Mall, the banks and grocery stores. At the edge of town the road inclined again, rising steadily toward the higher elevations of Blowing Rock.

It wasn't a place Mara thought of very often. It certainly wasn't a place she returned to. After her mother died and Mara left, her father had put the house up for sale. She was at Parsons then, staring at Rothkos and playing at being an art student, playing—in that way that is embarrassing if absolutely necessary—at life. When a lawyer informed her that $651,000 had been deposited into her account, she walked around for two days wondering what she should do, then realized she could simply do nothing. Her father was in Florida now, desiccating in the easy chair of a glass-paned study, his face lined with the ruined dignity of the well-read alcoholic, a Haitian woman stopping in every afternoon to clean—though there was nothing to clean—and cook—though he had long since lost interest in eating. So far as she knew, the house belonged to a retired real-estate agent and his orthopedic surgeon wife. Mara looked at Daniel in the backseat, no less distracted, no less happy, and decided she wanted to see it.

"Little detour for a second here, honey," she said.

He appeared not to have heard her.

She made the right by the Chetola Resort.

Mara must have believed that what you feel about your hometown is the surest articulation of how you feel about yourself. For my part, I believe that if you grow up in a small town in the South, if you grow up in a small town in America, if you grow up, perhaps, in a small town anywhere, you know what it is to hate not so much the thing you love as the thing you need. Your hometown is what you circle without ever quite landing. Yet Blowing Rock had attached itself to Mara's heart as much as to her memory. It was the place where things happened, where things changed. Blowing Rock before it became a ridgeline of second homes and ice cream shoppes, of wine cellars and B&Bs with their farm-to-table restaurants, everything sourced, everything local. Back then, the way Mara remembered it, Blowing Rock was simply a place. You worked there, went to church there, put up the Christmas tree, and bought the Easter dress. The high school, the municipal pool. The furniture factory on Aho Road where the wood dust was pulled from the air by giant fans, at least what hadn't already settled into your hair, your pores, your lungs.

None of this was true, of course.

Mara's parents were among the first wave of the rich to swoop down and buy up lots that overlooked the vast expanse of Pisgah National Forest or old farms fractured into communities gated and named like English hunting lodges. Already, the locals were being pushed deeper into the mountains or down toward Hickory and Lenoir, driving away with their buyout checks and resentment, maybe using some of it for cosmetic dentistry, some more for an above-ground pool, giving up Marlboros and anger for Nicorette and resignation. Which meant Mara grew up, at least to the extent she imagined it, remembered it, lied—but only to herself—about it, in a gauzy veil of wealth and Frasier Firs. Reading books in the hammock, walking barefoot to the city park. She didn't believe in the romance anymore, except when she wanted to, and that night she did.

She crossed New Year's Creek and made the left onto Wonderland Trail, the houses giant, shrouded in thickets and very nearly hidden, though now and then through a gap in the trees she could see the sky open above a sea of green, patched with a downy snow that seemed to float in the boughs of the countless trees.

The old house was more or less like she remembered it: stone and glass, a Christmas wreath still tacked to the red front door. She slowed, started to point it out to Daniel, but thought better of it. The complexity, the questions. She accelerated, but slowed again to make the left toward the Baptist church she'd attended that single summer. Sixteen years old and listening to her mother's Gram Parsons and Van Morrison, her mother's Stones. Her mother sitting outside the church with her cigarettes and judgment.

"Hungry," Daniel said from the backseat, and her eyes popped up to find him in the rearview.

"What would you like?"

"Food."

"Just food, huh?"

"Yeah." He laughed at his own cleverness. "Just food."

They drove to the Blowing Rock Brewery and sat at one of the high-tops, basketball on the TVs, the bar lively. In the corner sat a circle of well-dressed women holding what appeared to be a baby shower. Daniel wanted a cheeseburger. Mara ordered a kale caesar and a glass of Chardonnay.

"Want to text Dad?" she asked.

"Can I take a picture?"

"Sure."

He took the picture and sat absorbed by the phone while Mara ordered another glass. Their food came out and she thought back to that last summer, back to her mother's line—*my God is bigger than that*—to the excitement of being alone in that big house, the bluster of that trip to Daytona Beach they described as "mission work," to how she'd felt she'd gotten away with it, whatever *it* was, right up until the moment her mother died and the world assumed a different shape, something unknown, but not exactly unrecognizable. Something the shape of broken.

Sleeping with Chris.

Her mother's death.

Wasn't it all of a piece? That year had changed her, warped her in a sense, but it had also made her, and sitting there, watching her son run the last of his fries through the ketchup, happy and sleepy and by all measures moderately successful, she was glad not for her mother's death—she would never be glad about that—but glad she had survived it, glad she had survived all of it, survived and emerged so that she sat smiling dreamily over her third glass, her son beside her, while a woman came over to stand expectantly by the table.

"Hi, hello, I'm sorry to interrupt."

It was one of the women from the baby shower, *the* woman, Mara supposed, pretty and tall and very pregnant, the front of her red dress ballooning perfectly.

"You're Mara Wood, right?" the woman said.

"Yes, hi."

"Hi," she said. "I'm sorry to interrupt. I don't think we've actually met but I know your work, your art, I mean. I love it."

"Oh, thank you."

"I knew your husband too, a long time ago."

"Oh."

"We dated, actually. This is like light years ago. My name's Brandy." She extended her hand, small-boned, and, Mara noticed, almost shaking. "This is your son."

"It is," Mara said. "This is Daniel. It's his birthday."

"Almost," Daniel said.

"Well, happy almost birthday, Daniel," the woman said. "Let me guess. Eight?"

"Seven."

"Seven, wow."

"And you?" Mara asked

"Ah, yes" she said, and gently touched her stomach. "My second. Due like yesterday it feels like. A little boy like you, Daniel. My daughter's three."

"Well, congratulations," Mara said.

"Thank you," the woman said, "and, again, sorry to have interrupted. I just saw you, saw your boy and thought . . ."

"Sure."

"He looks just like Chris."

"I'm sorry?"

"I see you in him, too, of course," she said. "But those eyes. I can so see Chris."

"Oh, actually," Mara said, "I'm not married to Chris."

"Who's Chris?" Daniel asked.

"Chris Bright?" the woman said. "I thought . . ."

"No."

"You're not . . ."

"No."

"Oh, god. I'm so sorry."

"It's okay."

"I just saw and thought . . ."

"It's fine. I'm just not . . ."

"I am so . . ." The woman raised one hand and backed away. "I'm so sorry to have bothered you."

"I'm glad to meet you."

She nodded, began to speak but only smiled instead.

They were in the car when Daniel asked again.

"Who's Chris Bright?"

When you love someone, you want to know not just their significant days and moments but the everydayness of their lives. Where they have slept, laughed, traveled—the larger moments out of which we construct the narrative of a life. But also the way they enter a room or touch their hair or hide their mouth when they laugh: the smaller gestures out of which we construct a self. You want to know all of it not out of jealousy or possession but out of love. Ridiculous as that sounds, sentimental as it sounds. I've always thought that to be the true measure of a relationship: how you might forget it, you might let it slip for days, months, possibly years, but then it rushes back, the need, the awareness returning with such force its absence feels an absolute impossibility. You've always felt this way. You always will.

Mara had thought very little of Chris in the years since she'd abandoned him at a small hotel in the Sierra Gorda mountains of Mexico, but all at once, sitting in the car in the brewery parking lot, Daniel strapped in behind her, this must have seemed as positively unbearable as it did unbelievable. This must have seemed, at least in that moment, like the biggest mistake of her life.

She started the car.

"Want to ride around a little bit, honey?"

"Okay."

She dropped the car into reverse.

"Happy birthday."

"Not till Tuesday," he said.

"Happy early birthday then. I love you."

"I love you too."

She must have texted me from that parking lot.

Just checking in. love you

As for me, I was hunched over my laptop and sent a quick response—all good, love yall—and went back to work. I assume she texted me from the parking lot because there would have been no cell signal out at Chris Bright's farm, and that was where she went next.

The night was wildly dark.

I would sometimes forget about the darkness and then find myself on some narrow road and it would come back to me, the absolute absence of any light beyond the cones of my headlights. Mara drove slow, scanning the shoulders for deer. It wasn't late but the food from the brewery and the warmth from the heaters had put Daniel to sleep. She took her time. What must she have been thinking? That long-ago summer on the farm when we climbed the water tower near the Greenway with its giant American flag, prized open the hatch, and floated in the echoing metallic cool, something Chris said he'd first done with his teammate Bruce. Did she think of that? Or the time we picked wild blueberries on Roan Mountain in the pouring rain? Maybe she worried being found out for her double life, for the second heart she kept tucked behind her first, neither less real than the other. Or maybe she didn't worry at all. Maybe she just drove, the highway its own narcotic, the radio playing low, the heater cranked so that she could open the window a sliver to feel a blade of cold air just above her left eye.

When the road turned to gravel, she slowed, slowed again on the washed-out ruts of the driveway's long approach, and finally stopped, a hundred yards or so from the house. Did he wait for her? Had Chris somehow intuited her approach, inside with his stuffed mountain lion, a creature as sleek, dangerous, and gone as he must have imagined Mara?

She put the car in reverse but didn't yet move, checked the rearview mirror to see that Daniel was asleep.

He isn't yours, she thought, and then said it, whispered, because somehow speaking it made it true: "He isn't yours. He's mine."

The next night the nightmares began.

That was January.

In February, Mara and Daniel flew to Miami for her gallery show. The city had been just as she remembered it: the Brickell banks and high tide washing through the storm drains, the water sheeting off a balcony during a sudden rain. She'd watched the chosen sit in coffee shops drinking their five-dollar flat whites. The mojitos at sidewalk cafés. The Bugattis double-parked on Lincoln Drive. She and Daniel had driven to the gallery where she had sat outside and not cried, sat outside and felt nothing actually, except perhaps a vague disgust, this sense of near exhaustion that never quite bothered to articulate itself.

"Mom, what's wrong?"

It was almost but not quite raining. She looked out the window, bleared and streaked, and then down at her iPod plugged into the radio. She'd been stuck on the same Patsy Cline song for weeks—not the one you are thinking of.

"Mom?"

"I'm fine, honey. Really."

And she was, wasn't she? Because what she felt, wasn't it simply life in the Anthropocene, in the Sixth Extinction? The self-care while the dioxins flow into the groundwater. The meditation apps while the atmosphere ignites and the elephants die and we are all delivered to the grave via Amazon Prime.

"Let's go inside, okay?"

The show was a success and after they drove to Marathon Key where she had rented a small bungalow that sat beneath two loquat trees on the edge of the gulf. She and Daniel would spend a week there, volunteering at a bird sanctuary, driving down to Key West to snorkel and have dinner. I thought it was a good idea not only for the two of them to go but for them to go without me. Mara needed some time with Daniel as much as she needed to decompress. At the time I couldn't say exactly what was going on with her, but later, when she called from the gate at the Miami airport to tell me about her nightmare, she would admit that she had been thinking too much about the mountain lion she still believed was circling our house. There had been some premonitions, some bad moments when she thought . . .

"Thought what?" I asked her the day she called from the airport.

And here I imagine her standing, touching Daniel's head as he sits by the broad glass watching planes taxi. I imagine her walking a few steps away, just beyond earshot, dismissing what would prove to be an intuition as accurate as it was unthinkable.

"About Daniel," she said. "Like it's stalking him."

"A mountain lion?"

"Like it was going to take him from us."

"Like a mountain lion was going to take him? You mean physically?"

"I don't know, David. I just know I had this feeling last night like it was out there so I sat up reading about them online, sort of just waiting. I know it sounds crazy."

She told me a little more when they were back home, told me about the boat, the cage, showed me her feet, but mostly I am trying to conjure the night. How she reads about panthers on the bungalow porch after Daniel is asleep, alone with her laptop and a can of beer, a citronella candle. *Felis concolor coryi*, the cat of one color. How she walks inside to check on him where he sleeps beneath a sheet, the ceiling fan spinning just enough to allow the stolid air to circulate. I imagine her approaching him slowly, creeping closer, letting her hand drift toward his hair that appears damp. But she doesn't touch, won't touch, only lets her hand hang there, near him. She has him. He is safe.

When she walks back onto the porch, she feels at peace. She breathes deep and smells the loquats that have fallen from the limbs into the yard and shell driveway. The fruit is overripe and bursting, mawed open as if by disease or showing a single black spot out of which will occasionally rise a yellow jacket.

All week, she and Daniel have been collecting them, eating them, but more than that, Mara has been paying attention to them. The stem—if that's what you call it—the stem is thick and often comes off with the fruit, peeling the tree branch so that the waxy green of the wood is visible. It gives her pause. Seeing that raw green makes her question the damage done. It appears so vulnerable, like skin beneath a torn nail, and she has to be careful to twist the fruit, to let her thumbnail sink into the stem and cut it cleanly.

She walks barefoot into the dark yard and feels one break wetly beneath the arch of her foot.

The smell, sweet.

The juice, warm.

She slides her foot backward so that the crushed fruit streaks the pad of her foot and comes to rest between her toes.

And that is when she sees the cage.

I know it sounds crazy.

Out beneath the cabbage palms sits a large metal cage baited with a dead raccoon. She walks past it, touches it, the metal cool as shadow, the raccoon just beginning to smell. It is past the cage, deeper in the mangroves where she finds a second cage baited with dead birds, a small slaughter of crows. It occurs to her this is the kind of thing Daniel might try to crawl into, and then they'd have him.

But who, Mara? Who would have him?

She can't say, and instead stands there for some time, staring, not touching—afraid to touch.

It is when she looks up that she sees the lights visible through the brush. She can hear a woman's voice and beneath it the hum of a radio. She looks back at the bungalow and decides to walk over. *And yes, I knew it was stupid, David, and yes, I was barefoot, but I had this sudden need for adult company. A sudden need to tell someone what was happening. Because of—*

Because—god—I don't know. I just decided to—

She decides to walk over.

She can be back in what?

In twenty minutes, she thinks.

She's moved off the shell drive and into the loamy mangroves when she realizes she should have worn shoes. The ground thorny, everywhere dried palm fronds and cracked limbs, deadfall soft at first touch but beneath that hard and sharp. Still, she goes on, the lights assembling, the voices louder, almost intelligible. She comes out by the water, farther than she had thought. A sailboat is tied up in a glossy mirror of black glass. She can see the shapes of the man and the woman sitting on the dock in beach chairs. A radio plays Neil Young—her dead mother's music—and she knows them, these old hippies, realizes she has probably seen them at some point, beaded and bearded and dreadlocked, or seen people like them, since being an old hippie in the Keys is not a terribly unique thing. She hellos them and they call her up onto the dock.

"You came through those mangroves?" the man asks. "How far?"

"Not that far. My son and I are staying in a little house over there."

"Well, sister. Welcome to the Dreamcatcher," the man says grandly and takes a long pull off his beer. "A place of peace and harmony in our discordant times."

"Oh, god," the woman says. "I told him."

"What?"

"Saying shit like that to a stranger."

"She's not a stranger," the man says, "she's a fellow seeker."

And he's right, of course.

Mara talks to them while the woman packs and sparks a bowl and passes it to the man who is drinking Natural Light, the wreckage of cans beneath his chair. The woman sits beneath what appears to be a chenille bedspread, beside her a bottle of Seagram's.

The man hands Mara a beer and it feels so unaccountably wonderful there beneath the bright stars, so mysteriously right that she puts her head back against the pylon and closes her eyes only to open them on maybe a shooting star or maybe no more than light streaking beneath her eyelids. When the pipe comes her way, she decides to take it because with the weed makes it so easy to forget things, to stay here in this warm place. Back home it is still winter. Back home the mountains are white, the thread of the river sheeted in ice. I imagine her thinking of the way the current holds the cold, releasing it in gray breaths.

Inside, the piled quilts.

Outside, the thing that is already stalking our son.

She drinks her beer and the man passes her another.

"They're watching me," she says without actually meaning to. "They've sent a cat after me."

"What's that?" the man asks.

"A panther actually. *Felis* something. I think it followed me down here."

The woman looks at her.

"Like what do you mean followed you down here?"

"It creeps around the house. I think it wants my son."

"Your son? This is a metaphor or this is what?" the woman says, but the man nods.

"A panther," he says. "I hear ya."

"I think it has some message for me. But the thing is, I don't know what the message is. Like if it's a curse or a blessing."

"I hear ya, sister." Only the man isn't so much nodding as rocking. "The message is: it's the goddamn times. That's the message."

He says it like a benediction, like there is nothing left to be said, but when Mara stretches out her legs, the old woman suddenly bends forward, the oval of her face emerging in the wan light.

"Honey, your feet."

Mara's feet are cut and bleeding. She feels it but not really and holds her beer against first one arch and then the other.

"It's all right," she says.

She takes another beer, she keeps talking.

It's sometime later that she finds herself moving back through the mangroves. There had been some confusion, some sort of argument, perhaps. The man and woman wanting to keep her there, for her not to go, just sit still, drink some water. The woman trying to bandage her feet, saying the man would drive her home in the morning. His Grand Wagoneer right there by the dock if you'd just listen a minute. But there is Daniel. They seem not to understand about Daniel, seem not to believe in him, and Mara has to run, to go splashing into the forest only there is no splash, just the strangler vines, the same mangroves and cypress knees. She knows her feet are being torn deeper, shredded violently, but it registers more as pressure than pain, the sense that the skin is broken, and keeps breaking and will not fix, not now, not ever. *And I just didn't care, David. It didn't even occur to me to care. I just wanted to hurry.* So she does. She hurries, sees the light of the bungalow and then doesn't. Comes out of the mangroves past the second trap and into a sea of sawgrass and that isn't right, wrong direction, moving wrong, slicing herself—which is also wrong, the cuts on her arms and hands, the cuts on her throat.

Finally, she comes out on the shell road. The night is cool, but she is sweating, panting. She moves down the road and it's there, beneath the safety light of the bungalow, that she sees the tracks: the print of a housecat only twice the size. She can't tell if they lead toward or away from the house.

When she sees they lead in both directions, she starts running as hard as she can, harder still when she sees the front door is open, the screen torn. Then she sees the drag marks, the blood trail that leads into the mangroves *and I couldn't breathe, David,* sprinting now, the rough passage easy to follow though she doesn't have to think about following it or not. She has only to run, a wake of broken limbs and thrashed deadfall behind her while she screams Daniel's name and there is no feeling now beyond the sense she is moving on these pulpy stalks. The trail comes out on the road and moves back toward the house in one bloody loop.

She runs up the stairs and finds the screen intact, the door shut. Our son is asleep in bed, and standing there at the threshold she wants nothing more than to go to him, hold him, to smooth the damp pelt of his hair.

"But I couldn't, David. I had this feeling that if I did, he wouldn't be there."

"Mara, honey."

"I know it sounds crazy."

So instead of touching him, she stands crying until she is afraid her gasping will wake him. Only then does she walk on her heels to the bathroom where she fills the tub, the water going pink and then brown with blood and dirt. Later, she sits on the lowered toilet seat and cleans her wounds, tweezing thorns and shells shards. She takes three ibuprofens and checks a second time. Daniel is still asleep, and she arranges herself on the couch, props her feet on a pillow and shuts her eyes. The sweat and adrenaline and pot and beer and absolute exhaustion. It was fine, it was just a nightmare, a panic attack.

"Daniel was there," she will tell me later. "He was safe."

But six months later he isn't.

Six months later our son is dead.

Nearly eighteen months after that, she'll find the file I'd written on RAIN!

She'll remember those three cases of water I'd brought back as proof of my own misguided paranoia.

"You knew," she will say to me. "You knew and still you brought that into our house."

And then she leaves me to go to the Kinzers.

I had thought for a long time that Mara had gone back to Chris Bright, but with that, as with so many things, I was wrong. She went to the Kinzers and, at some point, she went to the group home.

"She just one day showed up, Mara did," the woman told me out by the dumpster behind the Dollar General. Lucille Duncan. Nana. "She said she'd seen Cory up by the falls. I'd seen her at the church, but we'd no more than nodded in each other's direction."

"She just showed up?"

She took a Kool from her pack.

"I figured those old Mennonites had set something in her head."

This was late November, a few weeks after I had come back first from meeting Toliver in Chicago and then making my ridiculous trip to Mexico. I'd been riding by the Dollar General since returning, stopping in, running off Java Energy Monsters and the possibilities that rested with the .357 I'd stolen from Jay and kept with me at all times.

"I got about two more minutes on my break," she said.

It was a cool day, the clouds low and gray and latched to the horizon. But thin enough for the sun to break through, a yellow day, breezy, loud with the eighteen-wheelers pulling into the QT to gas up.

Her lighter wouldn't spark so she put the cigarette in her apron pocket.

"They told me you come by here two, sometimes three times a day acting like don't nobody notice."

"I guess I have," I said.

"You guess?"

"I'm sorry."

She nodded, started to turn, and then stopped herself. Pushed the frosted hair from her face with one forearm.

"It weren't never for the money," she said. "I mean it started that way. Some crazy rich woman wants to pay to sit in my living room and watch the children out in the yard. But it changed after that. You could tell she needed something. Then I went and googled her, like you do. She said she was writing something and just needed to see that boy, to see Cory. But you could tell that wasn't it. Or wasn't the all of it, at least. It was almost like she started thinking that was her son out there in my yard."

"We had lost our son."

She looked away, took the cigarette from her apron pocket. "You don't have a light on you?"

"No."

"She said she had these wires drove down in her hands and feet. I could tell she'd got crazy, maybe always had been. But more than crazy, just flat-out sad. So when she asked to visit, it seemed Christian to let her. But have mercy, the way she sometimes talked—I asked her one day if she thought it was the Lord had put those wires in her. She didn't say anything for a minute, then later told me she thought it probably was. Either the Lord or the Devil, one. She said she was in a play."

"I used to write plays, one at least."

"Yeah, she said that too." She looked down at the cigarette in her hand. "Not a book of matches or anything?"

"I'm sorry."

"Just as well. Just as goddamn well." She tossed it away. "I got to go anyhow."

"Thank you for talking to me."

"Maybe don't come around so much anymore, all right?"

"I understand."

"Maybe like not at all." She turned and this time took two steps before she stopped. "You know it was hard on me, too."

"I won't come back."

"Cory was sick before Mara ever met him. Your boy dying didn't have nothing to do with that water no more than Cory did. People just get sick. Terrible things just happen. But you couldn't tell Mara that. She fixed on it like you do when nothing makes sense. She was sick herself, you know. Hurting. I'd watch her hand shake with the money so it got where I'd take it just to get her still. I wouldn't let her come with us to Duke. She was crazy by then. I was crazy too, Cory sick as he was." She looked out at another eighteen-wheeler pumping gas, MAYFLOWER down the side. "Then he went and died. I'm pretty certain she got into the house one night and took some of his things, some clothes, this little green bird he had. Then she went and did what she did."

She went and found "The Health Effects of Dioxin Poisoning: A Comprehensive Review" alongside the December 2001 report by the Virginia Department of Health indicating "substantial contamination" of the Tazewell County bottling plant alongside the May 2015 report, indicating the absence of said contaminants.

She went and found Chris.

I'd known that, of course.

It was the boy I hadn't considered.

It was Cory.

Go back to Cory.

Go back to the year after Daniel died, fourteen or so months before Mara would set off the bomb. Go back to the summer heat and the boy who emerges from the pool below Orchard Falls to find a woman staring at him. She follows him downriver where Lucille Duncan stands in the shade drinking a Mountain Dew and fingering down her phone. Mara must recognize her from church. She must already be thinking, imagining, dreaming, only I can't say exactly what.

—think eco-thriller by way of Sam Shepherd . . .
—think of Flannery O'Connor meets Rachel Carson (does that even make sense?)

ACT ONE, SCENE 1
August

He's playing rec football, walking to practice because "There ain't no gas in the tank to haul you around. You got money to put gas in the tank. I'll be more than happy to drive you."

So he (~~Daniel~~ Cory, the boy) is walking, some days he is walking. But it's almost three miles from the group home down to the Chicka-pea ballfield and by then what's the point? They play on the infield dirt and into the outfield, church league softball all around them. The sound of metal bats, the lights coming on at dusk.

Physical details:

You get red clay in the grooves of your hands.

You get it in your eyebrows to where it won't hardly come out. His football pants are more or less ruined with mud even though he keeps washing them with Clorox and hanging them on the line off the back porch. Three miles. Not even counting on you had to walk back in the dark.

SCENE 1
"DSS ain't no taxi service, son."

They are on the porch. ~~Daniel~~ Cory and Lucille Duncan, ~~Daniel~~ Cory and Nana.

"What's he wanting?"

The voice comes through the screen door, her husband, the one they

269

called Jeb, on the couch with a Natural Light and a rerun of *Dancing with the Stars*. Jeb will be gone for a week and then back for three or four days, his Peterbilt parked across the front lawn like a riding toy.

"Wants me to drive him to the ballfield."

"Down to Chickapea? Have his ass walk."

She (Nana, Lucille) has her phone out, scrolling through Craigslist.

"I told him."

"Ain't no gas for that."

"That's what I told him."

"He want all that exercise let him exercise his legs."

"That's what I just said, damn."

(He is ten years old, and very sick, though no one knows it yet.)

(His name is Cory, not Daniel.)

SCENE 2

Cory counts five boys in the group home, all of them older. Only Martin is his friend. Twelve and tiny for his age, he's in the self-contained class at school and is learning to read, and Cory sometimes helps him. They read Little Critter and Franklin, books discarded by the library because someone has scribbled *shit* with crayon on every page. Martin liking that owl they have for a teacher, one boy a fox, another a turtle in bifocals. MARTIN: *You reckon why that owl don't up and eat him?* Martin so simple and so small they let him play on the ten and under team.

The boys sit on the same stoop wearing the same kind of stained football pants and same kind of off-brand Under Armour shirts the rec department has given them. Their pads on the concrete walk clear of the fire ants, face masks pulled through the neck holes for carrying.

CORY: "They ain't gonna drive us."

MARTIN: "Don't matter if they do or if they don't. Speaking, like, in the grander scheme of things."

The house sits up in the holler enclosed by the mountains.

CORY: "We could just walk."

MARTIN: "Nah."

CORY: "We done it before."

MARTIN: "That ain't shit we need to be doing, walking like that."

Martin picks at his face. He has pink eye again.

A few days later he and Martin dye their hair with Kool-Aid. (*Show this?*)

SCENE 3 (*show? Or just imply?*)

Two days a week a van comes from town to take Cory and Martin
and one of the older boys to the services center downtown where they
drink Sam's Cola and write in their dream journals. It's a half-hour
ride, everything following the river, past farms and pastures and
chicken houses with giant ventilation fans. Churches everywhere.
Concrete blocks painted white. Picnic shelters and big two-by-four
crosses with a towel dyed purple and hung over the arms. Ingles.
Hardees. Town just one big parking lot with a Walmart and a crew of
Mexicans paving a new turn lane.

The one place in town Cory likes is the local history museum.
A concrete building off Short Street with high lunettes and an old
woman volunteering at the front desk. Now and then an old legion-
naire push-mows the grass in Dickies pants and a ballcap from the
VFW, arms liver-spotted and roped with veins (*show?*).

Inside are pioneer clothes—buckskin shirts and leggings in display cases meant for jewelry—Cherokee arrowheads knapped to
fine points, an ax-head grooved from its banding and pulled from
the Doe River. He walks past the maps and paintings depicting
long houses and encampments. A mountain lion stands in the corner,
mangy, but no less grand—a tawny queen in exile—and though a
sign reads DO NOT TOUCH, people have touched, people have rubbed
the right paw for good luck so that now the paw is bare and hairless,

271

wiped to its taxidermied shell. It seems to Cory like a disgrace, but the lioness appears unaware, its teeth bared, its eyes glossed to dark mirrors.

But it's the bird that holds him.

No more than four inches in height, it is carved from jade. A liquid green bird found in a plowed field a half century ago. A Carolina parakeet. Extinct now, last seen in Florida a century ago, having fled these mountains and flown south to the sea. Or so Cory likes to believe.

(*Note:* When you live in the mountains, you dream of the sea, that vastness. The hard sand, the tide. He likes to think the actual bird flew south following the water. There is no reason it might not have traveled as far as the Florida Keys except for the most fundamental reason of all: there is no flying free of this place. The mountains hold you. The mountains are greedy. They come up in green folds to move against you. The fog, too. He doesn't trust the fog.)

What follows is a quick montage, or separate scenes? (Not sure, continue to think on this.)

They walk to practice two days in a row and run suicides and do pushups in the dirt, and after the second night while everyone lines up for a Popsicle the coach comes over and pulls Cory over and says: "Somebody needs to talk to you a minute, son."

It's the woman from the river, dressed in a white blouse and black skirt with two pencils in her hair like chopsticks. (*two golf pencils, like from the putt-putt place in town*)

Detail: Her heels sink into the infield clay.

Mood: His body hurts.

Note: She isn't crying but her smile quivers, as if she might yet.

Revelation: He realizes he's been seeing her a lot lately. He realizes she's been following him.

One day his hair is different, peroxide blonde. The Kool-Aid having washed out at practice, staining the V-neck of the shirt he wears under his pads and turning it pink.

MARTIN: That's bullshit right there.

Meanwhile, Jeb is in Cleveland.

NANA: You wash that out your head before he gets back.

Jeb is in Milwaukee.

School starts back but they skip to dig potatoes with a beach shovel, a flimsy plastic thing meant for sand castles. They fill a plastic bag, Cory and Martin, some of the potatoes the size and hardness of marbles. Leave them in the kitchen sink, like an offering to the woman who is on the couch, watching him and not crying.

The next day the van takes him three hours to Durham where he has his blood drawn.

Jeb is somewhere along the I-55 corridor.

Note: They quit football sometime in October. They can't get to practice (show this?) and when the woman shows up at the ballfield to offer them a ride Cory decides to not go back. If anyone notices, no one says anything.

ACT TWO, SCENE 1

Halloween Nana paints their faces with some of her old makeup and drives them to town where the stores are giving out candy. She parks and says three hours, boys, and then walks to the Towne Tavern. Jeb is in Kansas City.

They carry plastic bags filled with Smarties and Tootsie Rolls and little miniature Snickers and Milky Ways. In the Walgreens, they stuff plastic masks down the front of their pants and put them on out in the street. Frankenstein's monster with stitches and a gray bolt. A pale zombie. The masks smell of rubber and they sweat makeup down their necks. Wind up pushing the masks up onto their foreheads like discarded skins. Wander off Main Street through a neighborhood of shabby duplexes with plywood stoops and porches made from raw lumber. Four of five cars on every lawn. Jack-o-lanterns. The sort of spider webs you sprayed from a can. He thinks maybe the woman from the river is following him but can't be sure.

Another quick montage:
 He goes back to see the parakeet.
 He would have taken it had it not been for the glass case.
 In his mind he does.

Really quick scene, maybe not even a scene:
 The woman comes to school and brings him a sandwich from Subway he picks at sitting under the playground trees while she stares at him.
 Jeb is in Phoenix, or Dallas it might be by then, drawing closer by the hour.
 ~~The next morning Cory wakes to find his body covered with a constellation of bruises that had not been there just hours before.~~

SCENE 2 (or maybe 3, depending . . .)
Thanksgiving dinner is turkey and dressing a woman from the church brought in a casserole dish.
 One of the older boys wears a leather thong around his neck, a sort of flower-child hippie thing.
 "Don't you wear that nasty thing at my table." JEB stares at the boy. "I will knock the ever-living shit out of you, you wear that at my table."
 (violence here? or leave implied?)
 Later, Cory sees the older boy in the yard sitting on the chrome passenger step of the Peterbilt. He has a pocketknife and has been

crying, and every now and then he takes the curly pig-tails of the
blue and green airbrake lines and makes to cut them.

But he never does.

SCENE 3 (or whatever)

In December, the van drives him to the hospital in Durham.

The woman from the ball field and school is coming around the
house more (*show this*), sitting in the living room, and very deliberately
not crying.

As for Jeb, Jeb is in Virginia, coming hard on I-81.

"When he comes back," NANA says, (she is counting the
money the woman gave her), "when Jeb comes back, you just keep your
mouth shut, all right? Much as you can you keep your mouth shut."

The boy goes back to the museum:

the jade parakeet . . .

the mountain lion . . .

ACT THREE, SCENE 1

January and they walk up the ridge below the dead oak (Cory and
Martin).

Around the tree are owl pellets, gray bundles of tiny bones swaddled
in what appear as grass twisted and thin as needles.

Back in the group home, long moment of watching the rain fall,
moody, melancholic—*or is that too much?*

SCENE 2

In February, they shoplift chocolate hearts and Robitussin from
the Walgreens in town, Cory and Martin. There are doctor ap-
pointments (many) and Sunday church services (a few) and the
woman who doesn't cry is everywhere. One day they (Cory and
Martin) swallow six gel caps and find a dead crow with one yellow

eye pecked from its head. Cory carries it in a Converse shoebox for three days before Nana finds it. He wonders could he take the parakeet without anyone ever knowing it?

SCENE 3 (with elements of a montage, maybe)
At the services center they write in their dream journals and after he and Martin sit on the front porch with their hot chocolate and Big Sixty cookies.

He is in Durham as often as not now, weak, possibly dying. They all know it, even the woman who is always around. Pack a bag, she tells him. Hide it. Be ready. I'll come for you.

It is June when he decides to steal the parakeet, to do it quick because standing there in front of the mirror he looks diminished, he looks smaller. He wears Jeb's work gloves, stiff and smelling of 3-in-One oil (*because, you know, fingerprints and all*), but Jeb is somewhere on I-95 and Nana is either working at the Dollar General or drinking at the Towne Tavern, depending. It is the woman who is there, the woman who is watching.

SCENE 4
Later that month they find the owl farther up the ridge, mummified and dragged between piles of granite that cropped between the big hardwoods and the dwarf pine. Cory carries it in the bowl of his hands like a (*metaphorical*) offering, down the slope and past the cellar and around the house where (*symbolically*) new grass sprouts over the lawn. He spreads its wings on the concrete walk and weighs each with a rock. The wings appear frayed. The moment is solemn. He looks close: the owl has been picked at by something, though not well. Tissue has been pulled from its open beak, a pinkish cord. Though some feathers were broken, its wings are as wide as Cory's arm.

Note:

He is exhausted by the walk and sits for a long time staring at it. He senses something all around him. Intuitively, we know that he knows it is EVIL. (*Or maybe it's the other way around?*)

Context:

Jeb is in Cleveland and Nana has a box of Franzia on the couch with her.

They heat a can of SpaghettiOs for dinner.

The woman says, be ready.

The woman says, I'll come like a thief in the night.

But by July he can't get out of bed.

By August, he is dead.

Just slipped away, just gone.

SCENE 5

But there is no scene 5. Only THE END. CURTAIN. WHATEVER, just know that the play is over, finished.

Note:

~~It's the boy who is dead.~~

~~It's the woman who goes on living.~~

~~The woman who wakes one day to the realization someone has anchored wires in her arms; that someone is controlling her.~~

~~The woman who wakes one day to the realization her husband has not only lied to her by omission but poisoned their son as well. And their son is dead. Thoroughly and completely.~~

THE END

Mara must have got into the group home just after that.

She must have found the bag, packed and ready and hidden beneath the bed, the stained T-shirt wrapped around the jade parakeet. She must have taken it.

That was August, maybe September. Right around the time I found her with the shotgun pressed beneath her chin.

In January, she left me to go to the Kinzers.

That summer she went looking for Chris.

She found him at his farm—*the* farm—everything exactly where she had left it. Only nothing was where she had left it. She noticed it as soon as she turned off the highway: the weeds swallowing the mailbox, the trash blown into the gully. The fields were not so much uncut as ignored. The apple trees shaggy. She was halfway down the rutted gravel drive when it occurred to her that maybe Chris wasn't here and maybe hadn't been for a long time. Maybe Chris was dead. She hadn't spoken to him, let alone seen him, since Mexico. Then she rounded the corner, past the dogwoods and white pines, and saw a line of thin smoke rising from the chimney. Which made no sense—it was 75 degrees—but did signal some sort of life.

She drove faster.

The wires must have been in her by then, her wrists, her feet and neck, only not yet tight: they weren't yet controlling her. But she must have known what was coming. She must have known she had to hurry. She pulled behind a battered Subaru Outback, the RAIN! file tucked into her bag on the seat beside her. She had dressed as if for business, blouse, pencil skirt—she was coming to him with a proposal after all—but when she saw the woman on the porch, she knew she had made a mistake. The woman was approximately Mara's age, long and angular and leaning against the balustrade, a cigarette burning down between her fingers. *Who the hell are you?* Which is how Mara met Tammy. Which was how Mara learned that Tammy only appeared the same age. Tammy was a decade younger. Only that decade had been particularly hard, what with Chris doing a year and a day in Caldwell Correctional on an intent to distribute charge, snagged by a narc while Tammy fucked a trucker in his sleeper cab in the Harrah's parking lot down in Cherokee. *Who the hell are you?* The flaking eyeliner. The pitted skin.

Hi, I'm Mara. I used to know Chris.

Used to.

It's been a while.

I know who you are.

And the woman, Tammy, giving her this look like *drive the hell on, bitch,* but she must have seen something in Mara's eyes, something that gave her pause enough to reconsider, to invite Mara in, but not before stopping there at the screen door to tell her *oh yeah, Chris is sick as hell, in case you didn't know it.*

That was the purpose of the fire going in the grate inside the house Mara had once lived in but no longer recognized: Chris's sickness. *We got shit everywhere,* Tammy said, which was true. A washer on the porch with its tangle of hoses. Boxes, newspapers, garbage bags of clothes. Narrow footpaths had been fashioned through the overheated room, the windows shut, the fire banked. The furniture was all found art: the tipped over cable spool, the church pew. The only thing missing was the lioness. Not that Mara couldn't imagine it, ragged from time but still golden and lean, head still cocked, ears still flat. All that austerity, Chris as monk, Chris as ascetic—gone, finished. What she found instead was Chris as dying, Chris on the couch with an afghan thrown over his legs right up to the point his flannel shirt bunched by the feeding port protruding from his stomach.

"Hello, Mara. It's been a while."

He weighed, she reckoned, one hundred pounds, no more, as close to death as his uncle had been all those years ago in the Johnson City VA hospital. Tammy stood behind him, blowing smoke past Mara's shoulder.

"Hadn't he hurt enough?" she asked.

They sat on the back porch just off the bedroom that had belonged to Chris's aunt that summer and fall so many years ago, the river just beyond them. The sound of the river, the idea of it, really—the grass was uncut and you could no longer see it from where they sat.

"I can't keep the place up anymore," Chris said.

"You don't look quite the same."

It was meant as a joke and he tried to muster something approaching a laugh.

"I look like shit. I look like stage 4 is what I look like."

"I didn't mean it to sound like that."

"Things change, Mara." He was smoking one of the American Spirits Mara had taken up after leaving me. "That's the nature of life, isn't it, change? The nature of the Tao."

"She said you did some time in prison."

"Did you know methamphetamine is a Schedule II drug? I'll bet you didn't, did you?" He took her fingers as if to examine her nails. "What with these clean hands."

"They're not so clean."

"If you're wondering did I say anything of course not. I never would. Not to Tammy, not to the police. I'll take it to my grave."

She pulled her hand away, gently, but she pulled it away all the same.

"Take what to your grave?"

It was only when he looked at her she recognized something of the old Chris still present in the icy blue of his eyes.

"All of it," he said. "Us."

They walked around the yard in the labored fashion that kept making her think she should take his arm, guide him, assist him, this man who'd once run across a desert on a broken ankle. He showed her the place, the collapsing buildings, the old Galaxie convertible beneath a tarp, the tires rotten and flat. The years had been hard.

"I sort of went off the rails for a bit."

He'd been a prepper for a while, reading the Book of Revelations and stocking up on canned beans and water purification tablets, ready in the next moment for the world to end. He had the bug-out bag. The forty-pound sacks of rice. The dealing had been a side gig, a one-time thing that ran on a little longer than intended. He'd been desperate for money, had needed to prepare, to buy things like a SIG 716 and a generator that ran on cooking oil, thinking any minute now the sky was going to open up with either Jesus or old Soviet warheads fallen into the hands of the Caliphate. It would be federal agents or Sharia law or a sun flare shutting down the power grid. He didn't know what, only that it would be something and it would be soon.

"I kind of lost myself there for a while."

It had been stupid, the dealing, but it was in prison that he'd gotten the diagnosis and started chemo so, stupid or not, it had also probably saved his life.

"Or at least extended it," he said, "however briefly."

They walked by the creek. Along with Chris's eyes, the water was the one thing that remained unchanged.

"You left David."

"Why would you say that?"

"So you didn't?"

"No, I did. I just couldn't . . ."

"You don't have to explain." They stopped on the sandy bank where we'd once sat, the three of us in camp chairs with our bourbon and bare feet. "How is he?"

"The same. Only maybe less so."

"Like all of us."

He looked back at the house and when Mara followed his gaze she saw Tammy framed by the bedroom window, watching them.

"When did you start?" she asked.

"I never did with meth. I was just Vics or Percs or whatever was around."

"Was it when he died?"

"It was trending already. It didn't exactly help things."

"He wasn't yours."

He nodded slowly.

"It's just like you to come out and say it."

"He was David's son," Mara said, "ours. Not yours."

"To lie knowingly," he said. "But also to believe it."

"Why did you come to Mexico? You knew what would happen."

"To lie knowingly and yet still believe the goddamn lie."

"You came to Mexico for me."

He looked off into space.

"Of course I came for you," he said finally. "So what are you doing coming here?"

Now it was her turn to stare into the distance.

"Remember when we set the animals free?" she said.

He smiled. "That sounds like a musical, something on Broadway."

"Remember the escape plan? We'd drive all night to the Keys?"

He took back his arm. "Mara, Christ. We couldn't even liberate a bunch of dying animals. We got a panther killed. So goddamn ineffective no one even cared."

"We sent a message."

"You're still telling yourself that, all these years later?"

"They knew, at least once, that someone was watching."

"They knew someone was pretending." He stopped, looked at the house, looked at the water. "Why are you here, Mara?"

"I know you have connections. I remember you mentioning a guy named Bruce."

"Why are you here?"

She took the RAIN! file from her bag, and if it sounded dramatic, she said it anyway.

"Because," she said, "I don't want to pretend anymore."

The drive to New Orleans takes thirteen hours in Mara's Sebring but then Bruce doesn't have the promised Semtex 10, just some unstable TATP, a few blasting caps, and the Tovex trigger.

("She was sort of lit. Internally, I mean," Bruce would tell me at the Dee-Luxe Inn. "The kind of glow you don't know where it's divine or just plain crazy.")

Chris refuses the TATP and she drives back, stopping only to allow him to vomit at an I-59 rest stop and again in the breakdown lane in Alabama. It slides past them, the world: the deer on the side of a night road in Louisiana. The motorcycles flying past in Tennessee, POW-MIA flags patched on leather vests. The women in Day-Glo Lycra and faded jeans. She has to hurry; she can feel the wires that have been implanted in her body, and though she doesn't yet feel them pulling she knows they're growing tighter by the day.

She makes her argument.

Lays out her case.

They pump water, she tells him as they drive. *They have all these friends who are hydrocarbons but they just pump water, Chris. They think it makes them pure.*

The FBI will show me the security footage of Mara pumping diesel at the Texaco in Hampton, Tennessee, and if I strain just right I can imagine I see Chris in the car. They will show me the receipts for the ammonium nitrate bought in Hot Springs. They'll show me the still images of Mara entering the 176 acres of the RAIN! bottling facility three times and leaving twice. They'll show me the files on Chris Bright, the time out west, the fires set at the summer home on Hawk Mountain and at the office park outside Johnson City. They'll show me how he changed his will, leaving everything to Tammy, just days before the fire. They'll show me everything except what I actually need to see. Which is what I don't know. I do not goddamn know.

Walk us through that last day, Mara.

That last day, they assembled the bomb out in the old greenhouse, some of the punched-out panes sheeted in Visqueen, some not, assembled it beneath the pull-chain bulb in the wavy heat of Indian summer. Chris's hands shook but he was steady: it came right back, the process. Which was a good thing, a relief. New Orleans had unsettled him. The noise of frat boys and drunk girls with their beads and go-cups, a *Tremé* walking tour out by the Desire line. Noise and more noise and how long since he had heard his father's voice, his mother's?

Now the day had its screws in him. Stupid to say, but it was true. Hot in the greenhouse, in the tent, in the painters suit and the sort of surgical mask you saw back then in the streets of Beijing or Seoul and now see everywhere.

Almost there, though. Almost finished.

Mara watching him, manic and more magnificent for it, that enforced calm, the kind of woman whose mother would shoot herself barefoot in a laurel thicket, makeup erased by the pellets that came up through her pallet and into the open cavities of her sinuses. The kind of woman who would do it without a shred of fear. Who would do it just because.

"What?" Mara wanted to know.

Chris shook his head, moved his eyes back to the bomb parts, the trigger and housing he was snapping into place.

"Never mind," he said.

"The way you're looking at me."

"I said never mind."

They'd met Bruce at a café in the Marigny, Chris running on Jack Daniels and Dexasone. Bruce appearing somehow smaller, a nub of his old self, some smoother incarnation, like a river rock rubbed down to near opacity, like he was returning to some base element. Nodding and drinking the pink slushy of a hurricane.

"I got what I could," he told them. But no C4. Just the TATP Chris refused, and the Tovex and blasting caps they tucked into the spare tire well.

"You'll be getting something in the mail from me," Chris said. "What?"

"It'll come via Mexico. Just be looking."

"I hope it isn't any sad shit," Bruce said.

But it was all sad shit now, and riding back Chris saw it everywhere. The billboards and mountain sides shaved for timber. The drive-throughs and brownfields and cancer clusters like interstate clover leaves. The big-ass concrete figurines—angels, cowboys, Bigfoot—outside a plant nursery in Hampton.

The geography of his childhood was gone.

The patio light, the carport—it wasn't even a thing anymore. The bug zapper with its blue hum. The Town Cars and Lincolns and secondhand shame. He was glad his aunt and uncle weren't alive to see it, his grandfather, his father and mother, none of them. The country was dying, the entire planet. He thought of that night on Big Bald with his father's ghost and the mountain lion down in the Scratch. All of it dead and forgotten, and hadn't he said it all along? How one day they'd turn on the pumps and one day not too long after that they'd turn them off. Chris had gotten prepared but then he'd gone and gotten sick too, so the propane canisters for the camp stove, the canned corn and 5.56 ammo—none of it mattered anymore. He might as well fit the trigger into the housing, which he did now. It would be a small blast, relatively speaking, but big enough to undo one small part of the failing. He snapped the parts into place. The world being not nearly as hard to take apart as put together.

So why not?

He wiped one forearm across his face.

Why the hell not?

If the seams were stripped of coal and the mountains of tops, the elephants of ivory, the blood streams of viable T cells, what did it matter? It must be God's work, this dismantling, or maybe the Devil's. Either way, it was getting done.

"Hold this," he told her.

"What is this?"

"A blasting cap. Just hold it."

He'd gotten out of jail and tried to go straight. Decided he'd be this white-bread minimum-wage washout, working beneath the heat lamp at Taco Bell, a loser, but a straight one, living right or maybe right-ish, having fully imbibed all the power of positive-thinking bullshit that got passed around group until you absorbed it fully enough to recite it to the parole board. But he'd overreached. He'd just goddamn overreached is what he'd done.

Turned out honesty was aspirational for a felon.

Turned out working fast food was aspirational for a felon.

He got work under the table with a team of Honduran roofers

until he passed out, nail gun in hand, cheek to the grit of an eleven-dollar architectural shingle. Got work on a state road crew until they finally got around to running the mandatory background check. So it was back to the small-time shit, sitting in the car with two dime bags outside the Dunkin Donuts, driving all night to make a pickup by a pay phone somewhere in Atlanta. He didn't pray. There was a God—he knew it now—but he was a small god with the silver eyes of rubbed coins, a killer.

He wasn't disappointed exactly.

It was fine; it was America. All the shit of the twenty-first century and who had gone to jail? Who had paid? Name the bitches doing time from Countrywide or Kellogg, Brown, and Root? How about Dick Cheney with his stolen transplanted heart? Name someone locked up from Blackwater or the Pentagon or the Heritage Foundation. How about Purdue Pharma? The answer was none of them, not a goddamn one. Donald J. Trump was in office for god's sake.

And who had paid?

Having made a dustbowl of America, a real desert of Iraq (and called it peace, just to drop some Tacitus like a leftover JDAM), having spewed oil through the gulf and foreclosures over the suburbs and opioids into every holler and town from Youngstown to Harlan to Winchester—who had paid? No one. That was who.

Yet there had to be a reckoning, surely there had to be. Which was what had led him to the first prepper message boards. He admired the foresight, but more than that the elegance: reading online about a kiddie pool carp tank with floating tomato plants fertilized by the fish shit. Admired it even if it wasn't true. Still, the bug-out bag, the compression bandages, and 9 easy tips for storing and cooking tubers. It lent a sense of purpose, a desired end. The bomb he was assembling was just a variation, another way to finish things.

"That's it," he said, and lowered the contraption back down to the quilt spread across the card table, the thing no bigger than a softball.

"It's ready?"

"We'll prime it tonight, but yeah, it's ready."

"Thank you."

He nodded and stepped outside, pulled the mask from his face, sweating, barely able to breathe. She followed him out and he heard the crinkle of her taking a cigarette from the pack.

"We'll go at dark," she said.

"All right."

"I won't need much time. I'll use the garden cart to get the diesel in. You just show me how to activate it or arm it or whatever you do."

He sat in the lawn chair by the garden gnome and put his head in his hands.

"But after," she said. "Chris, are you listening? You can still go with us."

"There's no us, Mara," saying this into his folded hands.

"Please."

"There's no us. Jesus. Besides, they'll be looking for a man and woman."

"We can be in Georgia before the fire department shows up. Be in the Keys before they think it's anything other than a mechanical fire."

"That's a child's plan."

"That was our plan."

"And we were children. Jesus, Mara. We were playing at life."

Which they had been. Which they were still.

He watched her walk to the house through the cage of his oily fingers, watched her walk away. They were approximately eight years past watching the birds murmurate on a dry lake bed in central Mexico. Approximately one lifetime past the birds and the sex and the way she'd abandoned him in a hotel room in Jalpan de Serra. After she'd left him, he'd stuck around for another year, volunteering at a healing center for wealthy Colombians and Venezuelans, driving the minibus down to Queretaro to pick up the infirm, pushing wheelchairs, cajoling, weeping, almost praying.

Now he was past that.

Now he was Bitcoin and the Free Clinic in Elizabethtown. Talk of Bitcoin, at least. The Bitcoin was theoretical. It was the clinic that was real. The chemo and anti-nausea meds, the shingles vaccine and the van that took him to the Tri-Cities Pharmacy and Discount Medical Supply. Got the hair falling out in clumps, got the laminated hang tag for the handicap spot just left of the door. You stop sleeping, you stop eating. Skin and bones they say, and you realize they mean it. *They* realize they mean it and suddenly it's not a joke anymore, it's not even an expression.

He looked for Mara through the windows but she was gone.

He didn't know what to think of the boy, her dead son, his dead son, maybe, were he willing to do the math which he wasn't, though a thousand times he had, over and over he had. The problem was his frayed heart, all bunched muscle and crimped nerve—it would no longer open. To even consider the possibility of a child required something he no longer possessed, could no longer even imagine. And what did it matter if he was going to die soon, the bomb, the cancer? What did any of it matter?

Tammy came out on the porch smoking one of Mara's American Spirits.

"She said she'd be back come evening."

"Okay."

"You all right?"

The rusted glider, the stiff curtains, the chrysanthemums brown and potted and dead.

"Chris?"

"I'm all right."

"She said come evening."

And then it was evening and Mara was driving north and thinking again of the woman she'd gradually come to almost not hate. Unbidden, these thoughts of Mara's mother. Intrusive and unwanted but there they were. Because she got her now, Mara must have finally understood. She tipped her cigarette out the two inches of open window and looked at Chris in the passenger seat.

"You all right?"

"Why do people keep asking me that?"

She laughed then, actually laughed.

"I can't imagine."

He looked away from her.

"Remember the Church of the Moving Waters?" he asked.

"What makes you ask that?"

"Do you?"

Of course she did. She remembered everything. Most certainly she remembered the dying. Her mother's death had come to seem less offensive over the years. Less offensive and more logical, the need for desperate measures, how eventually life came to that. Daniel's death, that was a different matter. Daniel's death was a crime. Mara's death would be no more than the tearing of paper. The thin membrane between her life here and her life there no more than a whisper, no more than a scratch. There were so many ways to consider it, but it all came down to a sort of grand nothing. A soap bubble drifting over the yard, glimmering and fragile and then gone.

But Daniel's death had been something else.

When Daniel had died, it was like the world ceased to rotate. It was only a moment, a sudden lag that gave way again to motion, but you felt it. You knew it had happened, that stutter she felt deep inside her chest.

My God is bigger than that.

But what if that isn't the case?

She believed in God. But it had occurred to her that what actually mattered was whether God believed in her.

Which was stupid.

She knew it was stupid.

But what can you do with such awareness?

You can live with it—that was all. Make accommodations for it. And ultimately that was what Mara had done: she had taken her stupid love and built her life over and around the very fear that sprang from it. But that life was over, or would be soon enough.

She'd left the greenhouse satisfied, if satisfaction was such a thing. Was John Brown satisfied? Again, stupid: there was no such thing as satisfaction. Still, the bomb was ready.

She'd been gathering her things when Tammy found her, chinning at the American Spirits in Mara's hand.

"Can I get one of those?"

Mara extended the box, flicked the Bic lighter, and Tammy leaned toward the steadying flame.

"I'm not here to hurt anyone," Mara said.

"Then what do you have him out there putting together?" Tammy moved to the couch, sank into the cushions. The fire was all ember and ash, the room too hot. "I saw your tree online, the purple petals and all, that's you?"

"Was," Mara said, "past tense. Tell him I'll be back come evening."

She had driven to the public library after that. She'd thought about going to the Kinzers but no, she wanted to be alone with it, whatever *it* was, whatever was coming. For maybe the hundredth time, she looked up "The Health Effects of Dioxin Poisoning: A

Comprehensive Review," didn't read it, just left the file there in front of her on the screen. It was like an old friend now, something whose grudge is so ancient it has become almost holy. Then she watched Richard Manley's YouTube confessional for the ten billionth time because it needed a face, what she was doing.

Now, driving north to the bottling plant, she pushed up the sleeves of her old cable-knit sweater, the wires in her arms loose, the lines binding her feet and rooted at the base of her skull gone slack. She looked again at Chris, sunken, dying, yet here they were, approaching some approximation of grace. She'd been sleeping for the last week on the couch in the overheated living room, waking now and then to the remembered presence of the old lioness arrested in mid-stride, waking one night to find Chris on all fours on the linoleum, trying to find his inhaler or keys or a dropped pill by the pale breath of refrigerator light.

"Remember when we climbed back up the hill above Tugg Wilson's?" she'd said. "I mean before we knew what happened. Remember how happy we were?"

"Go back to bed, Mara."

"What are you looking for?"

"Go back to sleep."

But she never slept, not anymore.

They passed under I-81, turned, turned again.

The Walmart garden cart lay across the back seats. The ANFO was in the trunk, the diesel and fertilizer, the assembled trigger of Tovex and blasting caps. The boy's clothes were in the trunk too, a small duffel bag she had taken from beneath his empty bed, his toothbrush, his comb. The carved jade bird. Everything she needed was in the trunk, now and forever. She thought that was the case, told herself it was the case.

It was beautiful, her plan. She'd set off the bomb and have him back; they'd run to Florida together, to the Keys, to the birds—beautiful, beautiful. But didn't Rilke say something about beauty being the last veil that envelops the monstrous?

The walk was harder than Chris had anticipated and he wound up outside the wire, hands planted on knees, panting and watching Mara roll the garden cart toward the bottling plant. In the time it took him to cross the rolling pasture toward the low-slung block building Mara made two trips, back and forth to the car, wheeling the fertilizer and diesel as if she were doing no more than working in a flowerbed. Chris moved slowly but steadily; he wouldn't stop. He knew she didn't really need him here but then he thought he needed to be here. Mara intended to set the timer but Chris had decided to do it himself. Activate the trigger, maybe hang around, maybe not. He would decide in the moment, or perhaps not decide, simply linger close, as if indecision wasn't itself a sort of decision.

By the time he reached the building, she was packing the well with the ANFO, her body hung into the borehole.

"This is right?" she said. "It'll collapse?"

He studied the arrangement though there was no need for study. They both reeked of diesel, the smell strong enough to burn the eyes and sinuses.

"Yeah. It'll collapse."

She climbed out and stood for a moment to stare back into it.

"Do you think he's in there?" she said.

"What are you talking about?"

She shook her head as if to loosen the thought. "Nothing," she said. "I just . . ."

"Mara?"

"One more trip," she said, a third trip, and slowly he followed her back out into the night. He was outside the building when he saw her coming again from the car, too quick, it seemed, to have made the trip.

293

"I dropped something," she said. "You see it?"

"What?"

"I don't know. The other flashlight."

"What other flashlight?"

"I heard it hit. Back on the knoll there. Can you?"

"Yeah," he said, and started toward the rise maybe one hundred meters away. He was nearly there when he understood what was happening and turned and ran, actually ran, and was almost back to the plant when the light erupted, a brilliance, a sparkle, a great glimmer of light and heat and then the blast wave that sent him collapsing backward into the dewy grass. He saw the glow settle into his eyes and then deeper. He saw the great flash of the explosion.

And then Chris Bright saw nothing at all.

But what is it he would have seen? There is no evidence she exited the building. There is no evidence she did anything other than crouch there by the well, thinking of our son, thinking, perhaps, of the mountain lion whose death she had insured all those years before. There is no evidence that she got out.

But there is no evidence that she didn't, either.

Maybe she walks away.

Maybe they both do.

I'm asking you to imagine such a thing as maybe exists.

Maybe it happens like this.

Maybe she drives the back roads—because there are only back roads—through southwest Virginia, beneath the I-81 overpass, and into Ashe County. She picks the boy up from the group home and he sleeps on the seat of her old Sebring, the bag of clothes she found hidden beneath his bed now resting at his feet, the jade parakeet wrapped in a T-shirt. Imagine her climbing out his window, easing his small body down into the dark yard. Imagine the deer grazing on the shoulder, the signs outside churches that read MAKE AMERICA GODLY AGAIN. The signs outside stores that read SNAP & EBT ACCEPTED HERE. That read AMUSEMENT WITHIN. Where is Chris at that moment? She doesn't know. (Poor blind Chris Bright will be arrested by the first sheriff's deputy responding to the fire just after 1 a.m., shivering and clutching himself as he walks barefoot along the shoulder of VA-632, a sheen of spilled diesel on his face and lips.) It's two, maybe three in the morning when she turns down the snaking drive of the Kinzers, headlights sweeping the signs she has erected over her months there—YOUR GPS IS WRONG and, a hundred meters down the gravel, YOU ARE FAR FROM GOD. Her headlights sweep the house where a single lamp burns in the front room, and by the time she has pulled behind the house the boy has stirred and two figures stand in the yard, the old man in his coveralls, the old woman with a shawl thrown over her shoulders.

Not there, the old man says, as Mara steps out. *Put it down in the barn.*

So she does, parks the car in the barn down behind the house. She reeks of diesel, so much so that the boy's eyes are watering.

Get inside and get cleaned up, the old woman tells her.

I don't have time.

They'll pull you over for the smell alone.

I don't have time.

Mama? the boy asks.

Take my truck, the old man says.

Mama?

Hold on, honey. I don't think—

I don't think you have time to argue, the old woman says, and she doesn't, Mara doesn't, and leaves in the Kinzers' pickup with what little clothes are left to them, her money, her cigarettes.

No stuffed mountain lion. She sees them watch her go, but by the time she hits the highway the old Mennonites are wiping her car down with alcohol swabs, vacuuming out the trunk, removing the tag, scratching off the VIN. The FBI will arrive two days later.

If you wonder why she's so adamant about nonviolence, it's because we weren't always.

By daylight she's in the parking lot of an abandoned KOA campground in south Georgia, maybe Folkston, maybe Vidalia. Mara can't be sure exactly, but exactly isn't the point. She's driven straight from North Carolina, drinking black coffee and once—when the boy was asleep—peeing onto the darkened highway's shoulder. What she does know is that for the last thirty miles she's been seeing signs for the Okefenokee Swamp so she's headed south, she's headed away, and *away* is the point.

This is the after part.

I'm asking you to imagine such a thing exists.

I'm asking you to imagine she's pulled the truck out of highway's sight, tucked beneath the plastic frame of a waterslide and a billboard that says WHITER SMILES IN JUST THREE VISITS, the lights of the Scotchman and Hardee's on GA-1 no more than a soft bruise above the trees, the fat head of a full moon no more than a luminous glow.

She's driven too fast, probably.

But the lines are beginning to tighten and she has to act, she has to drive too fast. Now she watches the traffic on GA-1, the pickups and minivans, an elderly man carrying his breakfast in a McDonald's bag. Watches until she feels dizzy with nicotine and exhaustion. Light is beginning to gather above the dark trees, the day assembling itself, and she knows she needs to get back on the road, be in the Keys by nightfall, before the wires tighten fully.

Hours later she watches him churn a spoon in his cereal on the Formica counter of a north Florida Denny's. He looks from his bowl, his mouth full of flakes—imagine the flakes.

"We should probably get going then," she tells him. "Go brush your teeth for me, okay?"

"Where?"

"The bathroom, honey. The men's room."

She watches him cross the room, his toothbrush in a Ziploc bag, his hair unbrushed, his body alive.

He's alive, she tells herself, though she never quite believes it, it never quite seems true.

They stop again in the late afternoon. Pull off I-95 somewhere around Daytona Beach beneath the palm trees and power lines. LPGA written in crushed shells on a grassy embankment. She needs some sleep. She needs some orientation. She is halfway to becoming a new person and it's tricky, the halfway part. The McDonald's dollar menu because that is not Mara. The Knights Inn at thirty-nine dollars a night because that is not Mara either, and while she is many things, she is no longer who she used to be. There is nothing on the news about the fire, nothing in the paper she buys. She could find it online, but knows not to look. Instead, she showers, puts the boy in the tub and washes his hair. They sleep through the afternoon and when she wakes it is night.

She sits on the stoop in a plastic lounge chair tipped against the block wall, perfectly still because if she's still enough the wires remain slack, because if she's still enough the mountain lion tracking her will remain just beyond sight.

She doesn't hear the door, but then he's standing there.

"Hey, honey." She can see the plastic triangle attached to the room key clutched in his right hand. "What are you doing up so late?"

"What are you doing out here?"

"Just sitting for a minute? What do you need, baby?"

"Where's Dad?"

She leads him back into the room, gets in bed beside him, and strokes his hair.

"Sleep, baby."

"Where's Dad?"

"He's waiting for us."

"Where?"

"Just down the road a little. Go to sleep, baby. He's waiting for us."

Imagine Highway 1. Miami, Homestead, Florida City. The cabbage palms and poincianas. Barred owls beneath the overpass. They cross the long bridges over water silvering in the dusk, stuck behind pickups pulling ski boats, the flashing of brake lights, the turn signals for vehicles that fail to turn. It doesn't matter. They are in no hurry. Their direction remains south and *that* is what matters.

The boy is buckled beside her, his lanky frame arranged beneath the seat belt.

"You okay?"

He shrugs and again she notices his skinniness, elbows and knees and the thin bones of his wrist.

"Rest and I'll wake you up when we get there."

"You promise?"

"I promise."

She feels the wires then, feels the back of her skull rising slightly.

It's dark when they reach Marathon and she drives the streets looking for a place they can afford. It's all neighborhood here, a sleepy quiet of bicycles on porches and trash cans rolled beneath streetlights. Chain-link fences and mailboxes shaped like mana-tees. She'll find a place here, they'll stay, disappear into the every-dayness of it all. And they do: the next day Mara finds them the rental, the bungalow with the porch where years later she finds the Key deer with the torn throat.

The Key deer being the other dead thing, the next dead thing, the only dead thing.

Not our son, never our son.

I'm asking you to imagine.

I didn't go straight home from the Dollar General, just drove around for a while, stopped by the liquor store and bought a fifth of bourbon. I kept thinking of something Toliver had told me that day in Chicago, about how it wasn't her grief or her anger so much as her vision. *Her vision*, he'd said, as if that clarified everything. So what had she seen? I think perhaps, it was greed, and how she must have come to believe it was greed that had killed our son. Our lives had been marked by the deification of the dollar. This has long been the world's trajectory, of course, a path we Ameri-cans have mapped with great diligence—we are a nation of grab-bers. But never had money outweighed all else. Now it was not God or family or even killing brown people in Japan or Vietnam or Iraq but the Dow Jones and interest rates, cash flow and work-ing capital versus fixed capital. Praise the Nasdaq. Praise Goldman and Blackrock from whom all blessings flow. Holy, holy, holy the GDP and the financial munificence it rains on us like manna.

Some of us, I mean. A few of us.

I drove the neglected roads past the trailers and caving homes with their Trump signs and Second Amendment flags, the aban-doned stores and empty parking lots. I'd looked at this all my adult life, but I was seeing it that evening for the first time. How half of America is a third-world country. How half of America

299

doesn't count, except when they are angry enough, and everyone was angry.

And all with cause.

All with goddamn cause.

I had made up my mind to go home when I found myself missing the turn onto 321 and heading toward Virginia. My GPS told me it was five hours but in the end the ride north felt longer than that, longer than possible actually, as if I were being given chance after chance to salvage my life. But there felt so little left to save. So it was I-81 where I stopped once for coffee and to piss and then I-66 and then I was gliding through horse country and downtown Middleburg. It was late, nearing midnight, and though the Christmas decorations twinkled in all their tasteful glory, the storefronts and restaurants were dark and the sidewalks empty. It seemed appropriate. I drove through town and made a left. The road here was gravel but well-groomed as it followed a white fence line. In two miles, my GPS told me, I would arrive at my destination.

It was marked by two stone horses the size of large dogs, mid-stride on their pedestals and bookending the driveway. I cut my lights and made the slow left onto the asphalt. The driveway rose over the swell of the pasture and in the distance stood the outline of the main house, a single copper light burning dimly in a downstairs room. I took Jay's .357 from the glove box and when the driveway dipped again I pulled onto the shoulder and got out.

It was maybe a quarter of a mile to the house.

The night was cold and bright with moonlight, the air sharp with manure.

I slipped the gun into my belt and walked up. I didn't know what I was doing but there is a logic to things that sooner or later takes over and once it does it's best to move quickly. Ahead, the single light appeared softer still, welcoming, as it was all waiting for me.

The way Daniel came from the tub smelling of coconut shampoo in his footed pajamas.

The old cable-knit sweater Mara wore until the very end.

The way she looked at me, the way she looked at him—it was all there. I sensed I was close and when I took the gun out I felt like I was carrying God. But it felt too heavy, too wrong, and I put it back in my waistband so that I felt it against my spine.

A motion light came on as I neared the garage and I froze for a moment before I realized it didn't matter. As if by magic, the door was unlocked. I moved past two gleaming Lexus SUVs and through a breezeway past the white wicker. It was dark but not impossibly so. In the kitchen, moonlight came through the windows to light the cookware hanging above a great tiled island, and again I touched the gun. Who do you pray to, I asked it, when the old God has not so much died as drifted into senescence and taken His people with Him? You pray to ghosts. And there I was, a ghost living in a ghost story, something I became aware of the way you are aware of a distant train: the unsteadiness, the weight of motion, but then it's gone, and maybe was never real in the first place. Maybe none of it is.

I found her in the living room.

Kathryn Banks sat in an armchair, frighteningly upright, the lamp beside her fringed and glowing.

"And you must be the aggrieved husband," she said.

I stopped when she spoke, maybe a dozen feet from her.

"I suppose I am," I said.

"The aggrieved husband with a gun it appears."

I hadn't realized I'd taken the gun back out, but there it was in my right hand.

"That too, it seems."

"It does indeed," she said, and stood and walked across the room. "I've been waiting on you quite calmly. But now I think I could stand a drink. You'll join me?"

"Sit back down."

"Don't be ludicrous, Mr. Wood. Bourbon is medicinal."

She poured two doubles and handed me one, settled back in her armchair, and crossed one leg, thigh to thigh.

"You're angry," she said, "thus you've come seeking solace or revenge. You need answers or meaning or what have you. You need someone to blame."

"Something like that."

"Of course." She sipped her drink. "I knew you'd come. As soon as they told me I knew we'd be meeting."

"Told you what?"

"About your wife."

"What about my wife?"

"That they found some of her tissue inside my water plant. Or did you not know that?"

"Her what?"

"They matched the DNA. Why don't you sit down."

"That can't be."

"Why don't you sit down, Mr. Wood."

"I don't believe you."

"Please, sit."

I lowered myself onto the arm of the couch.

"The FBI told me three days ago," she said. "I assumed they would have told you the same."

"No."

"A positive match. I've been leaving the door unlocked since then."

"I . . . I didn't know."

"What's that?"

"I said I didn't know."

"I can see that. I am sorry. For whatever that's worth."

I said nothing.

"Have a drink, Mr. Wood," she said to me, and like an obedient child, I did.

She put her glass by the lamp with what felt great formality.

"I have a theory," she said. "My theory is that you become American not by birth but by dint of will, by your rapacity, by your willingness to eat the world because why else were you put here? You are American. You are entitled. Does that sound harsh to you?"

"I don't know."

"Yes, you do. Answer me. It sounds harsh to your pampered ears, doesn't it?"

"It sounds evil."

She smiled. "It sounds honest. It sounds like this actual world when it isn't dressed up in your pieties and politics. That's the one thing my late husband taught me, Mr. Wood, bless him: that we're all of us the same, deep down. You might go crying for your Jesus or your Che, but in the end you are willing to take what you want not because you want it but because you, by god, deserve it." She touched her bourbon with a single fingertip, nothing more. "I think I would have liked your wife. I wish we had met under different circumstances."

"Our son died."

"Yet another thing I was sorry to learn."

"I know all about you too."

"Do you now?" she said, and looked almost amused. "Then I don't suppose you'd be surprised to know that one of my daughters went through a similar stage once. My oldest daughter, I'm talking about. Her freshman year of high school she started coming home talking about guilt and blame. About Matthew 25 and the World Trade Organization. About debt relief, for god's sake. It drove my husband mad, the poor man. He thought it was an attack on him, an indictment of his very life."

"Wasn't it?"

"An indictment? It was prattle, Mr. Wood. Teenage prattle. But I listened because she was fourteen and I am her mother and that is what mothers do. It was my husband, so tender, he was the one who couldn't bear it. But I heard it for what it was, the big-hearted rich girl crying Tiffany tears on her Chopard watch. Oh, the guilt. You should have seen it, the theatricality of all that guilt. Raging on her expensive Egyptian cotton sheets. All of it recorded on her iPhone for her friends on Instagram to cheer and support and ultimately ignore because what is more American than feeling horrible for stepping on the throats of the huddled masses without ever bothering to actually move your feet? What is more American than the child of privilege who, when faced with life, with actual real goddamn life, Mr. Wood, cannot believe a special dispensation hasn't been made for her? The petulant child suddenly realizes tragedy isn't just for the poor. So what does the petulant child do? She acts out. She lashes out. Does that sound like anyone you know?"

"You didn't know her."

"In fact—"

"You know nothing about her."

"In fact, Mr. Wood, I—" She looked past me for a moment. "Yes," she said, "come with me. I wasn't going to show you this, but I think now I will. Come with me, please."

"Where?"

"Just come, please. You can even bring your gun if you like."

I followed her through the living room, down a hall past

framed photographs and into a dark space. It was colder here, the floor unfinished cement.

"Wait," she said.

A moment later the lights flared and we were indeed in a cavernous room of naked drywall and exposed beams. I batted it all into focus. What I saw wasn't possible. Though of course it was: suspended and floating in the center of the room, just as it had been in her studio so many years before, was Mara's tree. *Alone Beneath the Tree of Knowledge.* I hadn't seen it since my visit to the High in Atlanta. Now I felt something deep inside my chest.

"How did you?"

"I had an auction house make some inquiries," she said. "It only arrived a few days ago. They hung it beautifully, I think."

"You're not going to—"

"I haven't decided what to do with it yet. But I knew I had to have it. What do you think?"

She stepped back so that I could see it. It appeared brighter than I remembered, the wood naked and gleaming beneath the lights. Glowing, it seemed. Brighter and then brighter still, so that I was squinting.

"I'm sorry about your son, Mr. Wood. I would say I lost my husband but I know it isn't the same. I suppose if I lost a child I might go crazy myself."

The tree appeared ablaze, as if lit from within.

"I'm not crazy," I said.

"Of course you aren't. But perhaps we aren't put here to recognize such distinctions. Perhaps we are put here only to recognize beauty."

"What did you say?"

"I think you heard me just fine. I said what if we are put here only to recognize beauty?" She canted her head as if I might come into better focus. "You didn't know it was there, did you? Look here."

I followed her past one tapering root to the trunk where in tiny leaning script Mara had carved *what if we are put here only to recognize beauty?* The words spiraled around a dark whorl in the wood so that they were nearly indistinguishable. Yet there they were; there they had been the entire time.

"You really didn't know?"

"No."

"Because," she told me, "you never looked. Let he with eyes see, Mr. Wood."

"All right."

"Let he with ears—"

"All right." I took a step back and realized I was still holding the .357.

The tree had grown brighter still and I raised the gun to shield my eyes.

I no longer felt like I was carrying God.

I felt like a fool.

She clucked her tongue.

"You and that gun. You didn't really come to shoot me, now did you?"

"I suppose not."

"I suppose you didn't come to be lectured either. So why come all this way? Was it just to stand there and point it at me?"

"I suppose," I said, only then realizing it, only then lowering the gun to my side, "I suppose I just wanted to know what it felt like."

For the briefest of moments, she looked at me like a woman caught in sudden rain, uncertain as to whether she should go forward or back, and I felt a flood of sympathy for both of us, for all of us. Then it passed and her face was hard and flat again.

"That's understandable perhaps," she said. "Nevertheless, it's time to go home, Mr. Wood. Time to go home, and no more coming back, do you understand? This fantasy is over. The children are no more dying in the Sahel than they are here." She looked at me then. "I mean, they're dying, just not like you think."

I walked out, left her standing by Mara's tree, got in my truck and drove down the winding driveway past the stables and paddock. The downstairs lights were all on now, but the field remained dark as an open grave. I stopped at the intersection between the stone horses and tossed Jay's pistol into the wet ditch where it disappeared into snowmelt and I left it to make my way back toward the interstate. The fantasy was over and I fixed my eyes on the mile markers flashing by.

The ride home felt shorter than possible, sadder, too.

It was dawn by the time I poured four fingers of Woodford, and piece by piece moved Mara and Daniel's "Tree of Heaven" into the living room, the sculpture tilted slightly to fit beneath two exposed beams, the bright birds, faded now, leaning until I turned the trunk and for a moment they took flight. When it slowed, I began to type furiously, Banjo at my feet, until it grew too cold and we moved to the bedroom.

In September of 2018, I typed, *nine months after she had left me, and just over two years after our son Daniel died of non-Hodgkin's lymphoma, a bomb went off at the RAIN! water-bottling plant in southwest Virginia, two hours north of the home I shared—or once shared—with my wife.*

I opened the windows and drank three fingers of bourbon.

I don't know how long it took, but when it was finished, I typed the completed RAIN! file she had left for me. I kept leaning closer to her pages, her handwriting difficult to read, crouched and leaning, not at all the elegant hand I remembered. Deciphering it felt almost like deciphering her, untangling a knot so thoroughly riddled it took the better part of two decades to realize as much. I worked all day and sometime that night the RAIN! file was complete and I was drunk. Banjo limped into the living room where he circled his bed twice and collapsed into it. I plugged the laptop into the phone line and emailed TheWaterOfLife.pdf to Bill Baker at the *Watauga Democrat*.

It was something like a rational decision, I think. I was no longer drunk, but simply exhausted. I could hear Banjo wheezing in the living room and gently pulled shut the bedroom door.

Outside, the moon wasn't quite full.

It must have been the crying that woke me, not barking or moaning so much as the sense that somewhere on the other side of the door the dog was weeping quietly. I sat up when I heard something fall over. What compelled me to reach for the .357 on the nightstand I don't know, fear, recognition. But the gun wasn't there. The gun was in a ditch on the edge of Kathryn Banks's fields. Something else toppled, crashed. I opened the door and reached for the light switch and maybe it was the sound of that crashing, the gravity of such, that made me go back and find the .410, Mara's gun. My gun, at least now.

The room was a wreck, the same shattered mess I remembered from the night before the FBI came. Bookshelves, chairs, cushions. Only now the tree too. It lay on its side, the birds scattered as if flung. Banjo lay on the rug by his bed, and it was only when he failed to rise I saw the animal in the center of the room. It was the trophy mountain lion Chris Bright had bought so many years ago, and it stood immobile in the living room. I hadn't seen it in almost twenty years but I knew it at once. Chris's lion, frozen by a hunter's bullet nearly a century ago, its head sleek and canted and perfectly still.

Then it moved.

Just the head, tilting, flashing those yellow eyes.

Then a slow step toward me, its body flattened to the ground, another.

Banjo whimpered and I lifted the gun.

Oh, Mara, I thought. Your GPS was wrong.

Oh, Mara, I said to the lion as it approached. Your God might have been bigger than that.

But you were still so far away.

part five

the tree of heaven

We are all now living in a different future, the one we knew was coming but has surprised us just the same. The waters rose—just as they said they would. The air is hotter and dirtier, the infections longer and deadlier. Those little surgical masks you saw now and then, sky blue and so unsettling—we are all now sweating beneath them. We are washing our hands. We are no longer praying. This is not another *maybe*. This is simply what we have woken to and will continue to wake to, each day a little warmer, a little grimmer, a little harder to breathe.

Still, there is one last thing to tell, and that is how the birds come at dusk, a dark train that flickers out of the East less like a river than a failing projector, the reel skipping with light over the dry lake bed, and then over the boy, and then over his mother. There are others up on the ridge, but the boy and his mother are alone there on the mud flat so that when the birds begin to bend and spiral it appears they are turning in recognition, as if they had almost made a mistake.

"Watch," Mara says quietly, reverently, almost silently.

The birds circle over the dry lake bed that floods at highest tide but otherwise is a field of gray muck with a single copse of banyan trees into which the birds eventually drop. She tells him this. How the birds circle until sunset, the holding pattern growing until overhead is a cyclone of perfect synchronicity, black one moment, silver the next. The idea is to confuse predators, the falcons that swoop in to snatch an isolated bird. But here no bird is isolated. Here there is safety in their anonymity.

"It's happening," she says.

The murmuration, she means. It isn't supposed to happen here in the Keys, something is failing within the birds, their interior mechanics skewed by the changing climate, their sense of navigation lost. Not only the cowbirds but all birds. Snowy owls drifting south. Magnificent Frigatebirds seen thousands of miles inland. It's like the Key deer coming north while the panther drifts south. What they are witnessing is confusion.

But it's the loveliest confusion she's ever seen.

The breeze comes off the gulf and her son's hair rides up off the top of his head and flattens when the direction changes.

She puts one hand on his shoulder.

"You okay?"

"I'm fine."

"Not cold?"

"I'm fine, mama. You okay?"

"I am," she says. "I'm just fine. I'm absolutely fine."

And she is, though she can't say how exactly. The sky bleeds in a way that doesn't lend itself to thought. It registers, though not in words, and she is lost in the sunset when the murmuration ends, the drop sudden, a great swooshing as the birds descend as one and the trees shake with arrival. After that the evening is still and quickly gone, the sun beneath the sea, darkness around them. And I ask you, what if it happens like this?

What if she puts her arm around him as they walk back up to where the truck is parked on the shoulder of the road? They are leaving; they cannot stay. Things will change, things will disappear. Everything you have loved, everything you have known— it cannot, it will not last. She knows this; we all know this. Still, what if she is content in that moment, together like that, happy and safe and beautiful?

And me, what if I have been put here only to recognize such?

What if that is enough?

acknowledgments

I am remarkably fortunate to live a life rich in friendship. My thanks to the Lost Mountain Adventure Club; the Monday Night Sewanee Crew; my colleagues at Appalachian State University, especially Caleb, Katy, Matthew, and Zack; the Romanian Fulbright Commission, Madison Bell, Clint Bentley, Wes Browne, Beverly Coyle, Dennis Covington, Jimmy Davidson, the Denner family, Chris Doucot, Patricia Engel, Leah Hampton, Drew Hildebrandt; Derek Krissoff, Sara Georgi, Sarah Munroe, and MaryAnn Steinmiller at WVU Press; Leigh Ann Henion, Jonathan Miles, Michael Nelson, Tom Perotta, Janisse Ray, Sam Slaughter, the Weiss family, Kayla Rae Whitaker, and, of course, my family, Denise, Silas, and Merritt, my parents and siblings and everyone else.

Portions of the book appeared previously in *Obra/Artifact*, *Appalachian Review*, *Mountains Piled upon Mountains*, and the *Oxford American*. Mara's Alone Beneath the Tree of Knowledge is inspired by Troy Norton's stark and stunning "Tree of Life." Find him at TroyNortonArt.com.

This novel is dedicated to my nana and in memory of my grandparents who have passed on. They loved the earth and sun and the animals, despised riches, and gave alms to everyone that asked—exactly as Whitman told us we should.